THE COMPLETE TALES OF HENRY JAMES
VOLUME FIVE: 1883–1884

THE COMPLETE TALES OF

HENRY JAMES

EDITED WITH AN

INTRODUCTION BY

LEON EDEL

5

1883–1884

J. B. LIPPINCOTT COMPANY
PHILADELPHIA AND NEW YORK

PRINTED IN THE UNITED STATES OF AMERICA
LIBRARY OF CONGRESS CATALOG CARD NUMBER 62-11335

CONTENTS

INTRODUCTION: 1883–1884

DURING the six years that followed the success of "Daisy Miller" Henry James devoted himself to the writing of "international" tales—that is, tales dealing with the contrast between "the distinctively American and the distinctively European outlook." His protagonist was usually an American girl, not always quite as limited in her perceptions as Daisy; sometimes indeed she was a figure largely endowed, facing her American-European destiny with an awareness of the values to which she aspired and with the egotistical belief that she was sufficiently equipped to assimilate them. James's concern was essentially with the "mixture of manners" on either side of the Atlantic; in this he found comedy and pathos and a series of little dramas that allowed him ample room for indulgent satire and delicate irony. By 1884, however, after two visits to the United States from his London perch in Bolton Street (during which he renewed acquaintance with the society of Boston and New York and for the first time studied society in Washington) he began to feel that he had "worked" the international theme to exhaustion. He had captured a transatlantic myth and found its many variations. He was ready to attempt new subjects.

His farewell to this first large phase of his career took the form of two brilliant stories of international marriages, and a tale of a self-made American girl. He was to return to the international marriages in later years, but there would never again be a period in which his tales reflected such an exuberant joy of creation, and such a spontaneous quality of wit. In "Lady Barberina" and "The Siege of London" he is writing at the top of his form and quite in the comic tradition of Molière —that is of Molière the moralist rather than the portrayer of

7

foibles and idiosyncrasies. James is concerned above all with
the anomalies and hypocrisies of society in London and New
York—with the ingrained habits and codes of the English
aristocracy and the attempts to mix these with the assumed
rigidities of the new American society and its eager aspirations.
But what is discernible in these tales is a disenchantment with
"society" altogether. As far as that of America is concerned,
James probably agreed with his friend Clarence King, the
geologist, that it was "far more Roman than English," in
its emphasis on growth and materialism, "size, brute mass, the
big figures of the Census" rather than civilization. Henry
James, however, focused on a smaller part of this social
organism, the American leisure class, and his concern was with
the levelling imposed by the democratic process. "Everyone
is Mr Jones, Mr Brown; and everyone looks like Mr Jones
and Mr Brown." And again, James could say, through the
lips of his European observer, that America was "the last word
of democracy, and that word is—*flatness.*"

One of James's remarks had been that "the first thing a
society does after it has left the aristocratic out is to put it in
again." He had argued also, in the 1870's, that a position in
society was "a legitimate object of ambition." Now—in the
1880's—his observer remarks in "The Siege of London": "I
hate that phrase, 'getting into society.' I don't think one ought
to attribute to one's self that sort of ambition. One ought to
assume that one is in society—that one *is* society—and to
hold that if one has good manners, one has, from the social
point of view, achieved the great thing." The observer accordingly has some wry remarks to make about Nancy Headway's
siege and conquest of London: her flamboyant manners, her
undisguised social ambition, her multiple American divorces.
Nancy seems to him the last person who might be allowed into a London drawing-room. And yet there she is, surrounded
by distinguished gentlemen, a source of their amusement, almost a freak of nature. Stranger things had happened in

London society: if it had rules, it also had a way of breaking them, and of closing its eyes to this contradiction; quite often it seemed arbitrarily to make its own rules. James had begun to wonder whether his own conquest of social as well as literary London had been achieved not on the ground of intrinsic charm or literary talent, but because he was yet another freak of nature, an amiable American artist, not too bohemian to be consorted with, and sufficiently amusing to be tolerated in the great houses. When Nancy discovers how heartily society can laugh at her American locutions and her American jokes, she begins to tell herself that this is really "success," and that "if she had only come to London five years sooner, she might have married a duke."

The disenchantment figures more subtly in "Lady Barberina," with its picture of the young and well-meaning doctor from New York, Jackson Lemon, who conceives of Lady Barberina as a certain high ideal of English womanhood and wants to place her in a grand mansion in Fifth Avenue. His American sensitivities are hurt that he must bargain for her with her aristocratic father and indulge in so commercial a treaty as a marriage-contract. But he is confident that once he has taken his prize home he and his English lady will live happily ever after. Lady Barb however refuses to be domesticated in Manhattan. She cannot accept Central Park as a substitute for Hyde Park. Manhattan society bores her. James shows us in this fashion the true incompatibility between an inflexible aristocracy of blood with its stratifications, and an aristocracy of wealth and its pretensions.

But what concerned James above all were the moral issues implicit in these tales and his sense that there could be no happy marriages between American and European—that they could not endure without serious compromise. It is Jackson Lemon, in the end, who must expatriate himself; and in the case of Mrs Headway, there is still another problem which deeply worries the irritated observer of the tale. This is whether a gentleman "tells" on a lady—even if she isn't a "lady" by social definition. In French plays they usually did; for the *demi-mondaine* was a creature proscribed, and it was indeed a gentleman's duty to tell. French morality seemed to James unnecessarily "ferocious." What he disliked above all in *Le Demi-Monde* by Dumas *fils* was the betrayal of the unhappy heroine by the very man whose mistress she had been. James's picture in "The Siege of London" of the frantic baronet's mother seeking to discover Nancy Headway's past in order to save her son from an "impossible" match, was as unflattering to English manners as Nancy herself was to those of America.

Henry James's last tale, in his long international series of the 1870's and 1880's, was "Pandora." The young lady who gives her name to the story is seen through the eyes of a young German diplomat bound for his post in Washington. The diplomat has been reading "Daisy Miller," and he wonders, as he surveys Pandora Day from his deck-chair, whether she is really like James's heroine. He will indeed see her dominating her parents and laying her siege to New York and Washington society; but he will discover her difference. She is "self-made." The tale was based on the novelist's recent visit to the American capital, and particularly his view of Washington society obtained from the vantage-point of the Henry Adams home in "H" Street. The Bonnycastles of this tale are a friendly sketch of the Adamses, and Pandora's encounter with the President of the United States has in it a little of Henry's meeting with President Chester Arthur at the home of Secretary Blaine. When the German diplomat has watched the enterprising Pandora obtain a position for her fiancé from the President himself, he begins to understand what is meant by the "self-made" American girl.

Of the remaining tales in this volume, "The Impressions of a Cousin" captures a few notes of the early 1880's in the life behind New York's brownstones. This is one of James's periodic experiments in first-person narration, the "impressions" serving not only to tell the tale but to characterise the diarist. "The Author of 'Beltraffio'," which James published in 1884, announced a new theme, and his venture into what he himself called the "fantastic-gruesome." Henry had been told by Edmund Gosse that the wife of John Addington Symonds, the historian of the Italian Renaissance, abhorred her husband's work and never read his books. James conceived his tale as "the opposition between the narrow, cold, Calvinistic wife, a rigid moralist; and the husband impregnated—even to morbidness—with the spirit of Italy, the love of beauty, of art, the aesthetic view of life, and aggravated by the sense of his wife's disapproval." To have this woman will the death of her child (by withholding medical help during an illness), rather than have the boy live to read the works of his father, seemed to James "too gruesome," and yet he attempted it. His fine-spun prose and the "distance" of his American narrator and observer, who tells the tale with an Olympian ambiguity, help to soften the horror. A superficial criticism has tended to call this tale one of James's "stories of writers"; but the author of *Beltraffio*'s being a writer is incidental to the central drama. It is in reality a Medea-tale, of a female figure who sacrifices innocence to her own cruel destructive vision; in this, and in certain of James's tales to come, the piping voice of childhood is smothered by a righteousness more evil than the evil it imagines and seeks to defy. "The Author of 'Beltraffio'" is a harbinger of "The Pupil" and "The Turn of the Screw," those stories in which an adult world makes its cruel offerings on the altars of its own egotism.

LEON EDEL

Gay Head, 1962

THE SIEGE OF LONDON

PART I

I

THAT solemn piece of upholstery, the curtain of the Comédie
Française, had fallen upon the first act of the piece, and our
two Americans had taken advantage of the interval to pass out
of the huge, hot theatre, in company with the other occupants of the stalls. But they were among the first to return,
and they beguiled the rest of the intermission with looking at
the house, which had lately been cleansed of its historic cob-
webs and ornamented with frescos illustrative of the classic
drama. In the month of September the audience at the Théâtre
Français is comparatively thin, and on this occasion the
drama—*L'Aventurière* of Emile Augier—had no pretensions
to novelty. Many of the boxes were empty, others were occupied by persons of provincial or nomadic appearance. The
boxes are far from the stage, near which our spectators were
placed; but even at a distance Rupert Waterville was able to
appreciate certain details. He was fond of appreciating details,
and when he went to the theatre he looked about him a good
deal, making use of a dainty but remarkably powerful glass.
He knew that such a course was wanting in true distinction,
and that it was indelicate to level at a lady an instrument which
was often only less injurious in effect than a double-barrelled
pistol; but he was always very curious, and he was sure, in any
case, that at that moment, at that antiquated play—so he was
pleased to qualify the masterpiece of an Academician—he
would not be observed by any one he knew. Standing up
therefore with his back to the stage, he made the circuit of the

boxes, while several other persons, near him, performed the same operation with even greater coolness.

"Not a single pretty woman," he remarked at last to his friend; an observation which Littlemore, sitting in his place and staring with a bored expression at the new-looking curtain, received in perfect silence. He rarely indulged in these optical excursions; he had been a great deal in Paris and had ceased to care about it, or wonder about it, much; he fancied that the French capital could have no more surprises for him, though it had had a good many in former days. Waterville was still in the stage of surprise; he suddenly expressed this emotion. "By Jove!" he exclaimed; "I beg your pardon—I beg *her* pardon—there is, after all, a woman that may be called"—he paused a little, inspecting her—"a kind of beauty!"

"What kind?" Littlemore asked, vaguely.

"An unusual kind—an indescribable kind." Littlemore was not heeding his answer, but he presently heard himself appealed to. "I say, I wish very much you would do me a favor."

"I did you a favor in coming here," said Littlemore. "It's insufferably hot, and the play is like a dinner that has been dressed by the kitchen-maid. The actors are all *doublures*."

"It's simply to answer me this: is *she* respectable, now?" Waterville rejoined, inattentive to his friend's epigram.

Littlemore gave a groan, without turning his head. "You are always wanting to know if they are respectable. What on earth can it matter?"

"I have made such mistakes—I have lost all confidence," said poor Waterville, to whom European civilization had not ceased to be a novelty, and who during the last six months had found himself confronted with problems long unsuspected. Whenever he encountered a very nice-looking woman, he was sure to discover that she belonged to the class represented by the heroine of M. Augier's drama; and whenever his attention rested upon a person of a florid style of attraction, there was the strongest probability that she would turn out to be a countess. The countesses looked so superficial and the others looked so exclusive. Now Littlemore distinguished at a glance; he never made mistakes.

"Simply for looking at them, it doesn't matter, I suppose," said Waterville, ingenuously, answering his companion's rather cynical inquiry.

"You stare at them all alike," Littlemore went on, still without moving; "except indeed when I tell you that they are not respectable—then your attention acquires a fixedness!"

"If your judgment is against this lady, I promise never to look at her again. I mean the one in the third box from the passage, in white, with the red flowers," he added, as Littlemore slowly rose and stood beside him. "The young man is leaning forward. It is the young man that makes me doubt of her. Will you have the glass?"

Littlemore looked about him without concentration. "No, I thank you, my eyes are good enough. The young man's a very good young man," he added in a moment.

"Very indeed; but he's several years younger than she. Wait till she turns her head."

She turned it very soon—she apparently had been speaking to the *ouvreuse*, at the door of the box—and presented her face to the public—a fair, well-drawn face, with smiling eyes, smiling lips, ornamented over the brow with delicate rings of black hair and, in each ear, with the sparkle of a diamond sufficiently large to be seen across the Théâtre Français. Littlemore looked at her; then, abruptly, he gave an exclamation. "Give me the glass!"

"Do you know her?" his companion asked, as he directed the little instrument.

Littlemore made no answer; he only looked in silence; then he handed back the glass. "No, she's not respectable," he said. And he dropped into his seat again. As Waterville remained standing, he added, "Please sit down; I think she saw me."

"Don't you want her to see you?" asked Waterville the interrogator, taking his seat.

Littlemore hesitated. "I don't want to spoil her game." By this time the *entr'acte* was at an end; the curtain rose again.

It had been Waterville's idea that they should go to the theatre. Littlemore, who was always for not doing a thing, had recommended that, the evening being lovely, they should simply sit and smoke at the door of the Grand Café, in a decent part of the Boulevard. Nevertheless Rupert Waterville enjoyed the second act even less than he had done the first, which he thought heavy. He began to wonder whether his companion would wish to stay to the end; a useless line of speculation, for now that he had got to the theatre, Littlemore's objection to doing things would certainly keep him from going. Waterville also wondered what he knew about the lady in the box. Once or twice he glanced at his friend, and then he saw that Littlemore was not following the play. He was thinking of something else; he was thinking of that woman. When the curtain fell again he sat in his place, making way for his neighbors, as usual, to edge past him, grinding his knees—his legs were long—with their own protuberances. When the two men were alone in the stalls, Littlemore said: "I think I should like to see her again, after all." He spoke as if Waterville might have known all about her. Waterville was conscious of not doing so, but as there was evidently a good deal to know, he felt that he should lose nothing by being a little discreet. So, for the moment, he asked no questions; he only said—

"Well, here's the glass."

Littlemore gave him a glance of good-natured compassion. "I don't mean that I want to stare at her with that beastly thing. I mean—to see her—as I used to see her."

"How did you use to see her?" asked Waterville, bidding farewell to discretion.

"On the back piazza, at San Diego." And as his interlocutor, in receipt of this information, only stared, he went on —"Come out where we can breathe, and I'll tell you more."
They made their way to the low and narrow door, more worthy of a rabbit-hutch than of a great theatre, by which you pass from the stalls of the Comédie to the lobby, and as Littlemore went first, his ingenuous friend, behind him, could see that he glanced up at the box in the occupants of which they were interested. The more interesting of these had her back to the house; she was apparently just leaving the box, after her companion; but as she had not put on her mantle it was evident that they were not quitting the theatre. Littlemore's pursuit of fresh air did not lead him into the street; he had passed his arm into Waterville's, and when they reached that fine frigid staircase which ascends to the Foyer, he began silently to mount it. Littlemore was averse to active pleasures, but his friend reflected that now at least he had launched himself—he was going to look for the lady whom, with a monosyllable, he appeared to have classified. The young man resigned himself for the moment to asking no questions, and the two strolled together into the shining saloon where Houdon's admirable statue of Voltaire, reflected in a dozen mirrors, is gaped at by visitors obviously less acute than the genius expressed in those living features. Waterville knew that Voltaire was very witty; he had read *Candide*, and had already had several opportunities of appreciating the statue. The Foyer was not crowded; only a dozen groups were scattered over the polished floor, several others having passed out to the balcony which overhangs the square of the Palais Royal. The windows were open, the brilliant lights of Paris made the dull summer evening look like an anniversary or a revolution; a murmur of voices seemed to come up from the streets, and even in the Foyer one heard the slow click of the horses and the rumble of the crookedly-driven fiacres on the hard, smooth asphalt. A lady and a gentleman, with their backs to

our friends, stood before the image of Voltaire; the lady was dressed in white, including a white bonnet. Littlemore felt, as so many persons feel in that spot, that the scene was conspicuously Parisian, and he gave a mysterious laugh.

"It seems comical to see her here! The last time was in New Mexico."

"In New Mexico?"

"At San Diego."

"Oh, on the back piazza," said Waterville, putting things together. He had not been aware of the position of San Diego, for if on the occasion of his lately being appointed to a subordinate diplomatic post in London, he had been paying a good deal of attention to European geography, he had rather neglected that of his own country.

They had not spoken loud, and they were not standing near her; but suddenly, as if she had heard them, the lady in white turned round. Her eye caught Waterville's first, and in that glance he saw that if she had heard them it was not because they were audible but because she had extraordinary quickness of ear. There was no recognition in it—there was none, at first, even when it rested lightly upon George Littlemore. But recognition flashed out a moment later, accompanied with a delicate increase of color and a quick extension of her apparently constant smile. She had turned completely round; she stood there in sudden friendliness, with parted lips, with a hand, gloved to the elbow, almost imperiously offered. She was even prettier than at a distance. "Well, I declare!" she exclaimed; so loud that every one in the room appeared to feel personally addressed. Waterville was surprised; he had not been prepared, even after the mention of the back piazza, to find her an American. Her companion turned round as she spoke; he was a fresh, lean young man, in evening dress; he kept his hands in his pockets; Waterville imagined that he at any rate was not an American. He looked very grave—for such a fair, festive young man—and gave Waterville and

Littlemore, though his height was not superior to theirs, a narrow, vertical glance. Then he turned back to the statue of Voltaire, as if it had been, after all, among his premonitions that the lady he was attending would recognize people he didn't know, and didn't even, perhaps, care to know. This possibly confirmed slightly Littlemore's assertion that she was not respectable. The young man was, at least; consummately so. "Where in the world did you drop from?" the lady inquired.

"I have been here some time," Littlemore said, going forward, rather deliberately, to shake hands with her. He smiled a little, but he was more serious than she; he kept his eye on her own as if she had been just a trifle dangerous; it was the manner in which a duly discreet person would have approached some glossy, graceful animal which had an occasional trick of biting.

"Here in Paris, do you mean?"

"No; here and there—in Europe generally."

"Well, it's queer I haven't met you."

"Better late than never!" said Littlemore. His smile was a little fixed.

"Well, you look very natural," the lady went on.

"So do you—or very charming—it's the same thing," Littlemore answered, laughing, and evidently wishing to be easy. It was as if, face to face, and after a considerable lapse of time, he had found her more imposing than he expected when, in the stalls below, he determined to come and meet her. As he spoke, the young man who was with her gave up his inspection of Voltaire and faced about, listlessly, without looking either at Littlemore or at Waterville.

"I want to introduce you to my friend," she went on. "Sir Arthur Demesne—Mr Littlemore. Mr Littlemore—Sir Arthur Demesne. Sir Arthur Demesne is an Englishman— Mr Littlemore is a countryman of mine, an old friend. I haven't seen him for years. For how long? Don't let's count!

—I wonder you knew me," she continued, addressing Little-more. "I'm fearfully changed." All this was said in a clear, gay tone, which was the more audible as she spoke with a kind of caressing slowness. The two men, to do honor to her introduction, silently exchanged a glance; the Englishman, perhaps, colored a little. He was very conscious of his companion. "I haven't introduced you to many people yet," she remarked.

"Oh, I don't mind," said Sir Arthur Demesne.

"Well, it's queer to see you!" she exclaimed, looking still at Littlemore. "You have changed, too—I can see that."

"Not where you are concerned."

"That's what I want to find out. Why don't you introduce your friend? I see he's dying to know me!"

Littlemore proceeded to this ceremony; but he reduced it to its simplest elements, merely glancing at Rupert Waterville, and murmuring his name.

"You didn't tell him *my* name," the lady cried, while Waterville made her a formal salutation. "I hope you haven't forgotten it!"

Littlemore gave her a glance which was intended to be more penetrating than what he had hitherto permitted himself; if it had been put into words it would have said, "Ah, but *which* name?"

She answered the unspoken question, putting out her hand, as she had done to Littlemore, "Happy to make your acquaintance, Mr Waterville. I'm Mrs Headway—perhaps you've heard of me. If you've ever been in America you must have heard of me. Not so much in New York, but in the Western cities. You *are* an American? Well, then, we are all compatriots—except Sir Arthur Demesne. Let me introduce you to Sir Arthur. Sir Arthur Demesne, Mr Waterville—Mr Waterville, Sir Arthur Demesne. Sir Arthur Demesne is a member of Parliament; don't he look young?" She waited for no answer to this question, but suddenly asked another, as she moved her bracelets back over her long, loose gloves. "Well, Mr Littlemore, what are you thinking of?"

He was thinking that he must indeed have forgotten her name, for the one that she had pronounced awakened no association. But he could hardly tell her that.

"I'm thinking of San Diego."

"The back piazza, at my sister's? Oh, don't; it was too horrid. She has left now. I believe every one has left."

Sir Arthur Demesne drew out his watch with the air of a man who could take no part in these domestic reminiscences; he appeared to combine a generic self-possession with a degree of individual shyness. He said something about its being time they should go back to their seats, but Mrs Headway paid no attention to the remark. Waterville wished her to linger; he felt in looking at her as if he had been looking at a charming picture. Her low-growing hair, with its fine dense undulations, was of a shade of blackness that has now become rare; her complexion had the bloom of a white flower; her profile, when she turned her head, was as pure and fine as the outline of a cameo.

"You know this is the first theatre," she said to Waterville, as if she wished to be sociable. "And this is Voltaire, the celebrated writer."

"I'm devoted to the Comédie Française," Waterville answered, smiling.

"Dreadfully bad house; we didn't hear a word," said Sir Arthur.

"Ah, yes, the boxes!" murmured Waterville.

"I'm rather disappointed," Mrs Headway went on. "But I want to see what becomes of that woman."

"Doña Clorinde? Oh, I suppose they'll shoot her; they generally shoot the women, in French plays," Littlemore said.

"It will remind me of San Diego!" cried Mrs Headway.

"Ah, at San Diego the women did the shooting."

"They don't seem to have killed you!" Mrs Headway rejoined, archly.

"No, but I am riddled with wounds."

"Well, this is very remarkable," the lady went on, turning to Houdon's statue. "It's beautifully modelled."

"You are perhaps reading M. de Voltaire," Littlemore suggested.

"No; but I've purchased his works."

"They are not proper reading for ladies," said the young Englishman, severely, offering his arm to Mrs Headway.

"Ah, you might have told me before I had bought them!" she exclaimed, in exaggerated dismay.

"I couldn't imagine you would buy a hundred and fifty volumes."

"A hundred and fifty? I have only bought two."

"Perhaps two won't hurt you?" said Littlemore with a smile. She darted him a reproachful ray. "I know what you mean, —that I'm too bad already. Well, bad as I am, you must come and see me." And she threw him the name of her hotel, as she walked away with her Englishman. Waterville looked after the latter with a certain interest; he had heard of him in London, and had seen his portrait in "Vanity Fair."

It was not yet time to go down, in spite of this gentleman's saying so, and Littlemore and his friend passed out on the balcony of the Foyer. "Headway—Headway? Where the deuce did she get that name?" Littlemore asked, as they looked down into the animated dusk.

"From her husband, I suppose," Waterville suggested.

"From her husband? From which? The last was named Beck."

"How many has she had?" Waterville inquired, anxious to hear how it was that Mrs Headway was not respectable.

"I haven't the least idea. But it wouldn't be difficult to find out, as I believe they are all living. She was Mrs Beck—Nancy Beck—when I knew her."

"Nancy Beck!" cried Waterville, aghast. He was thinking of her delicate profile, like that of a pretty Roman empress. There was a great deal to be explained.

Littlemore explained it in a few words before they returned to their places, admitting indeed that he was not yet able to elucidate her present situation. She was a memory of his Western days; he had seen her last some six years before. He had known her very well and in several places; the circle of her activity was chiefly the Southwest. This activity was of a vague character, except in the sense that it was exclusively social. She was supposed to have a husband, one Philadelphus Beck, the editor of a Democratic newspaper, the *Dakotah Sentinel;* but Littlemore had never seen him—the pair were living apart—and it was the impression at San Diego that matrimony, for Mr and Mrs Beck, was about played out. He remembered now to have heard afterwards that she was getting a divorce. She got divorces very easily, she was so taking in court. She had got one or two before from a man whose name he had forgotten, and there was a legend that even these were not the first. She had been exceedingly divorced! When he first met her in California, she called herself Mrs Grenville, which he had been given to understand was not an appellation acquired in matrimony, but her parental name, resumed after the dissolution of an unfortunate union. She had had these episodes—her unions were all unfortunate—and had borne half a dozen names. She was a charming woman, especially for New Mexico; but she had been divorced too often—it was a tax on one's credulity; she must have repudiated more husbands than she had married.

At San Diego she was staying with her sister, whose actual spouse (she, too, had been divorced), the principal man of the place, kept a bank (with the aid of a six-shooter), and who had never suffered Nancy to want for a home during her unattached periods. Nancy had begun very young; she must be about thirty-seven to-day. That was all he meant by her not being respectable. The chronology was rather mixed; her sister at least had once told him that there was one winter when she didn't know herself *who* was Nancy's husband. She had gone in mainly for editors—she esteemed the journalistic profession. They must all have been dreadful ruffians, for her own amiability was manifest. It was well known that whatever she had done she had done in self-defence. In fine, she had done things; that was the main point now! She was very pretty, good-natured and clever, and quite the best company in those parts. She was a genuine product of the far West—a flower of the Pacific slope; ignorant, audacious, crude, but full of pluck and spirit, of natural intelligence, and of a certain intermittent, haphazard good taste. She used to say that she only wanted a chance—apparently she had found it now. At one time, without her, he didn't see how he could have put up with the life. He had started a cattle-ranch, to which San Diego was the nearest town, and he used to ride over to see her. Sometimes he stayed there for a week; then he went to see her every evening. It was horribly hot; they used to sit on the back piazza. She was always as attractive, and very nearly as well-dressed, as they had just beheld her. As far as appearance went, she might have been transplanted at an hour's notice from that dusty old settlement to the city by the Seine.

"Some of those Western women are wonderful," Littlemore said. "Like her, they only want a chance."

He had not been in love with her—there never was anything of that sort between them. There might have been of course; but as it happened there was not. Headway apparently was the successor of Beck; perhaps there had been others between. She was in no sort of "society;" she only had a local reputation ("the elegant and accomplished Mrs Beck," the newspapers called her—the other editors, to whom she wasn't married), though, indeed, in that spacious civilization the locality was large. She knew nothing of the East, and to the best of his belief at that period had never seen New York.

Various things might have happened in those six years, however; no doubt she had "come up." The West was sending us everything (Littlemore spoke as a New Yorker); no doubt it would send us at last our brilliant women. This little woman used to look quite over the head of New York; even in those days she thought and talked of Paris, which there was no prospect of her knowing; that was the way she had got on in New Mexico. She had had her ambition, her presentiments; she had known she was meant for better things. Even at San Diego she had prefigured her little Sir Arthur; every now and then a wandering Englishman came within her range. They were not all baronets and M. P.'s, but they were usually a change from the editors. What she was doing with her present acquisition he was curious to see. She was certainly— if he had any capacity for that state of mind, which was not too apparent—making him happy. She looked very splendid; Headway had probably made a "pile," an achievement not to be imputed to any of the others. She didn't accept money— he was sure she didn't accept money.

On their way back to their seats Littlemore, whose tone had been humorous, but with that strain of the pensive which is inseparable from retrospect, suddenly broke into audible laughter.

"The modelling of a statue and the works of Voltaire!" he exclaimed, recurring to two or three things she had said. "It's comical to hear her attempt those flights, for in New Mexico she knew nothing about modelling."

"She didn't strike me as affected," Waterville rejoined, feeling a vague impulse to take a considerate view of her.

"Oh, no; she's only—as she says—fearfully changed."

They were in their places before the play went on again, and they both gave another glance at Mrs Headway's box. She leaned back, slowly fanning herself, and evidently watching Littlemore, as if she had been waiting to see him come in. Sir Arthur Demesne sat beside her, rather gloomily, resting a round pink chin upon a high stiff collar; neither of them seemed to speak.

"Are you sure she makes him happy?" Waterville asked.

"Yes—that's the way those people show it."

"But does she go about alone with him that way? Where's her husband?"

"I suppose she has divorced him."

"And does she want to marry the baronet?" Waterville asked, as if his companion were omniscient.

It amused Littlemore for the moment to appear so. "He wants to marry her, I guess."

"And be divorced, like the others?"

"Oh, no; this time she has got what she wants," said Littlemore, as the curtain rose.

He suffered three days to elapse before he called at the Hôtel Meurice, which she had designated, and we may occupy this interval in adding a few words to the story we have taken from his lips. George Littlemore's residence in the far West had been of the usual tentative sort—he had gone there to replenish a pocket depleted by youthful extravagance. His first attempts had failed; the days were passing away when a fortune was to be picked up even by a young man who might be supposed to have inherited from an honorable father, lately removed, some of those fine abilities, mainly dedicated to the importation of tea, to which the elder Mr Littlemore was indebted for the power of leaving his son well off. Littlemore had dissipated his patrimony, and he was not quick to discover his talents, which, consisting chiefly of an unlimited faculty for smoking and horse-breaking, appeared to lie in the direction of none of the professions called liberal. He had been sent to Harvard to have his aptitudes cultivated, but here they took such a form that repression had been found more necessary than stimulus—repression embodied in an occasional sojourn in one of the lovely villages of the Connecticut valley. Rustication saved him, perhaps, in the sense that it detached him; it destroyed his ambitions, which had been foolish. At the age of thirty, Littlemore had mastered none of the useful arts, unless we include in the number the great art of indifference. He was roused from his indifference by a stroke of good luck. To oblige a friend who was even in more pressing need of cash than himself, he had purchased for a moderate sum (the proceeds of a successful game of poker) a share in a silver-mine which the disposer, with unusual candor, admitted to be destitute of metal. Littlemore looked into his mine and recognized the truth of the contention, which, however, was demolished some two years later by a sudden revival of curiosity on the part of one of the other shareholders. This gentleman, convinced that a silver-mine without silver is as rare as an effect without a cause, discovered the sparkle of the precious element deep down in the reasons of things. The discovery was agreeable to Littlemore, and was the beginning of a fortune which, through several dull years and in many rough places, he had repeatedly despaired of, and which a man whose purpose was never very keen did not perhaps altogether deserve. It was before he saw himself successful that he had made the acquaintance of the lady now established at the Hôtel Meurice. To-day he owned the largest share in his mine, which remained perversely productive, and which enabled him to buy, among other things, in Montana, a cattle-ranch of much finer proportions than the dry acres near San Diego. Ranches and mines encourage security, and the consciousness of not having to watch the sources of his income too anxiously (an obligation which for a man of his disposition spoils everything) now added itself to his usual coolness. It was not that this same coolness had not been considerably tried. To take only one—the principal—instance: he had lost his wife after only a twelvemonth of marriage, some three years before the date at which we meet him. He was more than forty when he encountered and wooed a young girl of twenty-three, who, like himself, had consulted all the probabilities in expecting a succession of happy years. She left him a small daughter, now intrusted to the care of his only sister, the wife of an English squire and mistress of a dull park in Hampshire. This lady, Mrs Dolphin by name, had captivated her landowner during a journey in which Mr Dolphin had promised himself to examine the institutions of the United States. The institution on which he reported most favorably was the pretty girls of the larger towns, and he returned to New York a year or two later to marry Miss Littlemore, who, unlike her brother, had not wasted her patrimony. Her sister-in-law, married many years later, and coming to Europe on this occasion, had died in London—where she flattered herself the doctors were infallible—a week after the birth of her little girl; and poor Littlemore, though relinquishing his child for the moment, remained in these disappointing countries, to be within call of the Hampshire nursery. He was rather a noticeable man, especially since his hair and mustache had turned white. Tall and strong, with a good figure and a bad carriage, he looked capable but indolent, and was usually supposed to have an importance of which he was far from being conscious. His eye was at once keen and quiet, his smile dim and dilatory, but exceedingly genuine. His principal occupation to-day was doing nothing, and he did it with a sort of artistic perfection. This faculty excited real envy on the part of Rupert Waterville, who was ten years younger than he, and who had too many ambitions and anxieties—none of them very important, but making collectively a considerable incubus—to be able to wait for inspiration. He thought it a great accomplishment, he hoped some day to arrive at it; it made a man so independent; he had his resources within his own breast. Littlemore could sit for a whole evening, without utterance or movement, smoking cigars and looking absently at his finger-nails. As every one knew that he was a good fellow and had made his fortune, this dull behavior could not well be attributed to stupidity or to moroseness. It seemed to imply a fund of reminiscence, an experience of life which had left him hundreds of things to think about. Waterville felt that if he could make a good use of these present years, and keep a sharp look-out for experience, he too, at forty-five, might have time to look at his finger-nails. He had an idea that such contemplations—not of course in their literal, but in their symbolic intensity—were a sign of a man of the world. Waterville, reckoning possibly without an ungrateful Department of State, had also an idea that he had embraced the diplomatic career. He was the junior of the two Secretaries who render the *personnel* of the United States Legation in London exceptionally numerous, and was at present enjoying his annual leave of absence. It became a diplomatist to be inscrutable, and though he had by no means, as a whole, taken Littlemore as his model—there were much better ones in the diplomatic body in London—he thought he looked inscrutable when of an evening, in Paris, after he had been asked what he would like to do, he replied that he should like to do nothing, and simply sat for an interminable time in front of the Grand Café, on the Boulevard de la Madeleine (he was very fond of cafés), ordering a succession of *demitasses*. It was very rarely that Littlemore cared even to go to the theatre, and the visit to the Comédie Française, which we have described, had been undertaken at Waterville's instance. He had seen *Le Demi-Monde* a few nights before, and had been told that *L'Aventurière* would show him a particular treatment of the same subject—the justice to be meted out to unscrupulous women who attempt to thrust themselves into honorable families. It seemed to him that in both of these cases the ladies had deserved their fate, but he wished it might have been brought about by a little less lying on the part of the representatives of honor. Littlemore and he, without being intimate, were very good friends, and spent much of their time together. As it turned out, Littlemore was very glad he had gone to the theatre, for he found himself much interested in this new incarnation of Nancy Beck.

II

His delay in going to see her was nevertheless calculated; there were more reasons for it than it is necessary to mention. But when he went, Mrs Headway was at home, and Littlemore was not surprised to see Sir Arthur Demesne in her sitting-room. There was something in the air which seemed to in-dicate that this gentleman's visit had already lasted a certain time. Littlemore thought it probable that, given the circum-stances, he would now bring it to a close; he must have learned from their hostess that Littlemore was an old and familiar friend. He might of course have definite rights—he had every appearance of it; but the more definite they were the more gracefully he could afford to waive them. Littlemore made these reflections while Sir Arthur Demesne sat there looking at him without giving any sign of departure. Mrs Headway was very gracious—she had the manner of having known you a hundred years; she scolded Littlemore extravagantly for not having been to see her sooner, but this was only a form of the gracious. By daylight she looked a little faded; but she had an expression which could never fade. She had the best rooms in the hotel, and an air of extreme opulence and prosperity; her courier sat outside, in the ante-chamber, and she evidently knew how to live. She attempted to include Sir Arthur in the conversation, but though the young man remained in his place, he declined to be included. He smiled, in silence; but he was evidently uncomfortable. The conversation, therefore, remained superficial—a quality that, of old, had by no means belonged to Mrs Headway's interviews with her friends. The Englishman looked at Littlemore with a strange, perverse expression which Littlemore, at first, with a good deal of private amusement, simply attributed to jealousy.

"My dear Sir Arthur, I wish very much you would go," Mrs Headway remarked, at the end of a quarter of an hour.

Sir Arthur got up and took his hat. "I thought I should oblige you by staying."

"To defend me against Mr Littlemore? I've known him since I was a baby—I know the worst he can do." She fixed her charming smile for a moment on her retreating visitor, and she added, with much unexpectedness, "I want to talk to him about my past!"

"That's just what I want to hear," said Sir Arthur, with his hand on the door.

"We are going to talk American; you wouldn't understand us!—He speaks in the English style," she explained, in her little sufficient way, as the baronet, who announced that at all events he would come back in the evening, let himself out.

"He doesn't know about your past?" Littlemore inquired, trying not to make the question sound impertinent.

"Oh, yes; I've told him everything; but he doesn't understand. The English are so peculiar; I think they are rather stupid. He has never heard of a woman being—" But here Mrs Headway checked herself, while Littlemore filled out the blank. "What are you laughing at? It doesn't matter," she went on; "there are more things in the world than those people have heard of. However, I like them very much; at least I like him. He's such a gentleman; do you know what I mean? Only, he stays too long, and he isn't amusing. I'm very glad to see you, for a change."

"Do you mean I'm not a gentleman?" Littlemore asked.

"No indeed; you used to be, in New Mexico. I think you were the only one—and I hope you are still. That's why I recognized you the other night; I might have cut you, you know."

"You can still, if you like. It's not too late."

"Oh, no; that's not what I want. I want you to help me."

"To help you?"

Mrs Headway fixed her eyes for a moment on the door. "Do you suppose that man is there still?"

"That young man—your poor Englishman?"

"No; I mean Max. Max is my courier," said Mrs Headway, with a certain impressiveness.

"I haven't the least idea. I'll see, if you like."

"No; in that case I should have to give him an order, and I don't know what in the world to ask him to do. He sits there for hours; with my simple habits I afford him no employment. I am afraid I have no imagination."

"The burden of grandeur," said Littlemore.

"Oh yes, I'm very grand. But on the whole I like it. I'm only afraid he'll hear. I talk so very loud; that's another thing I'm trying to get over."

"Why do you want to be different?"

"Well, because everything else is different," Mrs Headway rejoined, with a little sigh. "Did you hear that I'd lost my husband?" she went on, abruptly.

"Do you mean—a—Mr——?" and Littlemore paused, with an effect that did not seem to come home to her.

"I mean Mr Headway," she said, with dignity. "I've been through a good deal since you saw me last: marriage, and death, and trouble, and all sorts of things."

"You had been through a good deal of marriage before that," Littlemore ventured to observe.

She rested her eyes on him with soft brightness, and without a change of color. "Not so much—not so much—"

"Not so much as might have been thought."

"Not so much as was reported. I forget whether I was married when I saw you last."

"It was one of the reports," said Littlemore. "But I never saw Mr Beck."

"You didn't lose much; he was a simple *wretch!* I have done certain things in my life which I have never understood; no wonder others can't understand them. But that's all over! Are you sure Max doesn't hear?" she asked, quickly.

"Not at all sure. But if you suspect him of listening at the keyhole, I would send him away."

"I don't think he does that. I am always rushing to the door."

"Then he doesn't hear. I had no idea you had so many secrets. When I parted with you, Mr Headway was in the future."

"Well, now he's in the past. He was a pleasant man—I can understand my doing that. But he only lived a year. He had neuralgia of the heart; he left me very well off." She mentioned these various facts as if they were quite of the same order.

"I'm glad to hear it; you used to have expensive tastes."

"I have plenty of money," said Mrs Headway. "Mr Headway had property at Denver, which has increased immensely in value. After his death I tried New York. But I don't like New York." Littlemore's hostess uttered this last sentence in a tone which was the *résumé* of a social episode. "I mean to live in Europe—I like Europe," she announced; and the manner of the announcement had a touch of prophecy, as the other words had had a reverberation of history.

Littlemore was very much struck with all this, and he was greatly entertained with Mrs Headway. "Are you travelling with that young man?" he inquired, with the coolness of a person who wishes to make his entertainment go as far as possible.

She folded her arms as she leaned back in her chair. "Look here, Mr Littlemore," she said; "I'm about as good-natured as I used to be in America, but I know a great deal more. Of course I ain't travelling with that young man; he's only a friend."

"He isn't a lover?" asked Littlemore, rather cruelly.

"Do people travel with their lovers? I don't want you to laugh at me—I want you to help me." She fixed her eyes on him with an air of tender remonstrance that might have touched him; she looked so gentle and reasonable. "As I tell you, I have taken a great fancy to this old Europe; I feel as if I should never go back. But I want to see something of the life. I think it would suit me—if I could get started a little. Mr Littlemore," she added, in a moment—"I may as well be frank, for I ain't at all ashamed. I want to get into society. That's what I'm after!"

Littlemore settled himself in his chair, with the feeling of a man who, knowing that he will have to pull, seeks to obtain a certain leverage. It was in a tone of light jocosity, almost of encouragement, however, that he repeated: "Into society? It seems to me you are in it already, with baronets for your adorers."

"That's just what I want to know!" she said, with a certain eagerness. "Is a baronet much?"

"So they are apt to think. But I know very little about it."

"Ain't you in society yourself?"

"I? Never in the world! Where did you get that idea? I care no more about society than about that copy of the *Figaro*."

Mrs Headway's countenance assumed for a moment a look of extreme disappointment, and Littlemore could see that, having heard of his silver-mine and his cattle-ranch, and knowing that he was living in Europe, she had hoped to find him immersed in the world of fashion. But she speedily recovered herself. "I don't believe a word of it. You know you're a gentleman—you can't help yourself."

"I may be a gentleman, but I have none of the habits of one." Littlemore hesitated a moment, and then he added—"I lived too long in the great Southwest."

She flushed quickly; she instantly understood—understood even more that he had meant to say. But she wished to make use of him, and it was of more importance that she should appear forgiving—especially as she had the happy consciousness of being so, than that she should punish a cruel speech. She could afford, however, to be lightly ironical. "That makes no difference—a gentleman is always a gentleman."

"Not always," said Littlemore, laughing.

"It's impossible that, through your sister, you shouldn't know something about European society," said Mrs Headway.

At the mention of his sister, made with a studied lightness of reference which he caught as it passed, Littlemore was unable to repress a start. "What in the world have you got to do with my sister?" he would have liked to say. The introduction of this lady was disagreeable to him; she belonged to quite another order of ideas, and it was out of the question that Mrs Headway should ever make her acquaintance—if this was what, as that lady would have said—she was "after." But he took advantage of a side-issue. "What do you mean by European society? One can't talk about that. It's a very vague phrase."

"Well, I mean English society—I mean the society your sister lives in—that's what I mean," said Mrs Headway, who was quite prepared to be definite. "I mean the people I saw in London last May—the people I saw at the opera and in the park, the people who go to the Queen's drawing-rooms. When I was in London I stayed at that hotel on the corner of Piccadilly—that looking straight down St James's Street—and I spent hours together at the window looking at the people in the carriages. I had a carriage of my own, and when I was not at my window I was driving all round. I was all alone; I saw every one, but I knew no one—I had no one to tell me. I didn't know Sir Arthur then—I only met him a month ago at Homburg. He followed me to Paris—that's how he came to be my guest." Serenely, prosaically, without any of the inflation of vanity, Mrs Headway made this last assertion; it was as if she were used to being followed, or as if a gentleman one met at Homburg would inevitably follow. In the same tone she went on: "I attracted a good deal of attention in London—I could easily see that."

"You'll do that wherever you go," Littlemore said, insufficiently enough, as he felt.

"I don't want to attract so much; I think it's vulgar," Mrs Headway rejoined, with a certain soft sweetness which seemed to denote the enjoyment of a new idea. She was evidently open to new ideas.

"Every one was looking at you the other night at the theatre," Littlemore continued. "How can you hope to escape notice?"

"I don't want to escape notice—people have always looked at me, and I suppose they always will. But there are different ways of being looked at, and I know the way I want. I mean to have it, too!" Mrs Headway exclaimed. Yes, she was very definite.

Littlemore sat there, face to face with her, and for some time he said nothing. He had a mixture of feelings, and the memory of other places, other hours, was stealing over him. There had been of old a very considerable absence of interposing surfaces between these two—he had known her as one knew people only in the great Southwest. He had liked her extremely, in a town where it would have been ridiculous to be difficult to please. But his sense of this fact was somehow connected with Southwestern conditions; his liking for Nancy Beck was an emotion of which the proper setting was a back piazza. She presented herself here on a new basis—she appeared to desire to be classified afresh. Littlemore said to himself that this was too much trouble; he had taken her in that way—he couldn't begin at this time of day to take her in another way. He asked himself whether she were going to be a bore. It was not easy to suppose Mrs Headway capable of this offence; but she might become tiresome if she were bent upon being different. It made him rather afraid when she began to talk about European society, about his sister, about things being vulgar. Littlemore was a very good fellow, and he had at least the average human love of justice; but there was in his composition an element of the indolent, the sceptical, perhaps even the brutal, which made him desire to preserve the simplicity of their former terms of intercourse. He had no particular desire to see a woman rise again, as the mystic process was called; he didn't believe in women's rising again. He believed in their not going down; thought it perfectly possible and eminently desirable, but held it was much better for society that they should not endeavor, as the French say, to *mêler les genres*. In general, he didn't pretend to say what was good for society—society seemed to him in rather a bad way; but he had a conviction on this particular point. Nancy Beck going in for the great prizes, that spectacle might be entertaining for a simple spectator; but it would be a nuisance, an embarrassment, from the moment anything more than contemplation should be expected of him. He had no wish to be rough, but it might be well to show her that he was not to be humbugged.

"Oh, if there's anything you want you'll have it," he said in answer to her last remark. "You have always had what you want."

"Well, I want something new this time. Does your sister reside in London?"

"My dear lady, what do you know about my sister?" Littlemore asked. "She's not a woman you would care for."

Mrs Headway was silent a moment. "You don't respect me!" she exclaimed suddenly in a loud, almost gay tone of voice. If Littlemore wished, as I say, to preserve the simplicity of their old terms of intercourse, she was apparently willing to humor him.

"Ah, my dear Mrs Beck . . .!" he cried, vaguely, protestingly, and using her former name quite by accident. At San

Diego he had never thought whether he respected her or not; that never came up.

"That's a proof of it—calling me by that hateful name! Don't you believe I'm married? I haven't been fortunate in my names," she added, pensively.

"You make it very awkward when you say such mad things. My sister lives most of the year in the country; she is very simple, rather dull, perhaps a trifle narrow-minded. You are very clever, very lively, and as wide as all creation. That's why I think you wouldn't like her."

"You ought to be ashamed to run down your sister!" cried Mrs Headway. "You told me once—at San Diego—that she was the nicest woman you knew. I made a note of that, you see. And you told me she was just my age. So that makes it rather uncomfortable for you, if you won't introduce me!" And Littlemore's hostess gave a pitiless laugh. "I'm not in the least afraid of her being dull. It's very distinguished to be dull. I'm ever so much too lively."

"You are indeed, ever so much! But nothing is more easy than to know my sister," said Littlemore, who knew perfectly that what he said was untrue. And then, as a diversion from this delicate topic, he suddenly asked, "Are you going to marry Sir Arthur?"

"Don't you think I've been married about enough?"

"Possibly; but this is a new line, it would be different. An Englishman—that's a new sensation."

"If I should marry, it would be a European," said Mrs Headway calmly.

"Your chance is very good; they are all marrying Americans."

"He would have to be some one fine, the man I should marry now. I have a good deal to make up for! That's what I want to know about Sir Arthur; all this time you haven't told me."

"I have nothing in the world to tell—I have never heard of him. Hasn't he told you himself?"

"Nothing at all; he is very modest. He doesn't brag, nor make himself out anything great. That's what I like him for: I think it's in such good taste. I like good taste!" exclaimed Mrs Headway. "But all this time," she added, "you haven't told me you would help me."

"How can I help you? I'm no one, I have no power."

"You can help me by not preventing me. I want you to promise not to prevent me." She gave him her fixed, bright gaze again; her eyes seemed to look far into his.

"Good Lord, how could I prevent you?"

"I'm not sure that you could. But you might try."

"I'm too indolent, and too stupid," said Littlemore jocosely.

"Yes," she replied, musing as she still looked at him. "I think you are too stupid. But I think you are also too kind," she added more graciously. She was almost irresistible when she said such a thing as that.

They talked for a quarter of an hour longer, and at last— as if she had had scruples—she spoke to him of his own marriage, of the death of his wife, matters to which she alluded more felicitously (as he thought) than to some other points. "If you have a little girl you ought to be very happy; that's what I should like to have. Lord, I should make her a nice woman! Not like me—in another style!" When he rose to leave her, she told him that he must come and see her very often; she was to be some weeks longer in Paris; he must bring Mr Waterville.

"Your English friend won't like that—our coming very often," Littlemore said, as he stood with his hand on the door.

"I don't know what he has got to do with it," she answered, staring.

"Neither do I. Only he must be in love with you."

"That doesn't give him any right. Mercy, if I had had to

put myself out for all the men that have been in love with me!"

"Of course you would have had a terrible life! Even doing as you please, you have had rather an agitated one. But your young Englishman's sentiments appear to give him the right to sit there, after one comes in, looking blighted and bored. That might become very tiresome."

"The moment he becomes tiresome I send him away. You can trust me for that."

"Oh," said Littlemore, "it doesn't matter, after all." He remembered that it would be very inconvenient to him to have undisturbed possession of Mrs Headway.

She came out with him into the antechamber. Mr Max, the courier, was fortunately not there. She lingered a little; she appeared to have more to say.

"On the contrary, he likes you to come," she remarked in a moment; "he wants to study my friends."

"To study them?"

"He wants to find out about me, and he thinks they may tell him something. Some day he will ask you right out, 'What sort of a woman is she, any way?'"

"Hasn't he found out yet?"

"He doesn't understand me," said Mrs Headway, survey-ing the front of her dress. "He has never seen any one like me."

"I should imagine not!"

"So he will ask you, as I say."

"I will tell him you are the most charming woman in Europe."

"That ain't a description! Besides, he knows it. He wants to know if I'm respectable."

"He's very curious!" Littlemore cried, with a laugh.

She grew a little pale; she seemed to be watching his lips. "Mind you tell him," she went on with a smile that brought none of her color back.

"Respectable? I'll tell him you're adorable!"

Mrs Headway stood a moment longer. "Ah, you're no

use!" she murmured. And she suddenly turned away and passed back into her sitting-room, slowly drawing her far-trailing skirts.

III

"*Elle ne se doute de rien!*" Littlemore said to himself as he walked away from the hotel; and he repeated the phrase in talking about her to Waterville. "She wants to be right," he added; "but she will never really succeed; she has begun too late, she will never be more than half-right. However, she won't know when she's wrong, so it doesn't signify!" And then he proceeded to assert that in some respects she would remain incurable; she had no delicacy; no discretion, no shading; she was a woman who suddenly said to you, "You don't respect me!" As if that were a thing for a woman to say!

"It depends upon what she meant by it." Waterville liked to see the meanings of things.

"The more she meant by it the less she ought to say it!" Littlemore declared.

But he returned to the Hôtel Meurice, and on the next occasion he took Waterville with him. The Secretary of Legation, who had not often been in close quarters with a lady of this ambiguous quality, was prepared to regard Mrs Headway as a very curious type. He was afraid she might be dangerous; but, on the whole, he felt secure. The object of his devotion at present was his country, or at least the Department of State; he had no intention of being diverted from that allegiance. Besides, he had his ideal of the attractive woman —a person pitched in a very much lower key than this shining, smiling, rustling, chattering daughter of the Territories. The woman he should care for would have repose, a certain love of privacy—she would sometimes let one alone. Mrs Headway was personal, familiar, intimate; she was always appealing or accusing, demanding explanations and pledges, saying things one had to answer. All this was accompanied with a hundred smiles and radiations and other natural graces, but the general effect of it was slightly fatiguing. She had certainly a great deal of charm, an immense desire to please, and a wonderful collection of dresses and trinkets; but she was eager and pre-occupied, and it was impossible that other people should share her eagerness. If she wished to get into society, there was no reason why her bachelor visitors should wish to see her there; for it was the absence of the usual social incumbrances which made her drawing-room attractive. There was no doubt whatever that she was several women in one, and she ought to content herself with that sort of numerical triumph. Littlemore said to Waterville that it was stupid of her to wish to scale the heights; she ought to know how much more she was in her place down below. She appeared vaguely to irritate him; even her fluttering attempts at self-culture—she had become a great critic, and handled many of the productions of the age with a bold, free touch—constituted a vague invocation, an appeal for sympathy which was naturally annoying to a man who disliked the trouble of revising old decisions, consecrated by a certain amount of reminiscence that might be called tender. She had, however, one palpable charm; she was full of surprises. Even Waterville was obliged to confess that an element of the unexpected was not to be excluded from his conception of the woman who should have an ideal repose. Of course there were two kinds of surprises, and only one of them was thoroughly pleasant, though Mrs Headway dealt impartially in both. She had the sudden delights, the odd exclamations, the queer curiosities of a person who has grown up in a country where everything is new and many things ugly, and who, with a natural turn for the arts and amenities of life, makes a tardy acquaintance with some of the finer usages, the higher pleasures. She was provincial

—it was easy to see that she was provincial; that took no great cleverness. But what was Parisian enough—if to be Parisian was the measure of success—was the way she picked up ideas and took a hint from every circumstance. "Only give me time, and I shall know all I have need of," she said to Littlemore, who watched her progress with a mixture of admiration and sadness. She delighted to speak of herself as a poor little barbarian who was trying to pick up a few crumbs of knowledge, and this habit took great effect from her delicate face, her perfect dress, and the brilliancy of her manners.

One of her surprises was that after that first visit she said no more to Littlemore about Mrs Dolphin. He did her perhaps the grossest injustice; but he had quite expected her to bring up this lady whenever they met. "If she will only leave Agnes alone, she may do what she will," he said to Waterville, expressing his relief. "My sister would never look at her, and it would be very awkward to have to tell her so." She expected assistance; she made him feel that simply by the way she looked at him; but for the moment she demanded no definite service. She held her tongue, but she waited, and her patience itself was a kind of admonition. In the way of society, it must be confessed, her privileges were meagre, Sir Arthur Demesne and her two compatriots being, so far as the latter could discover, her only visitors. She might have had other friends, but she held her head very high, and liked better to see no one than not to see the best company. It was evident that she flattered herself that she produced the effect of being, not neglected, but fastidious. There were plenty of Americans in Paris, but in this direction she failed to extend her acquaintance; the nice people wouldn't come and see her, and nothing would have induced her to receive the others. She had the most exact conception of the people she wished to see and to avoid. Littlemore expected every day that she would ask him why he didn't bring some of his friends, and he had his answer ready. It was a very poor one, for it consisted simply of a conventional assurance that he wished to keep her for himself. She would be sure to retort that this was very "thin," as, indeed, it was; but the days went by without her calling him to account. The little American colony in Paris is rich in amiable women, but there were none to whom Littlemore could make up his mind to say that it would be a favor to him to call on Mrs Headway. He shouldn't like them the better for doing so, and he wished to like those of whom he might ask a favor. Except, therefore, that he occasionally spoke of her as a little Western woman, very pretty and rather queer, who had formerly been a great chum of his, she remained unknown in the *salons* of the Avenue Gabriel and the streets that encircle the Arch of Triumph. To ask the men to go and see her, without asking the ladies, would only accentuate the fact that he didn't ask the ladies; so he asked no one at all. Besides, it was true—just a little—that he wished to keep her to himself, and he was fatuous enough to believe that she cared much more for him than for her Englishman. Of course, however, he would never dream of marrying her, whereas the Englishman apparently was immersed in that vision. She hated her past; she used to announce that very often, talking of it as if it were an appendage of the same order as a dishonest courier, or even an inconvenient protrusion of drapery. Therefore, as Littlemore was part of her past, it might have been supposed that she would hate him too, and wish to banish him, with all the images he recalled, from her sight. But she made an exception in his favor, and if she disliked their old relations as a chapter of her own history, she seemed still to like them as a chapter of his. He felt that she clung to him, that she believed he could help her and in the long run would. It was to the long run that she appeared little by little to have attuned herself.

She succeeded perfectly in maintaining harmony between Sir Arthur Desmesne and her American visitors, who spent much less time in her drawing-room. She had easily persuaded

him that there were no grounds for jealousy, and that they had
no wish, as she said, to crowd him out; for it was ridiculous to
be jealous of two persons at once, and Rupert Waterville,
after he had learned the way to her hospitable apartment,
appeared there as often as his friend Littlemore. The two, indeed, usually came together, and they ended by relieving their
competitor of a certain sense of responsibility. This amiable
and excellent but somewhat limited and slightly pretentious
young man, who had not yet made up his mind, was sometimes rather oppressed with the magnitude of his under-
taking, and when he was alone with Mrs Headway the
tension of his thoughts occasionally became quite painful. He
was very slim and straight, and looked taller than his height;
he had the prettiest, silkiest hair, which waved away from a
large white forehead, and he was endowed with a nose of the
so-called Roman model. He looked younger than his years
(in spite of those last two attributes), partly on account of the
delicacy of his complexion and the almost childlike candor of
his round blue eye. He was diffident and self-conscious; there
were certain letters he could not pronounce. At the same time
he had the manners of a young man who had been brought up
to fill a considerable place in the world, with whom a certain
correctness had become a habit, and who, though he might
occasionally be a little awkward about small things, would
be sure to acquit himself honorably in great ones. He was
very simple, and he believed himself very serious; he had the
blood of a score of Warwickshire squires in his veins; mingled
in the last instance with the somewhat paler fluid which animated the long-necked daughter of a banker who had expected
an earl for his son-in-law, but who had consented to regard
Sir Baldwin Demesne as the least insufficient of baronets. The
boy, the only one, had come into his title at five years of age;
his mother, who disappointed her auriferous sire a second
time when poor Sir Baldwin broke his neck in the hunting
field, watched over him with a tenderness that burned as

steadily as a candle shaded by a transparent hand. She never admitted, even to herself, that he was not the cleverest of men; but it took all her own cleverness, which was much greater than his, to maintain this appearance. Fortunately he was not wild, so that he would never marry an actress or a governess, like two or three of the young men who had been at Eton with him. With this ground of nervousness the less, Lady Demesne awaited with an air of confidence his promotion to some high office. He represented in Parliament the Conservative instincts and vote of a red-roofed market town, and sent regularly to his bookseller for all the new publications on economical subjects, for he was determined that his political attitude should have a firm statistical basis. He was not conceited; he was only misinformed—misinformed, I mean, about himself. He thought himself indispensable in the scheme of things—not as an individual, but as an institution. This conviction, however, was too sacred to betray itself by vulgar assumptions. If he was a little man in a big place, he never strutted nor talked loud; he merely felt it as a kind of luxury that he had a large social circumference. It was like sleeping in a big bed; one didn't toss about the more, but one felt a greater freshness.

He had never seen anything like Mrs Headway; he hardly knew by what standard to measure her. She was not like an English lady—not like those at least with whom he had been accustomed to converse; and yet it was impossible not to see that she had a standard of her own. He suspected that she was provincial, but as he was very much under the charm he compromised matters by saying to himself that she was only foreign. It was of course provincial to be foreign; but this was, after all, a peculiarity which she shared with a great many nice people. He was not wild, and his mother had flattered herself that in this all-important matter he would not be perverse; but it was all the same most unexpected that he should have taken a fancy to an American widow, five years older than himself, who knew no one and who sometimes didn't appear to understand exactly who he was. Though he disapproved of it, it was precisely her foreignness that pleased him; she seemed to be as little as possible of his own race and creed; there was not a touch of Warwickshire in her composition. She was like an Hungarian or a Pole, with the difference that he could almost understand her language. The unfortunate young man was fascinated, though he had not yet admitted to himself that he was in love. He would be very slow and deliberate in such a position, for he was deeply conscious of its importance. He was a young man who had arranged his life; he had determined to marry at thirty-two. A long line of ancestors was watching him; he hardly knew what they would think of Mrs Headway. He hardly knew what he thought himself; the only thing he was absolutely sure of was that she made the time pass as it passed in no other pursuit. He was vaguely uneasy; he was by no means sure it was right the time should pass like that. There was nothing to show for it but the fragments of Mrs Headway's conversation, the peculiarities of her accent, the sallies of her wit, the audacities of her fancy, her mysterious allusions to her past. Of course he knew that she had a past; she was not a young girl, she was a widow—and widows are essentially an expression of an accomplished fact. He was not jealous of her antecedents, but he wished to understand them, and it was here that the difficulty occurred. The subject was illumined with fitful flashes, but it never placed itself before him as a general picture. He asked her a good many questions, but her answers were so startling that, like sudden luminous points, they seemed to intensify the darkness round their edges. She had apparently spent her life in an inferior province of an inferior country; but it didn't follow from this that she herself had been low. She had been a lily among thistles; and there was something romantic in a man in his position taking an interest in such a woman. It pleased Sir Arthur to believe he was romantic; that had been the case with several of his ancestors, who supplied a precedent without which he would perhaps not have ventured to trust himself. He was the victim of perplexities from which a single spark of direct perception would have saved him. He took everything in the literal sense; he had not a grain of humor. He sat there vaguely waiting for something to happen, and not committing himself by rash declarations. If he was in love, it was in his own way, reflectively, inexpressively, obstinately. He was waiting for the formula which would justify his conduct and Mrs Headway's peculiarities. He hardly knew where it would come from; you might have thought from his manner that he would discover it in one of the elaborate *entrées* that were served to the pair when Mrs Headway consented to dine with him at Bignon's or the Café Anglais; or in one of the numerous bandboxes that arrived from the Rue de la Paix, and from which she often lifted the lid in the presence of her admirer. There were moments when he got weary of waiting in vain, and at these moments the arrival of her American friends (he often wondered that she had so few), seemed to lift the mystery from his shoulders and give him a chance to rest. This formula—she herself was not yet able to give it, for she was not aware how much ground it was expected to cover. She talked about her past, because she thought it the best thing to do; she had a shrewd conviction that it was better to make a good use of it than to attempt to efface it. To efface it was impossible, though that was what she would have preferred. She had no objection to telling fibs, but now that she was taking a new departure, she wished to tell only those that were necessary. She would have been delighted if it had been possible to tell none at all. A few, however, were indispensable, and we need not attempt to estimate more closely the ingenious re-arrangements of fact with which she entertained and mystified Sir Arthur. She knew of course that as a product of fashionable circles she was nowhere, but she might have great success as a child of nature.

IV

RUPERT WATERVILLE, in the midst of intercourse in which every one perhaps had a good many mental reservations, never forgot that he was in a representative position, that he was responsible, official; and he asked himself more than once how far it was permitted to him to countenance Mrs Headway's pretensions to being an American lady typical even of the newer phases. In his own way he was as puzzled as poor Sir Arthur, and indeed he flattered himself that he was as particular as any Englishman could be. Suppose that after all this free association Mrs Headway should come over to London and ask at the Legation to be presented to the Queen? It would be so awkward to refuse her—of course they would have to refuse her —that he was very careful about making tacit promises. She might construe anything as a tacit promise—he knew how the smallest gestures of diplomatists were studied and interpreted. It was his effort therefore to be really the diplomatist in his relations with this attractive but dangerous woman. The party of four used often to dine together—Sir Arthur pushed his confidence so far—and on these occasions Mrs Headway, availing herself of one of the privileges of a lady, even at the most expensive restaurant—used to wipe her glasses with her napkin. One evening, when after polishing a goblet she held it up to the light, giving it, with her head on one side, the least glimmer of a wink, he said to himself as he watched her that she looked like a modern bacchante. He noticed at this moment that the baronet was gazing at her too, and he wondered if the same idea had come to him. He often wondered what the baronet thought; he had devoted first and last a good deal of speculation to the baronial class. Littlemore, alone, at this moment, was not observing Mrs Headway; he never appeared to observe her, though she often observed him. Waterville asked himself among other things why Sir Arthur had not brought his own friends to see her, for Paris during the several weeks that now elapsed was rich in English visitors. He wondered whether she had asked him and he had refused; he would have liked very much to know whether she had asked him. He explained his curiosity to Littlemore, who, however, took very little interest in it. Littlemore said, nevertheless, that he had no doubt she had asked him; she never would be deterred by false delicacy.

"She has been very delicate with you," Waterville replied. "She hasn't been at all pressing of late."

"It is only because she has given me up; she thinks I'm a brute."

"I wonder what she thinks of me," Waterville said, pensively.

"Oh, she counts upon you to introduce her to the Minister. It's lucky for you that our representative here is absent."

"Well," Waterville rejoined, "the Minister has settled two or three difficult questions, and I suppose he can settle this one. I shall do nothing but by the orders of my chief." He was very fond of talking about his chief.

"She does me injustice," Littlemore added in a moment. "I have spoken to several people about her."

"Ah; but what have you told them?"

"That she lives at the Hôtel Meurice; and that she wants to know nice people."

"They are flattered, I suppose, at your thinking them nice, but they don't go," said Waterville.

"I spoke of her to Mrs Bagshaw, and Mrs Bagshaw has promised to go."

"Ah," Waterville murmured; "you don't call Mrs Bagshaw nice? Mrs Headway won't see her."

"That's exactly what she wants,—to be able to cut some one!"

Waterville had a theory that Sir Arthur was keeping Mrs Headway as a surprise—he meant perhaps to produce her during the next London season. He presently, however, learned as much about the matter as he could have desired to know. He had once offered to accompany his beautiful compatriot to the Museum of the Luxembourg and tell her a little about the modern French school. She had not examined this collection, in spite of her determination to see everything remarkable (she carried her *Murray* in her lap even when she went to see the great tailor in the Rue de la Paix, to whom, as she said, she had given no end of points); for she usually went to such places with Sir Arthur, and Sir Arthur was indifferent to the modern painters of France. "He says there are much better men in England. I must wait for the Royal Academy, next year. He seems to think one can wait for anything, but I'm not so good at waiting as he. I can't afford to wait—I've waited long enough." So much as this Mrs Headway said on the occasion of her arranging with Rupert Waterville that they should some day visit the Luxembourg together. She alluded to the Englishman as if he were her husband or her brother, her natural protector and companion.

"I wonder if she knows how that sounds?" Waterville said to himself. "I don't believe she would do it if she knew how it sounds." And he made the further reflection that when one arrived from San Diego there was no end to the things one had to learn: it took so many things to make a well-bred woman. Clever as she was, Mrs Headway was right in saying that she couldn't afford to wait. She must learn quickly. She wrote to Waterville one day to propose that they should go to the Museum on the morrow; Sir Arthur's mother was in Paris, on her way to Cannes, where she was to spend the winter. She was only passing through, but she would be there three days and he would naturally give himself up to her. She appeared to have the properest ideas as to what a gentleman would propose to do for his mother. She herself, therefore, would be free, and she named the hour at which she should expect him to call for her. He was punctual to the appointment, and they drove across the river in the large high-hung barouche in which she constantly rolled about Paris. With Mr Max on the box—the courier was ornamented with enormous whiskers—this vehicle had an appearance of great respectability, though Sir Arthur assured her—she repeated this to her other friends—that in London, next year, they would do the thing much better for her. It struck her other friends of course that the baronet was prepared to be very consistent, and this on the whole was what Waterville would have expected of him. Littlemore simply remarked that at San Diego she drove herself about in a rickety buggy, with muddy wheels, and with a mule very often in the shafts. Waterville felt something like excitement as he asked himself whether the baronet's mother would now consent to know her. She must of course be aware that it was a woman who was keeping her son in Paris at a season when English gentlemen were most naturally employed in shooting partridges.

"She is staying at the Hôtel du Rhin, and I have made him feel that he mustn't leave her while she is here," Mrs Headway said, as they drove up the narrow Rue de Seine. "Her name is Lady Demesne, but her full title is the Honorable Lady Demesne, as she's a Baron's daughter. Her father used to be a banker, but he did something or other for the Government —the Tories, you know, they call them—and so he was raised to the peerage. So you see one *can* be raised! She has a lady with her as a companion." Waterville's neighbor gave him this information with a seriousness that made him smile; he wondered whether she thought he didn't know how a Baron's daughter was addressed. In that she was very provincial; she had a way of exaggerating the value of her intellectual acquisitions and of assuming that others had been as ignorant as she. He noted, too, that she had ended by suppressing poor Sir Arthur's name altogether, and designating him only by a sort of conjugal pronoun. She had been so much, and so easily, married, that she was full of these misleading references to gentlemen.

V

THEY walked through the gallery of the Luxembourg, and except that Mrs Headway looked at everything at once and at nothing long enough, talked, as usual, rather too loud, and bestowed too much attention on the bad copies that were being made of several indifferent pictures, she was a very agreeable companion and a grateful recipient of knowledge. She was very quick to understand, and Waterville was sure that before she left the gallery she knew something about the French school. She was quite prepared to compare it critically with London exhibitions of the following year. As Littlemore and he had remarked more than once, she was a very odd mixture. Her conversation, her personality, were full of little joints and seams, all of them very visible, where the old and the new had been pieced together. When they had passed through the different rooms of the palace Mrs Headway proposed that instead of returning directly they should take a stroll in the adjoining gardens, which she wished very much to see and was sure she should like. She had quite seized the difference between the old Paris and the new, and felt the force of the romantic associations of the Latin quarter as perfectly as if she had enjoyed all the benefits of modern culture. The autumn sun was warm in the alleys and terraces of the Luxembourg; the masses of foliage above them, clipped and squared, rusty with ruddy patches, shed a thick lacework over the white sky, which was streaked with the palest blue. The beds of flowers near the palace were of the vividest yellow and red, and the sunlight rested on the smooth gray walls of those parts of its basement that looked south; in front of which, on the long green benches, a row of brown-cheeked nurses, in white caps and white aprons, sat offering nutrition to as many bundles of white drapery. There were other white caps wandering in the broad paths, attended by little brown French children; the small, straw-seated chairs were piled and stacked in some places and disseminated in others. An old lady in black, with white hair fastened over each of her temples by a large black comb, sat on the edge of a stone bench (too high for her delicate length), motionless, staring straight before her and holding a large door-key; under a tree a priest was reading—you could see his lips move at a distance; a young soldier, dwarfish and red-legged, strolled past with his hands in his pockets, which were very much distended. Waterville sat down with Mrs Headway on the straw-bottomed chairs, and she presently said, "I like this; it's even better than the pictures in the gallery. It's more of a picture."

"Everything in France is a picture—even things that are ugly," Waterville replied. "Everything makes a subject."

"Well, I like France!" Mrs Headway went on, with a little incongruous sigh. Then, suddenly, from an impulse eevn more inconsequent than her sigh, she added, "He asked me to go and see her, but I told him I wouldn't. She may come and see me if she likes." This was so abrupt that Waterville was slightly confounded; but he speedily perceived that she had returned by a short cut to Sir Arthur Demesne and his honorable mother. Waterville liked to know about other people's affairs, but he did not like this taste to be imputed to him; and therefore, though he was curious to see how the old lady, as he called her, would treat his companion, he was rather displeased with the latter for being so confidential. He had never imagined he was so intimate with her as that. Mrs Headway, however, had a manner of taking intimacy for granted; a manner which Sir Arthur's mother at least would be sure not to like. He pretended to wonder a little what she was talking about, but she scarcely explained. She only went on, through untraceable transitions: "The least she can do is to come. I have been very kind to her son. That's not a reason for my going to her—it's a reason for her coming to me. Besides, if she doesn't like what I've done, she can leave me alone. I want to get into European society, but I want to get in in my own way. I don't want to run after people; I want them to run after me. I guess they will, some day!" Waterville listened to this with his eyes on the ground; he felt himself blushing a little. There was something in Mrs Headway that shocked and mortified him, and Littlemore had been right in saying that she had a deficiency of shading. She was terribly distinct; her motives, her impulses, her desires were absolutely glaring. She needed to see, to hear, her own thoughts. Vehement thought, with Mrs Headway, was inevitably speech, though speech was not always thought, and now she had suddenly become vehement. "If she does once come—then, ah, then, I shall be too perfect with her; I sha'n't let her go! But she must take the first step. I confess, I hope she'll be nice."

"Perhaps she won't," said Waterville perversely.

"Well, I don't care if she isn't. He has never told me anything about her; never a word about any of his own belongings. If I wished, I might believe he's ashamed of them."

"I don't think it's that."

"I know it isn't. I know what it is. It's just modesty. He doesn't want to brag—he's too much of a gentleman. He doesn't want to dazzle me—he wants me to like him for himself. Well, I do like him," she added in a moment. "But I shall like him still better if he brings his mother. They shall know that in America."

"Do you think it will make an impression in America?" Waterville asked, smiling.

"It will show them that I am visited by the British aristocracy. They won't like that."

"Surely they grudge you no innocent pleasure," Waterville murmured, smiling still.

"They grudged me common politeness—when I was in New York! Did you ever hear how they treated me, when I came on from the West?"

Waterville stared; this episode was quite new to him. His companion had turned towards him; her pretty head was tossed back like a flower in the wind; there was a flush in her cheek, a sharper light in her eye. "Ah! my dear New Yorkers, they're incapable of rudeness!" cried the young man.

"You're one of them, I see. But I don't speak of the men. The men were well enough—though they did allow it."

"Allow what, Mrs Headway?" Waterville was quite in the dark.

She wouldn't answer at once; her eyes, glittering a little, were fixed upon absent images. "What did you hear about me over there? Don't pretend you heard nothing."

He had heard nothing at all; there had not been a word about Mrs Headway in New York. He couldn't pretend, and he was obliged to tell her this. "But I have been away," he added, "and in America I didn't go out. There's nothing to go out for in New York—only little boys and girls."

"There are plenty of old women! They decided I was improper. I'm very well known in the West—I'm known from Chicago to San Francisco—if not personally (in all cases), at least by reputation. People can tell you out there. In New York they decided I wasn't good enough. Not good enough for New York! What do you say to that?" And she gave a sweet little laugh. Whether she had struggled with her pride before making this avowal, Waterville never knew. The crudity of the avowal seemed to indicate that she had no pride, and yet there was a spot in her heart which, as he now perceived, was intensely sore and had suddenly begun to throb. "I took a house for the winter—one of the handsomest houses in the place— but I sat there all alone. They didn't think me proper. Such as you see me here, I wasn't a success! I tell you the truth, at whatever cost. Not a decent woman came to see me!"

Waterville was embarrassed; diplomatist as he was, he hardly knew what line to take. He could not see what need there was of her telling him the truth, though the incident appeared to have been most curious, and he was glad to know the facts on the best authority. It was the first he knew of this remarkable woman's having spent a winter in his native city—which was virtually a proof of her having come and gone in complete obscurity. It was vain for him to pretend that he had been a good deal away, for he had been appointed to his post in London only six months before, and Mrs Headway's social failure preceded that event. In the midst of these reflections he had an inspiration. He attempted neither to explain, to minimize, nor to apologize; he ventured simply to lay his hand for an instant on her own and to exclaim, as tenderly as possible, "I wish *I* had known you were there!"

"I had plenty of men—but men don't count. If they are not a positive help, they're a hinderance, and the more you have, the worse it looks. The women simply turned their backs."

"They were afraid of you—they were jealous," Waterville said.

"It's very good of you to try and explain it away; all I know is, not one of them crossed my threshold. You needn't try and tone it down; I know perfectly how the case stands. In New York, if you please, I was a failure!"

"So much the worse for New York!" cried Waterville, who, as he afterwards said to Littlemore, had got quite worked up.

"And now you know why I want to get nto society over here?" She jumped up and stood before him; with a dry, hard smile she looked down at him. Her smile itself was an answer to her question; it expressed an urgent desire for revenge. There was an abruptness in her movements which left Waterville quite behind; but as he still sat there, returning her glance, he felt that he at last, in the light of that smile, the flash of that almost fierce question, understood Mrs Headway.

She turned away, to walk to the gate of the garden, and he went with her, laughing vaguely, uneasily, at her tragic tone. Of course she expected him to help her to her revenge; but his female relations, his mother and his sisters, his innumerable cousins, had been a party to the slight she suffered, and he reflected as he walked along that after all they had been right. They had been right in not going to see a woman who could chatter that way about her social wrongs; whether Mrs Headway were respectable or not, they had a correct instinct, for at any rate she was vulgar. European society might let her in, but European society would be wrong. New York, Waterville said to himself with a glow of civic pride, was quite capable of taking a higher stand in such a matter than London. They went some distance without speaking; at last he said, expressing honestly the thought which at that moment was uppermost in his mind, "I hate that phrase, 'getting into society.' I don't think one ought to attribute to one's self that sort of ambition. One ought to assume that one is in society —that one *is* society—and to hold that if one has good manners, one has, from the social point of view, achieved the great thing. The rest regards others."

For a moment she appeared not to understand; then she broke out: "Well, I suppose I haven't good manners; at any rate, I'm not satisfied! Of course, I don't talk right—I know that very well. But let me get where I want to first— then I'll look after my expressions. If I once get there, I shall be perfect!" she cried with a tremor of passion. They reached the gate of the garden and stood a moment outside, opposite to the low arcade of the Odéon, lined with bookstalls at which Waterville cast a slightly wistful glance, waiting for Mrs Headway's carriage, which had drawn up at a short distance. The whiskered Max had seated himself within, and on the tense, elastic cushions had fallen into a doze. The carriage got into motion without his awaking; he came to his senses only as it stopped again. He started up, staring; then, without confusion, he proceeded to descend.

"I have learned it in Italy—they say the *siesta*," he remarked with an agreeable smile, holding the door open to Mrs Headway.

"Well, I should think you had!" this lady replied, laughing amicably as she got into the vehicle, whither Waterville followed her. It was not a surprise to him to perceive that she spoiled her courier; she naturally would spoil her courier. But civilization begins at home, said Waterville; and the incident threw an ironical light upon her desire to get into society. It failed, however, to divert her thoughts from the subject she was discussing with Waterville, for as Max ascended the box and the carriage went on its way, she threw out another little note of defiance. "If once I'm all right over here, I can snap my fingers at New York! You'll see the faces those women will make."

Waterville was sure his mother and sisters would make no faces; but he felt afresh, as the carriage rolled back to the Hôtel Meurice, that now he understood Mrs Headway. As they were about to enter the court of the hotel a closed carriage passed before them, and while a few moments later he helped his companion to alight, he saw that Sir Arthur Demesne had descended from the other vehicle. Sir Arthur perceived Mrs Headway, and instantly gave his hand to a lady seated in the *coupé*. This lady emerged with a certain slow impressiveness, and as she stood before the door of the hotel—a woman still young and fair, with a good deal of height, gentle, tranquil, plainly dressed, yet distinctly imposing—Waterville saw that the baronet had brought his mother to call upon Nancy Beck. Mrs Headway's triumph had begun; the Dowager Lady Demesne had taken the first step. Waterville wondered whether the ladies in New York, notified by some magnetic

wave, were distorting their features. Mrs Headway, quickly
conscious of what had happened, was neither too prompt to
appropriate the visit, nor too slow to acknowledge it. She just
paused, smiling at Sir Arthur.

"I wish to introduce my mother—she wants very much to
know you." He approached Mrs Headway; the lady had taken
his arm. She was at once simple and circumspect; she had all
the resources of an English matron.

Mrs Headway, without advancing a step, put out her hands
as if to draw her visitor quickly closer. "I declare, you're too
sweet!" Waterville heard her say.

He was turning away, as his own business was over; but
the young Englishman, who had surrendered his mother to
the embrace, as it might now almost be called, of their hostess,
just checked him with a friendly gesture. "I daresay I sha'n't
see you again—I'm going away."

"Good-by, then," said Waterville. "You return to England?"

"No; I go to Cannes with my mother."

"You remain at Cannes?"

"Till Christmas very likely."

The ladies, escorted by Mr Max, had passed into the hotel,
and Waterville presently quitted his interlocutor. He smiled
as he walked away reflecting that this personage had obtained
a concession from his mother only at the price of a concession.

The next morning he went to see Littlemore, from whom
he had a standing invitation to breakfast, and who, as usual,
was smoking a cigar and looking through a dozen newspapers.
Littlemore had a large apartment and an accomplished cook;
he got up late and wandered about his room all the morning,
stopping from time to time to look out of his windows which
overhung the Place de la Madeleine. They had not been seated
many minutes at breakfast when Waterville announced that
Mrs Headway was about to be abandoned by Sir Arthur,
who was going to Cannes.

"That's no news to me," Littlemore said. "He came last night to bid me good-by."

"To bid you good-by? He was very civil all of a sudden."

"He didn't come from civility—he came from curiosity. Having dined here, he had a pretext for calling."

"I hope his curiosity was satisfied," Waterville remarked, in the manner of a person who could enter into such a sentiment.

Littlemore hesitated. "Well, I suspect not. He sat here some time, but we talked about everything but what he wanted to know."

"And what did he want to know?"

"Whether I know anything against Nancy Beck."

Waterville stared. "Did he call her Nancy Beck?"

"We never mentioned her; but I saw what he wanted, and that he wanted me to lead up to her—only I wouldn't do it."

"Ah, poor man!" Waterville murmured.

"I don't see why you pity him," said Littlemore. "Mrs Beck's admirers were never pitied."

"Well, of course he wants to marry her."

"Let him do it, then. I have nothing to say to it."

"He believes there's something in her past that's hard to swallow."

"Let him leave it alone, then."

"How can he, if he's in love with her?" Waterville asked, in the tone of a man who could enter into that sentiment too.

"Ah, my dear fellow, he must settle it himself. He has no right, at any rate, to ask me such a question. There was a moment, just as he was going, when he had it on his tongue's end. He stood there in the doorway, he couldn't leave me—he was going to plump out with it. He looked at me straight, and I looked straight at him; we remained that way for almost a minute. Then he decided to hold his tongue, and took himself off."

Waterville listened to this little description with intense

interest. "And if he had asked you, what would you have said?"

"What do you think?"

"Well, I suppose you would have said that his question wasn't fair?"

"That would have been tantamount to admitting the worst."

"Yes," said Waterville, thoughtfully, "you couldn't do that. On the other hand, if he had put it to you on your honor whether she were a woman to marry, it would have been very awkward."

"Awkward enough. Fortunately, he has no business to put things to me on my honor. Moreover, nothing has passed between us to give him the right to ask me questions about Mrs Headway. As she is a great friend of mine, he can't pretend to expect me to give confidential information about her."

"You don't think she's a woman to marry, all the same," Waterville declared. "And if a man were to ask you that, you might knock him down, but it wouldn't be an answer."

"It would have to serve," said Littlemore. He added in a moment, "There are certain cases where it's a man's duty to commit perjury."

Waterville looked grave. "Certain cases?"

"Where a woman's honor is at stake."

"I see what you mean. That's of course if he has been himself concerned—"

"Himself or another. It doesn't matter."

"I think it does matter. I don't like perjury," said Waterville. "It's a delicate question."

They were interrupted by the arrival of the servant with a second course, and Littlemore gave a laugh as he helped himself. "It would be a joke to see her married to that superior being!"

"It would be a great responsibility."

"Responsibility or not, it would be very amusing."

"Do you mean to assist her, then?"

"Heaven forbid! But I mean to bet on her."

Waterville gave his companion a serious glance; he thought him strangely superficial. The situation, however, was difficult, and he laid down his fork with a little sigh.

PART II

VI

THE Easter holidays that year were unusually genial; mild, watery sunshine assisted the progress of the spring. The high, dense hedges, in Warwickshire, were like walls of hawthorn imbedded in banks of primrose, and the finest trees in England, springing out of them with a regularity which suggested conservative principles, began to cover themselves with a kind of green downiness. Rupert Waterville, devoted to his duties and faithful in attendance at the Legation, had had little time to enjoy that rural hospitality which is the great invention of the English people and the most perfect expression of their character. He had been invited now and then—for in London he commended himself to many people as a very sensible young man—but he had been obliged to decline more proposals than he accepted. It was still, therefore, rather a novelty to him to stay at one of those fine old houses, surrounded with hereditary acres, which from the first of his coming to England he had thought of with such curiosity and such envy. He proposed to himself to see as many of them as possible, but he disliked to do things in a hurry, or when his mind was preoccupied, as it was so apt to be, with what he believed to be business of importance. He kept the country-houses in reserve; he would take them up in their order, after he should have got a little more used to London. Without hesitation, however, he had accepted the invitation to Longlands; it had come to him in a simple and familiar note, from Lady Demesne, with whom he had no acquaintance. He knew of her return from Cannes, where she had spent the whole winter, for he had seen it related in a Sunday newspaper; yet it was with a certain surprise that he heard from her in these informal terms. "Dear Mr Waterville," she wrote, "my son tells me that you will perhaps be able to come down here on the 17th, to spend two or three days. If you can, it will give us much pleasure. We can promise you the society of your charming countrywoman, Mrs Headway."

He had seen Mrs Headway; she had written to him a fortnight before from an hotel in Cork Street, to say that she had arrived in London for the season and should be very glad to see him. He had gone to see her, trembling with the fear that she would break ground about her presentation; but he was agreeably surprised to observe that she neglected this topic. She had spent the winter in Rome, travelling directly from that city to England, with just a little stop in Paris, to buy a few clothes. She had taken much satisfaction in Rome, where she made many friends; she assured him that she knew half the Roman nobility. "They are charming people; they have only one fault, they stay too long," she said. And, in answer to his inquiring glance, "I mean when they come to see you," she explained. "They used to come every evening, and they wanted to stay till the next day. They were all princes and counts. I used to give them cigars, &c. I knew as many people as I wanted," she added, in a moment, discovering perhaps in Waterville's eye the traces of that sympathy with which six months before he had listened to her account of her discomfiture in New York. "There were lots of English; I knew all the English, and I mean to visit them here. The Americans waited to see what the English would do, so as to do the opposite. Thanks to that, I was spared some precious specimens. There are, you know, some fearful ones. Besides, in Rome, society doesn't matter, if you have a feeling for the ruins and the Campagna; I had an immense feeling for the Campagna. I was always mooning round in some damp old temple. It reminded me a good deal of the country round San Diego—if it hadn't been for the temples. I liked to think it all over, when I was driving round; I was always brooding over the past." At this moment, however, Mrs Headway had dismissed the past; she was prepared to give herself up wholly to the actual. She wished Waterville to advise her as to how she should live—what she should do. Should she stay at a hotel or should she take a house? She guessed she had better take a house, if she could find a nice one. Max wanted to look for one, and she didn't know but she'd let him; he got her such a nice one in Rome. She said nothing about Sir Arthur Demesne, who, it seemed to Waterville, would have been her natural guide and sponsor; he wondered whether her relations with the baronet had come to an end. Waterville had met him a couple of times since the opening of Parliament, and they had exchanged twenty words, none of which, however, had reference to Mrs Headway. Waterville had been recalled to London just after the incident of which he was witness in the court of the Hôtel Meurice; and all he knew of its consequence was what he had learned from Littlemore, who, on his way back to America, where he had suddenly ascertained that there were reasons for his spending the winter, passed through the British capital. Littlemore had reported that Mrs Headway was enchanted with Lady Demesne, and had no words to speak of her kindness and sweetness. "She told me she liked to know her son's friends, and I told her I liked to know my friends' mothers," Mrs Headway had related. "I should be willing to be old if I could be like that," she had added, oblivious for the moment that she was at least as near to the age of the mother as to that of the son. The mother and son, at any rate, had retired to Cannes together, and at this moment Littlemore had received letters from home which caused him to start for Arizona. Mrs Headway had accordingly been left to her own devices, and he was afraid she had bored herself, though Mrs Bagshaw had called upon her. In November she had travelled to Italy, not by way of Cannes.

"What do you suppose she'll do in Rome?" Waterville

had asked; his imagination failing him here, for he had not yet trodden the Seven Hills.

"I haven't the least idea. And I don't care!" Littlemore added in a moment. Before he left London he mentioned to Waterville that Mrs Headway, on his going to take leave of her in Paris, had made another, and a rather unexpected, attack. "About the society business—she said I must really do something—she couldn't go on in that way. And she appealed to me in the name—I don't think I quite know how to say it."

"I should be very glad if you would try," said Waterville, who was constantly reminding himself that Americans in Europe were, after all, in a manner, to a man in his position, as the sheep to the shepherd.

"Well, in the name of the affection that we had formerly entertained for each other."

"The affection?"

"So she was good enough to call it. But I deny it all. If one had to have an affection for every woman one used to sit up 'evenings' with—!" And Littlemore paused, not defining the result of such an obligation. Waterville tried to imagine what it would be; while his friend embarked for New York, without telling him how, after all, he had resisted Mrs Headway's attack.

At Christmas, Waterville knew of Sir Arthur's return to England, and believed that he also knew that the baronet had not gone down to Rome. He had a theory that Lady Demesne was a very clever woman—clever enough to make her son do what she preferred and yet also make him think it his own choice. She had been politic, accommodating, about going to see Mrs Headway; but, having seen her and judged her, she had determined to break the thing off. She had been sweet and kind, as Mrs Headway said, because for the moment that was easiest; but she had made her last visit on the same occasion as her first. She had been sweet and kind, but she had set her face as a stone, and if poor Mrs Headway, arriving in London for the season, expected to find any vague promises redeemed, she would taste of the bitterness of shattered hopes. He had made up his mind that, shepherd as he was, and Mrs Headway one of his sheep, it was none of his present duty to run about after her, especially as she could be trusted not to stray too far. He saw her a second time, and she still said nothing about Sir Arthur. Waterville, who always had a theory, said to himself that she was waiting, that the baronet had not turned up. She was also getting into a house; the courier had found her in Chesterfield Street, Mayfair, a little gem, which was to cost her what jewels cost. After all this, Waterville was greatly surprised at Lady Demesne's note, and he went down to Longlands with much the same impatience with which, in Paris, he would have gone, if he had been able, to the first night of a new comedy. It seemed to him that, through a sudden stroke of good fortune, he had received a *billet d'auteur*.

It was agreeable to him to arrive at an English country-house at the close of the day. He liked the drive from the station in the twilight, the sight of the fields and copses and cottages, vague and lonely in contrast to his definite, lighted goal; the sound of the wheels on the long avenue, which turned and wound repeatedly without bringing him to what he reached however at last—the wide, gray front, with a glow in its scattered windows and a sweep of still firmer gravel up to the door. The front at Longlands, which was of this sober complexion, had a grand, pompous air; it was attributed to the genius of Sir Christopher Wren. There were wings which came forward in a semicircle, with statues placed at intervals on the cornice; so that in the flattering dusk it looked like an Italian palace, erected through some magical evocation in an English park. Waterville had taken a late train, which left him but twenty minutes to dress for dinner. He prided himself considerably on the art of dressing both quickly and well; but this operation left him no time to inquire whether the apartment to which he had been assigned befitted the dignity of a Secretary of Legation. On emerging from his room he found there was an ambassador in the house, and this discovery was a check to uneasy reflections. He tacitly assumed that he would have had a better room if it had not been for the ambassador, who was of course counted first. The large, brilliant house gave an impression of the last century and of foreign taste, of light colors, high, vaulted ceilings, with pale mythological frescos, gilded doors, surmounted by old French panels, faded tapestries and delicate damasks, stores of ancient china, among which great jars of pink roses were conspicuous. The people in the house had assembled for dinner in the principal hall, which was animated by a fire of great logs, and the company was so numerous that Waterville was afraid he was the last. Lady Demesne gave him a smile and a touch of her hand; she was very tranquil, and, saying nothing in particular, treated him as if he had been a constant visitor. Waterville was not sure whether he liked this or hated it; but these alternatives mattered equally little to his hostess, who looked at her guests as if to see whether the number were right. The master of the house was talking to a lady before the fire; when he caught sight of Waterville across the room, he waved him "how d'ye do," with an air of being delighted to see him. He had never had that air in Paris, and Waterville had a chance to observe, what he had often heard, to how much greater advantage the English appear in their country houses. Lady Demesne turned to him again, with her sweet vague smile, which looked as if it were the same for everything.

"We are waiting for Mrs Headway," she said.

"Ah, she has arrived?" Waterville had quite forgotten her.

"She came at half-past five. At six she went to dress. She has had two hours."

"Let us hope that the results will be proportionate," said Waterville, smiling.

"Oh, the results; I don't know," Lady Demesne murmured,

without looking at him; and in these simple words Waterville saw the confirmation of his theory that she was playing a deep game. He wondered whether he should sit next to Mrs Headway at dinner, and hoped, with due deference to this lady's charms, that he should have something more novel. The results of a toilet which she had protracted through two hours were presently visible. She appeared on the staircase which descended to the hall, and which, for three minutes, as she came down rather slowly, facing the people beneath, placed her in considerable relief. Waterville, as he looked at her, felt that this was a moment of importance for her: it was virtually her entrance into English society. Mrs Headway entered English society very well, with her charming smile upon her lips and with the trophies of the Rue de la Paix trailing behind her. She made a portentous rustling as she moved. People turned their eyes toward her; there was soon a perceptible diminution of talk, though talk had not been particularly audible. She looked very much alone, and it was rather pretentious of her to come down last, though it was possible that this was simply because, before her glass, she had been unable to please herself. For she evidently felt the importance of the occasion, and Waterville was sure that her heart was beating. She was very valiant, however; she smiled more intensely, and advanced like a woman who was used to being looked at. She had at any rate the support of knowing that she was pretty; for nothing on this occasion was wanting to her prettiness, and the determination to succeed, which might have made her hard, was veiled in the virtuous consciousness that she had neglected nothing. Lady Demesne went forward to meet her; Sir Arthur took no notice of her; and presently Waterville found himself proceeding to dinner with the wife of an ecclesiastic, to whom Lady Demesne had presented him for this purpose when the hall was almost empty. The rank of this ecclesiastic in the hierarchy he learned early on the morrow; but in the mean time it seemed to him strange,

somehow, that in England ecclesiastics should have wives.
English life, even at the end of a year, was full of those surprises. The lady, however, was very easily accounted for; she
was in no sense a violent exception, and there had been no
need of the Reformation to produce her. Her name was Mrs
April; she was wrapped in a large lace shawl; to eat her dinner
she removed but one glove, and the other gave Waterville at
moments an odd impression that the whole repast, in spite of
its great completeness, was something of the picnic order.
Mrs Headway was opposite, at a little distance; she had been
taken in, as Waterville learned from his neighbor, by a general,
a gentleman with a lean, aquiline face and a cultivated whisker,
and she had on the other side a smart young man of an identity less definite. Poor Sir Arthur sat between two ladies
much older than himself, whose names, redolent of history,
Waterville had often heard, and had associated with figures
more romantic. Mrs Headway gave Waterville no greeting;
she evidently had not seen him till they were seated at table,
when she simply stared at him with a violence of surprise that
for a moment almost effaced her smile. It was a copious and
well-ordered banquet, but as Waterville looked up and down
the table he wondered whether some of its elements might
not be a little dull. As he made this reflection he became conscious that he was judging the affair much more from Mrs
Headway's point of view than from his own. He knew no one
but Mrs April, who, displaying an almost motherly desire to
give him information, told him the names of many of their
companions; in return for which he explained to her that he
was not in that set. Mrs Headway got on in perfection with
her general; Waterville watched her more than he appeared
to do, and saw that the general, who evidently was a cool
hand, was drawing her out. Waterville hoped she would be
careful. He was a man of fancy, in his way, and as he compared
her with the rest of the company he said to himself that she
was a very plucky little woman, and that her present under-

taking had a touch of the heroic. She was alone against many, and her opponents were a very serried phalanx; those who were there represented a thousand others. They looked so different from her that to the eye of the imagination she stood very much on her merits. All those people seemed so completely made up, so unconscious of effort, so surrounded with things to rest upon; the men with their clean complexions, their well-hung chins, their cold, pleasant eyes, their shoulders set back, their absence of gesture; the women, several very handsome, half strangled in strings of pearls, with smooth plain tresses, seeming to look at nothing in particular, supporting silence as if it were as becoming as candlelight, yet talking a little, sometimes, in fresh, rich voices. They were all wrapped in a community of ideas, of traditions; they understood each other's accent, even each other's variations. Mrs Headway, with all her prettiness, seemed to transcend these variations; she looked foreign, exaggerated; she had too much expression; she might have been engaged for the evening. Waterville remarked, moreover, that English society was always looking out for amusement and that its transactions were conducted on a cash basis. If Mrs Headway were amusing enough she would probably succeed, and her fortune—if fortune there was—would not be a hinderance.

In the drawing-room, after dinner, he went up to her, but she gave him no greeting. She only looked at him with an expression he had never seen before—a strange, bold expression of displeasure.

"Why have you come down here?" she asked. "Have you come to watch me?"

Waterville colored to the roots of his hair. He knew it was terribly little like a diplomatist; but he was unable to control his blushes. Besides, he was shocked, he was angry, and in addition he was mystified. "I came because I was asked," he said.

"Who asked you?"

"The same person that asked you, I suppose—Lady Desmesne,"

"She's an old cat!" Mrs Headway exclaimed, turning away from him.

He turned away from her as well. He didn't know what he had done to deserve such treatment. It was a complete surprise; he had never seen her like that before. She was a very vulgar woman; that was the way people talked, he supposed, at San Diego. He threw himself almost passionately into the conversation of the others, who all seemed to him, possibly a little by contrast, extraordinarily genial and friendly. He had not, however, the consolation of seeing Mrs Headway punished for her rudeness, for she was not in the least neglected. On the contrary, in the part of the room where she sat the group was denser, and every now and then it was agitated with unanimous laughter. If she should amuse them, he said to himself, she would succeed, and evidently she was amusing them.

VII

IF she was strange, he had not come to the end of her strangeness. The next day was a Sunday and uncommonly fine; he was down before breakfast, and took a walk in the park, stopping to gaze at the thin-legged deer, scattered like pins on a velvet cushion over some of the remoter slopes, and wandering along the edge of a large sheet of ornamental water, which had a temple, in imitation of that of Vesta, on an island in the middle. He thought at this time no more about Mrs Headway; he only reflected that these stately objects had for more than a hundred years furnished a background to a great deal of family history. A little more reflection would perhaps have suggested to him that Mrs Headway was possibly an incident of some importance in the history of a family. Two or three ladies failed to appear at breakfast; Mrs Headway was one of them.

"She tells me she never leaves her room till noon," he heard Lady Demesne say to the general, her companion of the previous evening, who had asked about her. "She takes three hours to dress."

"She's a monstrous clever woman!" the general exclaimed.

"To do it in three hours?"

"No, I mean the way she keeps her wits about her."

"Yes; I think she's very clever," said Lady Demesne, in a tone in which Waterville flattered himself that he saw more meaning than the general could see. There was something in this tall, straight, deliberate woman, who seemed at once benevolent and distant, that Waterville admired. With her delicate surface, her conventional mildness, he could see that she was very strong; she had set her patience upon a height, and she carried it like a diadem. She had very little to say to Waterville, but every now and then she made some inquiry of him that showed she had not forgotten him. Demesne himself was apparently in excellent spirits, though there was nothing bustling in his deportment, and he only went about looking very fresh and fair, as if he took a bath every hour or two, and very secure against the unexpected. Waterville had less conversation with him than with his mother; but the young man had found occasion to say to him the night before, in the smoking-room, that he was delighted Waterville had been able to come, and that if he was fond of real English scenery there were several things about there he should like very much to show him.

"You must give me an hour or two before you go, you know; I really think there are some things you'll like."

Sir Arthur spoke as if Waterville would be very fastidious; he seemed to wish to attach a vague importance to him. On the Sunday morning after breakfast he asked Waterville if he should care to go to church; most of the ladies and several of the men were going.

"It's just as you please, you know; but it's rather a pretty walk across the fields, and a curious little church of King Stephen's time."

Waterville knew what this meant; it was already a picture. Besides, he liked going to church, especially when he sat in the Squire's pew, which was sometimes as big as a boudoir. So he replied that he should be delighted. Then he added, without explaining his reason—

"Is Mrs Headway going?"

"I really don't know," said his host, with an abrupt change of tone—as if Waterville had asked him whether the house-keeper were going.

"The English are awfully queer!" Waterville indulged mentally in this exclamation, to which since his arrival in England he had had recourse whenever he encountered a gap in the consistency of things. The church was even a better picture than Sir Arthur's description of it, and Waterville said to himself that Mrs Headway had been a great fool not to come. He knew what she was after; she wished to study English life, so that she might take possession of it, and to pass in among a hedge of bobbing rustics, and sit among the monuments of the old Demesnes, would have told her a great deal about English life. If she wished to fortify herself for the struggle she had better come to that old church. When he returned to Longlands—he had walked back across the mea-dows with the canon's wife, who was a vigorous pedestrian—it wanted half an hour of luncheon, and he was unwilling to go indoors. He remembered that he had not yet seen the gardens, and he wandered away in search of them. They were on a scale which enabled him to find them without difficulty, and they looked as if they had been kept up unremittingly for a cen-tury or two. He had not advanced very far between their blooming borders when he heard a voice that he recognized, and a moment after, at the turn of an alley, he came upon Mrs Headway, who was attended by the master of Longlands. She was bareheaded beneath her parasol, which she flung back, stopping short, as she beheld her compatriot.

"Oh, it's Mr Waterville come to spy me out as usual!" It was with this remark that she greeted the slightly embarrassed young man.

"Hallo! you've come home from church," Sir Arthur said, pulling out his watch.

Waterville was struck with his coolness. He admired it; for, after all, he said to himself, it must have been disagreeable to him to be interrupted. He felt a little like a fool, and wished he had kept Mrs April with him, to give him the air of having come for her sake.

Mrs Headway looked adorably fresh, in a toilet which Waterville, who had his ideas on such matters, was sure would not be regarded as the proper thing for a Sunday morning in an English country house: a *négligé* of white flounces and frills, interspersed with yellow ribbons—a garment which Madame de Pompadour might have worn when she received a visit from Louis XV., but would probably not have worn when she went into the world. The sight of this costume gave the finishing touch to Waterville's impression that Mrs Headway knew, on the whole, what she was about. She would take a line of her own; she would not be too accommodating. She would not come down to breakfast; she would not go to church; she would wear on Sunday mornings little elaborately informal dresses, and look dreadfully un-British and un-Protestant. Perhaps, after all, this was better. She began to talk with a certain volubility.

"Isn't this too lovely? I walked all the way from the house. I'm not much at walking, but the grass in this place is like a parlor. The whole thing is beyond everything. Sir Arthur, you ought to go and look after the Ambassador; it's shameful the way I've kept you. You didn't care about the Ambassador? You said just now you had scarcely spoken to him, and you must make it up. I never saw such a way of neglecting your guests. Is that the usual style over here? Go and take him out for a ride, or make him play a game of billiards. Mr Waterville will take me home; besides, I want to scold him for spying on me."

Waterville sharply resented this accusation. "I had no idea you were here," he declared.

"We weren't hiding," said Sir Arthur quietly. "Perhaps you'll see Mrs Headway back to the house. I think I ought to look after old Davidoff. I believe lunch is at two."

He left them, and Waterville wandered through the gardens with Mrs Headway. She immediately wished to know if he had come there to look after her; but this inquiry was accompanied, to his surprise, with the acrimony she had displayed the night before. He was determined not to let that pass, however; when people had treated him in that way they should not be allowed to forget it.

"Do you suppose I am always thinking of you?" he asked. "You're out of my mind sometimes. I came here to look at the gardens, and if you hadn't spoken to me I should have passed on."

Mrs Headway was perfectly good-natured; she appeared not even to hear his defence. "He has got two other places," she simply rejoined. "That's just what I wanted to know."

But Waterville would not be turned away from his grievance. That mode of reparation to a person whom you had insulted which consisted in forgetting that you had done so, was doubtless largely in use in New Mexico; but a person of honor demanded something more. "What did you mean last night by accusing me of having come down here to watch you? You must excuse me if I tell you that I think you were rather rude." The sting of this accusation lay in the fact that there was a certain amount of truth in it; yet for a moment

Mrs Headway, looking very blank, failed to recognize the allusion. "She's a barbarian, after all," thought Waterville. "She thinks a woman may slap a man's face and run away!"

"Oh!" cried Mrs Headway, suddenly, "I remember, I was angry with you; I didn't expect to see you. But I didn't really care about it at all. Every now and then I am angry, like that, and I work it off on any one that's handy. But it's over in three minutes, and I never think of it again. I was angry last night; I was furious with the old woman."

"With the old woman?"

"With Sir Arthur's mother. She has no business here, any way. In this country, when the husband dies, they're expected to clear out. She has a house of her own, ten miles from here, and she has another in Portman Square; so she's got plenty of places to live. But she sticks—she sticks to him like a plaster. All of a sudden it came over me that she didn't invite me here because she liked me, but because she suspects me. She's afraid we'll make a match, and she thinks I ain't good enough for her son. She must think I'm in a great hurry to get hold of him. I never went after him, he came after me. I should never have thought of anything if it hadn't been for him. He began it last summer at Homburg; he wanted to know why I didn't come to England; he told me I should have great success. He doesn't know much about it, any way; he hasn't got much gumption. But he's a very nice man, all the same; it's very pleasant to see him surrounded by his—" And Mrs Headway paused a moment, looking admiringly about her—"Surrounded by all his old heirlooms. I like the old place," she went on; "it's beautifully mounted; I'm quite satisfied with what I've seen. I thought Lady Demesne was very friendly; she left a card on me in London, and very soon after, she wrote to me to ask me here. But I'm very quick; I sometimes see things in a flash. I saw something yesterday, when she came to speak to me at dinner-time. She saw I looked pretty, and it made her blue with rage; she hoped I would be ugly. I should like very much to oblige her; but what can one do? Then I saw that she had asked me here only because he insisted. He didn't come to see me when I first arrived—he never came near me for ten days. She managed to prevent him; she got him to make some promise. But he changed his mind after a little, and then he had to do something really polite. He called three days in succession, and he made her come. She's one of those women that resists as long as she can, and then seems to give in, while she's really resisting more than ever. She hates me like poison; I don't know what she thinks I've done. She's very underhand; she's a regular old cat. When I saw you last night at dinner, I thought she had got you here to help her."

"To help her?" Waterville asked.

"To tell her about me. To give her information, that she can make use of against me. You may tell her what you like!"

Waterville was almost breathless with the attention he had given this extraordinary burst of confidence, and now he really felt faint. He stopped short; Mrs Headway went on a few steps, and then, stopping too, turned and looked at him. "You're the most unspeakable woman!" he exclaimed. She seemed to him indeed a barbarian.

She laughed at him—he felt she was laughing at his expression of face—and her laugh rang through the stately gardens. "What sort of a woman is that?"

"You've got no delicacy," said Waterville, resolutely.

She colored quickly, though, strange to say, she appeared not to be angry. "No delicacy?" she repeated.

"You ought to keep those things to yourself."

"Oh, I know what you mean; I talk about everything. When I'm excited I've got to talk. But I must do things in my own way. I've got plenty of delicacy, when people are nice to me. Ask Arthur Demesne if I ain't delicate—ask George Littlemore if I ain't. Don't stand there all day; come in to lunch!" And Mrs Headway resumed her walk, while Rupert Waterville, raising his eyes for a moment, slowly overtook her.

"Wait till I get settled; then I'll be delicate," she pursued. "You can't be delicate when you're trying to save your life. It's very well for *you* to talk, with the whole American Legation to back you. Of course I'm excited. I've got hold of this thing, and I don't mean to let go!" Before they reached the house she told him why he had been invited to Longlands at the same time as herself. Waterville would have liked to believe that his personal attractions sufficiently explained the fact; but she took no account of this supposition. Mrs Headway preferred to think that she lived in an element of ingenious machination, and that most things that happened had reference to herself. Waterville had been asked because he represented, however modestly, the American Legation, and their host had a friendly desire to make it appear that this pretty American visitor, of whom no one knew anything, was under the protection of that establishment. "It would start me better," said Mrs Headway, serenely. "You can't help yourself—you've helped to start me. If he had known the Minister he would have asked him—or the first secretary. But he don't know them."

They reached the house by the time Mrs Headway had developed this idea, which gave Waterville a pretext more than sufficient for detaining her in the portico. "Do you mean to say Sir Arthur told you this?" he inquired, almost sternly.

"Told me? Of course not! Do you suppose I would let him take the tone with me that I need any favors? I should like to hear him tell me that I'm in want of assistance!"

"I don't see why he shouldn't—at the pace you go yourself. You say it to every one."

"To every one? I say it to you, and to George Littlemore —when I'm nervous. I say it to you because I like you, and to him because I'm afraid of him. I'm not in the least afraid of you, by the way. I'm all alone—I haven't got any one. I must have some comfort, mustn't I? Sir Arthur scolded me for putting you off last night—he noticed it; and that was what made me guess his idea."

"I'm much obliged to him," said Waterville, rather bewildered.

"So mind you answer for me. Don't you want to give me your arm, to go in?"

"You're a most extraordinary combination," he murmured, as she stood smiling at him.

"Oh, come, don't *you* fall in love with me!" she cried, with a laugh; and, without taking his arm, passed in before him.

That evening, before he went to dress for dinner, Waterville wandered into the library, where he felt sure that he should find some superior bindings. There was no one in the room, and he spent a happy half-hour among the treasures of literature and the triumphs of old morocco. He had a great esteem for good literature; he held that it should have handsome covers. The daylight had begun to wane, but whenever, in the rich-looking dimness, he made out the glimmer of a well-gilded back, he took down the volume and carried it to one of the deep-set windows. He had just finished the inspection of a delightfully fragrant folio, and was about to carry it back to its niche, when he found himself standing face to face with Lady Demesne. He was startled for a moment, for her tall, slim figure, her fair visage, which looked white in the high, brown room, and the air of serious intention with which she presented herself, gave something spectral to her presence. He saw her smile, however, and heard her say, in that tone of hers which was sweet almost to sadness, "Are you looking at our books? I'm afraid they are rather dull."

"Dull? Why, they are as bright as the day they were bound." And he turned the glittering panels of his folio towards her.

"I'm afraid I haven't looked at them for a long time," she murmured, going nearer to the window, where she stood looking out. Beyond the clear pane the park stretched away, with the grayness of evening beginning to hang itself on the great limbs of the oaks. The place appeared cold and empty, and the trees had an air of conscious importance, as if nature herself had been bribed somehow to take the side of county families. Lady Demesne was not an easy person to talk with; she was neither spontaneous nor abundant; she was conscious of herself, conscious of many things. Her very simplicity was conventional, though it was rather a noble convention. You might have pitied her, if you had seen that she lived in constant unrelaxed communion with certain rigid ideals. This made her at times seem tired, like a person who has undertaken too much. She gave an impression of still brightness, which was not at all brilliancy, but a carefully preserved purity. She said nothing for a moment, and there was an appearance of design in her silence, as if she wished to let him know that she had a certain business with him, without taking the trouble to announce it. She had been accustomed to expect that people would suppose things, and to be saved the trouble of explanations. Waterville made some hap-hazard remark about the beauty of the evening (in point of fact, the weather had changed for the worse), to which she vouchsafed no reply. Then, presently, she said, with her usual gentleness, "I hoped I should find you here—I wish to ask you something."

"Anything I can tell you—I shall be delighted!" Waterville exclaimed.

She gave him a look, not imperious, almost appealing, which seemed to say—"Please be very simple—very simple indeed." Then she glanced about her, as if there had been other people in the room; she didn't wish to appear closeted with him, or to have come on purpose. There she was, at any rate, and she went on. "When my son told me he should ask you to come down, I was very glad. I mean, of course, that we were delighted—" And she paused a moment. Then she added, simply, "I want to ask you about Mrs Headway."

"Ah, here it is!" cried Waterville within himself. More

superficially, he smiled, as agreeably as possible, and said, "Ah yes, I see!"

"Do you mind my asking you? I hope you don't mind. I haven't any one else to ask."

"Your son knows her much better than I do." Waterville said this without an intention of malice, simply to escape from the difficulties of his situation; but after he had said it, he was almost frightened by its mocking sound.

"I don't think he knows her. She knows him, which is very different. When I ask him about her, he merely tells me she is fascinating. She *is* fascinating," said her ladyship, with inimitable dryness.

"So I think, myself. I like her very much," Waterville rejoined, cheerfully.

"You are in all the better position to speak of her, then."

"To speak well of her," said Waterville, smiling.

"Of course, if you can. I should be delighted to hear you do that. That's what I wish—to hear some good of her."

It might have seemed, after this, that nothing would have remained but for Waterville to launch himself in a panegyric of his mysterious countrywoman; but he was no more to be tempted into that danger than into another. "I can only say I like her," he repeated. "She has been very kind to me."

"Every one seems to like her," said Lady Demesne, with an unstudied effect of pathos. "She is certainly very amusing."

"She is very good-natured; she has lots of good intentions."

"What do you call good intentions?" asked Lady Demesne, very sweetly.

"Well, I mean that she wants to be friendly and pleasant."

"Of course you have to defend her. She's your countrywoman."

"To defend her—I must wait till she's attacked," said Waterville, laughing.

"That's very true. I needn't call your attention to the fact that I am not attacking her. I should never attack a person staying in this house. I only want to know something about her, and if you can't tell me, perhaps at least you can mention some one who will."

"She'll tell you herself. Tell you by the hour!"

"What she has told my son? I shouldn't understand it. My son doesn't understand it. It's very strange. I rather hoped you might explain it."

Waterville was silent a moment. "I'm afraid I can't explain Mrs Headway," he remarked at last.

"I see you admit she is very peculiar."

Waterville hesitated again. "It's too great a responsibility to answer you." He felt that he was very disobliging; he knew exactly what Lady Demesne wished him to say. He was unprepared to blight the reputation of Mrs Headway to accommodate Lady Demesne; and yet, with his active little imagination, he could enter perfectly into the feelings of this tender, formal, serious woman, who—it was easy to see—had looked for her own happiness in the cultivation of duty and in extreme constancy to two or three objects of devotion chosen once for all. She must, indeed, have had a vision of things which would represent Mrs Headway as both displeasing and dangerous. But he presently became aware that she had taken his last words as a concession in which she might find help.

"You know why I ask you these things, then?"

"I think I have an idea," said Waterville, persisting in irrelevant laughter. His laugh sounded foolish in his own ears.

"If you know that, I think you ought to assist me." Her tone changed as she spoke these words; there was a quick tremor in it; he could see it was a confession of distress. Her distress was deep; he immediately felt that it must have been, before she made up her mind to speak to him. He was sorry for her, and determined to be very serious.

"If I could help you I would. But my position is very difficult."

"It's not so difficult as mine!" She was going all lengths; she was really appealing to him. "I don't imagine that you are under any obligation to Mrs Headway—you seem to me very different," she added.

Waterville was not insensible to any discrimination that told in his favor; but these words gave him a slight shock, as if they had been an attempt at bribery. "I am surprised that you don't like her," he ventured to observe.

Lady Demesne looked out of the window a little. "I don't think you are really surprised, though possibly you try to be. I don't like her, at any rate, and I can't fancy why my son should. She's very pretty, and she appears to be very clever; but I don't trust her. I don't know what has taken possession of him; it is not usual in his family to marry people like that. I don't think she's a lady. The person I should wish for him would be so very different—perhaps you can see what I mean. There's something in her history that we don't understand. My son understands it no better than I. If you could only explain to us, that might be a help. I treat you with great confidence the first time I see you; it's because I don't know where to turn. I am exceedingly anxious."

It was very plain that she was anxious; her manner had become more vehement; her eyes seemed to shine in the thickening dusk. "Are you very sure there is danger?" Waterville asked. "Has he asked her to marry him, and has she consented?"

"If I wait till they settle it all, it will be too late. I have reason to believe that my son is not engaged, but he is terribly entangled. At the same time he is very uneasy, and that may save him yet. He has a great sense of honor. He is not satisfied about her past life; he doesn't know what to think of what we have been told. Even what she admits is so strange. She has been married four or five times—she has been divorced again and again—it seems so extraordinary. She tells him that in America it is different, and I daresay you have not our ideas; but really there is a limit to everything. There must have been some great irregularities—I am afraid some great scandals. It's dreadful to have to accept such things. He has not told me all this; but it's not necessary he should tell me; I know him well enough to guess."

"Does he know that you have spoken to me?" Waterville asked.

"Not in the least. But I must tell you that I shall repeat to him anything that you may say against her."

"I had better say nothing, then. It's very delicate. Mrs Headway is quite undefended. One may like her or not, of course. I have seen nothing of her that is not perfectly correct."

"And you have heard nothing?"

Waterville remembered Littlemore's assertion that there were cases in which a man was bound in honor to tell an untruth, and he wondered whether this were such a case. Lady Demesne imposed herself, she made him believe in the reality of her grievance, and he saw the gulf that divided her from a pushing little woman who had lived with Western editors. She was right to wish not to be connected with Mrs Headway. After all, there had been nothing in his relations with that lady to make it incumbent on him to lie for her. He had not sought her acquaintance, she had sought his; she had sent for him to come and see her. And yet he couldn't give her away, as they said in New York; that stuck in his throat. "I am afraid I really can't say anything. And it wouldn't matter. Your son won't give her up because I happen not to like her."

"If he were to believe she has done wrong, he would give her up."

"Well, I have no right to say so," said Waterville.

Lady Demesne turned away; she was much disappointed in him. He was afraid she was going to break out—"Why, then, do you suppose I asked you here?" She quitted her place near the window and was apparently about to leave the room. But she stopped short. "You know something against her, but you won't say it."

Waterville hugged his folio and looked awkward. "You attribute things to me. I shall never say anything."

"Of course you are perfectly free. There is some one else who knows, I think—another American—a gentleman who was in Paris when my son was there. I have forgotten his name."

"A friend of Mrs Headway's? I suppose you mean George Littlemore."

"Yes—Mr Littlemore. He has a sister, whom I have met; I didn't know she was his sister till to-day. Mrs Headway spoke of her, but I find she doesn't know her. That itself is a proof, I think. Do you think *he* would help me?" Lady Demesne asked, very simply.

"I doubt it, but you can try."

"I wish he had come with you. Do you think he would come?"

"He is in America at this moment, but I believe he soon comes back."

"I shall go to his sister; I will ask her to bring him to see me. She is extremely nice; I think she will understand. Unfortunately there is very little time."

"Don't count too much on Littlemore," said Waterville, gravely.

"You men have no pity."

"Why should we pity you? How can Mrs Headway hurt such a person as you?"

Lady Demesne hesitated a moment. "It hurts me to hear her voice."

"Her voice is very sweet."

"Possibly. But she's horrible!"

This was too much, it seemed to Waterville; poor Mrs Headway was extremely open to criticism, and he himself had declared she was a barbarian. Yet she was not horrible. "It's for your son to pity you. If he doesn't, how can you expect it of others?'"

"Oh, but he does!" And with a majesty that was more striking even than her logic, Lady Demesne moved towards the door.

Waterville advanced to open it for her, and as she passed out he said, "There's one thing you can do—try to like her!"

She shot him a terrible glance. "That would be worst of all!"

VIII

GEORGE LITTLEMORE arrived in London on the twentieth of May, and one of the first things he did was to go and see Waterville at the Legation, where he made known to him that he had taken for the rest of the season a house at Queen Anne's Gate, so that his sister and her husband, who, under the pressure of diminished rents, had let their own town-residence, might come up and spend a couple of months with him.

"One of the consequences of your having a house will be that you will have to entertain Mrs Headway," Waterville said.

Littlemore sat there with his hands crossed upon his stick; he looked at Waterville with an eye that failed to kindle at the mention of this lady's name. "Has she got into European society?" he asked, rather languidly.

"Very much, I should say. She has a house, and a carriage, and diamonds, and everything handsome. She seems already to know a lot of people; they put her name in the *Morning Post*. She has come up very quickly; she's almost famous. Every one is asking about her—you'll be plied with questions."

Littlemore listened gravely. "How did she get in?"

"She met a large party at Longlands, and made them all think her great fun. They must have taken her up; she only wanted a start."

Littlemore seemed suddenly to be struck with the grotesqueness of this news, to which his first response was a burst of quick laughter. "To think of Nancy Beck! The people here are queer people. There's no one they won't go after. They wouldn't touch her in New York."

"Oh, New York's old-fashioned," said Waterville; and he announced to his friend that Lady Demesne was very eager for his arrival, and wanted to make him help her prevent her son's bringing such a person into the family. Littlemore apparently was not alarmed at her ladyship's projects, and intimated, in the manner of a man who thought them rather impertinent, that he could trust himself to keep out of her way. "It isn't a proper marriage, at any rate," Waterville declared.

"Why not, if he loves her?"

"Oh, if that's all you want!" cried Waterville, with a degree of cynicism that rather surprised his companion. "Would you marry her yourself?"

"Certainly, if I were in love with her."

"You took care not to be that."

"Yes, I did—and so Demesne had better have done. But since he's bitten—!" and Littlemore terminated his sentence in a suppressed yawn.

Waterville presently asked him how he would manage, in view of his sister's advent, about asking Mrs Headway to his house; and he replied that he would manage by simply not asking her. Upon this, Waterville declared that he was very inconsistent; to which Littlemore rejoined that it was very possible. But he asked whether they couldn't talk about something else than Mrs Headway. He couldn't enter into the young man's interest in her, and was sure to have enough of her later.

Waterville would have been sorry to give a false idea of his interest in Mrs Headway; for he flattered himself the feeling had definite limits. He had been two or three times to see her; but it was a relief to think that she was now quite independent of him. There had been no revival of that intimate intercourse which occurred during the visit to Longlands. She could dispense with assistance now; she knew herself that she was in the current of success. She pretended to be surprised at her good fortune, especially at its rapidity; but she was really surprised at nothing. She took things as they came, and, being essentially a woman of action, wasted almost as little time in elation as she would have done in despondence. She talked a great deal about Lord Edward and Lady Margaret, and about such other members of the nobility as had shown a desire to cultivate her acquaintance; professing to understand perfectly the sources of a popularity which apparently was destined to increase. "They come to laugh at me," she said; "they come simply to get things to repeat. I can't open my mouth but they burst into fits. It's a settled thing that I'm an American humorist; if I say the simplest things, they begin to roar. I must express myself somehow; and indeed when I hold my tongue they think me funnier than ever. They repeat what I say to a great person, and a great person told some of them the other night that he wanted to hear me for himself. I'll do for him what I do for the others; no better and no worse. I don't know how I do it; I talk the only way I can. They tell me it isn't so much the things I say as the way I say them. Well, they're very easy to please. They don't care for me; it's only to be able to repeat Mrs Headway's 'last.' Every one wants to have it first; it's a regular race." When she found what was expected of her, she undertook to supply the article in abundance; and the poor little woman really worked hard at her Americanisms. If the taste of London lay that way, she would do her best to gratify it; it was only a pity she hadn't known it before; she would have made more extensive preparations. She thought it a disadvantage, of old, to live in

Arizona, in Dakotah, in the newly admitted States; but now she perceived that, as she phrased it to herself, this was the best thing that ever had happened to her. She tried to remember all the queer stories she had heard out there, and keenly regretted that she had not taken them down in writing; she drummed up the echoes of the Rocky Mountains and practised the intonations of the Pacific slope. When she saw her audience in convulsions, she said to herself that this was success, and believed that, if she had only come to London five years sooner, she might have married a duke. That would have been even a more absorbing spectacle for the London world than the actual proceedings of Sir Arthur Demesne, who, however, lived sufficiently in the eye of society to justify the rumor that there were bets about town as to the issue of his already protracted courtship. It was food for curiosity to see a young man of his pattern—one of the few "earnest" young men of the Tory side, with an income sufficient for tastes more marked than those by which he was known—make up to a lady several years older than himself, whose fund of Californian slang was even larger than her stock of dollars. Mrs Headway had got a good many new ideas since her arrival in London, but she also retained several old ones. The chief of these—it was now a year old—was that Sir Arthur Demesne was the most irreproachable young man in the world. There were, of course, a good many things that he was not. He was not amusing; he was not insinuating; he was not of an absolutely irrepressible ardor. She believed he was constant; but he was certainly not eager. With these things, however, Mrs Headway could perfectly dispense; she had, in particular, quite outlived the need of being amused. She had had a very exciting life, and her vision of happiness at present was to be magnificently bored. The idea of complete and uncriticised respectability filled her soul with satisfaction; her imagination prostrated itself in the presence of this virtue. She was aware that she had achieved it but ill in her own person; but she could now, at least, connect herself with it by sacred ties. She could prove in that way what was her deepest feeling. This was a religious appreciation of Sir Arthur's great quality—his smooth and rounded, his blooming, lily-like exemption from social flaws.

She was at home when Littlemore went to see her, and surrounded by several visitors, to whom she was giving a late cup of tea and to whom she introduced her compatriot. He stayed till they dispersed, in spite of the manœuvres of a gentleman who evidently desired to outstay him, but who, whatever might have been his happy fortune on former visits, received on this occasion no encouragement from Mrs Headway. He looked at Littlemore slowly, beginning with his boots and travelling upwards, as if to discover the reason of so unexpected a preference, and then, without a salutation, left him face to face with their hostess.

"I'm curious to see what you'll do for me, now that you've got your sister with you," Mrs Headway presently remarked, having heard of this circumstance from Rupert Waterville. "I suppose you'll have to do something, you know. I'm sorry for you; but I don't see how you can get off. You might ask me to dine some day when she's dining out. I would come even then, I think, because I want to keep on the right side of you."

"I call that the wrong side," said Littlemore.

"Yes, I see. It's your sister that's on the right side. You're in rather an embarrassing position, ain't you? However, you take those things very quietly. There's something in you that exasperates me. What does your sister think of me? Does she hate me?"

"She knows nothing about you."

"Have you told her nothing?"

"Never a word."

"Hasn't she asked you? That shows that she hates me. She thinks I ain't creditable to America. I know all that. She wants to show people over here that, however they may be taken in by me, she knows much better. But she'll have to ask you about me; she can't go on for ever. Then what'll you say?"

"That you're the most successful woman in Europe."

"Oh, bother!" cried Mrs Headway, with irritation.

"Haven't you got into European society?"

"Maybe I have, maybe I haven't. It's too soon to see. I can't tell this season. Every one says I've got to wait till next, to see if it's the same. Sometimes they take you up for a few weeks, and then never know you again. You've got to fasten the thing somehow—to drive in a nail."

"You speak as if it were your coffin," said Littlemore.

"Well, it is a kind of coffin. I'm burying my past!"

Littlemore winced at this. He was tired to death of her past. He changed the subject, and made her talk about London, a topic which she treated with a great deal of humor. She entertained him for half an hour, at the expense of most of her new acquaintances and of some of the most venerable features of the great city. He himself looked at England from the outside, as much as it was possible to do; but in the midst of her familiar allusions to people and things known to her only since yesterday, he was struck with the fact that she would never really be initiated. She buzzed over the surface of things like a fly on a window-pane. She liked it immensely; she was flattered, encouraged, excited; she dropped her confident judgments as if she were scattering flowers, and talked about her intentions, her prospects, her wishes. But she knew no more about English life than about the molecular theory. The words in which he had described her of old to Waterville came back to him: "*Elle ne se doute de rien!*" Suddenly she jumped up; she was going out to dine, and it was time to dress. "Before you leave I want you to promise me something," she said off-hand, but with a look which he had seen before and which meant that the point was important. "You'll be sure to be questioned about me." And then she paused.

"How do people know I know you?"

"You haven't bragged about it? Is that what you mean? You can be a brute when you try. They do know it, at any rate. Possibly I may have told them. They'll come to you, to ask about me. I mean from Lady Demesne. She's in an awful state—she's so afraid her son'll marry me."

Littlemore was unable to control a laugh. "I'm not, if he hasn't done it yet."

"He can't make up his mind. He likes me so much, yet he thinks I'm not a woman to marry." It was positively grotesque, the detachment with which she spoke of herself.

"He must be a poor creature if he won't marry you as you are," Littlemore said.

This was not a very gallant form of speech; but Mrs Headway let it pass. She only replied, "Well, he wants to be very careful, and so he ought to be!"

"If he asks too many questions, he's not worth marrying."

"I beg your pardon—he's worth marrying whatever he does—he's worth marrying for me. And I want to marry him—that's what I want to do."

"Is he waiting for me, to settle it?"

"He's waiting for I don't know what—for some one to come and tell him that I'm the sweetest of the sweet. Then he'll believe it. Some one who has been out there and knows all about me. Of course you're the man, you're created on purpose. Don't you remember how I told you in Paris that he wanted to ask you? He was ashamed, and he gave it up; he tried to forget me. But now it's all on again; only, meanwhile, his mother has been at him. She works at him night and day, like a weasel in a hole, to persuade him that I'm far beneath him. He's very fond of her, and he's very open to influence —I mean from his mother, not from any one else. Except me, of course. Oh, I've influenced him, I've explained everything fifty times over. But some things are rather complicated, don't you know; and he keeps coming back to them. He wants every little speck explained. He won't come to you himself, but his mother will, or she'll send some of her people. I guess she'll send the lawyer—the family solicitor, they call him. She wanted to send him out to America to make inquiries, only she didn't know where to send. Of course I couldn't be expected to give the places, they've got to find them out for themselves. She knows all about you, and she has made the acquaintance of your sister. So you see how much I know. She's waiting for you; she means to catch you. She has an idea she can fix you—make you say what'll meet her views. Then she'll lay it before Sir Arthur. So you'll be so good as to deny everything."

Littlemore listened to this little address attentively, but the conclusion left him staring. "You don't mean that anything I can say will make a difference?"

"Don't be affected! You know it will as well as I."

"You make him out a precious idiot."

"Never mind what I make him out. I want to marry him, that's all. And I appeal to you solemnly. You can save me, as you can lose me. If you lose me, you'll be a coward. And if you say a word against me, I shall be lost."

"Go and dress for dinner, that's your salvation," Littlemore answered, separating from her at the head of the stairs.

IX

It was very well for him to take that tone; but he felt as he walked home that he should scarcely know what to say to people who were determined, as Mrs Headway put it, to catch him. She had worked a certain spell; she had succeeded in making him feel responsible. The sight of her success, however, rather hardened his heart; he was irritated by her ascending movement. He dined alone that evening, while his sister and her husband, who had engagements every day for a month, partook of their repast at the expense of some friends. Mrs Dolphin, however, came home rather early, and immediately sought admittance to the small apartment at the foot of the staircase, which was already spoken of as Littlemore's den. Reginald had gone to a "squash" somewhere, and she had returned without delay, having something particular to say to her brother. She was too impatient even to wait till the next morning. She looked impatient; she was very unlike George Littlemore. "I want you to tell me about Mrs Headway," she said, while he started slightly at the coincidence of this remark with his own thoughts. He was just making up his mind at last to speak to her. She unfastened her cloak and tossed it over a chair, then pulled off her long tight black gloves, which were not so fine as those Mrs Headway wore; all this as if she were preparing herself for an important interview. She was a small, neat woman, who had once been pretty, with a small, thin voice, a sweet, quiet manner, and a perfect knowledge of what it was proper to do on every occasion in life. She always did it, and her conception of it was so definite that failure would have left her without excuse. She was usually not taken for an American, but she made a point of being one, because she flattered herself that she was of a type which, in that nationality, borrowed distinction from its rarity. She was by nature a great conservative, and had ended by being a better Tory than her husband. She was thought by some of her old friends to have changed immensely since her marriage. She knew as much about English society as if she had invented it; had a way, usually, of looking as if she were dressed for a ride; had also thin lips and pretty teeth; and was as positive as she was amiable. She told her brother that Mrs Headway had given out that he was her most intimate friend, and she thought it rather odd he had never spoken of her. He admitted that he had known her a long time, referred to the circumstances in which the acquaintance had sprung up, and added that he had seen her that afternoon. He sat there smoking his cigar and looking at the ceiling, while Mrs Dolphin delivered herself of a series of questions. Was it true that he liked her so much, was it true he thought her a possible woman to marry, was it not true that her antecedents had been most peculiar?

"I may as well tell you that I have a letter from Lady Demesne," Mrs Dolphin said. "It came to me just before I went out, and I have it in my pocket."

She drew forth the missive, which she evidently wished to read to him; but he gave her no invitation to do so. He knew that she had come to him to extract a declaration adverse to Mrs Headway's projects, and however little satisfaction he might take in this lady's upward flight, he hated to be urged and pushed. He had a great esteem for Mrs Dolphin, who, among other Hampshire notions, had picked up that of the preponderance of the male members of a family, so that she treated him with a consideration which made his having an English sister rather a luxury. Nevertheless he was not very encouraging about Mrs Headway. He admitted once for all that she had not behaved properly—it wasn't worth while to split hairs about that—but he couldn't see that she was much worse than many other women, and he couldn't get up much feeling about her marrying or not marrying. Moreover, it was none of his business, and he intimated that it was none of Mrs Dolphin's.

"One surely can't resist the claims of common humanity!" his sister replied; and she added that he was very inconsistent. He didn't respect Mrs Headway, he knew the most dreadful things about her, he didn't think her fit company for his own flesh and blood. And yet he was willing to let poor Arthur Demesne be taken in by her!

"Perfectly willing!" Littlemore exclaimed. "All I've got to do is not to marry her myself."

"Don't you think we have any responsibilities, any duties?"

"I don't know what you mean. If she can succeed, she's welcome. It's a splendid sight in its way."

"How do you mean splendid?'"

"Why, she has run up the tree as if she were a squirrel!"

"It's very true that she has an audacity à *toute épreuve*. But English society has become scandalously easy. I never saw anything like the people that are taken up. Mrs Headway has had only to appear to succeed. If they think there's something bad about you they'll be sure to run after you. It's like the decadence of the Roman Empire. You can see to look at Mrs Headway that she's not a lady. She's pretty, very pretty, but she looks like a dissipated dressmaker. She failed absolutely in New York. I have seen her three times—she apparently goes everywhere. I didn't speak of her—I was wanting to see what you would do. I saw that you meant to do nothing, then this letter decided me. It's written on purpose to be shown to you; it's what she wants you to do. She wrote to me before I came to town, and I went to see her as soon as I arrived. I think it very important. I told her that if she would draw up a little statement I would put it before you as soon as we got settled. She's in real distress. I think you ought to feel for her. You ought to communicate the facts exactly as they stand. A woman has no right to do such things and come and ask to be accepted. She may make it up with her conscience, but she can't make it up with society. Last night at Lady Dovedale's I was afraid she would know who I was and come and speak to me. I was so frightened that I went away. If Sir Arthur wishes to marry her for what she is, of course he's welcome. But at least he ought to know."

Mrs Dolphin was not excited nor voluble; she moved from point to point with a calmness which had all the air of being used to have reason on its side. She deeply desired, however, that Mrs Headway's triumphant career should be checked; she had sufficiently abused the facilities of things. Herself a party to an international marriage, Mrs Dolphin naturally wished that the class to which she belonged should close its ranks and carry its standard high.

"It seems to me that she's quite as good as the little baronet," said Littlemore, lighting another cigar.

"As good? What do you mean? No one has ever breathed a word against him."

"Very likely. But he's a nonentity, and she at least is somebody. She's a person, and a very clever one. Besides, she's quite as good as the women that lots of them have married. I never heard that the British gentry were so unspotted."

"I know nothing about other cases," Mrs Dolphin said, "I only know about this one. It so happens that I have been brought near to it, and that an appeal has been made to me. The English are very romantic—the most romantic people in the world, if that's what you mean. They do the strangest things, from the force of passion—even those from whom you would least expect it. They marry their cooks—they marry their coachmen—and their romances always have the most miserable end. I'm sure this one would be most wretched. How can you pretend that such a woman as that is to be trusted? What I see is a fine old race—one of the oldest and most honorable in England, people with every tradition of good conduct and high principle—and a dreadful, disreputable, vulgar little woman, who hasn't an idea of what such things are, trying to force her way into it. I hate to see such things—I want to go to the rescue!"

"I don't—I don't care anything about the fine old race."

"Not from interested motives, of course, any more than I. But surely, on artistic grounds, on grounds of decency?"

"Mrs Headway isn't indecent—you go too far. You must remember that she's an old friend of mine." Littlemore had become rather stern; Mrs Dolphin was forgetting the consideration due, from an English point of view, to brothers.

She forgot it even a little more. "Oh, if you are in love with her, too!" she murmured, turning away.

He made no answer to this, and the words had no sting for him. But at last, to finish the affair, he asked what in the world the old lady wanted him to do. Did she want him to go out into Piccadilly and announce to the passers-by that there was one winter when even Mrs Headway's sister didn't know who was her husband?

Mrs Dolphin answered this inquiry by reading out Lady Demesne's letter, which her brother, as she folded it up again, pronounced one of the most extraordinary letters he had ever heard.

"It's very sad—it's a cry of distress," said Mrs Dolphin. "The whole meaning of it is that she wishes you would come and see her. She doesn't say so in so many words, but I can read between the lines. Besides, she told me she would give anything to see you. Let me assure you it's your duty to go."

"To go and abuse Nancy Beck?"

"Go and praise her, if you like!" This was very clever of Mrs Dolphin, but her brother was not so easily caught. He didn't take that view of his duty, and he declined to cross her ladyship's threshold. "Then she'll come and see you," said Mrs Dolphin, with decision.

"If she does, I'll tell her Nancy's an angel."

"If you can say so conscientiously, she'll be delighted to hear it," Mrs Dolphin replied, as she gathered up her cloak and gloves.

Meeting Rupert Waterville the next day, as he often did, at the St George's Club, which offers a much-appreciated hospitality to secretaries of legation and to the natives of the countries they assist in representing, Littlemore let him know that his prophecy had been fulfilled and that Lady Demesne had been making proposals for an interview. "My sister read me a most remarkable letter from her," he said.

"What sort of a letter?"

"The letter of a woman so scared that she will do anything. I may be a great brute, but her fright amuses me."

"You're in the position of Olivier de Jalin, in the *Demi-Monde*," Waterville remarked.

"In the *Demi-Monde?*" Littlemore was not quick at catching literary allusions.

"Don't you remember the play we saw in Paris? Or like Don Fabrice in *L'Aventurière*. A bad woman tries to marry an honorable man, who doesn't know how bad she is, and they who do know step in and push her back."

"Yes, I remember. There was a good deal of lying, all round."

"They prevented the marriage, however, which is the great thing."

"The great thing, if you care about it. One of them was the intimate friend of the fellow, the other was his son. Demesne's nothing to me."

"He's a very good fellow," said Waterville.

"Go and tell him, then."

"Play the part of Olivier de Jalin? Oh, I can't; I'm not Olivier. But I wish he would come along. Mrs Headway oughtn't really to be allowed to pass."

"I wish to heaven they'd let me alone," Littlemore murmured, ruefully, staring for a while out of the window.

"Do you still hold to that theory you propounded in Paris? Are you willing to commit perjury?" Waterville asked.

"Of course I can refuse to answer questions—even that one."

"As I told you before, that will amount to a condemnation."

"It may amount to what it pleases. I think I will go to Paris."

"That will be the same as not answering. But it's quite the best thing you can do. I have been thinking a great deal about it, and it seems to me, from the social point of view, that, as I say, she really oughtn't to pass." Waterville had the air of looking at the thing from a great elevation; his tone, the expression of his face, indicated this lofty flight; the effect of which, as he glanced down at his didactic young friend, Littlemore found peculiarly irritating.

"No, after all, hanged if they shall drive me away!" he exclaimed abruptly; and walked off, while his companion looked after him.

X

THE morning after this Littlemore received a note from Mrs Headway—a short and simple note, consisting merely of the words, "I shall be at home this afternoon; will you come and see me at five? I have something particular to say to you." He sent no answer to this inquiry, but he went to the little house in Chesterfield Street at the hour that its mistress had designated.

"I don't believe you know what sort of woman I am!" she exclaimed, as soon as he stood before her.

"Oh, Lord!" Littlemore groaned, dropping into a chair. Then he added, "Don't begin on that sort of thing!"

"I shall begin—that's what I wanted to say. It's very important. You don't know me—you don't understand me. You think you do—but you don't."

"It isn't for the want of your having told me—many, many times!" And Littlemore smiled, though he was bored at the prospect that opened before him. The last word of all was, decidedly, that Mrs Headway was a nuisance. She didn't deserve to be spared!

She glared at him a little, at this; her face was no longer the face that smiled. She looked sharp and violent, almost old; the change was complete. But she gave a little angry laugh. "Yes, I know; men are so stupid. They know nothing about women but what women tell them. And women tell them things on purpose, to see how stupid they can be. I've told you things like that, just for amusement, when it was dull. If you believed them, it was your own fault. But now I am serious, I want you really to know."

"I don't want to know. I know enough."

"How do you mean, you know enough?" she cried, with a flushed face. "What business have you to know anything?" The poor little woman, in her passionate purpose, was not obliged to be consistent, and the loud laugh with which Littlemore greeted this interrogation must have seemed to her unduly harsh. "You shall know what I want you to know, however. You think me a bad woman—you don't respect me; I told you that in Paris. I have done things I don't understand, myself, to-day; that I admit, as fully as you please. But I've completely changed, and I want to change everything. You ought to enter into that; you ought to see what I want. I hate everything that has happened to me before this; I loathe it, I despise it. I went on that way trying—one thing and another. But now I've got what I want. Do you expect me to go down on my knees to you? I believe I will, I'm so anxious. You can help me—no one else can do a thing—no one can do anything—they are only waiting to see if he'll do it. I told you in Paris you could help me, and it's just as true now. Say a good word for me, for God's sake! You haven't lifted your little finger, or I should know it by this time. It will just make the difference. Or if your sister would come and see me, I should be all right. Women are pitiless, pitiless, and you are pitiless too. It isn't that she's anything so great, most of my friends are better than that!—but she's the one woman who *knows*, and people know that she knows. *He* knows that she knows, and he knows she doesn't come. So she kills me—she kills me! I understand perfectly what he wants—I shall do everything, be anything, I shall be the most perfect wife. The old woman will adore me when she knows me—it's too stupid of her not to see. Everything in the past is over; it has all fallen away from me; it's the life of another woman. This was what I wanted; I knew I should find it some day. What could I do in those horrible places? I had to take what I could. But now I've got a nice country. I want you to do me justice; you have never done me justice; that's what I sent for you for."

Littlemore suddenly ceased to be bored; but a variety of feelings had taken the place of a single one. It was impossible not to be touched; she really meant what she said. People don't change their nature; but they change their desires, their ideal, their effort. This incoherent and passionate protestation was an assurance that she was literally panting to be respectable. But the poor woman, whatever she did, was condemned, as Littlemore had said of old, in Paris, to Waterville, to be only half-right. The color rose to her visitor's face as he listened to this outpouring of anxiety and egotism; she had not managed her early life very well, but there was no need of her going down on her knees. "It's very painful to me to hear all this," he said. "You are under no obligation to say such things to me. You entirely misconceive my attitude—my influence."

"Oh yes, you shirk it—you only wish to shirk it!" she cried, flinging away fiercely the sofa-cushion on which she had been resting.

"Marry whom you please!" Littlemore almost shouted, springing to his feet.

He had hardly spoken when the door was thrown open, and the servant announced Sir Arthur Demesne. The baronet entered with a certain briskness, but he stopped short on seeing that Mrs Headway had another visitor. Recognizing Littlemore, however, he gave a slight exclamation, which might have passed for a greeting. Mrs Headway, who had risen as he came in, looked with extraordinary earnestness from one of the men to the other; then, like a person who had a sudden inspiration, she clasped her hands together and cried out, "I'm so glad you've met; if I had arranged it, it couldn't be better!"

"If you had arranged it?" said Sir Arthur, crinkling a little his high, white forehead, while the conviction rose before Littlemore that she had indeed arranged it.

"I'm going to do something very strange," she went on, and her eye glittered with a light that confirmed her words.

"You're excited, I'm afraid you're ill." Sir Arthur stood there with his hat and his stick; he was evidently much annoyed.

"It's an excellent opportunity; you must forgive me if I take advantage." And she flashed a tender, touching ray at the baronet. "I have wanted this a long time—perhaps you have seen I wanted it. Mr Littlemore has known me a long, long time; he's an old, old friend. I told you that in Paris, don't you remember? Well, he's my only one, and I want him to speak for me." Her eyes had turned now to Littlemore; they rested upon him with a sweetness that only made the whole proceeding more audacious. She had begun to smile again, though she was visibly trembling. "He's my only one," she continued; "it's a great pity, you ought to have known others. But I'm very much alone, I must make the best of what I have. I want so much that some one else than myself should speak for me. Women usually can ask that service of a relative, or of another woman. I can't; it's a great pity, but it's not my fault, it's my misfortune. None of my people are here; and I'm terribly alone in the world. But Mr Littlemore will tell you; he will say he has known me for years. He will tell you whether he knows any reason—whether he knows anything against me. He's been wanting the chance; but he thought he couldn't begin himself. You see I treat you as an old friend, dear Mr Littlemore. I will leave you with Sir Arthur. You will both excuse me." The expression of her face, turned towards Littlemore, as she delivered herself of this singular proposal had the intentness of a magician who wishes to work a spell. She gave Sir Arthur another smile, and then she swept out of the room.

The two men remained in the extraordinary position that

she had created for them; neither of them moved even to open the door for her. She closed it behind her, and for a moment there was a deep, portentous silence. Sir Arthur Demesne, who was very pale, stared hard at the carpet.

"I am placed in an impossible situation," Littlemore said at last, "and I don't imagine that you accept it any more than I do."

The baronet kept the same attitude; he neither looked up nor answered. Littlemore felt a sudden gush of pity for him. Of course he couldn't accept the situation; but all the same, he was half sick with anxiety to see how this nondescript American, who was both so valuable and so superfluous, so familiar and so inscrutable, would consider Mrs Headway's challenge.

"Have you any question to ask me?" Littlemore went on.

At this Sir Arthur looked up. Littlemore had seen the look before; he had described it to Waterville after the baronet came to call on him in Paris. There were other things mingled with it now—shame, annoyance, pride; but the great thing, the intense desire to *know*, was paramount.

"Good God, how can I tell him?" Littlemore exclaimed to himself.

Sir Arthur's hesitation was probably extremely brief; but Littlemore heard the ticking of the clock while it lasted. "Certainly, I have no question to ask," the young man said in a voice of cool, almost insolent surprise.

"Good-day, then."

"Good-day."

And Littlemore left Sir Arthur in possession. He expected to find Mrs Headway at the foot of the staircase; but he quitted the house without interruption.

On the morrow, after lunch, as he was leaving the little mansion at Queen Anne's Gate, the postman handed him a letter. Littlemore opened and read it on the steps of his house, an operation which took but a moment. It ran as follows:—

"Dear Mr Littlemore,—It will interest you to know that I am engaged to be married to Sir Arthur Demesne, and that our marriage is to take place as soon as their stupid old Parliament rises. But it's not to come out for some days, and I am sure that I can trust meanwhile to your complete discretion.

"Yours very sincerely,
"Nancy H.

"P.S.—He made me a terrible scene for what I did yesterday, but he came back in the evening and made it up. That's how the thing comes to be settled. He won't tell me what passed between you—he requested me never to allude to the subject. I don't care; I was bound you should speak!"

Littlemore thrust this epistle into his pocket and marched away with it. He had come out to do various things, but he forgot his business for the time, and before he knew it had walked into Hyde Park. He left the carriages and riders to one side of him and followed the Serpentine into Kensington Gardens, of which he made the complete circuit. He felt annoyed, and more disappointed than he understood—than he would have understood if he had tried. Now that Nancy Beck had succeeded, her success seemed offensive, and he was almost sorry he had not said to Sir Arthur—"Oh, well, she was pretty bad, you know." However, now the thing was settled, at least they would leave him alone. He walked off his irritation, and before he went about the business he had come out for, had ceased to think about Mrs Headway. He went home at six o'clock, and the servant who admitted him informed him in doing so that Mrs Dolphin had requested he should be told on his return that she wished to see him in the drawing-room. "It's another trap!" he said to himself, instinctively; but, in spite of this reflection, he went upstairs. On entering the apartment in which Mrs Dolphin was accustomed to sit, he found that she had a visitor. This visitor, who was apparently on the point of departing, was a tall, elderly woman, and the two ladies stood together in the middle of the room.

"I'm so glad you've come back," said Mrs Dolphin, without meeting her brother's eye. "I want so much to introduce you to Lady Demesne, and I hoped you would come in. Must you really go—won't you stay a little?" she added, turning to her companion; and without waiting for an answer, went on hastily—"I must leave you a moment—excuse me. I will come back!" Before he knew it, Littlemore found himself alone with Lady Demesne, and he understood that, since he had not been willing to go and see her, she had taken upon herself to make an advance. It had the queerest effect, all the same, to see his sister playing the same tricks as Nancy Beck!

"Ah, she must be in a fidget!" he said to himself as he stood before Lady Demesne. She looked delicate and modest, even timid, as far as a tall, serene woman who carried her head very well could look so; and she was such a different type from Mrs Headway that his present vision of Nancy's triumph gave her by contrast something of the dignity of the vanquished. It made him feel sorry for her. She lost no time; she went straight to the point. She evidently felt that in the situation in which she had placed herself, her only advantage could consist in being simple and business-like.

"I'm so glad to see you for a moment. I wish so much to ask you if you can give me any information about a person you know and about whom I have been in correspondence with Mrs Dolphin. I mean Mrs Headway."

"Won't you sit down?" asked Littlemore.

"No, I thank you. I have only a moment,"

"May I ask you why you make this inquiry?"

"Of course I must give you my reason. I am afraid my son will marry her."

Littlemore was puzzled for a moment; then he felt sure that she was not yet aware of the fact imparted to him in Mrs

Headway's note. "You don't like her?" he said, exaggerating in spite of himself the interrogative inflexion.

"Not at all," said Lady Demesne, smiling and looking at him. Her smile was gentle, without rancor; Littlemore thought it almost beautiful.

"What would you like me to say?" he asked.

"Whether you think her respectable."

"What good will that do you? How can it possibly affect the event?"

"It will do me no good, of course, if your opinion is favorable. But if you tell me it is not, I shall be able to say to my son that the one person in London who has known her more than six months thinks her a bad woman."

This epithet, on Lady Demesne's clear lips, evoked no protest from Littlemore. He had suddenly become conscious of the need to utter the simple truth with which he had answered Rupert Waterville's first question at the Théâtre Français. "I don't think Mrs Headway respectable," he said.

"I was sure you would say that." Lady Demesne seemed to pant a little.

"I can say nothing more—not a word. That's my opinion. I don't think it will help you."

"I think it will. I wished to have it from your own lips. That makes all the difference," said Lady Demesne. "I am exceedingly obliged to you." And she offered him her hand; after which he accompanied her in silence to the door.

He felt no discomfort, no remorse, at what he had said; he only felt relief. Perhaps it was because he believed it would make no difference. It made a difference only in what was at the bottom of all things—his own sense of fitness. He only wished he had remarked to Lady Demesne that Mrs Headway would probably make her son a capital wife. But that, at least, would make no difference. He requested his sister, who had wondered greatly at the brevity of his interview with Lady Demesne, to spare him all questions on this subject; and Mrs

Dolphin went about for some days in the happy faith that there were to be no dreadful Americans in English society compromising her native land.

Her faith, however, was short-lived. Nothing had made any difference; it was, perhaps, too late. The London world heard in the first days of July, not that Sir Arthur Demesne was to marry Mrs Headway, but that the pair had been privately, and it was to be hoped, as regards Mrs Headway, on this occasion indissolubly, united. Lady Demesne gave neither sign nor sound; she only retired to the country.

"I think you might have done differently," said Mrs Dolphin, very pale, to her brother. "But of course everything will come out now."

"Yes, and make her more the fashion than ever!" Littlemore answered, with cynical laughter. After his little interview with the elder Lady Demesne, he did not feel himself at liberty to call again upon the younger; and he never learned—he never even wished to know—whether in the pride of her success she forgave him.

Waterville—it was very strange—was positively scandalized at this success. He held that Mrs Headway ought never to have been allowed to marry a confiding gentleman; and he used, in speaking to Littlemore, the same words as Mrs Dolphin. He thought Littlemore might have done differently. He spoke with such vehemence that Littlemore looked at him hard—hard enough to make him blush.

"Did you want to marry her yourself?" his friend inquired. "My dear fellow, you're in love with her! That's what's the matter with you."

This, however, blushing still more, Waterville indignantly denied. A little later he heard from New York that people were beginning to ask who in the world was Mrs Headway.

THE IMPRESSIONS OF A COUSIN

I

NEW YORK, *April* 3, 1873.—There are moments when I feel that she has asked too much of me—especially since our arrival in this country. These three months have not done much toward making me happy here. I don't know what the difference is—or rather I do; and I say this only because it's less trouble. It is no trouble, however, to say that I like New York less than Rome: that, after all, *is* the difference. And then there's nothing to sketch! For ten years I have been sketching, and I really believe I do it very well. But how can I sketch Fifty-third Street? There are times when I even say to myself, How can I even inhabit Fifty-third Street? When I turn into it from the Fifth Avenue the vista seems too hideous: the narrow, impersonal houses, with the dry, hard tone of their brown-stone, a surface as uninteresting as that of sandpaper; their steep, stiff stoops, giving you such a climb to the door; their lumpish balustrades, porticoes, and cornices, turned out by the hundred and adorned with heavy excrescences—such an eruption of ornament and such a poverty of effect! I suppose my superior tone would seem very pretentious if anybody were to read this shameless record of personal emotion; and I should be asked why an expensive up-town residence is not as good as a slimy Italian palazzo. My answer, of course, is that I can sketch the palazzo and can do nothing with the up-town residence. I can live in it, of course, and be very grateful for the shelter; but that doesn't count. Putting aside that odious fashion of popping into the "parlours" as soon as you cross the threshold—no interval, no approach—these places are wonderfully comfortable. This one of Eunice's is perfectly arranged; and we have so much space that she has given me a sitting-room of my own—an immense luxury. Her kindness, her affection, are the most charming, delicate, natural thing I ever conceived. I don't know what can have put it into her head to like me so much; I suppose I should say into her heart, only I don't like to write about Eunice's heart —that tender, shrinking, shade-loving, and above all fresh and youthful, organ. There is a certain self-complacency, perhaps, in my assuming that her generosity is mere affection; for her conscience is so inordinately developed that she attaches the idea of duty to everything—even to her relations to a poor, plain, unloved and unlovable third-cousin. Whether she is fond of me or not, she thinks it right to be fond of me; and the effort of her life is to do what is right. In matters of duty, in short, she is a real little artist; and her masterpiece (in that way) is coming back here to live. She can't like it; her tastes are not here. If she did like it, I am sure she would never have invented such a phrase as the one of which she delivered herself the other day—"I think one's life has more dignity in one's own country." That's a phrase made up after the fact. No one ever gave up living in Europe because there is a want of dignity in it. Poor Eunice talks of "one's own country" as if she kept the United States in the back-parlour. I have yet to perceive the dignity of living in Fifty-third Street. This, I suppose, is very treasonable; but a woman isn't obliged to be patriotic. I believe I should be a good patriot if I could sketch my native town. But I can't make a picture of the brown-stone stoops in the Fifth Avenue, or the platform of the elevated railway in the Sixth. Eunice has suggested to me that I might find some subjects in the Park, and I have been there to look for them. But somehow the blistered *sentiers* of asphalt, the rock-work caverns, the huge iron bridges spanning little muddy lakes, the whole crowded, cockneyfied place, making up so many faces to look pretty, don't appeal

to me—haven't, from beginning to end, a discoverable "bit."
Besides, it's too cold to sit on a campstool under this clean-
swept sky, whose depths of blue air do very well, doubtless,
for the floor of heaven, but are quite too far away for the ceiling of earth. The sky over here seems part of the world at
large; in Europe it's part of the particular place. In summer, I
dare say, it will be better; and it will go hard with me if I
don't find somewhere some leafy lane, some cottage roof,
something in some degree mossy or mellow. Nature here, of
course, is very fine, though I am afraid only in large pieces;
and with my little yard-measure (it used to serve for the
Roman Campagna!) I don't know what I shall be able to do.
I must try to rise to the occasion.

The Hudson is beautiful; I remember that well enough;
and Eunice tells me that when we are in *villeggiatura* we shall
be close to the loveliest part of it. Her cottage, or villa, or
whatever they call it (Mrs Ermine, by the way, always speaks
of it as a "country-seat"), is more or less opposite to West
Point, where it makes one of its grandest sweeps. Unfortunately, it has been let these three years that she has been
abroad, and will not be vacant till the first of June. Mr Caliph,
her trustee, took upon himself to do that; very impertinently,
I think, for certainly if I had Eunice's fortune I shouldn't
let my houses—I mean, of course, those that are so
personal. Least of all should I let my "country-seat." It's
bad enough for people to appropriate one's sofas and tables,
without appropriating one's flowers and trees and even one's
views. There is nothing so personal as one's horizon,—the
horizon that one commands, whatever it is, from one's window. Nobody else has just that one. Mr Caliph, by the way, is
apparently a person of the incalculable, irresponsible sort. It
would have been natural to suppose that having the greater
part of my cousin's property in his care, he would be in
New York to receive her at the end of a long absence and a
boisterous voyage. Common civility would have suggested

that, especially as he was an old friend, or rather a young friend, of both her parents. It was an odd thing to make him sole trustee; but that was Cousin Letitia's doing: "she thought it would be so much easier for Eunice to see only one person." I believe she had found that effort the limit of her own energy; but she might have known that Eunice would have given her best attention, every day, to twenty men of business, if such a duty had been presented to her. I don't think poor Cousin Letitia knew very much; Eunice speaks of her much less than she speaks of her father, whose death would have been the greater sorrow if she dared to admit to herself that she preferred one of her parents to the other. The number of things that the poor girl doesn't dare to admit to herself! One of them, I am sure, is that Mr Caliph is acting improperly in spending three months in Washington, just at the moment when it would be most convenient to her to see him. He has pressing business there, it seems (he is a good deal of a politician—not that I know what people do in Washington), and he writes to Eunice every week or two that he will "finish it up" in ten days more, and then will be completely at her service; but he never finishes it up —never arrives. She has not seen him for three years; he certainly, I think, ought to have come out to her in Europe. She doesn't know that, and I haven't cared to suggest it, for she wishes (very naturally) to think him a pearl of trustees. Fortunately he sends her all the money she needs; and the other day he sent her his brother, a rather agitated (though not in the least agitating) youth, who presented himself about lunch-time—Mr Caliph having (as he explained) told him that this was the best hour to call. What does Mr Caliph know about it, by the way? It's little enough he has tried! Mr Adrian Frank had of course nothing to say about business; he only came to be agreeable, and to tell us that he had just seen his brother in Washington—as if that were any comfort! They are brothers only in the sense that they are children of the same mother; Mrs Caliph having accepted consolations in her widowhood and produced this blushing boy, who is ten years younger than the accomplished Caliph. (I say accomplished Caliph for the phrase. I haven't the least idea of his accomplishments. Somehow, a man with that name ought to have a good many.) Mr Frank, the second husband, is dead as well as herself, and the young man has a very good fortune. He is shy and simple, colours immensely and becomes alarmed at his own silences; but is tall and straight and clear-eyed, and is, I imagine, a very estimable youth. Eunice says that he is as different as possible from his step-brother; so that perhaps, though she doesn't mean it in that way, his step-brother is not estimable. I shall judge of that for myself, if he ever gives me a chance.

Young Frank, at any rate, is a gentleman, and in spite of his blushes has seen a great deal of the world. Perhaps that is what he is blushing for: there are so many things we humans have no reason to be proud of. He stayed to lunch, and talked a little about the far East—Babylon, Palmyra, Ispahan, and that sort of thing—from which he is lately returned. He also is a sketcher, though evidently he doesn't show. He asked to see my things, however; and I produced a few old water-colours, of other days and other climes, which I have luckily brought to America—produced them with my usual calm assurance. It was clear he thought me very clever; so I suspect that in not showing he himself is rather wise. When I said there was nothing here to sketch, that rectangular towns won't do, etc., he asked me why I didn't try people. What people? the people in the Fifth Avenue? They are even less pictorial than their houses. I don't perceive that those in the Sixth are any better, or those in the Fourth and Third, or in the Seventh and Eighth. Good heavens! what a nomenclature! The city of New York is like a tall sum in addition, and the streets are like columns of figures. What a place for me to live, who hate arithmetic! I have tried Mrs Ermine, but that is only because she asked me to: Mrs Ermine asks for whatever she wants. I don't think she cares for it much, for though it's bad, it's not bad enough to please her. I thought she would be rather easy to do, as her countenance is made up largely of negatives—no colour, no form, no intelligence; I should simply have to leave a sort of brilliant blank. I found, however, there was difficulty in representing an expression which consisted so completely of the absence of that article. With her large, fair, featureless face, unillumined by a ray of meaning, she makes the most incoherent, the most unexpected, remarks. She asked Eunice, the other day, whether she should not bring a few gentlemen to see her—she seemed to know so few, to be so lonely. Then when Eunice thanked her, and said she needn't take that trouble: she was not lonely, and in any case did not desire her solitude to be peopled in that manner—Mrs Ermine declared blandly that it was all right, but that she supposed this was the great advantage of being an orphan, that you might have gentlemen brought to see you. "I don't like being an orphan, even for that," said Eunice; who indeed does not like it at all, though she will be twenty-one next month, and has had several years to get used to it. Mrs Ermine is very vulgar, yet she thinks she has high distinction. I am very glad our cousinship is not on the same side. Except that she is an idiot and a bore, however, I think there is no harm in her. Her time is spent in contemplating the surface of things—and for that I don't blame her, for I myself am very fond of the surface. But she doesn't see what she looks at, and in short is very tiresome. That is one of the things poor Eunice won't admit to herself—that Lizzie Ermine will end by boring us to death. Now that both her daughters are married, she has her time quite on her hands; for the sons-in-law, I am sure, can't encourage her visits. She may, however, contrive to be with them as well as here, for, as a poor young husband once said to me, a *belle-mère*, after marriage, is as inevitable as stickiness after eating honey. A fool can do plenty of harm without deep intentions. After all, intentions fail; and what you know an accident by is that it doesn't. Mrs Ermine doesn't like me; she thinks she ought to be in my shoes—that when Eunice lost her old governess, who had remained with her as "companion," she ought, instead of picking me up in Rome, to have come home and thrown herself upon some form of kinship more cushiony. She is jealous of me, and vexed that I don't give her more opportunities; for I know that she has made up her mind that I ought to be a Bohemian: in that case she could persuade Eunice that I am a very unfit sort of person. I am single, not young, not pretty, not well off, and not very desirous to please; I carry a palette on my thumb, and very often have stains on my apron—though except for those stains I pretend to be immaculately neat. What right have I *not* to be a Bohemian, and not to teach Eunice to make cigarettes? I am convinced Mrs Ermine is disappointed that I don't smoke. Perhaps, after all, she is right, and that I am too much a creature of habits, of rules. A few people have been good enough to call me an artist; but I am not. I am only, in a small way, a worker. I walk too straight; it's ten years since any one asked me to dance! I wish I could oblige you, Mrs Ermine, by dipping into Bohemia once in a while. But one can't have the defects of the qualities one doesn't possess. I am not an artist, I am too much of a critic. I suppose a she-critic is a kind of monster; women should only be criticised. That's why I keep it all to myself—myself being this little book. I grew tired of myself some months ago, and locked myself up in a desk. It was a kind of punishment, but it was also a great rest, to stop judging, to stop caring, for a while. Now that I have come out, I suppose I ought to take a vow not to be ill-natured.

As I read over what I have written here, I wonder whether it was worth while to have reopened my journal. Still, why not have the benefit of being thought disagreeable—the luxury of recorded observation? If one is poor, plain, proud—

and in this very private place I may add, clever—there are certain necessary revenges!

April 10.—Adrian Frank has been here again, and we rather like him. (That will do for the first note of a more genial tone.) His eyes are very blue, and his teeth very white—two things that always please me. He became rather more communicative, and almost promised to show me his sketches—in spite of the fact that he is evidently as much as ever struck with my own ability. Perhaps he has discovered that I am trying to be genial! He wishes to take us to drive—that is, to take Eunice; for of course I shall go only for propriety. She doesn't go with young men alone; that element was not included in her education. She said to me yesterday, "The only man I shall drive alone with will be the one I marry." She talks so little about marrying that this made an impression on me. That subject is supposed to be a girl's inevitable topic; but no young women could occupy themselves with it less than she and I do. I think I may say that we never mention it at all. I suppose that if a man were to read this he would be greatly surprised and not particularly edified. As there is no danger of any man's reading it, I may add that I always take tacitly for granted that Eunice will marry. She doesn't in the least pretend that she won't; and if I am not mistaken she is capable of the sort of affection that is expected of a good wife. The longer I live with her the more I see that she is a dear girl. Now that I know her better, I perceive that she is perfectly natural. I used to think that she tried too much—that she watched herself, perhaps, with a little secret admiration. But that was because I couldn't conceive of a girl's motives being so simple. She only wants not to suffer—she is immensely afraid of that. Therefore, she wishes to be universally tender—to mitigate the general sum of suffering, in the hope that she herself may come off easily. Poor thing! she doesn't know that we can diminish the amount of suffering for others only by taking to ourselves a part of their share. The amount of that commodity in the world is always the same; it is only the distribution that varies. We all try to dodge our portion, and some of us succeed. I find the best way is not to think about it, and to make little water-colours. Eunice thinks that the best way is to be very generous, to condemn no one unheard.

A great many things happen that I don't mention here; incidents of social life, I believe they call them. People come to see us, and sometimes they invite us to dinner. We go to certain concerts, many of which are very good. We take a walk every day; and I read to Eunice, and she plays to me. Mrs Ermine makes her appearance several times a week, and gives us the news of the town—a great deal more of it than we have any use for. She thinks we live in a hole; and she has more than once expressed her conviction that I can do nothing socially for Eunice. As to that, she is perfectly right; I am aware of my social insignificance. But I am equally aware that my cousin has no need of being pushed. I know little of the people and things of this place; but I know enough to see that, whatever they are, the best of them are at her service. Mrs Ermine thinks it a great pity that Eunice should have come too late in the season to "go out" with her; for after this there are few entertainments at which my protecting presence is not sufficient. Besides, Eunice isn't eager; I often wonder at her indifference. She never thinks of the dances she has missed, nor asks about those at which she still may figure. She isn't sad, and it doesn't amount to melancholy; but she certainly is rather detached. She likes to read, to talk with me, to make music, and to dine out when she supposes there will be "real conversation." She is extremely fond of real conversation; and we flatter ourselves that a good deal of it takes place between us. We talk about life and religion and art and George Eliot; all that, I hope, is sufficiently real. Eunice understands everything, and has a great many opinions; she is quite the modern young woman, though she hasn't modern manners. But all this doesn't explain to me why, as Mrs Ermine says, she should wish to be so dreadfully quiet. That lady's suspicion to the contrary notwithstanding, it is not I who make her so. I would go with her to a party every night if she should wish it, and send out cards to proclaim that we "receive." But her ambitions are not those of the usual girl; or, at any rate, if she is waiting for what the usual girl waits for, she is waiting very patiently. As I say, I can't quite make out the secret of her patience. However, it is not necessary I should; it was no part of the bargain on which I came to her that we were to conceal nothing from each other. I conceal a great deal from Eunice; at least I hope I do: for instance, how fearfully I am bored. I think I am as patient as she; but then I have certain things to help me—my age, my resignation, my ability, and, I suppose I may add, my conceit. Mrs Ermine doesn't bring the young men, but she talks about them, and calls them Harry and Freddy. She wants Eunice to marry, though I don't see what she is to gain by it. It is apparently a disinterested love of matrimony—or rather, I should say, a love of weddings. She lives in a world of "engagements," and announces a new one every time she comes in. I never heard of so much marrying in all my life before. Mrs Ermine is dying to be able to tell people that Eunice is engaged; that distinction should not be wanting to a cousin of hers. Whoever marries her, by the way, will come into a very good fortune. Almost for the first time, three days ago, she told me about her affairs.

She knows less about them than she believes—I could see that; but she knows the great matter; which is, that in the course of her twenty-first year, by the terms of her mother's will she becomes mistress of her property, of which for the last seven years Mr Caliph has been sole trustee. On that day Mr Caliph is to make over to her three hundred thousand dollars, which he has been nursing and keeping safe. So much on every occasion seems to be expected of this wonderful man! I call him so because I think it was wonderful of him to have been appointed sole depositary of the property of an orphan by a very anxious, scrupulous, affectionate mother, whose one desire, when she made her will, was to prepare for her child a fruitful majority, and whose acquaintance with him had not been of many years, though her esteem for him was great. He had been a friend—a very good friend—of her husband, who, as he neared his end, asked him to look after his widow. Eunice's father didn't however make him trustee of his little estate; he put that into other hands, and Eunice has a very good account of it. It amounts, unfortunately, but to some fifty thousand dollars. Her mother's proceedings with regard to Mr Caliph were very feminine—so I may express myself in the privacy of these pages. But I believe all women are very feminine in their relations with Mr Caliph. "Haroun-al-Raschid" I call him to Eunice; and I suppose he expects to find us in a state of Oriental prostration. She says, however, that he is not the least of a Turk, and that nothing could be kinder or more considerate than he was three years ago, before she went to Europe. He was constantly with her at that time, for many months; and his attentions have evidently made a great impression on her. That sort of thing naturally would, on a girl of seventeen; and I have told her she must be prepared to think him much less brilliant a personage to-day. I don't know what he will think of some of her plans of expenditure, —laying out an Italian garden at the house on the river, founding a cot at the children's hospital, erecting a music room in the rear of this house. Next winter Eunice proposes to receive; but she wishes to have an originality, in the shape of really good music. She will evidently be rather extravagant, at least at first. Mr Caliph of course will have no more authority; still, he may advise her as a friend.

April 23.—This afternoon, while Eunice was out, Mr Frank made his appearance, having had the civility, as I afterwards learned, to ask for me, in spite of the absence of the *padronina*. I told him she was at Mrs Ermine's, and that Mrs Ermine was her cousin.

"Then I can say what I should not be able to say if she were here," he said, smiling that singular smile which has the effect of showing his teeth and drawing the lids of his eyes together. If he were a young countryman, one would call it a grin. It is not exactly a grin, but it is very simple.

"And what may that be?" I asked, with encouragement.

He hesitated a little, while I admired his teeth, which I am sure he has no wish to exhibit; and I expected something wonderful. "Considering that she is fair, she is really very pretty," he said at last.

I was rather disappointed, and I went so far as to say to him that he might have made that remark in her presence.

This time his blue eyes remained wide open: "So you really think so?"

"'Considering that she's fair,' that part of it, perhaps, might have been omitted; but the rest surely would have pleased her."

"Do you really think so?"

"Well, 'really very pretty' is, perhaps, not quite right; it seems to imply a kind of surprise. You might have omitted the 'really.'"

"You want me to omit everything," he said, laughing, as if he thought me wonderfully amusing.

"The gist of the thing would remain, 'You are very pretty;' that would have been unexpected and agreeable."

"I think you are laughing at me!" cried poor Mr Frank, without bitterness. "I have no right to say that till I know she likes me."

"She does like you; I see no harm in telling you so." He seemed to me so modest, so natural, that I felt as free to say this to him as I would have been to a good child: more, indeed, than to a good child, for a child to whom one would say that would be rather a prig, and Adrian Frank is not a prig. I could see this by the way he answered; it was rather odd.

"It will please my brother to know that!"

"Does he take such an interest in the impressions you make?"

"Oh yes; he wants me to appear well." This was said with the most touching innocence; it was a complete confession of inferiority. It was, perhaps, the tone that made it so; at any rate, Adrian Frank has renounced the hope of ever appearing as well as his brother. I wonder if a man must be really inferior, to be in such a state of mind as that. He must at all events be very fond of his brother, and even, I think, have sacrificed himself a good deal. This young man asked me ever so many questions about my cousin; frankly, simply; as if, when one wanted to know, it was perfectly natural to ask. So it is, I suppose; but why should he want to know? Some of his questions were certainly idle. What can it matter to him whether she has one little dog or three, or whether she is an admirer of the music of the future? "Does she go out much, or does she like a quiet evening at home?" "Does she like living in Europe, and what part of Europe does she prefer?" "Has she many relatives in New York, and does she see a great deal of them?" On all these points I was obliged to give Mr Frank a certain satisfaction; and after that, I thought I had a right to ask why he wanted to know. He was evidently surprised at being challenged, blushed a good deal, and made me feel for a moment as if I had asked a vulgar question. I saw he had no particular reason; he only wanted to be civil, and that is the way best known to him of expressing an interest. He was confused; but he was not so confused that he took his departure. He sat half an hour longer, and let me make up to him by talking very agreeably for the shock I had administered. I may mention here—for I like to see it in black and white—that I *can* talk very agreeably. He listened with the most flattering attention, showing me his blue eyes and his white teeth in alternation, and laughing largely, as if I had a command of the comical. I am not conscious of that. At last, after I had paused a little, he said to me, apropos of nothing:

"Do you think the realistic school are—a—to be admired?"
Then I saw that he had already forgotten my earlier check—
such was the effect of my geniality—and that he would ask
me as many questions about myself as I would let him. I
answered him freely, but I answered him as I chose. There
are certain things about myself I never shall tell, and the
simplest way not to tell is to say the contrary. If people are
indiscreet, they must take the consequences. I declared that I
held the realistic school in horror; that I found New York the
most interesting, the most sympathetic of cities; and that I
thought the American girl the finest result of civilisation. I am
sure I convinced him that I am a most remarkable woman.
He went away before Eunice returned. He is a charming
creature—a kind of Yankee Donatello. If I could only be his
Miriam, the situation would be almost complete, for Eunice is
an excellent Hilda.

April 26.—Mrs Ermine was in great force to-day; she described all the fine things Eunice can do when she gets her
money into her own hands. A set of Mechlin lace, a *rivière* of
diamonds which she saw the other day at Tiffany's, a set of
Russian sables that she knows of somewhere else, a little
English phaeton with a pair of ponies and a tiger, a family of
pugs to waddle about in the drawing-room—all these luxuries
Mrs Ermine declares indispensable. "I should like to know
that you have them—it would do me real good," she said to
Eunice. "I like to see people with handsome things. It would
give me more pleasure to know you have that set of Mechlin
than to have it myself. I can't help that—it's the way I am
made. If other people have handsome things I see them more;
and then I do want the good of others—I don't care if you
think me vain for saying so. I shan't be happy till I see you in
an English phaeton. The groom oughtn't to be more than
three feet six. I think you ought to show for what you
are."

"How do you mean, for what I am?" Eunice asked.

"Well, for a charming girl, with a very handsome fortune."

"I shall never show any more than I do now."

"I will tell you what you do—you show Miss Condit." And Mrs Ermine presented me her large, foolish face. "If you don't look out, she'll do you up in Morris papers, and then all the Mechlin lace in the world won't matter!"

"I don't follow you at all—I never follow you," I said, wishing I could have sketched her just as she sat there. She was quite grotesque.

"I would rather go without you," she repeated.

"I think that after I come into my property I shall do just as I do now," said Eunice. "After all, where will the difference be? I have to-day everything I shall ever have. It's more than enough."

"You won't have to ask Mr Caliph for everything."

"I ask him for nothing now."

"Well, my dear," said Mrs Ermine, "you don't deserve to be rich."

"I am not rich," Eunice remarked.

"Ah, well, if you want a million!"

"I don't want anything," said Eunice.

That's not exactly true. She does want something, but I don't know what it is.

May 2.—Mr Caliph is really very delightful. He made his appearance to-day and carried everything before him. When I say he carried everything, I mean he carried me; for Eunice had not my prejudices to get over. When I said to her after he had gone, "Your trustee is a very clever man," she only smiled a little, and turned away in silence. I suppose she was amused with the air of importance with which I announced this discovery. Eunice had made it several years ago, and could not be excited about it. I had an idea that some allusion would be made to the way he has neglected her—some apology at least for his long absence. But he did something better than this. He made no definite apology; he only expressed, in his

manner, his look, his voice, a tenderness, a charming benevolence, which included and exceeded all apologies. He looks
rather tired and preoccupied; he evidently has a great many
irons of his own in the fire, and has been thinking these last
weeks of larger questions than the susceptibilities of a little
girl in New York who happened several years ago to have an
exuberant mother. He is thoroughly genial, and is the best
talker I have seen since my return. A totally different type from
the young Adrian. He is not in the least handsome—is, indeed, rather ugly; but with a fine, expressive, pictorial ugli-
ness. He is forty years old, large and stout, may even be pronounced fat; and there is something about him that I don't
know how to describe except by calling it a certain richness. I
have seen Italians who have it, but this is the first American.
He talks with his eyes, as well as with his lips, and his features
are wonderfully mobile. His smile is quick and delightful;
his hands are well-shaped, but distinctly fat; he has a pale
complexion and a magnificent brown beard—the beard of
Haroun-al-Raschid. I suppose I must write it very small;
but I have an intimate conviction that he is a Jew, or of Jewish
origin. I see that in his plump, white face, of which the tone
would please a painter, and which suggests fatigue, but is
nevertheless all alive; in his remarkable eye, which is full of
old expressions—expressions which linger there from the
past, even when they are not active to-day; in his profile, in
his anointed beard, in the very rings on his large pointed
fingers. There is not a touch of all this in his step-brother;
so I suppose the Jewish blood is inherited from his father.
I don't think he looks like a gentleman; he is something apart
from all that. If he is not a gentleman, he is not in the least a
bourgeois—neither is he of the Bohemian type. In short, as I
say, he is a Jew; and Jews of the upper class have a style of their
own. He is very clever, and I think genuinely kind. Nothing
could be more charming than his way of talking to Eunice—
a certain paternal interest mingled with an air of respectful

gallantry (he gives her good advice, and at the same time pays her compliments); the whole thing being not in the least over-done. I think he found her changed—"more of a person," as Mrs Ermine says; I even think he was a little surprised. She seems slightly afraid of him, which rather surprised me—she was, from her own account, so familiar with him of old. He is decidedly florid, and was very polite to me; that was a part of the floridity. He asked if we had seen his step-brother; begged us to be kind to him and to let him come and see us often. He doesn't know many people in New York, and at that age it is everything (I quote Mr Caliph) for a young fellow to be at his ease with one or two charming women. "Adrian takes a great deal of knowing; is horribly shy; but is most intelligent, and has one of the sweetest natures! I'm very fond of him—he's all I've got. Unfortunately the poor boy is cursed with a competence. In this country there is nothing for such a young fellow to do; he hates business, and has absolutely no talent for it. I shall send him back here the next time I see him." Eunice made no answer to this, and, in fact, had little answer to make to most of Mr Caliph's remarks, only sitting looking at the floor with a smile. I thought it proper therefore to reply that we had found Mr Frank very pleasant, and hoped he would soon come again. Then I mentioned that the other day I had had a long visit from him alone; we had talked for an hour, and become excellent friends. Mr Caliph, as I said this, was leaning forward with his elbow on his knee and his hand up-lifted, grasping his thick beard. The other hand, with the elbow out, rested on the other knee; his head was turned to-ward me, askance. He looked at me a moment with his deep bright eye—the eye of a much older man than he; he might have been posing for a water-colour. If I had painted him, it would have been in a high-peaked cap, and an amber-coloured robe, with a wide girdle of pink silk wound many times round his waist, stuck full of knives with jewelled handles. Our eyes met, and we sat there exchanging a glance. I don't know whether he's vain, but I think he must see I appreciate him; I am sure he understands everything.

"I like you when you say that," he remarked at the end of a minute.

"I am glad to hear you like me!" This sounds horrid and pert as I relate it.

"I don't like every one," said Mr Caliph.

"Neither do Eunice and I; do we, Eunice?"

"I am afraid we only try to," she answered, smiling her most beautiful smile.

"Try to? Heaven forbid! I protest against that," I cried. I said to Mr Caliph that Eunice was too good.

"She comes honestly by that. Your mother was an angel, my child," he said to her.

Cousin Letitia was not an angel, but I have mentioned that Mr Caliph is florid. "You used to be very good to her," Eunice murmured, raising her eyes to him.

He had got up; he was standing there. He bent his head, smiling like an Italian. "You must be the same, my child."

"What can I do?" Eunice asked.

"You can believe in me—you can trust me."

"I do, Mr Caliph. Try me and see!"

This was unexpectedly gushing, and I instinctively turned away. Behind my back, I don't know what he did to her—I think it possible he kissed her. When you call a girl "my child," I suppose you may kiss her; but that may be only my bold imagination. When I turned round he had taken up his hat and stick, to say nothing of buttoning a very tightly-fitting coat round a very spacious person, and was ready to offer me his hand in farewell.

"I am so glad you are with her. I am so glad she has a companion so accomplished—so capable."

"So capable of what?" I said, laughing; for the speech was absurd, as he knows nothing about my accomplishments.

There is nothing solemn about Mr Caliph; but he gave me

a look which made it appear to me that my levity was in bad taste. Yes, humiliating as it is to write it here, I found myself rebuked by a Jew with fat hands! "Capable of advising her well!" he said softly.

"Ah, don't talk about advice," Eunice exclaimed. "Advice always gives an idea of trouble, and I am very much afraid of trouble."

"You ought to get married," he said, with his smile coming back to him.

Eunice coloured and turned away, and I observed—to say something—that this was just what Mrs Ermine said.

"Mrs Ermine? ah, I hear she's a charming woman!" And shortly after that he went away.

That was almost the only weak thing he said—the only thing for mere form, for of course no one can really think her charming; least of all a clever man like that. I don't like Americans to resemble Italians, or Italians to resemble Americans; but putting that aside, Mr Caliph is very prepossessing. He is wonderfully good company; he will spoil us for other people. He made no allusion to business, and no appointment with Eunice for talking over certain matters that are pending; but I thought of this only half an hour after he had gone. I said nothing to Eunice about it, for she would have noticed the omission herself, and that was enough. The only other point in Mr Caliph that was open to criticism is his asking Eunice to believe in him—to trust him. Why shouldn't she, pray? If that speech was curious—and, strange to say, it almost appeared so—it was incredibly naïf. But this quality is insupposable of Mr Caliph; who ever heard of a naïf Jew? After he had gone I was on the point of saying to Eunice, "By the way, why did you never mention that he is a Hebrew? That's an important detail." But an impulse that I am not able to define stopped me, and now I am glad I didn't speak. I don't believe Eunice ever made the discovery, and I don't think she would like it if she did make it. That I should have done so on the instant only proves that I am in the habit of studying the human profile!

May 9.—Mrs Ermine must have discovered that Mr Caliph has heard she is charming, for she is perpetually coming in here with the hope of meeting him. She appears to think that he comes every day; for when she misses him, which she has done three times (that is, she arrives just after he goes), she says that if she doesn't catch him on the morrow she will go and call upon him. She is capable of that, I think; and it makes no difference that he is the busiest of men and she the idlest of women. He has been here four times since his first call, and has the air of wishing to make up for the neglect that preceded it. His manner to Eunice is perfect; he continues to call her "my child," but in a superficial, impersonal way, as a Catholic priest might do it. He tells us stories of Washington, describes the people there, and makes us wonder whether we should care for K Street and 14½ Street. As yet, to the best of my knowledge, not a word about Eunice's affairs; he behaves as if he had simply forgotten them. It was, after all, not out of place the other day to ask her to "believe in him;" the faith wouldn't come as a matter of course. On the other hand he is so pleasant that one would believe in him just to oblige him. He has a great deal of trust-business, and a great deal of law-business of every kind. So at least he says; we really know very little about him but what he tells us. When I say "we," of course I speak mainly for myself, as I am perpetually forgetting that he is not so new to Eunice as he is to me. She knows what she knows, but I only know what I see. I have been wondering a good deal what is thought of Mr. Caliph "down-town," as they say here, but without much result, for naturally I can't go down-town and see. The appearance of the thing prevents my asking questions about him; it wonld be very compromising to Eunice, and make people think that she complains of him—which is so far from being the case. She likes him just as he is, and is appa-

rently quite satisfied. I gather, moreover, that he is thought
very brilliant, though a little peculiar, and that he has made
a great deal of money. He has a way of his own of doing
things, and carries imagination and humour, and a sense of
the beautiful, into Wall Street and the Stock Exchange. Mrs
Ermine announced the other day that he is "considered the
most fascinating man in New York;" but that is the romantic
up-town view of him, and not what I want. His brother has
gone out of town for a few days, but he continues to recommend the young Adrian to our hospitality. There is something really touching in his relation to that rather limited
young man.

May 11.—Mrs Ermine is in high spirits; she has met Mr
Caliph—I don't know where—and she quite confirms the up-
town view. She thinks him the most fascinating man she has
ever seen, and she wonders that we should have said so little
about him. He is so handsome, so high-bred; his manners are
so perfect; he's a regular old dear. I think, of course ill-
naturedly, several degrees less well of him since I have heard
Mrs Ermine's impressions. He is not handsome, he is not high-
bred, and his manners are not perfect. They are original, and
they are expressive; and if one likes him there is an interest in
looking for what he will do and say. But if one should happen
to dislike him, one would detest his manners and think them
familiar and vulgar. As for breeding, he has about him, indeed,
the marks of antiquity of race; yet I don't think Mrs Ermine
would have liked me to say, "Oh yes, all Jews have blood!"
Besides, I couldn't before Eunice. Perhaps I consider
Eunice too much; perhaps I am betrayed by my old habit of
trying to see through millstones; perhaps I interpret things too
richly—just as (I know) when I try to paint an old wall I
attempt to put in too much "character;" character being in
old walls, after all, a finite quantity. At any rate she seems to
me rather nervous about Mr Caliph: that appeared after a
little when Mrs Ermine came back to the subject. She had a

great deal to say about the oddity of her never having seen him before, of old, "for after all," as she remarked, "we move in the same society—he moves in the very best." She used to hear Eunice talk about her trustee, but she supposed a trustee must be some horrid old man with a lot of papers in his hand, sitting all day in an office. She never supposed he was a prince in disguise. "We've got a trustee somewhere, only I never see him; my husband does all the business. No wonder he keeps him out of the way if he resembles Mr Caliph." And then suddenly she said to Eunice, "My dear, why don't you marry him? I should think you would want to." Mrs Ermine doesn't look through millstones; she contents herself with giving them a poke with her parasol. Eunice coloured, and said she hadn't been asked; she was evidently not pleased with Mrs Ermine's joke, which was of course as flat as you like. Then she added in a moment—"I should be very sorry to marry Mr Caliph, even if he were to ask me. I like him, but I don't like him enough for that."

"I should think he would be quite in your style—he's so literary. They say he writes," Mrs Ermine went on.

"Well, I don't write," Eunice answered, laughing.

"You could if you would try. I'm sure you could make a lovely book." Mrs Ermine's amiability is immense.

"It's safe for you to say that—you never read."

"I have no time," said Mrs Ermine, "but I like literary conversation. It saves time, when it comes in that way. Mr Caliph has ever so much."

"He keeps it for you. With us he is very frivolous," I ventured to observe.

"Well, what you call frivolous! I believe you think the prayer-book frivolous."

"Mr Caliph will never marry any one," Eunice said, after a moment. "That I am very sure of."

Mrs Ermine stared; there never is so little expression in her face as when she is surprised. But she soon recovered herself.

"Don't you believe that! He will take some quiet little woman, after you have all given him up."

Eunice was sitting at the piano, but had wheeled round on the stool when her cousin came in. She turned back to it and struck a few vague chords, as if she were feeling for something. "Please don't speak that way; I don't like it," she said, as she went on playing.

"I will speak any way you like!" Mrs Ermine cried, with her vacant laugh.

"I think it very low." For Eunice this was severe. "Girls are not always thinking about marriage. They are not always thinking of people like Mr Caliph—that way."

"They must have changed then, since my time! Wasn't it so in yours, Miss Condit?" She's so stupid that I don't think she meant to make a point.

"I had no 'time,' Mrs Ermine. I was born an old maid."

"Well, the old maids are the worst. I don't see why it's low to talk about marriage. It's thought very respectable to marry. You have only to look round you."

"I don't want to look round me; it's not always so beautiful, what you see," Eunice said, with a small laugh and a good deal of perversity, for a young woman so reasonable.

"I guess you read too much," said Mrs Ermine, getting up and setting her bonnet-ribbons at the mirror.

"I should think he would hate them!" Eunice exclaimed, striking her chords.

"Hate who?" her cousin asked.

"Oh, all the silly girls."

"Who is 'he,' pray?" This ingenious inquiry was mine.

"Oh, the Grand Turk!" said Eunice, with her voice covered by the sound of her piano. Her piano is a great resource.

May 12.—This afternoon, while we were having our tea, the Grand Turk was ushered in, carrying the most wonderful bouquet of Boston roses that seraglio ever produced. (That image, by the way, is rather mixed; but as I write for myself alone, it may stand.) At the end of ten minutes he asked Eunice if he might see her alone—"on a little matter of business." I instantly rose to leave them, but Eunice said that she would rather talk with him in the library; so she led him off to that apartment. I remained in the drawing-room, saying to myself that I had at last discovered the *fin mot* of Mr Caliph's peculiarities, which is so very simple that I am a great goose not to have perceived it before. He is a man with a system; and his system is simply to keep business and entertainment perfectly distinct. There may be pleasure for him in his figures, but there are no figures in his pleasure—which has hitherto been to call upon Eunice as a man of the world. To-day he was to be the trustee; I could see it in spite of his bouquet, as soon as he came in. The Boston roses didn't contradict that, for the excellent reason that as soon as he had shaken hands with Eunice, who looked at the flowers and not at him, he presented them to Catherine Condit. Eunice then looked at this lady; and as I took the roses I met her eyes, which had a charming light of pleasure. It would be base in me, even in this strictly private record, to suggest that she might possibly have been displeased; but if I cannot say that the expression of her face was lovely without appearing in some degree to point to an ignoble alternative, it is the fault of human nature. Why Mr Caliph should suddenly think it necessary to offer flowers to Catherine Condit—that is a line of inquiry by itself. As I said some time back, it's a part of his floridity. Besides, any presentation of flowers seems sudden; I don't know why, but it's always rather a *coup de théâtre*. I am writing late at night; they stand on my table, and their fragrance is in the air. I don't say it for the flowers, but no one has ever treated poor Miss Condit with such consistent consideration as Mr Caliph. Perhaps she is morbid: this is probably the Diary of a Morbid Woman; but in such a matter as that she admires consistency. That little glance of Eunice comes back to me as I write; she is a pure, enchanting soul. Mrs Ermine came in while she was in the library with Mr Caliph, and immediately noticed the Boston roses, which effaced all the other flowers in the room.

"Were they sent from her seat?" she asked. Then, before I could answer, "I am going to have some people to dinner to-day; they would look very well in the middle."

"If you wish me to offer them to you, I really can't; I prize them too much."

"Oh, are they yours? Of course you prize them! I don't suppose you have many."

"These are the first I have ever received—from Mr Caliph."

"From Mr Caliph? Did he give them to *you*?" Mrs Ermine's intonations are not delicate. That "*you*" should be in enormous capitals.

"With his own hand—a quarter of an hour ago." This sounds triumphant, as I write it; but it was no great sensation to triumph over Mrs Ermine.

She laid down the bouquet, looking almost thoughtful. "He *does* want to marry Eunice," she declared in a moment. This is the region in which, after a flight of fancy, she usually alights. I am sick of the irrepressible verb; just at that moment, however, it was unexpected, and I answered that I didn't understand.

"That's why he gives you flowers," she explained. But the explanation made the matter darker still, and Mrs Ermine went on: "Isn't there some French proverb about paying one's court to the mother in order to gain the daughter? Eunice is the daughter, and you are the mother."

"And you are the grandmother, I suppose! Do you mean that he wishes me to intercede?"

"I can't imagine why else!" and smiling, with her wide lips, she stared at the flowers.

"At that rate you too will get your bouquet," I said.

"Oh, I have no influence! You ought to do something in return—to offer to paint his portrait."

"I don't offer that, you know; people ask me. Besides, you have spoiled me for common models!"

It strikes me, as I write this, that we had gone rather far—farther than it seemed at the time. We might have gone farther yet, however, if at this moment Eunice had not come back with Mr Caliph, who appeared to have settled his little matter of business briskly enough. He remained the man of business to the end, and, to Mrs Ermine's evident disappointment, declined to sit down again. He was in a hurry; he had an engagement.

"Are you going up or down? I have a carriage at the door," she broke in.

"At Fifty-third Street one is usually going down;" and he gave his peculiar smile, which always seems so much beyond the scope of the words it accompanies. "If you will give me a lift I shall be very grateful."

He went off with her, she being much divided between the prospect of driving with him and her loss of the chance to find out what he had been saying to Eunice. She probably believed he had been proposing to her, and I hope he mystified her well in the carriage.

He had not been proposing to Eunice; he had given her a cheque, and made her sign some papers. The cheque was for a thousand dollars, but I have no knowledge of the papers. When I took up my abode with her I made up my mind that the only way to preserve an appearance of disinterestedness was to know nothing whatever of the details of her pecuniary affairs. She has a very good little head of her own, and if she shouldn't understand them herself it would be quite out of my power to help her. I don't know why I should care about *appearing* disinterested, when I have in quite sufficient measure the consciousness of being so; but in point of fact I do, and I value that purity as much as any other. Besides, Mr

Caliph is her supreme adviser, and of course makes everything clear to her. At least I hope he does. I couldn't help saying as much as this to Eunice.

"My dear child, I suppose you understand what you sign. Mr Caliph ought to be—what shall I call it?—crystalline."

She looked at me with the smile that had come into her face when she saw him give me the flowers. "Oh yes, I think so. If I didn't, it's my own fault. He explains everything so beautifully that it's a pleasure to listen. I always read what I sign."

"Je l'espère bien!" I said, laughing.

She looked a little grave. "The closing up a trust is very complicated."

"Yours is not closed yet? It strikes me as very slow."

"Everything can't be done at once. Besides, he has asked for a little delay. Part of my affairs, indeed, are now in my own hands; otherwise I shouldn't have to sign."

"Is that a usual request—for delay?"

"Oh yes, perfectly. Besides, I don't want everything in my own control. That is, I want it some day, because I think I ought to accept the responsibilities, as I accept all the pleasures; but I am not in a hurry. This way is so comfortable, and Mr Caliph takes so much trouble for me."

"I suppose he has a handsome commission," I said, rather crudely.

"He has no commission at all; he would never take one."

"In your place, I would much rather he should take one."

"I have asked him to, but he won't!" Eunice said, looking now extremely grave.

Her gravity indeed was so great that it made me smile. "He is wonderfully generous!"

"He is indeed."

"And is it to be indefinitely delayed—the termination of his trust?"

"Oh no; only a few months, 'till he gets things into shape,' as he says."

"He has had several years for that, hasn't he?"

Eunice turned away; evidently our talk was painful to her. But there was something that vaguely alarmed me in her taking, or at least accepting, the sentimental view of Mr Caliph's services. "I don't think you are kind, Catherine; you seem to suspect him," she remarked, after a little.

"Suspect him of what?"

"Of not wishing to give up the property."

"My dear Eunice, you put things into terrible words! Seriously, I should never think of suspecting him of anything so silly. What could his wishes count for? Is not the thing regulated by law—by the terms of your mother's will? The trust expires of itself at a certain period, doesn't it? Mr Caliph, surely, has only to act accordingly."

"It is just what he is doing. But there are more papers necessary, and they will not be ready for a few weeks more."

"Don't have too many papers; they are as bad as too few. And take advice of some one else—say of your cousin Ermine, who is so much more sensible than his wife."

"I want no advice," said Eunice, in a tone which showed me that I had said enough. And presently she went on, "I thought you liked Mr Caliph."

"So I do, immensely. He gives beautiful flowers."

"Ah, you are horrid!" she murmured.

"Of course I am horrid. That's my business—to be horrid." And I took the liberty of being so again, half an hour later, when she remarked that she must take good care of the cheque Mr Caliph had brought her, as it would be a good while before she should have another. "Why should it be longer than usual?" I asked. "Is he going to keep your income for himself?"

"I am not to have any till the end of the year—any from the trust, at least. Mr Caliph has been converting some old houses into shops, so that they will bring more rent. But the alterations have to be paid for—and he takes part of my income to do it."

"And pray what are you to live on meanwhile?"

"I have enough without that; and I have savings."

"It strikes me as a cool proceeding, all the same."

"He wrote to me about it before we came home, and I thought that way was best."

"I don't think he ought to have asked you," I said. "As your trustee, he acts in his discretion."

"You are hard to please," Eunice answered.

That is perfectly true; but I rejoined that I couldn't make out whether he consulted her too much or too little. And I don't know that my failure to make it out in the least matters!

May 13.—Mrs Ermine turned up to-day at an earlier hour than usual, and I saw as soon as she got into the room that she had something to announce. This time it was not an engagement. "He sent me a bouquet—Boston roses—quite as many as yours! They arrived this morning, before I had finished breakfast." This speech was addressed to me, and Mrs Ermine looked almost brilliant. Eunice scarcely followed her.

"She is talking about Mr Caliph," I explained.

Eunice stared a moment; then her face melted into a deep little smile. "He seems to give flowers to every one but to me." I could see that this reflection gave her remarkable pleasure.

"Well, when he gives them, he's thinking of you," said Mrs Ermine. "He wants to get us on his side."

"On his side?"

"Oh yes; some day he will have need of us!" And Mrs Ermine tried to look sprightly and insinuating. But she is too utterly *fade*, and I think it is not worth while to talk any more to Eunice just now about her trustee. So, to anticipate Mrs Ermine, I said to her quickly, but very quietly—

"He sent you flowers simply because you had taken him

into your carriage last night. It was an acknowledgment of your great kindness."

She hesitated a moment. "Possibly. We had a charming drive—ever so far down-town." Then, turning to Eunice, she exclaimed, "My dear, you don't know that man till you have had a drive with him!" When does one know Mrs Ermine? Every day she is a surprise!

May 19.—Adrian Frank has come back to New York, and has been three times at this house—once to dinner, and twice at tea-time. After his brother's strong expression of the hope that we should take an interest in him, Eunice appears to have thought that the least she could do was to ask him to dine. She appears never to have offered this privilege to Mr Caliph, by the way; I think her view of his cleverness is such that she imagines she knows no one sufficiently brilliant to be invited to meet him. She thought Mrs Ermine good enough to meet Mr Frank, and she had also young Woodley—Willie Woodley, as they call him—and Mr Latrobe. It was not very amusing. Mrs Ermine made love to Mr Woodley, who took it serenely; and the dark Latrobe talked to me about the Seventh Regiment—an impossible subject. Mr Frank made an occasional remark to Eunice, next whom he was placed; but he seemed constrained and frightened, as if he knew that his step-brother had recommended him highly and felt it was impossible to come up to the mark. He is really very modest; it is impossible not to like him. Every now and then he looked at me, with his clear blue eye conscious and expanded, as if to beg me to help him on with Eunice; and then, when I threw in a word, to give their conversation a push, he looked at her in the same way, as if to express the hope that she would not abandon him. There was no danger of this, she only wished to be agreeable to him; but she was nervous and preoccupied, as she always is when she has people to dinner—she is so afraid they may be bored—and I think that half the time she didn't understand what he said. She told me afterwards that she liked him more even than she liked him at first; that he has, in her opinion, better manners, in spite of his shyness, than any of the young men; and that he must have a nice nature to have such a charming face;—all this she told me, and she added that, notwithstanding all this, there is something in Mr Adrian Frank that makes her uncomfortable. It is perhaps rather heartless, but after this, when he called two days ago, I went out of the room and left them alone together. The truth is, there is something in this tall, fair, vague, inconsequent youth, who would look like a Prussian lieutenant if Prussian lieutenants ever hesitated, and who is such a singular mixture of confusion and candour—there is something about him that is not altogether to my own taste, and that is why I took the liberty of leaving him. Oddly enough, I don't in the least know what it is; I usually know why I dislike people. I don't dislike the blushing Adrian, however—that is, after all, the oddest part. No, the oddest part of it is that I think I have a feeling of pity for him; that is probably why (if it were not my duty sometimes to remain) I should always depart when he comes. I don't like to see the people I pity; to be pitied by me is too low a depth. Why I should lavish my compassion on Mr Frank of course passes my comprehension. He is young, intelligent, in perfect health, master of a handsome fortune, and favourite brother of Haroun-al-Raschid. Such are the consequences of being a woman of imagination. When, at dinner, I asked Eunice if he had been as interesting as usual, she said she would leave it to me to judge; he had talked altogether about Miss Condit! He thinks her very attractive! Poor fellow, when it is necessary he doesn't hesitate, though I can't imagine why it should be necessary. I think that *au fond* he bores Eunice a little; like many girls of the delicate, sensitive kind, she likes older, more confident men.

May 24.—He has just made me a remarkable communication! This morning I went into the Park in quest of a "bit," with some colours and brushes in a small box, and that wonderfully compressible campstool which I can carry in my pocket. I wandered vaguely enough, for half an hour, through the carefully-arranged scenery, the idea of which appears to be to represent the earth's surface *en raccourci*, and at last discovered a small clump of birches which, with their white stems and their little raw green bristles, were not altogether uninspiring. The place was quiet—there were no nurse-maids nor bicycles; so I took up a position and enjoyed an hour's successful work. At last I heard some one say behind me, "I think I ought to tell you I'm looking!" It was Adrian Frank, who had recognised me at a distance, and, without my hearing him, had walked across the grass to where I sat. This time I couldn't leave him, for I hadn't finished my sketch. He sat down near me, on an artistically-preserved rock, and we ended by having a good deal of talk—in which, however, I did the listening, for I can't express myself in two ways at once. What I listened to was this—that Mr Caliph wishes his step-brother to "make up" to Eunice, and that the candid Adrian wishes to know what I think of his chances.

"Are you in love with her?" I asked.

"Oh dear, no! If I were in love with her I should go straight in, without—without this sort of thing."

"You mean without asking people's opinion?"

"Well, yes. Without even asking yours."

I told him that he needn't say "even" mine; for mine would not be worth much. His announcement rather startled me at first, but after I had thought of it a little, I found in it a good deal to admire. I have seen so many "arranged" marriages that have been happy, and so many "sympathetic" unions that have been wretched, that the political element doesn't altogether shock me. Of course I can't imagine Eunice making a political marriage, and I said to Mr Frank, very promptly, that she might consent if she could be induced to love him, but would never be governed in her choice by his advantages. I said "advantages" in order to be polite; the singular number would have served all the purpose. His only advantage is his fortune; for he has neither looks, talents, nor position that would dazzle a girl who is herself clever and rich. This, then, is what Mr Caliph has had in his head all this while—this is what has made him so anxious that we should like his step-brother. I have an idea that I ought to be rather scandalised, but I feel my pulse and find that I am almost pleased. I don't mean at the idea of her marrying poor Mr Frank; I mean at such an indication that Mr Caliph takes an interest in her. I don't know whether it is one of the regular duties of a trustee to provide the trustful with a husband; perhaps in that case his merit may be less. I suppose he has said to himself that if she marries his step-brother she won't marry a worse man. Of course it is possible that he may not have thought of Eunice at all, and may simply have wished the guileless Adrian to do a good thing without regard to Eunice's point of view. I am afraid that even this idea doesn't shock me. Trying to make people marry is, under any circumstances, an unscrupulous game; but the offence is minimised when it is a question of an honest man marrying an angel. Eunice is the angel, and the young Adrian has all the air of being honest. It would, naturally, not be the union of her secret dreams, for the hero of those pure visions would have to be clever and distinguished. Mr Frank is neither of these things, but I believe he is perfectly good. Of course he is weak—to come and take a wife simply because his brother has told him to—or is he doing it simply for form, believing that she will never have him, that he consequently doesn't expose himself, and that he will therefore have on easy terms, since he seems to value it, the credit of having obeyed Mr Caliph? Why he should value it is a matter between themselves, which I am not obliged to know. I don't think I care at all for the relations of men between themselves. Their relations with women are bad enough, but when there is no woman to save it a little— *merci!* I shouldn't think that the young Adrian would care to subject himself to a simple refusal, for it is not gratifying to receive the cold shoulder, even from a woman you don't want to marry. After all, he may want to marry her; there are all sorts of reasons in things. I told him I wouldn't undertake to do anything, and the more I think of it the less I am willing. It would be a weight off my mind to see her comfortably settled in life, beyond the possibility of marrying some highly varnished brute—a fate in certain circumstances quite open to her. She is perfectly capable—with her folded angel's wings—of bestowing herself upon the baker, upon the fishmonger, if she were to take a fancy to him. The clever man of her dreams might beat her or get tired of her; but I am sure that Mr Frank, if he should pronounce his marriage-vows, would keep them to the letter. From that to pushing her into his arms, however, is a long way. I went so far as to tell him that he had my good wishes; but I made him understand that I can give him no help. He sat for some time poking a hole in the earth with his stick and watching the operation. Then he said, with his wide, exaggerated smile—the one thing in his face that recalls his brother, though it is so different—"I think I should like to try." I felt rather sorry for him, and made him talk of something else; and we separated without his alluding to Eunice, though at the last he looked at me for a moment intently, with something on his lips, which was probably a return to his idea. I stopped him; I told him I always required solitude for my finishing-touches. He thinks me *brusque* and queer, but he went away. I don't know what he means to do; I am curious to see whether he will begin his siege. It can scarcely be said, as yet, to have begun—Eunice, at any rate, is all unconscious.

June 6.—Her unconsciousness is being rapidly dispelled; Mr Frank has been here every day since I last wrote. He is a singular youth, and I don't make him out; I think there is more in him than I supposed at first. He doesn't bore us, and he has become, to a certain extent, one of the family. I like him very much, and he excites my curiosity. I don't quite see where he expects to come out. I mentioned some time back that Eunice had told me he made her uncomfortable; and now, if that continues, she appears to have resigned herself. He has asked her repeatedly to drive with him, and twice she has consented; he has a very pretty pair of horses, and a vehicle that holds but two persons. I told him I could give him no positive help, but I do leave them together. Of course Eunice has noticed this—it is the only intimation I have given her that I am aware of his intentions. I have constantly expected her to say something, but she has said nothing, and it is possible that Mr Frank is making an impression. He makes love very reasonably; evidently his idea is to be intensely gradual. Of course it isn't gradual to come every day; but he does very little on any one occasion. That, at least, is my impression; for when I talk of his making love I don't mean that I see it. When the three of us are together he talks to me quite as much as to her, and there is no difference in his manner from one of us to the other. His shyness is wearing off, and he blushes so much less that I have discovered his natural hue. It has several shades less of crimson than I supposed. I have taken care that he should not see me alone, for I don't wish him to talk to me of what he is doing—I wish to have nothing to say about it. He has looked at me several times in the same way in which he looked just before we parted, that day he found me sketching in the Park; that is, as if he wished to have some special understanding with me. But I don't want a special understanding, and I pretend not to see his looks. I don't exactly see why Eunice doesn't speak to me, and why she expresses no surprise at Mr Frank's sudden devotion. Perhaps Mr Caliph has notified her, and she is prepared for everything—prepared even to accept the young Adrian. I have an idea he will be rather taken in if she does. Perhaps the day will come soon when I shall think it well to say: "Take care, take care; you *may* succeed!" He improves on acquaintance; he knows a great many things, and he is a gentleman to his finger-tips. We talk very often about Rome; he has made out every inscription for himself, and has got them all written down in a little book. He brought it the other afternoon and read some of them out to us, and it was more amusing than it may sound. I listen to such things because I can listen to anything about Rome; and Eunice listens possibly because Mr Caliph has told her to. She appears ready to do anything he tells her; he has been sending her some more papers to sign. He has not been here since the day he gave me the flowers; he went back to Washington shortly after that. She has received several letters from him, accompanying documents that look very legal. She has said nothing to me about them, and since I uttered those words of warning which I noted here at the time, I have asked no questions and offered no criticism. Sometimes I wonder whether I myself had not better speak to Mr Ermine; it is only the fear of being idiotic and meddle-some that restrains me. It seems to me so odd there should be no one else; Mr Caliph appears to have everything in his own hands. We are to go down to our "seat," as Mrs Ermine says, next week. That brilliant woman has left town herself, like many other people, and is staying with one of her daughters. Then she is going to the other, and then she is coming to Eunice, at Cornerville.

II

June 8.—Late this afternoon—about an hour before dinner—Mr Frank arrived with what Mrs Ermine calls his equipage, and asked her to take a short drive with him. At first she declined—said it was too hot, too late, she was too tired; but he seemed very much in earnest and begged her to think better of it. She consented at last, and when she had left the room to arrange herself, he turned to me with a little grin of elation. I saw he was going to say something about his prospects, and I determined, this time, to give him a chance. Besides, I was curious to know how he believed himself to be getting on. To my surprise, he disappointed my curiosity; he only said, with his timid brightness, "I am always so glad when I carry my point."

"Your point? Oh yes. I think I know what you mean."

"It's what I told you that day." He seemed slightly surprised that I should be in doubt as to whether he had really presented himself as a lover.

"Do you mean to ask her to marry you?"

He stared a little, looking graver. "Do you mean to-day?"

"Well, yes, to-day, for instance; you have urged her so to drive."

"I don't think I will do it to-day; it's too soon."

His gravity was natural enough, I suppose; but it had suddenly become so intense that the effect was comical, and I could not help laughing. "Very good; whenever you please."

"Don't you think it's too soon?" he asked.

"Ah, I know nothing about it."

"I have seen her alone only four or five times."

"You must go on as you think best," I said.

"It's hard to tell. My position is very difficult." And then he began to smile again. He is certainly very odd.

It is my fault, I suppose, that I am too impatient of what I don't understand; and I don't understand this odd mixture of calculation and passion, or the singular alternation of Mr Frank's confessions and reserves. "I can't enter into your position," I said; "I can't advise you or help you in any way." Even to myself my voice sounded a little hard as I spoke, and he was evidently discomposed by it.

He blushed as usual, and fell to putting on his gloves. "I think a great deal of your opinion, and for several days I have wanted to ask you."

"Yes, I have seen that."

"How have you seen it?"

"By the way you have looked at me."

He hesitated a moment. "Yes, I have looked at you—I know that. There is a great deal in your face to see."

This remark, under the circumstances, struck me as absurd; I began to laugh again. "You speak of it as if it were a collection of curiosities." He looked away now, he wouldn't meet my eye, and I saw that I had made him feel thoroughly uncomfortable. To lead the conversation back into the commonplace, I asked him where he intended to drive.

"It doesn't matter much where we go—it's so pretty everywhere now." He was evidently not thinking of his drive, and suddenly he broke out, "I want to know whether you think she likes me."

"I haven't the least idea. She hasn't told me."

"Do you think she knows that I mean to propose to her?"

"You ought to be able to judge of that better than I."

"I am afraid of taking too much for granted; also of taking her by surprise."

"So that—in her agitation—she might accept you? Is that what you are afraid of?"

"I don't know what makes you say that. I wish her to accept me."

"Are you very sure?"

"Perfectly sure. Why not? She is a charming creature."

"So much the better, then; perhaps she will."

"You don't believe it," he exclaimed, as if it were very clever of him to have discovered that.

"You think too much of what I believe. That has nothing to do with the matter."

"No, I suppose not," said Mr Frank, apparently wishing very much to agree with me.

"You had better find out as soon as possible from Eunice herself," I added.

"I haven't expected to know—for some time."

"Do you mean for a year or two? She will be ready to tell you before that."

"Oh no—not a year or two; but a few weeks."

"You know you come to the house every day. You ought to explain to her."

"Perhaps I had better not come so often."

"Perhaps not!"

"I like it very much," he said, smiling.

I looked at him a moment; I don't know what he has got in his eyes. "Don't change! You are such a good young man that I don't know what we should do without you." And I left him to wait alone for Eunice.

From my window, above, I saw them leave the door; they make a fair, bright young couple as they sit together. They had not been gone a quarter of an hour when Mr Caliph's name was brought up to me. He had asked for me—me alone; he begged that I would do him the favour to see him for ten minutes. I don't know why this announcement should have made me nervous; but it did. My heart beat at the prospect of entering into direct relations with Mr Caliph. He is very clever, much thought of, and talked of; and yet I had vaguely suspected him—of I don't know what! I became conscious of that, and felt the responsibility of it; though I didn't foresee, and indeed don't think I foresee yet, any danger of a collision between us. It is to be noted, moreover, that even a woman who is both plain and conceited must feel a certain agitation at entering the presence of Haroun-al-Raschid. I had begun to dress for dinner, and I kept him waiting till I had taken my usual time to finish. I always take some such revenge as that upon men who make me nervous. He is the sort of man who feels immediately whether a woman is well-dressed or not; but I don't think this reflection really had much to do with my putting on the freshest of my three little French gowns.

He sat there, watch in hand; at least he slipped it into his pocket as I came into the room. He was not pleased at having had to wait, and when I apologised, hypocritically, for having kept him, he answered, with a certain dryness, that he had come to transact an important piece of business in a very short space of time. I wondered what his business could be, and whether he had come to confess to me that he had spent Eunice's money for his own purposes. Did he wish me to use my influence with her not to make a scandal? He didn't look like a man who has come to ask a favour of that kind; but I am sure that if he ever does ask it he will not look at all as he might be expected to look. He was clad in white garments, from head to foot, in recognition of the hot weather, and he had half a dozen roses in his button-hole. This time his flowers were for himself. His white clothes made him look as big as Henry VIII.; but don't tell me he is not a Jew! He's a Jew of the artistic, not of the commercial type; and as I stood there I thought him a very strange person to have as one's trustee. It seemed to me that he would carry such an office into transcendental regions, out of all common jurisdictions; and it was a comfort to me to remember that I have no property to be taken care of. Mr Caliph kept a pocket-handkerchief, with an enormous monogram, in his large tapering hand, and every other moment he touched his face with it. He evidently suffers from the heat. With all that, *il est bien beau*. His business was not what had at first occurred to me; but I don't know that it was much less strange.

"I knew I should find you alone, because Adrian told me this morning that he meant to come and ask our young friend to drive. I was glad of that; I have been wishing to see you alone, and I didn't know how to manage it."

"You see it's very simple. Didn't you send your brother?" I asked. In another place, to another person, this might have sounded impertinent; but evidently, addressed to Mr Caliph, things have a special measure, and this I instinctively felt. He will take a great deal, and he will give a great deal.

He looked at me a moment, as if he were trying to measure what I would take. "I see you are going to be a very satisfactory person to talk with," he answered. "That's exactly what I counted on. I want you to help me."

"I thought there was some reason why Mr Frank should urge Eunice so to go," I went on; refreshed a little, I admit, by these words of commendation. "At first she was unwilling."

"Is she usually unwilling—and does he usually have to be urgent?" he asked, like a man pleased to come straight to the point.

'What does it matter, so long as she consents in the end?" I responded, with a smile that made him smile. There is a singular stimulus, even a sort of excitement, in talking with him; he makes one wish to venture. And this not as women usually venture, because they have a sense of impunity, but, on the contrary, because one has a prevision of penalties— those penalties which give a kind of dignity to sarcasm. He must be a dangerous man to irritate.

"Do you think she will consent, in the end?" he inquired; and though I had now foreseen what he was coming to, I felt that, even with various precautions, which he had plainly decided not to take, there would still have been a certain crudity in it when, a moment later, he put his errand into words. "I want my little brother to marry her, and I want you to help me bring it about." Then he told me that he knew his brother had already spoken to me, but that he believed I had not promised him much countenance. He wished me to think well of the plan; it would be a delightful marriage.

"Delightful for your brother, yes. That's what strikes me most."

"Delightful for him, certainly; but also very pleasant for Eunice, as things go here. Adrian is the best fellow in the world; he's a gentleman; he hasn't a vice or a fault; he is very well educated; and he has twenty thousand a year. A lovely property."

"Not in trust?" I said, looking into Mr Caliph's extraordinary eyes.

"Oh no; he has full control of it. But he is wonderfully careful."

"He doesn't trouble you with it?"

"Oh, dear, no; why should he? Thank God, I haven't got that on my back. His property comes to him from his father, who had nothing to do with me; didn't even like me, I think. He has capital advisers—presidents of banks, overseers of hospitals, and all that sort of thing. They have put him in the way of some excellent investments."

As I write this, I am surprised at my audacity; but, somehow, it didn't seem so great at the time, and he gave absolutely no sign of seeing more in what I said than appeared. He evidently desires the marriage immensely, and he was thinking only of putting it before me so that I too should think well of it; for evidently, like his brother, he has the most exaggerated opinion of my influence with Eunice. On Mr Frank's part this doesn't surprise me so much; but I confess it seems to me odd that a man of Mr Caliph's acuteness should make the mistake of taking me for one of those persons who covet influence and like to pull the wires of other people's actions. I have a horror of influence, and should never have consented to come and live with Eunice if I had not seen that she is at bottom much stronger than I, who am not at all strong, in spite of my grand airs. Mr Caliph, I suppose, cannot conceive of a woman in my dependent position being indifferent to opportunities for working in the dark; but he ought to leave those vulgar imputations to Mrs Ermine. He ought, with his intelligence, to see one as one is; or do I possibly exaggerate that intelligence? "Do you know I feel as if you were asking me to take part in a conspiracy?" I made that announcement with as little delay as possible.

He stared a moment, and then he said that he didn't in the least repudiate that view of his proposal. He admitted that he was a conspirator—in an excellent cause. All match-making was conspiracy. It was impossible that as a superior woman I should enter into his ideas, and he was sure that I had seen too much of the world to say anything so *banal* as that the young people were not in love with each other. That was only a basis for marriage when better things were lacking. It was decent, it was fitting, that Eunice should be settled in life; his conscience would not be at rest about her until he should see that well arranged. He was not in the least afraid of that word "arrangement;" a marriage was an eminently practical matter, and it could not be too much arranged. He confessed that he took the European view. He thought that a young girl's elders ought to see that she marries in a way in which certain definite proprieties are observed. He was sure of his brother; he knew how faultless Adrian was. He talked for some time, and said a great deal that I had said to myself the other day, after Mr Frank spoke to me; said, in particular, very much what I had thought, about the beauty of arrangements—that there are far too few among Americans who marry, that we are the people in the world who divorce and separate most, that there would be much less of this sort of thing if young people were helped to choose; if marriages were, as one might say, presented to them. I listened to Mr Caliph with my best attention, thinking it was odd that, on his lips, certain things which I had phrased to myself in very much the same way should sound so differently. They ought to have sounded better, uttered as they were with the energy, the authority, the lucidity, of a man accustomed to making arguments; but somehow they didn't. I am afraid I am very perverse. I answered—I hardly remember what; but there was a taint of that perversity in it. As he rejoined, I felt that he was growing urgent—very urgent; he has an immense desire that something may be done. I remember saying at last, "What I don't understand is why your brother should wish to marry my cousin. He has told me he is not in love with her. Has your presentation of the idea, as you call it —has that been enough? Is he acting simply at your request?"

I saw that his reply was not perfectly ready, and for a moment those strange eyes of his emitted a ray that I had not seen before. They seemed to say, "Are you really taking liberties with me? Be on your guard; I may be dangerous." But he always smiles. Yes, I think he is dangerous, though I don't know exactly what he could do to me. I believe he would smile at the hangman, if he were condemned to meet him. He is very angry with his brother for having admitted to me that the sentiment he entertains for Eunice is not a passion; as if it would have been possible for him, under my eyes, to pretend that he is in love! I don't think I am afraid of Mr Caliph; I don't desire to take liberties with him (as his eyes seemed to call it) or with any one; but, decidedly, I am not afraid of him. If it came to protecting Eunice, for instance; to demanding justice—But what extravagances am I writing? He answered, in a moment, with a good deal of dignity, and even a good deal of reason, that his brother has the greatest admiration for my cousin, that he agrees fully and cordially with everything he (Mr Caliph) has said to him about its being an excellent match, that he wants very much to marry, and wants to marry as a gentleman should. If he is not in love with Eunice, moreover, he is not in love with any one else.

"I hope not!" I said, with a laugh; whereupon Mr Caliph got up, looking, for him, rather grave.

"I can't imagine why you should suppose that Adrian is not acting freely. I don't know what you imagine my means of coercion to be."

"I don't imagine anything. I think I only wish he had thought of it himself."

"He would never think of anything that is for his good. He is not in the least interested."

"Well, I don't know that it matters, because I don't think Eunice will see it—as we see it."

"Thank you for saying 'we.' Is she in love with some one else?"

"Not that I know of; but she may expect to be, some day. And better than that, she may expect—very justly—some one to be in love with her."

"Oh, in love with her! How you women talk! You all of you want the moon. If she is not content to be thought of as Adrian thinks of her, she is a very silly girl. What will she have more than tenderness? That boy is all tenderness."

"Perhaps he is too tender," I suggested. "I think he is afraid to ask her."

"Yes, I know he is nervous—at the idea of a refusal. But I should like her to refuse him once."

"It is not of that he is afraid—it is of her accepting him."

Mr Caliph smiled, as if he thought this very ingenious. "You don't understand him. I'm so sorry! I had an idea that —with your knowledge of human nature, your powers of observation—you would have perceived how he is made. In fact, I rather counted on that." He said this with a little tone of injury which might have made me feel terribly inadequate if it had not been accompanied with a glance that seemed to say that, after all, he was generous and he forgave me. "Adrian's is one of those natures that are inflamed by not succeeding. He doesn't give up; he thrives on opposition. If she refuses him three or four times he will adore her!"

"She is sure then to be adored—though I am not sure it will make a difference with her. I haven't yet seen a sign that she cares for him."

"Why then does she go out to drive with him?" There was nothing brutal in the elation with which Mr Caliph made this point; still, he looked a little as if he pitied me for exposing myself to a refutation so prompt.

"That proves nothing, I think. I would go to drive with Mr Frank, if he should ask me, and I should be very much surprised if it were regarded as an intimation that I am ready to marry him."

Mr Caliph had his hands resting on his thighs, and in this position, bending forward a little, with his smile he said, "Ah, but he doesn't want to marry *you!*"

That was a little brutal, I think; but I should have appeared ridiculous if I had attempted to resent it. I simply answered that I had as yet seen no sign even that Eunice is conscious of Mr Frank's intentions. I think she is, but I don't think so from anything she has said or done. Mr Caliph maintains that she is capable of going for six months without betraying herself, all the while quietly considering and making up her mind. It is possible he is right—he has known her longer than I. He is far from wishing to wait for six months, however; and the part I must play is to bring matters to a crisis. I told him that I didn't see why he did not speak to her directly—why he should operate in this roundabout way. Why shouldn't he say to her all that he had said to me—tell her that she would make him very happy by marrying his little brother? He answered that this is impossible, that the nearness of relationship would make it unbecoming; it would look like a kind of nepotism. The thing must appear to come to pass of itself—and I, somehow, must be the author of that appearance! I was too much a woman of the world, too acquainted with life, not to see the force of all this. He had a great deal to say about my being a woman of the world; in one sense it is not all complimentary; one would think me some battered old dowager who had married off fifteen daughters. I feel that I am far from all that when Mr Caliph leaves me so mystified. He has some other reason for wishing these nuptials than love of the two young people, but I am unable to put my hand on it. Like the children at hide-and-seek, however, I think I "burn." I don't like him, I mistrust him; but he is a very charming man. His geniality, his richness, his magnetism, I suppose I should say, are extraordinary; he fascinates me, in spite of my suspicions. The truth is, that in his way he is an artist, and in my little way I am also one; and the artist in me recognises the artist in him, and cannot quite resist the temptation to foregather. What is more than this, the artist in him has recognised the artist in me—it is very good of him—and would like to establish a certain freemasonry. "Let us take together the artistic view of life;" that is simply the meaning of his talking so much about my being a woman of the world. That is all very well; but it seems to me there would be a certain baseness in our being artists together at the expense of poor little Eunice. I should like to know some of Mr Caliph's secrets, but I don't wish to give him any of mine in return for them. Yet I gave him something before he departed; I hardly know what, and hardly know how he extracted it from me. It was a sort of promise that I would after all speak to Eunice,—"as I should like to have you, you know." He remained there for a quarter of an hour after he got up to go; walking about the room with his hands on his hips; talking, arguing, laughing, holding me with his eyes, his admirable face—as natural, as dramatic, and at the same time as diplomatic, as an Italian. I am pretty sure he was trying to produce a certain effect, to entangle, to magnetise me. Strange to say, Mr Caliph compromises himself, but he doesn't compromise his brother. He has a private reason, but his brother has nothing to do with his privacies. That was my last word to him.

"The moment I feel sure that I may do something for your brother's happiness—your brother's alone—by pleading his cause with Eunice—that moment I will speak to her. But I can do nothing for yours."

In answer to this, Mr Caliph said something very unexpected. "I wish I had known you five years ago!"

There are many meanings to that; perhaps he would have liked to put me out of the way. But I could take only the polite meaning. "Our acquaintance could never have begun too soon."

"Yes, I should have liked to know you," he went on, "in spite of the fact that you are not kind, that you are not just. Have I asked you to do anything for my happiness? My happiness is nothing. I have nothing to do with happiness. I don't deserve it. It is only for my little brother—and for your charming cousin."

I was obliged to admit that he was right; that he had asked nothing for himself. "But I don't want to do anything for you even by accident!" I said—laughing, of course.

This time he was grave. He stood looking at me a moment, then put out his hand. "Yes, I wish I had known you!"

There was something so expressive in his voice, so handsome in his face, so tender and respectful in his manner, as he said this, that for an instant I was really moved, and I was on the point of saying with feeling, "I wish indeed you had!" But that instinct of which I have already spoken checked me— the sense that somehow, as things stand, there can be no *rapprochement* between Mr Caliph and me that will not involve a certain sacrifice of Eunice. So I only replied, "You seem to me strange, Mr Caliph. I must tell you that I don't understand you."

He kept my hand, still looking at me, and went on as if he had not heard me. "I am not happy—I am not wise nor good." Then suddenly, in quite a different tone, "For God's sake, let her marry my brother!"

There was a quick passion in these words which made me say, "If it is so pressing as that, you certainly ought to speak to her. Perhaps she'll do it to oblige you!"

We had walked into the hall together, and the last I saw of him he stood in the open doorway, looking back at me with his smile. "Hang the nepotism! I *will* speak to her!"

Cornerville, July 6.—A whole month has passed since I have made an entry; but I have a good excuse for this dreadful gap.

Since we have been in the country I have found subjects
enough and to spare, and I have been painting so hard that my
hand, of an evening, has been glad to rest. This place is very
lovely, and the Hudson is as beautiful as the Rhine. There are
the words, in black and white, over my signature; I can't do
more than that. I have said it a dozen times, in answer to as
many challenges, and now I record the opinion with all the
solemnity I can give it. May it serve for the rest of the summer! This is an excellent old house, of the style that was
thought impressive, in this country, forty years ago. It is
painted a cheerful slate-colour, save for a multitude of pilasters
and facings which are picked out in the cleanest and freshest
white. It has a kind of clumsy gable or apex, on top; a sort of
roofed terrace, below, from which you may descend to a lawn
dotted with delightful old trees; and between the two, in the
second story, a deep verandah, let into the body of the building, and ornamented with white balustrades, considerably
carved, and big blue stone jars. Add to this a multitude of green
shutters and striped awnings, and a mass of Virginia creepers
and wisterias, and fling over it the lavish light of the American
summer, and you have a notion of some of the conditions of
our *villeggiatura*. The great condition, of course, is the splendid river, lying beneath our rounded headland in vast silvery
stretches and growing almost vague on the opposite shore. It
is a country of views; you are always peeping down an avenue,
or ascending a mound, or going round a corner, to look at one.
They are rather too shining, too high-pitched, for my little
purposes; all nature seems glazed with light and varnished
with freshness. But I manage to scrape something off. Mrs
Ermine is here, as brilliant as her setting; and so, strange to
say, is Adrian Frank. Strange, for this reason, that the night
before we left town I went into Eunice's room and asked her
whether she knew, or rather whether she suspected, what was
going on. A sudden impulse came to me; it seemed to me unnatural that in such a situation I should keep anything from

her. I don't want to interfere, but I think I want even less to carry too far my aversion to interference, and without pretending to advise Eunice, it was revealed to me that she ought to know that Mr Caliph had come to see me on purpose to induce me to work upon her. It was not till after he was gone that it occurred to me he had sent his brother in advance, on purpose to get Eunice out of the way, and that this was the reason the young Adrian would take no refusal. He was really in excellent training. It was a very hot night. Eunice was alone in her room, without a lamp; the windows were wide open, and the dusk was clarified by the light of the street. She sat there, among things vaguely visible, in a white wrapper, with her fair hair on her shoulders, and I could see her eyes move toward me when I asked her whether she knew that Mr Frank wished to marry her. I could see her smile, too, as she answered that she knew he thought he did, but also knew he didn't.

"Of course I have only his word for it," I said.

"Has he told you?"

"Oh yes, and his brother, too."

"His brother?" And Eunice slowly got up.

"It's an idea of Mr Caliph's as well. Indeed Mr Caliph may have been the first. He came here to-day, while you were out, to tell me how much he should like to see it come to pass. He has set his heart upon it, and he wished me to engage to do all in my power to bring it about. Of course I can't do anything, can I?"

She had sunk into her chair again as I went on; she sat there looking before her, in the dark. Before she answered me she gathered up her thick hair with her hands, twisted it together, and holding it in place on top of her head, with one hand, tried to fasten a comb into it with the other. I passed behind her to help her; I could see she was agitated. "Oh no, you can't do anything," she said, after a moment, with a laugh that was not like her usual laughter. "I know all about it; they have told me, of course." Her tone was forced, and I could see

that she had not really known all about it—had not known that
Mr Caliph is pushing his brother. I went to the window and
looked out a little into the hot, empty street, where the gas
lamps showed me, up and down, the hundred high stoops,
exactly alike, and as ugly as a bad dream. While I stood there
a thought suddenly dropped into my mind, which has lain
ever since where it fell. But I don't wish to move it, even to
write it here. I stayed with Eunice for ten minutes; I told her
everything that Mr Caliph had said to me. She listened in
perfect silence—I could see that she was glad to listen. When
I related that he didn't wish to speak to her himself on behalf
of his brother, because that would seem indelicate, she broke
in, with a certain eagerness, "Yes, that is very natural!"

"And now you can marry Mr Frank without my help!" I
said, when I had done.

She shook her head sadly, though she was smiling again.
"It's too late for your help. He has asked me to marry him,
and I have told him he can hope for it—never!"

I was surprised to hear he had spoken, and she said nothing
about the time or place. It must have been that afternoon,
during their drive. I said that I was rather sorry for our poor
young friend, he was such a very nice fellow. She agreed that
he was remarkably nice, but added that this was not a sufficient
reason for her marrying him; and when I said that he would
try again, that I had Mr Caliph's assurance that he would not
be easy to get rid of, and that a refusal would only make him
persist, she answered that he might try as often as he liked;
he was so little disagreeable to her that she would take even
that from him. And now, to give him a chance to try again,
she has asked him down here to stay, thinking apparently that
Mrs Ermine's presence puts us *en règle* with the proprieties. I
should add that she assured me there was no real danger of his
trying again; he had told her he meant to, but he had said it
only for form. Why should he, since he was not in love with
her? It was all an idea of his brother's, and she was much

obliged to Mr Caliph, who took his duties much too seriously and was not in the least bound to provide her with a husband. Mr Frank and she had agreed to remain friends, as if nothing had happened; and I think she then said something about her intending to ask him to this place. A few days after we got here, at all events, she told me that she had written to him, proposing his coming; whereupon I intimated that I thought it a singular overture to make to a rejected lover whom one didn't wish to encourage. He would take it as encouragement, or at all events Mr Caliph would. She answered that she didn't care what Mr Caliph thinks, and that she knew Mr Frank better than I, and knew therefore that he had absolutely no hope. But she had a particular reason for wishing him to be here. That sounded mysterious, and she couldn't tell me more; but in a month or two I would guess her reason. As she said this she looked at me with a brighter smile than she has had for weeks; for I protest that she is troubled—Eunice is greatly troubled. Nearly a month has elapsed, and I haven't guessed that reason. Here is Adrian Frank, at any rate, as I say; and I can't make out whether he persists or renounces. His manner to Eunice is just the same; he is always polite and always shy, never inattentive and never unmistakable. He has not said a word more to me about his suit. Apart from this he is very sympathetic, and we sit about sketching together in the most fraternal manner. He made to me a day or two since a very pretty remark; viz., that he would rather copy a sketch of mine than try, himself, to do the place from nature. This perhaps does not look so *galant* as I repeat it here; but with the tone and glance with which he said it, it really almost touched me. I was glad, by the way, to hear from Eunice the night before we left town that she doesn't care what Mr Caliph thinks; only, I should be gladder still if I believed it. I don't, unfortunately; among other reasons because it doesn't at all agree with that idea which descended upon me with a single jump—from heaven knows where—while I looked out of her window at the stoops. I observe with pleasure, however, that he doesn't send her any more papers to sign. These days pass softly, quickly, but with a curious, an unnatural, stillness. It is as if there were something in the air—a sort of listening hush. That sounds very fantastic, and I suppose such remarks are only to be justified by my having the artistic temperament —that is, if I have it! If I haven't, there is no excuse; unless it be that Eunice is distinctly uneasy, and that it takes the form of a voluntary, exaggerated calm, of which I feel the contact, the tension. She is as quiet as a mouse and yet as restless as a flame. She is neither well nor happy; she doesn't sleep. It is true that I asked Mr Frank the other day what impression she made on him, and he replied, with a little start, and a smile of alacrity, "Oh, delightful, as usual!"—so that I saw he didn't know what he was talking about. He is tremendously sunburnt, and as red as a tomato. I wish he would look a little less at my daubs and a little more at the woman he wishes to marry. In summer I always suffice to myself, and I am so much interested in my work that if I hope, devoutly, as I do, that nothing is going to happen to Eunice, it is probably quite as much from selfish motives as from others. If anything were to happen to her I should be immensely interrupted. Mrs Ermine is bored, *par exemple!* She is dying to have a garden-party, at which she can drag a long train over the lawn; but day follows day and this entertainment does not take place. Eunice has promised it, however, for another week, and I believe means to send out invitations immediately. Mrs Ermine has offered to write them all; she has, after all, *du bon*. But the fatuity of her misunderstandings of everything that surrounds her passes belief. She sees nothing that really occurs, and gazes complacently into the void. Her theory is always that Mr Caliph is in love with Eunice,—she opened up to me on the subject only yesterday, because with no one else to talk to but the young Adrian, who dodges her, she doesn't in the least mind that she hates me, and that I think her a goose—that

Mr Caliph is in love with Eunice, but that Eunice, who is queer enough for anything, doesn't like him, so that he has sent down his step-brother to tell stories about the good things he has done, and to win over her mind to a more favourable view. Mrs Ermine believes in these good things, and appears to think such action on Mr Caliph's part both politic and dramatic. She has not the smallest suspicion of the real little drama that has been going on under her nose. I wish I had that absence of vision; it would be a great rest. Heaven knows I see more than I want—for instance when I see that my poor little cousin is pinched with pain, and yet that I can't relieve her, can't even advise her. I couldn't do the former even if I would, and she wouldn't let me do the latter even if I could. It seems too pitiful, too incredible, that there should be no one to turn to. Surely, if I go up to town for a day next week, as seems probable, I may call upon William Ermine. Whether I *may* or not, I will.

July 11.—She has been getting letters, and they have made her worse. Last night I spoke to her—I asked her to come into my room. I told her that I saw she was in distress; that it was terrible to me to see it; that I was sure that she has some miserable secret. Who was making her suffer this way? No one had the right—not even Mr Caliph, if Mr Caliph it was, to whom she appeared to have conceded every right. She broke down completely, burst into tears, confessed that she is troubled about money. Mr Caliph has again requested a delay as to his handing in his accounts, and has told her that she will have no income for another year. She thinks it strange; she is afraid that everything isn't right. She is not afraid of being poor; she holds that it's vile to concern one's self so much about money. But there is something that breaks her heart in thinking that Mr Caliph should be in fault. She had always admired him, she had always believed in him, she had always—— What it was, in the third place, that she had always done I didn't learn, for at this point she buried her head

still deeper in my lap and sobbed for half an hour. Her grief
was melting. I was never more troubled, and this in spite of
the fact that I was furious at her strange air of acceptance of a
probable calamity. She is afraid that everything isn't right, for-
sooth! I should think it was not, and should think it hadn't
been for heaven knows how long. This is what has been in
the air; this is what was hanging over us. But Eunice is simply
amazing. She declines to see a lawyer; declines to hold Mr
Caliph accountable; declines to complain, to inquire, to in-
vestigate in any way. I am sick, I am terribly perplexed—I
don't know what to do. Her tears dried up in an instant as
soon as I made the very obvious remark that the beautiful,
the mysterious, the captivating Caliph is no better than a
common swindler; and she gave me a look which might have
frozen me if, when I am angry, I were freezable. She took it
de bien haut; she intimated to me that if I should ever speak
in that way again of Mr Caliph we must part company for ever.
She was distressed; she admitted that she felt injured. I had
seen for myself how far that went. But she didn't pretend to
judge him. He had been in trouble,—he had told her that; and
his trouble was worse than hers, inasmuch as his honour was
at stake, and it had to be saved.

"It's charming to hear you speak of his honour," I cried,
quite regardless of the threat she had just uttered. "Where was
his honour when he violated the most sacred of trusts? Where
was his honour when he went off with your fortune? Those
are questions, my dear, that the courts will make him answer.
He shall make up to you every penny that he has stolen, or
my name is not Catherine Condit!"

Eunice gave me another look, which seemed meant to let
me know that I had suddenly become in her eyes the most
indecent of women; and then she swept out of the room. I
immediately sat down and wrote to Mr Ermine, in order to
have my note ready to send up to town at the earliest hour the
next morning. I told him that Eunice was in dreadful trouble

about her money-matters, and that I believed he would render her a great service, though she herself had no wish to ask it, by coming down to see her at his first convenience. I reflected, of course, as I wrote, that he could do her no good if she should refuse to see him; but I made up for this by saying to myself that I at least should see him, and that he would do me good. I added in my note that Eunice had been despoiled by those who had charge of her property; but I didn't mention Mr Caliph's name. I was just closing my letter when Eunice came into my room again. I saw in a moment that she was different from anything she had ever been before—or at least had ever seemed. Her excitement, her passion, had gone down; even the traces of her tears had vanished. She was perfectly quiet, but all her softness had left her. She was as solemn and impersonal as the priestess of a cult. As soon as her eyes fell upon my letter she asked me to be so good as to inform her to whom I had been writing. I instantly satisfied her, telling her what I had written; and she asked me to give her the document. "I must let you know that I shall immediately burn it up," she added; and she went on to say that if I should send it to Mr Ermine she herself would write to him by the same post that he was to heed nothing I had said. I tore up my letter, but I announced to Eunice that I would go up to town and see the person to whom I had addressed it. "That brings us precisely to what I came in to say," she answered; and she proceeded to demand of me a solemn vow that I would never speak to a living soul of what I had learned in regard to her affairs. They were her affairs exclusively, and no business of mine or of any other human being; and she had a perfect right to ask and to expect this promise. She has, indeed—more's the pity; but it was impossible to me to admit just then—indignant and excited as I was—that I recognised the right. I did so at last, however, and I made the promise. It seems strange to me to write it here; but I am pledged by a tremendous vow, taken in this "intimate" spot, in the small hours of the morning, never to lift a finger, never to speak a word, to redress any wrong that Eunice may have received at the hands of her treacherous trustee, to bring it to the knowledge of others, or to invoke justice, compensation or pity. How she extorted this concession from me is more than I can say: she did so by the force of her will, which, as I have already had occasion to note, is far stronger than mine; and by the vividness of her passion, which is none the less intense because it burns inward and makes her heart glow while her face remains as clear as an angel's. She seated herself with folded hands, and declared she wouldn't leave the room until I had satisfied her. She is in a state of extraordinary exaltation, and from her own point of view she was eloquent enough. She returned again and again to the fact that she did not judge Mr Caliph; that what he may have done is between herself and him alone; and that if she had not been betrayed to speaking of it to me in the first shock of finding that certain allowances would have to be made for him, no one need ever have suspected it. She was now perfectly ready to make those allowances. She was unspeakably sorry for Mr Caliph. He had been in urgent need of money, and he had used hers: pray, whose else would I have wished him to use? Her money had been an insupportable bore to him from the day it was thrust into his hands. To make him her trustee had been in the worst possible taste; he was not the sort of person to make a convenience of, and it had been odious to take advantage of his good nature. She had always been ashamed of owing him so much. He had been perfect in all his relations with her, though he must have hated her and her wretched little investments from the first. If she had lost money, it was not his fault; he had lost a great deal more for himself than he had lost for her. He was the kindest, the most delightful, the most interesting of men. Eunice brought out all this with pure defiance; she had never treated herself before to the luxury of saying it, and it was singular to think that she found her first pretext, her first boldness, in the fact that he had ruined her. All this looks almost grotesque as I write it here; but she imposed it upon me last night with all the authority of her passionate little person. I agreed, as I say, that the matter was none of my business; that is now definite enough. Two other things are equally so. One is that she is to be plucked like a chicken; the other is that she is in love with the precious Caliph, and has been so for years! I didn't dare to write that the other night, after the beautiful idea had suddenly flowered in my mind; but I don't care what I write now. I am so horribly tongue-tied that I must at least relieve myself here. Of course I wonder now that I never guessed her secret before; especially as I was perpetually hovering on the edge of it. It explains many things, and it is very terrible. In love with a pick-pocket! *Merci!* I am glad fate hasn't played me that trick.

July 14.—I can't get over the idea that he is to go scot-free. I grind my teeth at it as I sit at work, and I find myself using the most livid, the most indignant colours. I have had another talk with Eunice, but I don't in the least know what she is to live on. She says she has always her father's pro-perty, and that this will be abundant; but that of course she cannot pretend to live as she has lived hitherto. She will have to go abroad again and economise; and she will probably have to sell this place—that is, if she can. "If she can," of course means if there is anything to sell; if it isn't devoured with mortgages. What I want to know is, whether Justice, in such a case as this, will not step in, notwithstanding the silence of the victim. If I could only give her a hint—the angel of the scales and sword—in spite of my detestable promise! I can't find out about Mr Caliph's impunity, as it is impossible for me to allude to the matter to any one who would be able to tell me. Yes, the more I think of it the more reason I see to rejoice that fate hasn't played me that trick of making me fall in love with a common thief! Suffering keener than my poor little cousin's I cannot possibly imagine, or a power of self-sacrifice more

awful. Fancy the situation, when the only thing one can do for
the man one loves is to forgive him for stealing! What a delicate attention, what a touching proof of tenderness! This
Eunice can do; she has waited all these years to do something.
I hope she is pleased with her opportunity. And yet when I
say she has forgiven him for stealing, I lose myself in the
mystery of her exquisite spirit. Who knows what it is she has
forgiven—does she even know herself? She consents to being
injured, despoiled, and finds in consenting a kind of rapture.
But I notice that she has said no more about Mr Caliph's
honour. That substantive she condemns herself never to hear
again without a quiver, for she has condoned something too
ignoble. What I further want to know is, what conceivable
tone he has taken—whether he has made a clean breast of it,
and thrown himself upon her mercy; or whether he has sought
refuge in bravado, in prevarication? Not indeed that it matters,
save for the spectacle of the thing, which I find rich. I should
also like much to know whether everything has gone, whether
something may yet be saved. It is safe to say that she doesn't
know the worst, and that if he has admitted the case is bad,
we may take for granted that it leaves nothing to be desired.
Let him alone to do the thing handsomely! I have a right to be
violent, for there was a moment when he made me like him,
and I feel as if he had cheated me too. Her being in love with
him makes it perfect; for of course it was in that that he saw
his opportunity to fleece her. I don't pretend to say how he
discovered it, for she has watched herself as a culprit watches
a judge; but from the moment he guessed it he must have seen
that he could do what he liked. It is true that this doesn't agree
very well with his plan that she should marry his step-brother;
but I prefer to believe it, because it makes him more horrible.
And apropos of Adrian Frank, it is very well I like *him* so
much (that comes out rather plump, by the way), inasmuch as
if I didn't it would be quite open to me to believe that he is in
league with Caliph. There has been nothing to prove that he

has not said to his step-brother, "Very good; you take all you can get, and I will marry her, and being her husband, hush it up,"—nothing but the expression of his blue eyes. That is very little, when we think that expressions and eyes are a specialty of the family, and haven't prevented Mr Caliph from being a robber. It is those eyes of his that poor Eunice is in love with, and it is for their sake that she forgives him. But the young Adrian's are totally different, and not nearly so fine, which I think a great point in his favour. Mr Caliph's are southern eyes, and the young Adrian's are eyes of the north. Moreover, though he is so amiable and obliging, I don't think he is amiable enough to *endosser* his brother's victims to that extent, even to save his brother's honour. He needn't care so much about that honour, since Mr Caliph's name is not his name. And then, poor fellow, he is too stupid; he is almost as stupid as Mrs Ermine. The two have sat together directing cards for Eunice's garden-party as placidly as if no one had a sorrow in life. Mrs Ermine proposed this pastime to Mr Frank; and as he has nothing in the world to do, it is as good an employment for him as another. But it exasperates me to see him sitting at the big table in the library, opposite to Mrs E., while they solemnly pile one envelope on top of another. They have already a heap as high as their heads; they must have invited a thousand people. I can't imagine who they all are. It is an extraordinary time for Eunice to be giving a party— the day after she discovers that she is penniless; but of course it isn't Eunice, it's Mrs Ermine. I said to her yesterday that if she was to change her mode of life—simple enough already, poor thing—she had better begin at once; and that her garden-party under Mrs Ermine's direction would cost her a thousand dollars. She answered that she must go on, since it had already been talked about; she wished no one to know anything—to suspect anything. This would be her last extravagance, her farewell to society. If such resources were open to us poor heretics, I should suppose she meant to go into a convent. She exasperates me too—every one exasperates me. It is some satisfaction, however, to feel that my exasperation clears up my mind. It is Caliph who is "sold," after all. He would not have invented this alliance for his brother if he had known— if he had faintly suspected—that Eunice was in love with him, inasmuch as in this case he had assured impunity. Fancy his not knowing it—the idiot!

July 10.—They are still directing cards, and Mrs Ermine has taken the whole thing on her shoulders. She has invited people that Eunice has never heard of—a pretty rabble she will have made of it! She has ordered a band of music from New York, and a new dress for the occasion—something in the last degree *champêtre*. Eunice is perfectly indifferent to what she does; I have discovered that she is thinking only of one thing. Mr Caliph is coming, and the bliss of that idea fills her mind. The more people the better; she will not have the air of making petty economies to afflict him with the sight of what he has reduced her to!

"This is the way Eunice ought to live," Mrs Ermine said to me this afternoon, rubbing her hands, after the last invitation had departed. When I say the last, I mean the last till she had remembered another that was highly important, and had floated back into the library to scribble it off. She writes a regular invitation-hand—a vague, sloping, silly hand, that looks as if it had done nothing all its days but write, "Mr and Mrs Ermine request the pleasure;" or, "Mr and Mrs Ermine are delighted to accept." She told me that she knew Eunice far better than Eunice knew herself, and that her line in life was evidently to "receive." No one better than she would stand in a doorway and put out her hand with a smile; no one would be a more gracious and affable hostess, or make a more generous use of an ample fortune. She is really very trying, Mrs Ermine, with her ample fortune; she is like a clock striking impossible hours. I think she must have engaged a special train for her guests—a train to pick up people up and down the river. Adrian Frank went to town to-day; he comes back on the 23d, and the festival takes place the next day. The festival,—Heaven help us! Eunice is evidently going to be ill; it's as much as I can do to keep from adding that it serves her right! It's a great relief to me that Mr Frank has gone; this has ceased to be a place for him. It is ever so long since he has said anything to me about his "prospects." They are charming, his prospects!

July 26.—The garden-party has taken place, and a great deal more besides. I have been too agitated, too fatigued and bewildered, to write anything here; but I can't sleep to-night —I'm too nervous—and it is better to sit and scribble than to toss about. I may as well say at once that the party was very pretty—Mrs Ermine may have that credit. The day was lovely; the lawn was in capital order; the music was good, and the *buffet* apparently inexhaustible. There was an immense number of people; some of them had come even from Albany —many of them strangers to Eunice, and protegés only of Mrs Ermine; but they dispersed themselves on the grounds, and I have not heard as yet that they stole the spoons or plucked up the plants. Mrs Ermine, who was exceedingly *champêtre*—white muslin and corn-flowers—told me that Eunice was "receiving adorably," was in her native element. She evidently inspired great curiosity; that was why every one had come. I don't mean because every one suspects her situation, but because as yet, since her return, she has been little seen and known, and is supposed to be a distinguished figure —clever, beautiful, rich, and a *parti*. I think she satisfied every one; she was voted most interesting, and except that she was deadly pale, she was prettier than any one else. Adrian Frank did not come back on the 23d, and did not arrive for the festival. So much I note without as yet understanding it. His absence from the garden-party, after all his exertions under the orders of Mrs Ermine, is in need of an explanation. Mr Caliph could give none, for Mr Caliph was there. He professed surprise at not finding his brother; said he had not seen him in town, that he had no idea what had become of him. This is probably perfectly false. I am bound to believe that everything he says and does is false; and I have no doubt that they met in New York, and that Adrian told him his reason—whatever it was—for not coming back. I don't know how to relate what took place between Mr Caliph and me; we had an extraordinary scene—a scene that gave my nerves the shaking from which they have not recovered. He is truly a most amazing personage. He is altogether beyond me; I don't pretend to fathom him. To say that he has no moral sense is nothing. I have seen other people who have had no moral sense; but I have seen no one with that impudence, that cynicism, that remorseless cruelty. We had a tremendous encounter; I thank heaven that strength was given me! When I found myself face to face with him, and it came over me that, blooming there in his diabolical assurance, it was he—he with his smiles, his bows, his gorgeous *bontonnière*, the wonderful air he has of being anointed and gilded—he that had ruined my poor Eunice, who grew whiter than ever as he approached: when I felt all this my blood began to tingle, and if I were only a handsome woman I might believe that my eyes shone like those of an avenging angel. He was as fresh as a day in June, enormous, and more than ever like Haroun-al-Raschid. I asked him to take a walk with me; and just for an instant, before accepting, he looked at me, as the French say, in the white of the eyes. But he pretended to be delighted, and we strolled away together to the path that leads down to the river. It was difficult to get away from the people—they were all over the place; but I made him go so far that at the end of ten minutes we were virtually alone together. It was delicious to see how he hated it. It was then that I asked him what had become of his step-brother, and that he professed, as I have said, the utmost ignorance of Adrian's whereabouts. I hated him; it was odious to me to be so close to him; yet I could have endured this for hours in order to make him feel that I despised him. To make him feel it without saying it—there was an inspiration in that idea; but it is very possible that it made me look more like a demon than like the angel I just mentioned. I told him in a moment, abruptly, that his step-brother would do well to remain away altogether in future; it was a farce his pretending to make my cousin reconsider her answer.

"Why, then, did she ask him to come down here?" He launched this inquiry with confidence.

"Because she thought it would be pleasant to have a man in the house; and Mr Frank is such a harmless, discreet, accommodating one."

"Why, then, do you object to his coming back?"

He had made me contradict myself a little, and of course he enjoyed that. I was confused—confused by my agitation; and I made the matter worse. I was furious that Eunice had made me promise not to speak, and my anger blinded me, as great anger always does, save in organisations so fine as Mr Caliph's.

"Because Eunice is in no condition to have company. She is very ill; you can see for yourself."

"Very ill? with a garden-party and a band of music! Why, then, did she invite us all?"

"Because she is a little crazy, I think."

"You are very consistent!" he cried, with a laugh. "I know people who think every one crazy but themselves. I have had occasion to talk business with her several times of late, and I find her mind as clear as a bell."

"I wonder if you will allow me to say that you talk business too much? Let me give you a word of advice: wind up her affairs at once without any more procrastination, and place them in her own hands. She is very nervous; she knows this ought to have been done already. I recommend you strongly to make an end of the matter."

I had no idea I could be so insolent, even in conversation

with a swindler. I confess I didn't do it so well as I might, for my voice trembled perceptibly in the midst of my efforts to be calm. He had picked up two or three stones and was tossing them into the river, making them skim the surface for a long distance. He held one poised a moment, turning his eye askance on me; then he let it fly, and it danced for a hundred yards. I wondered whether in what I had just said I broke my vow to Eunice; and it seemed to me that I didn't, inasmuch as I appeared to assume that no irreparable wrong had been done her.

"Do you wish yourself to get control of her property?" Mr Caliph inquired, after he had made his stone skim. It was magnificently said, far better than anything I could do; and I think I answered it—though it made my heart beat fast— almost with a smile of applause.

"Aren't you afraid?" I asked in a moment, very gently.

"Afraid of what—of you?"

"Afraid of justice—of Eunice's friends?"

"That means you, of course. Yes, I am very much afraid. When was a man not, in the presence of a clever woman?"

"I am clever; but I am not clever enough. If I were, you should have no doubt of it."

He folded his arms as he stood there before me, looking at me in that way I have mentioned more than once—like a genial Mephistopheles. "I must repeat what I have already told you, that I wish I had known you ten years ago!"

"How you must hate me to say that!" I exclaimed. "That's some comfort, just a little—your hating me."

"I can't tell you how it makes me feel to see you so indiscreet," he went on, as if he had not heard me. "Ah, my dear lady, don't meddle—a woman like you! Think of the bad taste of it."

"It's bad if you like; but yours is far worse."

"Mine! What do you know about mine? What do you know about me? See how superficial it makes you." He paused a moment, smiling almost compassionately; and then he said, with an abrupt change of tone and manner, as if our conversation wearied him and he wished to sum up and return to the house, "See that she marries Adrian; that's all you have to do!"

"That's a beautiful idea of yours! You know you don't believe in it yourself!" These words broke from me as he turned away, and we ascended the hill together.

"It's the only thing I believe in," he answered, very gravely.

"What a pity for you that your brother doesn't! For he doesn't—I persist in that!" I said this because it seemed to me just then to be the thing I could think of that would exasperate him most. The event proved I was right.

He stopped short in the path—gave me a very bad look. "Do you want him for yourself? Have *you* been making love to him?"

"Ah, Mr Caliph, for a man who talks about taste!" I answered.

"Taste be damned!" cried Mr Caliph, as we went on again.

"That's quite my idea!" He broke into an unexpected laugh, as if I had said something very amusing, and we proceeded in silence to the top of the hill. Then I suddenly said to him, as we emerged upon the lawn, "Aren't you really a little afraid?"

He stopped again, looking toward the house and at the brilliant groups with which the lawn was covered. We had lost the music, but we began to hear it again. "Afraid? of course I am! I'm immensely afraid. It comes over me in such a scene as this. But I don't see what good it does you to know."

"It makes me rather happy." That was a fib; for it didn't, somehow, when he looked and talked in that way. He has an absolutely bottomless power of mockery; and really, absurd as it appears, for that instant I had a feeling that it was quite magnanimous of him not to let me know what he thought of my idiotic attempt to frighten him. He feels strong and safe somehow, somewhere; but I can't discover why he should, inasmuch as he certainly doesn't know Eunice's secret, and it is only her state of mind that gives him impunity. He believes her to be merely credulous; convinced by his specious arguments that everything will be right in a few months; a little nervous, possibly—to justify my account of her—but for the present, at least, completely at his mercy. The present, of course, is only what now concerns him; for the future he has invented Adrian Frank. How he clings to this invention was proved by the last words he said to me before we separated on the lawn; they almost indicate that he has a conscience, and this is so extraordinary—

"She must marry Adrian! She must marry Adrian!"

With this he turned away and went to talk to various people whom he knew. He talked to every one; diffused his genial influence all over the place, and contributed greatly to the brilliancy of the occasion. I hadn't therefore the comfort of feeling that Mrs Ermine was more of a waterspout than usual, when she said to me afterwards that Mr Caliph was a man to adore, and that the party would have been quite "ordinary" without him. "I mean in comparison, you know." And then she said to me suddenly, with her blank impertinence: "Why don't you set your cap at him? I should think you would!"

"Is it possible you have not observed my frantic efforts to captivate him?" I answered. "Didn't you notice how I drew him away and made him walk with me by the river? It's too soon to say, but I really think I am gaining ground." For so mild a pleasure it really pays to mystify Mrs Ermine! I kept away from Eunice till almost every one had gone. I knew that she would look at me in a certain way, and I didn't wish to meet her eyes. I have a bad conscience, for turn it as I would I *had* broken my vow. Mr Caliph went away without my meeting him again; but I saw that half an hour before he left he strolled to a distance with Eunice. I instantly guessed what his business was; he had made up his mind to present to her directly, and in person, the question of her marrying his step-brother. What a happy inspiration, and what a well-selected occasion! When she came back I saw that she had been crying, though I imagine no one else did. I know the signs of her tears, even when she has checked them as quickly as she must have done to-day. Whatever it was that had passed between them, it diverted her from looking at me, when we were alone together, in that way I was afraid of. Mrs Ermine is prolific; there is no end to the images that succeed each other in her mind. Late in the evening, after the last carriage had rolled away, we went up the staircase together, and at the top she detained me a moment.

"I have been thinking it over, and I am afraid that there is no chance for you. I have reason to believe that he proposed to-day to Eunice!"

August 19.—Eunice is very ill, as I was sure she would be, after the effort of her horrible festival. She kept going for three days more; then she broke down completely, and for a week now she has been in bed. I have had no time to write, for I have been constantly with her, in alternation with Mrs Ermine. Mrs Ermine was about to leave us after the garden-party, but when Eunice gave up she announced that she would stay and take care of her. Eunice tells me that she is a good nurse, except that she talks too much, and of course she gives me a chance to rest. Eunice's condition is strange; she has no fever, but her life seems to have ebbed away. She lies with her eyes shut, perfectly conscious, answering when she is spoken to, but immersed in absolute rest. It is as if she had had some terrible strain or fatigue, and wished to steep herself in obli-vion. I am not anxious about her—am much less frightened than Mrs Ermine or the doctor, for whom she is apparently dying of weakness. I tell the doctor I understand her condi-tion—I have seen her so before. It will last probably a month, and then she will slowly pull herself together. The poor man accepts this theory for want of a better, and evidently depends upon me to see her through, as he says. Mrs Ermine wishes to send for one of the great men from New York, but I have opposed this idea, and shall continue to oppose it. There is (to my mind) a kind of cruelty in exhibiting the poor girl to more people than are absolutely necessary. The dullest of them would see that she is in love. The seat of her illness is in her mind, in her soul, and no rude hands must touch her there. She herself has protested—she has murmured a prayer that she may be forced to see no one else. "I only want to be left alone—to be left alone." So we leave her alone—that is, we simply watch and wait. She will recover—people don't die of these things; she will live to suffer—to suffer always. I am tired to-night, but Mrs Ermine is with her, and I shall not be wanted till morning; therefore, before I lie down, I will repair in these remarkable pages a serious omission. I scarcely know why I should have written all this, except that the history of things interests me, and I find that it is even a greater pleasure to write it than to read it. If what I have committed to this little book hitherto has not been profitless, I must make a note of an incident which I think more curious than any of the scenes I have described.

Adrian Frank reappeared the day after the garden-party— late in the afternoon, while I sat in the verandah and watched the sunset and Eunice strolled down to the river with Mrs Ermine. I had heard no sound of wheels, and there was no evidence of a vehicle or of luggage. He had not come through the house, but walked round it from the front, having apparently been told by one of the servants that we were in the grounds. On seeing me he stopped, hesitated a moment, then came up to the steps, shook hands in silence, seated himself near me and looked at me through the dusk. This was all tolerably mysterious, and it was even more so after he had explained a little. I told him that he was a day after the fair, that he had been considerably missed, and even that he was slightly wanting in respect to Eunice. Since he had absented himself from her party it was not quite delicate to assume that she was ready to receive him at his own time. I don't know what made me so truculent—as if there were any danger of his having really not considered us, or his lacking a good reason. It was simply, I think, that my talk with Mr Caliph the evening before had made me so much bad blood and left me in a savage mood. Mr Frank answered that he had not stayed away by accident—he had stayed away on purpose; he had been for several days at Saratoga, and on returning to Cornerville had taken quarters at the inn in the village. He had no intention of presuming further on Eunice's hospitality, and had walked over from the hotel simply to bid us good-evening and give an account of himself.

"My dear Mr Frank, your account is not clear!" I said, laughing. "What in the world were you doing at Saratoga?" I must add that his humility had completely disarmed me; I was ashamed of the brutality with which I had received him, and convinced afresh that he was the best fellow in the world.

"What was I doing at Saratoga? I was trying hard to forget you!"

This was Mr Frank's rejoinder; and I give it exactly as he uttered it; or rather, not exactly, inasmuch as I cannot give the tone—the quick, startling tremor of his voice. But those are the words with which he answered my superficially-intended question. I saw in a moment that he meant a great deal by them—I became aware that we were suddenly in deep waters; that *he* was, at least, and that he was trying to draw me into the stream. My surprise was immense, complete; I had absolutely not suspected what he went on to say to me. He said many things—but I needn't write them here. It is not in detail that I see the propriety of narrating this incident; I suppose a woman may be trusted to remember the form of such assurances. Let me simply say that the poor dear young

man has an idea that he wants to marry me. For a moment,—
just a moment—I thought he was jesting; then I saw, in the
twilight, that he was pale with seriousness. He is perfectly
sincere. It is strange, but it is real, and, moreover, it is his own
affair. For myself, when I have said I was amazed, I have said
everything; *en tête-à-tête* with myself I needn't blush and
protest. I was not in the least annoyed or alarmed; I was filled
with kindness and consideration, and I was extremely interested. He talked to me for a quarter of an hour; it seemed a
very long time. I asked him to go away; not to wait till Eunice
and Mrs Ermine should come back. Of course I refused him,
by the way.

It was the last thing I was expecting at this time of day, and
it gave me a great deal to think of. I lay awake that night;
I found I was more agitated than I supposed, and all sorts of
visions came and went in my head. I shall not marry the
young Adrian: I am bound to say that vision was not one of
them; but as I thought over what he had said to me it became
more clear, more conceivable. I began now to be a little surprised at my surprise. It appears that I have had the honour
to please him from the first; when he began to come to see us
it was not for Eunice, it was for me. He made a general confession on this subject. He was afraid of me; he thought me
proud, sarcastic, cold, a hundred horrid things; it didn't seem
to him possible that we should ever be on a footing of familiarity which would enable him to propose to me. He regarded me,
in short, as unattainable, out of the question, and made up
his mind to admire me for ever in silence. (In plain English, I
suppose he thought I was too old, and he has simply got used
to the difference in our years.) But he wished to be near me,
to see me, and hear me (I am really writing more details than
seem worth while); so that when his step-brother recommended
him to try and marry Eunice he jumped at the opportunity to
make good his place. This situation reconciled everything. He
could oblige his brother, he could pay a high compliment

to my cousin, and he could see me every day or two. He was convinced from the first that he was in no danger; he was morally sure that Eunice would never smile upon his suit. He didn't know why, and he doesn't know why yet; it was only an instinct. That suit was avowedly perfunctory; still the young Adrian has been a great comedian. He assured me that if he had proved to be wrong, and Eunice had suddenly accepted him, he would have gone with her to the altar and made her an excellent husband; for he would have acquired in this manner the certainty of seeing for the rest of his life a great deal of me! To think of one's possessing, all unexpected, this miraculous influence! When he came down here, after Eunice had refused him, it was simply for the pleasure of living in the house with me; from that moment there was no comedy —everything was clear and comfortable betwixt him and Eunice. I asked him if he meant by this that she knew of the sentiments he entertained for her companion, and he answered that he had never breathed a word on this subject, and flattered himself that he had kept the thing dark. He had no reason to believe that she guessed his motives, and I may add that I have none either; they are altogether too extraordinary! As I have said, it was simply time, and the privilege of seeing more of me, that had dispelled his hesitation. I didn't reason with him; and though, once I was fairly enlightened, I gave him the most respectful attention, I didn't appear to consider his request too seriously. But I *did* touch upon the fact that I am five or six years older than he: I suppose I needn't mention that it was not in a spirit of coquetry. His rejoinder was very gallant; but it belongs to the class of details. He is really in love—heaven forgive him! but I shall not marry him. How strange are the passions of men!

I saw Mr Frank the next day; I had given him leave to come back at noon. He joined me in the grounds, where as usual I had set up my easel. I left it to his discretion to call first at the house and explain both his absence and his presence to Eunice and Mrs Ermine—the latter especially—ignorant as yet of his visit the night before, of which I had not spoken to them. He sat down beside me on a garden-chair and watched me as I went on with my work. For half an hour very few words passed between us; I felt that he was happy to sit there, to be near me, to see me—strange as it seems! and for myself there was a certain sweetness in knowing it, though it was the sweetness of charity, not of elation or triumph. He must have seen I was only pretending to paint—if he followed my brush, which I suppose he didn't. My mind was full of a determination I had arrived at after many waverings in the hours of the night. It had come to me toward morning as a kind of inspiration. I could never marry him, but was there not some way in which I could utilise his devotion? At the present moment, only forty-eight hours later, it seems strange, unreal, almost grotesque; but for ten minutes I thought I saw the light. As we sat there under the great trees, in the stillness of the noon, I suddenly turned and said to him—

"I thank you for everything you have told me; it gives me very nearly all the pleasure you could wish. I believe in you; I accept every assurance of your devotion. I think that devotion is capable of going very far; and I am going to put it to a tremendous test, one of the greatest, probably, to which a man was ever subjected."

He stared, leaning forward, with his hands on his knees. "Any test—any test——" he murmured.

"Don't give up Eunice, then; make another trial; I wish her to marry you!"

My words may have sounded like an atrocious joke, but they represented for me a great deal of hope and cheer. They brought a deep blush into Adrian Frank's face; he winced a little, as if he had been struck by a hand whose blow he could not return, and the tears suddenly started to his eyes. "Oh, Miss Condit!" he exclaimed.

What I saw before me was bright and definite; his distress

seemed to me no obstacle, and I went on with a serenity of which I longed to make him perceive the underlying support. "Of course what I say seems to you like a deliberate insult; but nothing would induce me to give you pain if it were possible to spare you. But it isn't possible, my dear friend; it isn't possible. There is pain for you in the best thing I can say to you; there are situations in life in which we can only accept our pain. I can never marry you; I shall never marry any one. I am an old maid, and how can an old maid have a husband? I will be your friend, your sister, your brother, your mother, but I will never be your wife. I should like immensely to be your brother, for I don't like the brother you have got, and I think you deserve a better one. I believe, as I tell you, in everything you have said to me—in your affection, your tenderness, your honesty, the full consideration you have given to the whole matter. I am happier and richer for knowing it all; and I can assure you that it gives something to life which life didn't have before. We shall be good friends, dear friends, always, whatever happens. But I can't be your wife— I want you for some one else. You will say I have changed— that I ought to have spoken in this way three months ago. But I haven't changed—it is circumstances that have changed. I see reasons for your marrying my cousin that I didn't see then. I can't say that she will listen to you now, any more than she did then; I don't speak of her; I speak only of you and of myself. I wish you to make another attempt; and I wish you to make it, this time, with my full confidence and support. Moreover, I attach a condition to it—a condition I will tell you presently. Do you think me slightly demented, malignantly perverse, atrociously cruel? If you could see the bottom of my heart you would find something there which, I think, would almost give you joy. To ask you to do something you don't want to do as a substitute for something you desire, and to attach to the hard achievement a condition which will require a good deal of thinking of and will certainly make it harder—you may well believe I have some extraordinary reason for taking such a line as this. For remember, to begin with, that I can never marry you."

"Never—never—never?"

"Never, never, never."

"And what is your extraordinary reason?"

"Simply that I wish Eunice to have your protection, your kindness, your fortune."

"My fortune?"

"She has lost her own. She will be poor."

"Pray, how has she lost it?" the poor fellow asked, beginning to frown, and more and more bewildered.

"I can't tell you that, and you must never ask. But the fact is certain. The greater part of her property has gone; she has known it for some little time."

"For some little time? Why, she never showed any change."

"You never saw it, that was all! You were thinking of me," and I believe I accompanied this remark with a smile—a smile which was most inconsiderate, for it could only mystify him more.

I think at first he scarcely believed me. "What a singular time to choose to give a large party!" he exclaimed, looking at me with eyes quite unlike his old—or rather his young—ones; eyes that, instead of overlooking half the things before them (which was their former habit), tried to see a great deal more in my face, in my words, than was visible on the surface. I don't know what poor Adrian Frank saw—I shall never know all that he saw.

"I agree with you that it was a very singular time," I said. "You don't understand me—you can't—I don't expect you to;" I went on. "That is what I mean by devotion, and that is the kind of appeal I make to you: to take me on trust, to act in the dark, to do something simply because I wish it."

He looked at me as if he would fathom the depths of my

soul, and my soul had never seemed to myself so deep. "To marry your cousin—that's all?" he said, with a strange little laugh.

"Oh no, it's not all: to be very kind to her as well."

"To give her plenty of money, above all?"

"You make me feel very ridiculous; but I should not make this request of you if you had not a fortune."

"She can have my money without marrying me."

"That's absurd. How could she take your money?"

"How, then, can she take me?"

"That's exactly what I wish to see. I told you with my own lips, weeks ago, that she would only marry a man she should love; and I may seem to contradict myself in taking up now a supposition so different. But, as I tell you, everything has changed."

"You think her capable, in other words, of marrying for money."

"For money? Is your money all there is of you? Is there a better fellow than you—is there a more perfect gentleman?"

He turned away his face at this, leaned it in his hands and groaned. I pitied him, but I wonder now that I shouldn't have pitied him more; that my pity should not have checked me. But I was too full of my idea. "It's like a fate," he murmured; "first my brother, and then you. I can't understand."

"Yes, I know your brother wants it—wants it now more than ever. But I don't care what your brother wants; and my idea is entirely independent of his. I have not the least conviction that you will succeed at first any better than you have done already. But it may be only a question of time, if you will wait and watch, and let me help you. You know you asked me to help you before, and then I wouldn't. But I repeat it again and again, at present everything is changed. Let me wait with you, let me watch with you. If you succeed, you will be very dear to me; if you fail, you will be still more so. You see it's an act of devotion, if there ever was one. I am quite aware that I ask of you something unprecedented and extraordinary. Oh, it may easily be too much for you. I can only put it before you—that's all; and as I say, I can help you. You will both be my children—I shall be near you always. If you can't marry me, perhaps you will make up your mind that this is the next best thing. You know you said that last night, yourself."

He had begun to listen to me a little, as if he were being persuaded. "Of course, I should let her know that I love you."

"She is capable of saying that you can't love me more than she does."

"I don't believe she is capable of saying any such folly. But we shall see."

"Yes; but not to-day, not to-morrow. Not at all for the present. You must wait a great many months."

"I will wait as long as you please."

"And you mustn't say a word to me of the kind you said last night."

"Is that your condition?"

"Oh no; my condition is a very different matter, and very difficult. It will probably spoil everything."

"Please, then, let me hear it at once."

"It is very hard for me to mention it; you must give me time." I turned back to my little easel and began to daub again; but I think my hand trembled, for my heart was beating fast. There was a silence of many moments; I couldn't make up my mind to speak.

"How in the world has she lost her money?" Mr Frank asked, abruptly, as if the question had just come into his mind. "Hasn't my brother the charge of her affairs?"

"Mr Caliph is her trustee. I can't tell you how the losses have occurred."

He got up quickly. "Do you mean that they have occurred through *him*?"

I looked up at him, and there was something in his face

which made me leave my work and rise also. "I will tell you my condition now," I said. "It is that you should ask no questions—not one!" This was not what I had had in my mind; but I had not courage for more, and this had to serve.

He had turned very pale, and I laid my hand on his arm, while he looked at me as if he wished to wrest my secret out of my eyes. My secret, I call it, by courtesy; God knows I had come terribly near telling it. God will forgive me, but Eunice probably will not. Had I broken my vow, or had I kept it? I asked myself this, and the answer, so far as I read it in Mr Frank's eyes, was not reassuring. I dreaded his next question; but when it came it was not what I had expected. Something violent took place in his own mind—something I couldn't follow.

"If I do what you ask me, what will be my reward?"

"You will make me very happy."

"And what shall I make your cousin?—God help us!"

"Less wretched than she is to-day."

"Is she 'wretched'?" he asked, frowning as he did before —a most distressing change in his mild mask.

"Ah, when I think that I have to tell you that—that you have never noticed it—I despair!" I exclaimed, with a laugh.

I had laid my hand on his arm, and he placed his right hand upon it, holding it there. He kept it a moment in his grasp, and then he said, "Don't despair!"

"Promise me to wait," I answered. "Everything is in your waiting."

"I promise you!" After which he asked me to kiss him, and I did so, on the lips. It was as if he were starting on a journey —leaving me for a long time.

"Will you come when I send for you?" I asked.

"I adore you!" he said; and he turned quickly away, to leave the place without going near the house. I watched him, and in a moment he was gone. He has not reappeared; and when I found, at lunch, that neither Eunice nor Mrs Ermine alluded to his visit, I determined to keep the matter to myself. I said nothing about it, and up to the moment Eunice was taken ill—the next evening—he was not mentioned between us. I believe Mrs Ermine more than once gave herself up to wonder as to his whereabouts, and declared that he had not the perfect manners of his step-brother, who was a religious observer of the *convenances;* but I think I managed to listen without confusion. Nevertheless, I had a bad conscience, and I have it still. It throbs a good deal as I sit there with Eunice in her darkened room. I *have* given her away; I *have* broken my vow. But what I wrote above is not true; she *will* forgive me! I sat at my easel for an hour after Mr Frank left me, and then suddenly I found that I had cured myself of my folly by giving it out. It was the result of a sudden passion of desire to do something for Eunice. Passion is blind, and when I opened my eyes I saw ten thousand difficulties; that is, I saw one, which contained all the rest. That evening I wrote to Mr Frank, to his New York address, to tell him that I had had a fit of madness, and that it had passed away; but that I was sorry to say it was not any more possible for me to marry him. I have had no answer to this letter; but what answer can he make to that last declaration? He will continue to adore me. How strange are the passions of men!

New York, November 20.—I have been silent for three months, for good reasons. Eunice was ill for many weeks, but there was never a moment when I was really alarmed about her; I knew she would recover. In the last days of October she was strong enough to be brought up to town, where she had business to transact, and now she is almost herself again. I say almost, advisedly; for she will never be herself,—her old, sweet, trustful self, so far as I am concerned. She has simply not forgiven me! Strange things have happened—things that I don't dare to consider too closely, lest I should not forgive myself. Eunice is in complete possession of her property! Mr Caliph has made over to her everything—

everything that had passed away; everything of which, three months ago, he could give no account whatever. He was with her in the country for a long day before we came up to town (during which I took care not to meet her), and after our return he was in and out of this house repeatedly. I once asked Eunice what he had to say to her, and she answered that he was "explaining." A day or two later she told me that he had given a complete account of her affairs; everything was in order; she had been wrong in what she told me before. Beyond this little statement, however, she did no further penance for the impression she had given of Mr Caliph's earlier conduct. She doesn't yet know what to think; she only feels that if she has recovered her property there has been some interference; and she traces, or at least imputes, such interference to me. If I have interfered, I have broken my vow; and for this, as I say, the gentle creature can't forgive me. If the passions of men are strange, the passions of women are stranger still! It was sweeter for her to suffer at Mr Caliph's hands than to receive her simple dues from them. She looks at me askance, and her coldness shows through a conscientious effort not to let me see the change in her feeling. Then she is puzzled and mystified; she can't tell what has happened, or how and why it has happened. She has waked up from her illness into a different world—a world in which Mr Caliph's accounts were correct after all; in which, with the washing away of his stains, the colour has been quite washed out of his rich physiognomy. She vaguely feels that a sacrifice, a great effort of some kind, has been made for her, whereas her plan of life was to make the sacrifices and efforts herself. Yet she asks me no questions; the property is her right, after all, and I think there are certain things she is afraid to know. But I am more afraid than she, for it comes over me that a great sacrifice has indeed been made. I have not seen Adrian Frank since he parted from me under the trees three months ago. He has gone to Europe, and the day before he left I got a note from him. It contained only these words: "When you send for me I will come. I am waiting, as you told me." It is my belief that up to the moment I spoke of Eunice's loss of money and requested him to ask no questions, he had not definitely suspected his noble kinsman, but that my words kindled a train that lay all ready. He went away then to his shame, to the intolerable weight of it, and to heaven knows what sickening explanations with his step-brother! That gentleman has a still more brilliant bloom; he looks to my mind exactly as people look who have accepted a sacrifice; and he hasn't had another word to say about Eunice's marrying Mr Adrian Frank. Mrs Ermine sticks to her idea that Mr Caliph and Eunice will make a match; but my belief is that Eunice is cured. Oh yes, she is cured! But I have done more than I meant to do, and I have not done it as I meant to do it; and I am very weary, and I shall write no more.

November 27.—Oh yes, Eunice is cured! And that is what she has not forgiven me. Mr Caliph told her yesterday that Mr Frank meant to spend the winter in Rome.

December 3.—I have decided to return to Europe, and have written about my apartment in Rome. I shall leave New York, if possible, on the 10th. Eunice tells me she can easily believe I shall be happier there.

December 7.—I *must* note something I had the satisfaction to-day to say to Mr Caliph. He has not been here for three weeks, but this afternoon he came to call. He is no longer the trustee; he is only the visitor. I was alone in the library, into which he was ushered; and it was ten minutes before Eunice appeared. We had some talk, though my disgust for him is now unspeakable. At first it was of a very perfunctory kind; but suddenly he said, with more than his old impudence, "That was a most extraordinary interview of ours, at Cornerville!" I was surprised at his saying only this, for I expected him to take his revenge on me by some means or other for having put his brother on the scent of his misdeeds. I can only account for his silence on that subject by the supposition that Mr Frank has been able to extract from him some pledge that I shall not be molested. He was, however, such an image of unrighteous success that the sight of him filled me with gall, and I tried to think of something which would make him smart.

"I don't know what you have done, nor how you have done it," I said; "but you took a very roundabout way to arrive at certain ends. There was a time when you might have married Eunice."

It was of course nothing new that we were frank with each other, and he only repeated, smiling, "Married Eunice?"

"She was very much in love with you last spring."

"Very much in love with me?"

"Oh, it's over now. Can't you imagine that? She's cured."

He broke into a laugh, but I felt I had startled him.

"You are the most delightful woman!" he cried.

"Think how much simpler it would have been—I mean originally, when things were right, if they ever were right. Don't you see my point? But now it's too late. She has seen you when you were not on show. I assure you she is cured!"

At this moment Eunice came in, and just afterwards I left the room. I am sure it was a revelation, and that I have given him a *mauvais quart d'heure*.

Rome, February 23.—When I came back to this dear place Adrian Frank was not here, and I learned that he had gone to Sicily. A week ago I wrote to him: "You said you would come if I should send for you. I should be glad if you would come now." Last evening he appeared, and I told him that I could no longer endure my suspense in regard to a certain subject. Would he kindly inform me what he had done in New York after he left me under the trees at Cornerville? Of what sacrifice had he been guilty; to what high generosity—terrible to me to think of—had he committed himself? He would tell me very little; but he is almost a poor man. He has just enough income to live in Italy.

May 9.—Mrs Ermine has taken it into her head to write to me. I have heard from her three times; and in her last letter, received yesterday, she returns to her old refrain that Eunice and Mr Caliph will soon be united. I don't know what may be going on; but can it be possible that I put it into his head? Truly, I have a felicitous touch!

May 15.—I told Adrian yesterday that I would marry him if ever Eunice should marry Mr Caliph. It was the first time I had mentioned his step-brother's name to him since the explanation I had attempted to have with him after he came back to Rome; and he evidently didn't like it at all.

In the Tyrol, August.—I sent Mrs Ermine a little water-colour in return for her last letter, for I can't write to her, and that is easier. She now writes me again, in order to get another water-colour. She speaks of course of Eunice and Mr Caliph, and for the first time there appears a certain reality in what she says. She complains that Eunice is very slow in coming to the point, and relates that poor Mr Caliph, who has taken her into his confidence, seems at times almost to despair. Nothing would suit him better of course than to appropriate two fortunes: two are so much better than one. But however much he may have explained, he can hardly have explained everything. Adrian Frank is in Scotland; in writing to him three days ago I had occasion to repeat that I will marry him on the day on which a certain other marriage takes place. In that way I am safe. I shall send another water-colour to Mrs Ermine. Water-colours or no, Eunice doesn't write to me. It is clear that she hasn't forgiven me! She regards me as perjured; and of course I am. Perhaps she will marry him after all.

LADY BARBERINA

I

It is well known that there are few sights in the world more brilliant than the main avenues of Hyde Park of a fine afternoon in June. This was quite the opinion of two persons who, on a beautiful day at the beginning of that month, four years ago, had established themselves under the great trees in a couple of iron chairs (the big ones with arms, for which, if I mistake not, you pay twopence), and sat there with the slow procession of the Drive behind them, while their faces were turned to the more vivid agitation of the Row. They were lost in the multitude of observers, and they belonged, superficially, at least, to that class of persons who, wherever they may be, rank rather with the spectators than with the spectacle. They were quiet, simple, elderly, of aspect somewhat neutral; you would have liked them extremely, but you would scarcely have noticed them. Nevertheless, in all that shining host, it is to them, obscure, that we must give our attention. The reader is begged to have confidence; he is not asked to make vain concessions. There was that in the faces of our friends which indicated that they were growing old together, and that they were fond enough of each other's company not to object (if it was a condition) even to that. The reader will have guessed that they were husband and wife; and perhaps while he is about it he will have guessed that they were of that nationality for which Hyde Park at the height of the season is most completely illustrative. They were familiar strangers, as it were; and people at once so initiated and so detached could only be Americans. This reflection, indeed, you would have made only after some delay; for it must be admitted that they carried few patriotic signs on the surface. They had the American turn of mind, but that was very subtle; and to your eye—if your eye had cared about it—they might have been of English, or even of Continental, parentage. It was as if it suited them to be colourless; their colour was all in their talk. They were not in the least verdant; they were gray, rather, of monotonous hue. If they were interested in the riders, the horses, the walkers, the great exhibition of English wealth and health, beauty, luxury and leisure, it was because all this referred itself to other impressions, because they had the key to almost everything that needed an answer—because, in a word, they were able to compare. They had not arrived, they had only returned; and recognition much more than surprise was expressed in their quiet gaze. It may as well be said outright that Dexter Freer and his wife belonged to that class of Americans who are constantly "passing through" London. Possessors of a fortune of which, from any standpoint, the limits were plainly visible, they were unable to command that highest of luxuries —a habitation in their own country. They found it much more possible to economise at Dresden or Florence than at Buffalo or Minneapolis. The economy was as great, and the inspiration was greater. From Dresden, from Florence, moreover, they constantly made excursions which would not have been possible in those other cities; and it is even to be feared that they had some rather expensive methods of saving. They came to London to buy their portmanteaus, their toothbrushes, their writing-paper; they occasionally even crossed the Atlantic to assure themselves that prices over there were still the same. They were eminently a social pair; their interests were mainly personal. Their point of view always was so distinctly human that they passed for being fond of gossip; and they certainly knew a good deal about the affairs of other people. They had friends in every country, in every town; and it was not their fault if people told them their secrets. Dexter Freer was a tall, lean man, with an interested eye, and a nose that rather aspired than drooped, yet was salient withal. He brushed his hair, which was streaked with white, forward over his ears, in those locks which are represented in the portraits of clean-shaven gentlemen who flourished fifty years ago, and wore an old-fashioned neckcloth and gaiters. His wife, a small, plump person, of superficial freshness, with a white face, and hair that was still perfectly black, smiled perpetually, but had never laughed since the death of a son whom she had lost ten years after her marriage. Her husband, on the other hand, who was usually quite grave, indulged on great occasions in resounding mirth. People confided in her less than in him; but that mattered little, as she confided sufficiently in herself. Her dress, which was always black or dark gray, was so harmoniously simple that you could see she was fond of it; it was never smart by accident. She was full of intentions, of the most judicious sort; and though she was perpetually moving about the world she had the air of being perfectly stationary. She was celebrated for the promptitude with which she made her sitting-room at an inn, where she might be spending a night or two, look like an apartment long inhabited. With books, flowers, photographs, draperies, rapidly distributed—she had even a way, for the most part, of having a piano—the place seemed almost hereditary. The pair were just back from America, where they had spent three months, and now were able to face the world with something of the elation which people feel who have been justified in a prevision. They had found their native land quite ruinous.

"There he is again!" said Mr Freer, following with his eyes a young man who passed along the Row, riding slowly. "That's a beautiful thoroughbred!"

Mrs Freer asked idle questions only when she wished for time to think. At present she had simply to look and see who it was her husband meant. "The horse is too big," she remarked, in a moment.

"You mean that the rider is too small," her husband rejoined; "he is mounted on his millions."

"Is it really millions?"

"Seven or eight, they tell me."

"How disgusting!" It was in this manner that Mrs Freer usually spoke of the large fortunes of the day. "I wish he would see us," she added.

"He does see us, but he doesn't like to look at us. He is too conscious; he isn't easy."

"Too conscious of his big horse?"

"Yes, and of his big fortune; he is rather ashamed of it."

"This is an odd place to come, then," said Mrs Freer.

"I am not sure of that. He will find people here richer than himself, and other big horses in plenty, and that will cheer him up. Perhaps, too, he is looking for that girl."

"The one we heard about? He can't be such a fool."

"He isn't a fool," said Dexter Freer. "If he is thinking of her, he has some good reason."

"I wonder what Mary Lemon would say."

"She would say it was right, if he should do it. She thinks he can do no wrong. He is exceedingly fond of her."

"I shan't be sure of that if he takes home a wife who will despise her."

"Why should the girl despise her? She is a delightful woman."

"The girl will never know it—and if she should, it would make no difference; she will despise everything."

"I don't believe it, my dear; she will like some things very much. Every one will be very nice to her."

"She will despise them all the more. But we are speaking as if it were all arranged; I don't believe in it at all," said Mrs Freer.

"Well, something of the sort—in this case or in some other —is sure to happen sooner or later," her husband replied, turning round a little toward the part of the delta which is formed, near the entrance to the Park, by the divergence of the two great vistas of the Drive and the Row.

Our friends had turned their backs, as I have said, to the solemn revolution of wheels and the densely-packed mass of spectators who had chosen that part of the show. These spectators were now agitated by a unanimous impulse: the pushing back of chairs, the shuffle of feet, the rustle of garments and the deepening murmur of voices sufficiently expressed it. Royalty was approaching—royalty was passing —royalty had passed. Freer turned his head and his ear a little; but he failed to alter his position further, and his wife took no notice of the flurry. They had seen royalty pass, all over Europe, and they knew that it passed very quickly. Sometimes it came back; sometimes it didn't; for more than once they had seen it pass for the last time. They were veteran tourists, and they knew perfectly when to get up and when to remain seated. Mr Freer went on with his proposition: "Some young fellow is certain to do it, and one of these girls is certain to take the risk. They must take risks, over here, more and more."

"The girls, I have no doubt, will be glad enough; they have had very little chance as yet. But I don't want Jackson to begin."

"Do you know I rather think I do?" said Dexter Freer; "It will be very amusing."

"For us, perhaps, but not for him; he will repent of it, and be wretched. He is too good for that."

"Wretched, never! He has no capacity for wretchedness; and that's why he can afford to risk it."

"He will have to make great concessions," Mrs Freer remarked.

"He won't make one."

"I should like to see."

"You admit, then, that it will be amusing, which is all I contend for. But, as you say, we are talking as if it were settled, whereas there is probably nothing in it, after all. The best stories always turn out false. I shall be sorry in this case."

They relapsed into silence, while people passed and repassed them—continuous, successive, mechanical, with strange sequences of faces. They looked at the people, but no one looked at them, though every one was there so admittedly to see what was to be seen. It was all striking, all pictorial, and it made a great composition. The wide, long area of the Row, its red-brown surface dotted with bounding figures, stretched away into the distance and became suffused and misty in the bright, thick air. The deep, dark English verdure that bordered and overhung it, looked rich and old, revived and refreshed though it was by the breath of June. The mild blue of the sky was spotted with great silvery clouds, and the light drizzled down in heavenly shafts over the quieter spaces of the Park, as one saw them beyond the Row. All this, however, was only a background, for the scene was before everything personal; superbly so, and full of the gloss and lustre, the contrasted tones, of a thousand polished surfaces. Certain things were salient, pervasive—the shining flanks of the perfect horses, the twinkle of bits and spurs, the smoothness of fine cloth adjusted to shoulders and limbs, the sheen of hats and boots, the freshness of complexions, the expression of smiling, talking faces, the flash and flutter of rapid gallops. Faces were everywhere, and they were the great effect; above all, the fair faces of women on tall horses, flushed a little under their stiff black hats, with figures stiffened, in spite of much definition of curve, by their tight-fitting habits. Their hard little helmets; their neat, compact heads; their straight necks; their firm, tailor-made armour; their blooming, competent physique, made them look doubly like amazons about to ride a charge. The men, with their eyes before them, with hats of undulating brim, good profiles, high collars, white flowers on their chests, long legs and long feet, had an air more elaborately decorative, as they jolted beside the ladies, always out of step. These were youthful types; but it was not all youth, for many a saddle was surmounted by a richer rotundity; and ruddy faces, with short white whiskers or with matronly chins, looked down comfortably from an equilibrium which was moral and social as well as physical. The walkers differed from the riders only in being on foot, and in looking at the riders more than these looked at them; for they would have done as well in the saddle and ridden as the others ride. The women had tight little bonnets and still tighter little knots of hair; their round chins rested on a close swathing of lace, or, in some cases, of silver chains and circlets. They had flat backs and small waists; they walked slowly, with their elbows out, carrying vast parasols, and turning their heads very little to the right or the left. They were amazons unmounted, quite ready to spring into the saddle. There was a great deal of beauty and a general look of successful development, which came from clear, quiet eyes, and from well-cut lips, on which syllables were liquid and sentences brief. Some of the young men, as well as the women, had the happiest proportions and oval faces, in which line and colour were pure and fresh and the idea of the moment was not very intense.

"They are very good-looking," said Mr Freer, at the end of ten minutes; "they are the finest whites."

"So long as they remain white they do very well; but when they venture upon colour!" his wife replied. She sat with her eyes on a level with the skirts of the ladies who passed her; and she had been following the progress of a green velvet robe, enriched with ornaments of steel and much gathered up in the hands of its wearer, who, herself apparently in her teens, was accompanied by a young lady draped in scanty pink muslin, embroidered, æsthetically, with flowers that simulated the iris.

"All the same, in a crowd, they are wonderfully well turned out," Dexter Freer went on; "take the men, and women, and horses together. Look at that big fellow on the light chestnut: what could be more perfect? By the way, it's

Lord Canterville," he added in a moment, as if the fact were
of some importance.

Mrs Freer recognised its importance to the degree of raising
her glass to look at Lord Canterville. "How do you know it's
he?" she asked, with her glass still up.

"I heard him say something the night I went to the House
of Lords. It was very few words, but I remember him. A
man who was near me told me who he was."

"He is not so handsome as you," said Mrs Freer, dropping
her glass.

"Ah, you're too difficult!" her husband murmured. "What
a pity the girl isn't with him," he went on; "we might see
something."

It appeared in a moment that the girl was with him. The
nobleman designated had ridden slowly forward from the
start, but just opposite our friends he pulled up to look behind
him, as if he had been waiting for some one. At the same
moment a gentleman in the Walk engaged his attention, so
that he advanced to the barrier which protects the pedestrians,
and halted there, bending a little from his saddle and talking
with his friend, who leaned against the rail. Lord Canterville
was indeed perfect, as his American admirer had said. Upwards of sixty, and of great stature and great presence, he was
really a splendid apparition. In exquisite preservation, he had
the freshness of middle life, and would have been young to
the eye if the lapse of years were not needed to account for
his considerable girth. He was clad from head to foot in garments of a radiant gray, and his fine florid countenance was
surmounted with a white hat, of which the majestic curves
were a triumph of good form. Over his mighty chest was
spread a beard of the richest growth, and of a colour, in spite
of a few streaks, vaguely grizzled, to which the coat of his
admirable horse appeared to be a perfect match. It left no
opportunity, in his uppermost button-hole, for the customary
gardenia; but this was of comparatively little consequence,

as the vegetation of the beard itself was tropical. Astride his great steed, with his big fist, gloved in pearl-gray, on his swelling thigh, his face lighted up with good-humoured indifference, and all his magnificent surface reflecting the mild sunshine, he was a very imposing man indeed, and visibly, incontestably, a personage. People almost lingered to look at him as they passed. His halt was brief, however, for he was almost immediately joined by two handsome girls, who were as well turned out, in Dexter Freer's phrase, as himself. They had been detained a moment at the entrance to the Row, and now advanced side by side, their groom close behind them. One was taller and older than the other, and it was apparent at a glance that they were sisters. Between them, with their charming shoulders, contracted waists, and skirts that hung without a wrinkle, like a plate of zinc, they represented in a singularly complete form the pretty English girl in the position in which she is prettiest.

"Of course they are his daughters," said Dexter Freer, as they rode away with Lord Canterville; "and in that case one of them must be Jackson Lemon's sweetheart. Probably the bigger; they said it was the eldest. She is evidently a fine creature."

"She would hate it over there," Mrs Freer remarked, for all answer to this cluster of inductions.

"You know I don't admit that. But granting she should, it would do her good to have to accommodate herself."

"She wouldn't accommodate herself."

"She looks so confoundedly fortunate, perched up on that saddle," Dexter Freer pursued, without heeding his wife's rejoinder.

"Aren't they supposed to be very poor?"

"Yes, they look it!" And his eyes followed the distinguished trio, as, with the groom, as distinguished in his way as any of them, they started on a canter.

The air was full of sound, but it was low and diffused; and

when, near our friends, it became articulate, the words were simple and few.

"It's as good as the circus, isn't it, Mrs Freer?" These words correspond to that description, but they pierced the air more effectually than any our friends had lately heard. They were uttered by a young man who had stopped short in the path, absorbed by the sight of his compatriots. He was short and stout, he had a round, kind face, and short, stiff-looking hair, which was reproduced in a small bristling beard. He wore a double-breasted walking-coat, which was not, however, buttoned, and on the summit of his round head was perched a hat of exceeding smallness, and of the so-called "pot" category. It evidently fitted him, but a hatter himself would not have known why. His hands were encased in new gloves, of a dark-brown colour, and they hung with an air of un-accustomed inaction at his sides. He sported neither umbrella nor stick. He extended one of his hands, almost with eager-ness, to Mrs Freer, blushing a little as he became aware that he had been eager.

"Oh, Doctor Feeder!" she said, smiling at him. Then she repeated to her husband, "Doctor Feeder, my dear!" and her husband said, "Oh, Doctor, how d'ye do?" I have spoken of the composition of his appearance; but the items were not perceived by these two. They saw only one thing, his delightful face, which was both simple and clever, and un-reservedly good. They had lately made the voyage from New York in his company, and it was plain that he would be very genial at sea. After he had stood in front of them a moment, a chair beside Mrs Freer became vacant, on which he took pos-session of it, and sat there telling her what he thought of the Park and how he liked London. As she knew every one she had known many of his people at home; and while she listened to him she remembered how large their contribution had been to the virtue and culture of Cincinnati. Mrs Freer's social horizon included even that city; she had been on terms almost familiar with several families from Ohio, and was acquainted with the position of the Feeders there. This family, very numerous, was interwoven into an enormous cousinship. She herself was quite out of such a system, but she could have told you whom Doctor Feeder's great-grandfather had married. Every one, indeed, had heard of the good deeds of the descendants of this worthy, who were generally physicians, excellent ones, and whose name expressed not inaptly their numerous acts of charity. Sidney Feeder, who had several cousins of this name established in the same line at Cincinnati, had transferred himself and his ambition to New York, where his practice, at the end of three years, had begun to grow. He had studied his profession at Vienna, and was impregnated with German science; indeed, if he had only worn spectacles, he might perfectly, as he sat there watching the riders in Rotten Row as if their proceedings were a successful demonstration, have passed for a young German of distinction. He had come over to London to attend a medical congress which met this year in the British capital; for his interest in the healing art was by no means limited to the cure of his patients; it embraced every form of experiment, and the expression of his honest eyes would almost have reconciled you to vivisection. It was the first time he had come to the Park; for social experiments he had little leisure. Being aware, however, that it was a very typical, and as it were symptomatic, sight, he had conscientiously reserved an afternoon, and had dressed himself carefully for the occasion. "It's quite a brilliant show," he said to Mrs Freer; "it makes me wish I had a mount." Little as he resembled Lord Canterville, he rode very well.

"Wait till Jackson Lemon passes again, and you can stop him and make him let you take a turn." This was the jocular suggestion of Dexter Freer.

"Why, is he here? I have been looking out for him; I should like to see him."

"Doesn't he go to your medical congress?" asked Mrs Freer.

"Well, yes, he attends; but he isn't very regular. I guess he goes out a good deal."

"I guess he does," said Mr Freer; "and if he isn't very regular, I guess he has a good reason. A beautiful reason, a charming reason," he went on, bending forward to look down toward the beginning of the Row. "Dear me, what a lovely reason!"

Doctor Feeder followed the direction of his eyes, and after a moment understood his allusion. Little Jackson Lemon, on his big horse, passed along the avenue again, riding beside one of the young girls who had come that way shortly before in the company of Lord Canterville. His lordship followed, in conversation with the other, his younger daughter. As they advanced, Jackson Lemon turned his eyes toward the multitude under the trees, and it so happened that they rested upon the Dexter Freers. He smiled, and raised his hat with all possible friendliness; and his three companions turned to see to whom he was bowing with so much cordiality. As he settled his hat on his head he espied the young man from Cincinnati, whom he had at first overlooked; whereupon he smiled still more brightly and waved Sidney Feeder an airy salutation with his hand, reining in a little at the same time just for an instant, as if he half expected the Doctor to come and speak to him. Seeing him with strangers, however, Sidney Feeder hung back, staring a little as he rode away.

It is open to us to know that at this moment the young lady by whose side he was riding said to him, familiarly enough: "Who are those people you bowed to?"

"Some old friends of mine—Americans," Jackson Lemon answered.

"Of course they are Americans; there is nothing but Americans nowadays."

"Oh yes, our turn's coming round!" laughed the young man.

"But that doesn't say who they are," his companion continued. "It's so difficult to say who Americans are," she added, before he had time to answer her.

"Dexter Freer and his wife—there is nothing difficult about that; every one knows them."

"I never heard of them," said the English girl.

"Ah, that's your fault. I assure you everybody knows them."

"And does everybody know the little man with the fat face whom you kissed your hand to?"

"I didn't kiss my hand, but I would if I had thought of it. He is a great chum of mine,—a fellow-student at Vienna."

"And what's *his* name?"

"Doctor Feeder."

Jackson Lemon's companion was silent a moment. "Are *all* your friends doctors?" she presently inquired.

"No; some of them are in other businesses."

"Are they all in some business?"

"Most of them; save two or three, like Dexter Freer."

"Dexter Freer? I thought you said Doctor Freer."

The young man gave a laugh. "You heard me wrong. You have got doctors on the brain, Lady Barb."

"I am rather glad," said Lady Barb, giving the rein to her horse, who bounded away.

"Well, yes, she's very handsome, the reason," Doctor Feeder remarked, as he sat under the trees.

"Is he going to marry her?" Mrs Freer inquired.

"Marry her? I hope not."

"Why do you hope not?"

"Because I know nothing about her. I want to know something about the woman that man marries."

"I suppose you would like him to marry in Cincinnati," Mrs Freer rejoined lightly.

"Well, I am not particular where it is; but I want to know her first." Doctor Feeder was very sturdy.

"We were in hopes you would know all about it," said Mr Freer.

"No; I haven't kept up with him there."

"We have heard from a dozen people that he has been always with her for the last month; and that kind of thing, in England, is supposed to mean something. Hasn't he spoken of her when you have seen him?"

"No, he has only talked about the new treatment of spinal meningitis. He is very much interested in spinal meningitis."

"I wonder if he talks about it to Lady Barb," said Mrs Freer.

"Who is she, any way?" the young man inquired.

"Lady Barberina Clement."

"And who is Lady Barberina Clement?"

"The daughter of Lord Canterville."

"And who is Lord Canterville?"

"Dexter must tell you that," said Mrs Freer.

And Dexter accordingly told him that the Marquis of Canterville had been in his day a great sporting nobleman and an ornament to English society, and had held more than once a high post in her Majesty's household. Dexter Freer knew all these things—how his lordship had married a daughter of Lord Treherne, a very serious, intelligent and beautiful woman, who had redeemed him from the extravagance of his youth and presented him in rapid succession with a dozen little tenants for the nurseries at Pasterns—this being, as Mr Freer also knew, the name of the principal seat of the Cantervilles. The Marquis was a Tory, but very liberal for a Tory, and very popular in society at large; good-natured, good-looking, knowing how to be genial and yet remain a *grand seigneur*, clever enough to make an occasional speech, and much associated with the fine old English pursuits, as well as with many of the new improvements—the purification of the Turf, the opening of the museums on Sunday, the propagation of coffee-taverns, the latest ideas on sanitary reform. He disapproved of the extension of the suffrage, but he positively had drainage on the brain. It had been said of him at least once (and I think in print) that he was just the man to convey to the popular mind the impression that the British aristocracy is still a living force. He was not very rich, unfortunately (for a man who had to exemplify such truths), and of his twelve children no less than seven were daughters. Lady Barberina, Jackson Lemon's friend, was the second; the eldest had married Lord Beauchemin. Mr Freer had caught quite the right pronunciation of this name: he called it Bitumen. Lady Louisa had done very well, for her husband was rich, and she had brought him nothing to speak of; but it was hardly to be expected that the others would do so well. Happily the younger girls were still in the school-room; and before they had come up, Lady Canterville, who was a woman of resources, would have worked off the two that were out. It was Lady Agatha's first season; she was not so pretty as her sister, but she was thought to be cleverer. Half a dozen people had spoken to him of Jackson Lemon's being a great deal at the Cantervilles. He was supposed to be enormously rich.

"Well, so he is," said Sidney Feeder, who had listened to Mr Freer's little recital with attention, with eagerness even, but with an air of imperfect apprehension.

"Yes, but not so rich as they probably think."

"Do they want his money? Is that what they're after?"

"You go straight to the point," Mrs Freer murmured.

"I haven't the least idea," said her husband. "He is a very nice fellow in himself."

"Yes, but he's a doctor," Mrs Freer remarked.

"What have they got against that?" asked Sidney Feeder.

"Why, over here, you know, they only call them in to prescribe," said Dexter Freer; "the profession isn't—a— what you'd call aristocratic."

"Well, I don't know it, and I don't know that I want to

know it. How do you mean, aristocratic? What profession is? It would be rather a curious one. Many of the gentlemen at the congress there are quite charming."

"I like doctors very much," said Mrs Freer; "my father was a doctor. But they don't marry the daughters of marquises."

"I don't believe Jackson wants to marry that one."

"Very possibly not—people are such asses," said Dexter Freer. "But he will have to decide. I wish you would find out, by the way; you can if you will."

"I will ask him—up at the congress; I can do that. I suppose he has got to marry some one," Sidney Feeder added, in a moment, "and she may be a nice girl."

"She is said to be charming."

"Very well, then; it won't hurt him. I must say, however, I am not sure I like all that about her family."

"What I told you? It's all to their honour and glory."

"Are they quite on the square? It's like those people in Thackeray."

"Oh, if Thackeray could have done this!" Mrs Freer exclaimed, with a good deal of expression.

"You mean all this scene?" asked the young man.

"No; the marriage of a British noblewoman and an American doctor. It would have been a subject for Thackeray."

"You see you do want it, my dear," said Dexter Freer quietly.

"I want it as a story, but I don't want it for Doctor Lemon."

"Does he call himself 'Doctor' still?" Mr Freer asked of young Feeder.

"I suppose he does; I call him so. Of course he doesn't practise. But once a doctor, always a doctor."

"That's doctrine for Lady Barb!"

Sidney Feeder stared. "Hasn't she got a title too? What would she expect him to be? President of the United States?

He's a man of real ability; he might have stood at the head of his profession. When I think of that, I want to swear. What did his father want to go and make all that money for?"

"It must certainly be odd to them to see a 'medical man' with six or eight millions," Mr Freer observed.

"They use the same term as the Choctaws," said his wife.

"Why, some of their own physicians make immense fortunes," Sidney Feeder declared.

"Couldn't he be made a baronet by the Queen?" This suggestion came from Mrs Freer.

"Yes, then he would be aristocratic," said the young man.

·"But I don't see why he should want to marry over here; it seems to me to be going out of his way. However, if he is happy, I don't care. I like him very much; he has got lots of ability. If it hadn't been for his father he would have made a splendid doctor. But, as I say, he takes a great interest in medical science, and I guess he means to promote it all he can—with his fortune. He will always be doing something in the way of research. He thinks we *do* know something, and he is bound we shall know more. I hope she won't prevent him, the young marchioness—is that her rank? And I hope they are really good people. He ought to be very useful. I should want to know a good deal about the family I was going to marry into."

"He looked to me, as he rode there, as if he knew a good deal about the Clements," Dexter Freer said, rising, as his wife suggested that they ought to be going; "and he looked to me pleased with the knowledge. There they come, down on the other side. Will you walk away with us, or will you stay?"

"Stop him and ask him, and then come and tell us—in Jermyn Street." This was Mrs Freer's parting injunction to Sidney Feeder.

"He ought to come himself—tell him that," her husband added.

"Well, I guess I'll stay," said the young man, as his companions merged themselves in the crowd that now was tending toward the gates. He went and stood by the barrier, and saw Doctor Lemon and his friends pull up at the entrance to the Row, where they apparently prepared to separate. The separation took some time, and Sidney Feeder became interested. Lord Canterville and his younger daughter lingered to talk with two gentlemen, also mounted, who looked a good deal at the legs of Lady Agatha's horse. Jackson Lemon and Lady Barberina were face to face, very near each other; and she, leaning forward a little, stroked the overlapping neck of his glossy bay. At a distance he appeared to be talking, and she to be listening and saying nothing. "Oh yes, he's making love to her," thought Sidney Feeder. Suddenly her father turned away, to leave the Park, and she joined him and disappeared, while Doctor Lemon came up on the left again, as if for a final gallop. He had not gone far before he perceived his *confrère*, who awaited him at the rail; and he repeated the gesture which Lady Barberina had spoken of as a kissing of his hand, though it must be added that, to his friend's eyes, it had not quite that significance. When he reached the point where Feeder stood he pulled up.

"If I had known you were coming here I would have given you a mount," he said. There was not in his person that irradiation of wealth and distinction which made Lord Canterville glow like a picture; but as he sat there with his little legs stuck out, he looked very bright and sharp and happy, wearing in his degree the aspect of one of Fortune's favourites. He had a thin, keen, delicate face, a nose very carefully finished, a rapid eye, a trifle hard in expression, and a small moustache, a good deal cultivated. He was not striking, but he was very positive, and it was easy to see that he was full of purpose.

"How many horses have you got—about forty?" his compatriot inquired, in response to his greeting.

"About five hundred," said Jackson Lemon.

"Did you mount your friends—the three you were riding with?"

"Mount them? They have got the best horses in England."

"Did they sell you this one?" Sidney Feeder continued in the same humorous strain.

"What do you think of him?" said his friend, not deigning to answer this question.

"He's an awful old screw; I wonder he can carry you."

"Where did you get your hat?" asked Doctor Lemon, in return.

"I got it in New York. What's the matter with it?"

"It's very beautiful; I wish I had bought one like it."

"The head's the thing—not the hat. I don't mean yours, but mine. There is something very deep in your question; I must think it over."

"Don't—don't," said Jackson Lemon; "you will never get to the bottom of it. Are you having a good time?"

"A glorious time. Have you been up to-day?"

"Up among the doctors? No; I have had a lot of things to do."

"We had a very interesting discussion. I made a few remarks."

"You ought to have told me. What were they about?"

"About the intermarriage of races, from the point of view——" And Sidney Feeder paused a moment, occupied with the attempt to scratch the nose of his friend's horse.

"From the point of view of the progeny, I suppose?"

"Not at all; from the point of view of the old friends."

"Damn the old friends!" Doctor Lemon exclaimed, with jocular crudity.

"Is it true that you are going to marry a young marchioness?"

The face of the young man in the saddle became just a

trifle rigid, and his firm eyes fixed themselves on Doctor Feeder.

"Who has told you that?"

"Mr and Mrs Freer, whom I met just now."

"Mr and Mrs Freer be hanged! And who told them?"

"Ever so many people; I don't know who."

"Gad, how things are tattled!" cried Jackson Lemon, with some asperity.

"I can see it's true, by the way you say that."

"Do Freer and his wife believe it?" Jackson Lemon went on impatiently.

"They want you to go and see them: you can judge for yourself."

"I will go and see them, and tell them to mind their business."

"In Jermyn Street; but I forget the number. I am sorry the marchioness isn't American," Sidney Feeder continued.

"If I should marry her, she would be," said his friend. "But I don't see what difference it can make to you."

"Why, she'll look down on the profession; and I don't like that from your wife."

"That will touch me more than you."

"Then it *is* true?" cried Feeder, more seriously looking up at his friend.

"She won't look down; I will answer for that."

"You won't care; you are out of it all now."

"No, I am not; I mean to do a great deal of work."

"I will believe that when I see it," said Sidney Feeder, who was by no means perfectly incredulous, but who thought it salutary to take that tone. "I am not sure that you have any right to work—you oughtn't to have everything; you ought to leave the field to us. You must pay the penalty of being so rich. You would have been celebrated if you had continued to practise—more celebrated than any one. But you won't be now—you can't be. Some one else will be, in your place."

Jackson Lemon listened to this, but without meeting the eyes of the speaker; not, however, as if he were avoiding them, but as if the long stretch of the Ride, now less and less obstructed, invited him and made his companion's talk a little retarding. Nevertheless, he answered, deliberately and kindly enough: "I hope it will be you;" and he bowed to a lady who rode past.

"Very likely it will. I hope I make you feel badly—that's what I'm trying to do."

"Oh, awfully!" cried Jackson Lemon; "all the more that I am not in the least engaged."

"Well, that's good. Won't you come up to-morrow?" Doctor Feeder went on.

"I'll try, my dear fellow; I can't be sure. By-by!"

"Oh, you're lost anyway!" cried Sidney Feeder, as the other started away.

II

IT was Lady Marmaduke, the wife of Sir Henry Marmaduke, who had introduced Jackson Lemon to Lady Beauchemin; after which Lady Beauchemin had made him acquainted with her mother and sisters. Lady Marmaduke was also transatlantic; she had been for her conjugal baronet the most permanent consequence of a tour in the United States. At present, at the end of ten years, she knew her London as she had never known her New York, so that it had been easy for her to be, as she called herself, Jackson Lemon's social godmother. She had views with regard to his career, and these views fitted into a social scheme which, if our space permitted, I should be glad to lay before the reader in its magnitude. She wished to add an arch or two to the bridge on which she had effected her transit from America, and it was her belief that

Jackson Lemon might furnish the materials. This bridge, as yet a somewhat sketchy and rickety structure, she saw (in the future) boldly stretching from one solid pillar to another. It would have to go both ways, for reciprocity was the keynote of Lady Marmaduke's plan. It was her belief that an ultimate fusion was inevitable, and that those who were the first to understand the situation would gain the most. The first time Jackson Lemon had dined with her, he met Lady Beauchemin, who was her intimate friend. Lady Beauchemin was remarkably gracious; she asked him to come and see her as if she really meant it. He presented himself, and in her drawing-room met her mother, who happened to be calling at the same moment. Lady Canterville, not less friendly than her daughter, invited him down to Pasterns for Easter week; and before a month had passed it seemed to him that, though he was not what he would have called intimate at any house in London, the door of the house of Clement opened to him pretty often. This was a considerable good fortune, for it always opened upon a charming picture. The inmates were a blooming and beautiful race, and their interior had an aspect of the ripest comfort. It was not the splendour of New York (as New York had lately begun to appear to the young man), but a splendour in which there was an unpurchasable ingredient of age. He himself had a great deal of money, and money was good, even when it was new; but old money was the best. Even after he learned that Lord Canterville's fortune was more ancient than abundant, it was still the mellowness of the golden element that struck him. It was Lady Beauchemin who had told him that her father was not rich; having told him, besides this, many surprising things—things that were surprising in themselves or surprising on her lips. This struck him afresh later that evening—the day he met Sidney Feeder in the Park. He dined out, in the company of Lady Beauchemin, and afterward, as she was alone—her husband had gone down to listen to a debate—she offered to "take him on." She was going to several places, and he must be going to some of them. They compared notes, and it was settled that they should proceed together to the Trumpingtons', whither, also, it appeared at eleven o'clock that all the world was going, the approach to the house being choked for half a mile with carriages. It was a close, muggy night; Lady Beauchemin's chariot, in its place in the rank, stood still for long periods. In his corner beside her, through the open window, Jackson Lemon, rather hot, rather oppressed, looked out on the moist, greasy pavement, over which was flung, a considerable distance up and down, the flare of a public-house. Lady Beauchemin, however, was not impatient, for she had a purpose in her mind, and now she could say what she wished.

"Do you really love her?" That was the first thing she said.

"Well, I guess so," Jackson Lemon answered, as if he did not recognise the obligation to be serious.

Lady Beauchemin looked at him a moment in silence; he felt her gaze, and turning his eyes, saw her face, partly shadowed, with the aid of a street-lamp. She was not so pretty as Lady Barberina; her countenance had a certain sharpness; her hair, very light in colour and wonderfully frizzled, almost covered her eyes, the expression of which, however, together with that of her pointed nose, and the glitter of several diamonds, emerged from the gloom. "You don't seem to know. I never saw a man in such an odd state," she presently remarked.

"You push me a little too much; I must have time to think of it," the young man went on. "You know in my country they allow us plenty of time." He had several little oddities of expression, of which he was perfectly conscious, and which he found convenient, for they protected him in a society in which a lonely American was rather exposed; they gave him the advantage which corresponded with certain drawbacks. He had very few natural Americanisms, but the occasional use of one, discreetly chosen, made him appear simpler than he really was, and he had his reasons for wishing this result. He was not simple; he was subtle, circumspect, shrewd, and perfectly aware that he might make mistakes. There was a danger of his making a mistake at present—a mistake which would be immensely grave. He was determined only to succeed. It is true that for a great success he would take a certain risk; but the risk was to be considered, and he gained time while he multiplied his guesses and talked about his country.

"You may take ten years if you like," said Lady Beauchemin. "I am in no hurry whatever to make you my brother-in-law. Only you must remember that you spoke to me first."

"What did I say?"

"You told me that Barberina was the finest girl you had seen in England."

"Oh, I am willing to stand by that; I like her type."

"I should think you might!"

"I like her very much—with all her peculiarities."

"What do you mean by her peculiarities?"

"Well, she has some peculiar ideas," said Jackson Lemon, in a tone of the sweetest reasonableness; "and she has a peculiar way of speaking."

"Ah, you can't expect us to speak as well as you!" cried Lady Beauchemin.

"I don't know why not; you do some things much better."

"We have our own ways, at any rate, and we think them the best in the world. One of them is not to let a gentleman devote himself to a girl for three or four months without some sense of responsibility. If you don't wish to marry my sister you ought to go away."

"I ought never to have come," said Jackson Lemon.

"I can scarcely agree to that; for I should have lost the pleasure of knowing you."

"It would have spared you this duty, which you dislike very much."

"Asking you about your intentions? I don't dislike it at all; it amuses me extremely."

"Should you like your sister to marry me?" asked Jackson Lemon, with great simplicity.

If he expected to take Lady Beauchemin by surprise he was disappointed; for she was perfectly prepared to commit herself. "I should like it very much. I think English and American society ought to be but one—I mean the best of each—a great whole."

"Will you allow me to ask whether Lady Marmaduke suggested that to you?"

"We have often talked of it."

"Oh yes, that's her aim."

"Well, it's my aim too. I think there's a great deal to be done."

"And you would like me to do it?"

"To begin it, precisely. Don't you think we ought to see more of each other?—I mean the best in each country."

Jackson Lemon was silent a moment. "I am afraid I haven't any general ideas. If I should marry an English girl it wouldn't be for the good of the species."

"Well, we want to be mixed a little; that I am sure of," Lady Beauchemin said.

"You certainly got that from Lady Marmaduke."

"It's too tiresome, your not consenting to be serious! But my father will make you so," Lady Beauchemin went on. "I may as well let you know that he intends in a day or two to ask you your intentions. That's all I wished to say to you. I think you ought to be prepared."

"I am much obliged to you; Lord Canterville will do quite right."

There was, to Lady Beauchemin, something really unfathomable in this little American doctor, whom she had taken up on grounds of large policy, and who, though he was assumed to have sunk the medical character, was neither handsome nor distinguished, but only immensely rich and quite original, for he was not insignificant. It was unfathomable, to begin with, that a medical man should be so rich, or that so rich a man should be medical; it was even, to an eye which was always gratified by suitability, rather irritating. Jackson Lemon himself could have explained it better than any one else, but this was an explanation that one could scarcely ask for. There were other things; his cool acceptance of certain situations; his general indisposition to explain; his way of taking refuge in jokes which at times had not even the merit of being American; his way, too, of appearing to be a suitor without being an aspirant. Lady Beauchemin, however, was, like Jackson Lemon, prepared to run a certain risk. His reserves made him slippery; but that was only when one pressed. She flattered herself that she could handle people lightly. "My father will be sure to act with perfect tact," she said; "of course, if you shouldn't care to be questioned, you can go out of town." She had the air of really wishing to make everything easy for him.

"I don't want to go out of town; I am enjoying it far too much here," her companion answered. "And wouldn't your father have a right to ask me what I meant by that?"

Lady Beauchemin hesitated; she was slightly perplexed. But in a moment she exclaimed: "He is incapable of saying anything vulgar!"

She had not really answered his inquiry, and he was conscious of that; but he was quite ready to say to her, a little later, as he guided her steps from the brougham to the strip of carpet which, between a somewhat rickety border of striped cloth and a double row of waiting footmen, policemen and dingy amateurs of both sexes, stretched from the curbstone to the portal of the Trumpingtons, "Of course I shall not wait for Lord Canterville to speak to me."

He had been expecting some such announcement as this from Lady Beauchemin, and he judged that her father would do no more than his duty. He knew that he ought to be prepared with an answer to Lord Canterville, and he wondered at himself for not yet having come to the point. Sidney Feeder's question in the Park had made him feel rather pointless; it was the first allusion that had been made to his possible marriage, except on the part of Lady Beauchemin. None of his own people were in London; he was perfectly independent, and even if his mother had been within reach he could not have consulted her on the subject. He loved her dearly, better than any one; but she was not a woman to consult, for she approved of whatever he did: it was her standard. He was careful not to be too serious when he talked with Lady Beauchemin; but he was very serious indeed as he thought over the matter within himself, which he did even among the diversions of the next half-hour, while he squeezed obliquely and slowly through the crush in Mrs Trumpington's drawing-room. At the end of the half-hour he came away, and at the door he found Lady Beauchemin, from whom he had separated on entering the house, and who, this time with a companion of her own sex, was awaiting her carriage and still "going on." He gave her his arm into the street, and as she stepped into the vehicle she repeated that she wished he would go out of town for a few days.

"Who, then, would tell me what to do?" he asked, for answer, looking at her through the window.

She might tell him what to do, but he felt free, all the same; and he was determined this should continue. To prove it to himself he jumped into a hansom and drove back to Brook Street, to his hotel, instead of proceeding to a bright-windowed house in Portland Place, where he knew that after midnight he should find Lady Canterville and her daughters. There had been a reference to the subject between Lady Barberina and himself during their ride, and she would probably expect him; but it made him taste his liberty not to go, and he liked to taste his liberty. He was aware that to taste it in perfection he ought to go to bed; but he did not go to bed, he did not even take off his hat. He walked up and down his sitting-room, with his head surmounted by this ornament, a good deal tipped back, and his hands in his pockets. There were a good many cards stuck into the frame of the mirror, over his chimney-piece, and every time he passed the place he seemed to see what was written on one of them—the name of the mistress of the house in Portland Place, his own name, and, in the lower left-hand corner, the words: "A small Dance." Of course, now, he must make up his mind; he would make it up to the next day: that was what he said to himself as he walked up and down; and according to his decision he would speak to Lord Canterville or he would take the night-express to Paris. It was better meanwhile that he should not see Lady Barberina. It was vivid to him, as he paused occasionally, looking vaguely at that card in the chimney-glass, that he had come pretty far; and he had come so far because he was under the charm—yes, he was in love with Lady Barb. There was no doubt whatever of that; he had a faculty for diagnosis, and he knew perfectly well what was the matter with him. He wasted no time in musing upon the mystery of this passion, in wondering whether he might not have escaped it by a little vigilance at first, or whether it would die out if he should go away. He accepted it frankly, for the sake of the pleasure it gave him—the girl was the delight of his eyes—and confined himself to considering whether such a marriage would square with his general situation. This would not at all necessarily follow from the fact that he was in love; too many other things would come in between. The most important of these was the change, not only of the geographical, but of the social, standpoint for his wife, and a certain readjustment that it would involve in his own relation to things. He was not inclined to readjustments, and there was no reason why he should be; his own position was in most respects so advantageous. But the girl tempted him almost irresistibly, satisfying his imagination both as a lover and as a student of the human organism; she was so blooming, so complete, of a type so rarely encountered in that degree of perfection. Jackson Lemon was not an Anglo-maniac, but he admired the physical conditions of the English—their complexion, their temperament, their tissue; and Lady Barberina struck him, in flexible, virginal form, as a wonderful compendium of these elements. There was something simple and robust in her beauty; it had the quietness of an old Greek statue, without the vulgarity of the modern simper or of contemporary prettiness. Her head was antique; and though her conversation was quite of the present period, Jackson Lemon had said to himself that there was sure to be in her soul a certain primitive sincerity which would match with her facial mould. He saw her as she might be in the future, the beautiful mother of beautiful children, in whom the look of race should be conspicuous. He should like his children to have the look of race, and he was not unaware that he must take his precautions accordingly. A great many people had it in England; and it was a pleasure to him to see it, especially as no one had it so unmistakably as the second daughter of Lord Canterville. It would be a great luxury to call such a woman one's own; nothing could be more evident than that, because it made no difference that she was not strikingly clever. Striking cleverness was not a part of harmonious form and the English complexion; it was associated with the modern simper, which was a result of modern nerves. If Jackson Lemon had wanted a nervous wife, of course he could have found her at home; but this tall, fair girl, whose character, like her figure, appeared mainly to have been formed by riding across country, was differently put together. All the same, would it suit his book, as they said in London, to marry her and transport her to New York? He came back to this question; came back to it with a persistency which, had she been admitted to a view of it, would have tried the patience of Lady Beauchemin. She had been irritated, more than once, at his appearing to attach himself so exclusively to this horn of the dilemma—as if it could possibly fail to be a good thing for a little American doctor to marry the daughter of an English peer. It would have been more becoming, in her ladyship's eyes, that he should take that for granted a little more, and the consent of her ladyship's—of their ladyships'—family a little less. They looked at the matter so differently! Jackson Lemon was conscious that if he should marry Lady Barberina Clement it would be because it suited him, and not because it suited his possible sisters-in-law. He believed that he acted in all things by his own will—an organ for which he had the highest respect.

It would have seemed, however, that on this occasion it was not working very regularly, for though he had come home to go to bed, the stroke of half-past twelve saw him jump, not into his couch, but into a hansom which the whistle of the porter had summoned to the door of his hotel, and in which he rattled off to Portland Place. Here he found—in a very large house—an assembly of three hundred people, and a band of music concealed in a bower of azaleas. Lady Canterville had not arrived; he wandered through the rooms and assured himself of that. He also discovered a very good conservatory, where there were banks and pyramids of azaleas. He watched the top of the staircase, but it was a long time before he saw what he was looking for, and his impatience at last was extreme. The reward, however, when it came, was all that he could have desired. It was a little smile from Lady Barberina, who stood behind her mother while the latter extended her finger-tips to the hostess. The entrance of this charming woman, with her beautiful daughters—always a noticeable incident—was effected with a certain brilliancy, and just now it was agreeable to Jackson Lemon to think that it concerned him more than any one else in the house. Tall, dazzling, indifferent, looking about her as if she saw very little, Lady Barberina was certainly a figure round which a young man's fancy might revolve. She was very quiet and simple, had little manner and little movement; but her detachment was not a vulgar art. She appeared to efface herself, to wait till, in the natural course, she should be attended to; and in this there was evidently no exaggeration, for she was too proud not to have perfect confidence. Her sister, smaller, slighter, with a little surprised smile, which seemed to say that in her extreme innocence she was yet prepared for anything, having heard, indirectly, such extraordinary things about society, was much more impatient and more expressive, and projected across a threshold the pretty radiance of her eyes and teeth before her mother's name was announced. Lady Canterville was thought by many persons to be very superior to her daughters; she had kept even more beauty than she had given them; and it was a beauty which had been called intellectual. She had extraordinary sweetness, without any definite professions; her manner was mild almost to tenderness; there was even a kind of pity in it. Moreover, her features were perfect, and nothing could be more gently gracious than a way she had of speaking, or rather, of listening, to people, with her head inclined a little to one side. Jackson Lemon liked her very much, and she had certainly been most kind to him. He approached Lady Barberina as soon as he could do so without an appearance of precipitation, and said to her that he hoped very much she would not dance. He was a master of the art which flourishes in New York above every other, and he had guided her through a dozen waltzes with a skill which, as she felt, left absolutely nothing to be desired. But dancing was not his business to-night. She smiled a little at the expression of his hope.

"That is what mamma has brought us here for," she said; "she doesn't like it if we don't dance."

"How does she know whether she likes it or not? You have always danced."

"Once I didn't," said Lady Barberina.

He told her that, at any rate, he would settle it with her mother, and persuaded her to wander with him into the conservatory, where there were coloured lights suspended among the plants, and a vault of verdure overhead. In comparison with the other rooms the conservatory was dusky and remote. But they were not alone; half a dozen other couples were in possession. The gloom was rosy with the slopes of azalea, and suffused with mitigated music, which made it possible to talk without consideration of one's neighbours. Nevertheless, though it was only in looking back on the scene later that Lady Barberina perceived this, these dispersed couples were talking very softly. She did not look at them; it seemed to her that, virtually, she was alone with Jackson Lemon. She said something about conservatories, about the fragrance of the air; for all answer to which he asked her, as he stood there before her, a question by which she might have been exceedingly startled.

"How do people who marry in England ever know each other before marriage? They have no chance."

"I am sure I don't know," said Lady Barberina; "I never was married."

"It's very different in my country. There a man may see much of a girl; he may come and see her, he may be constantly alone with her. I wish you allowed that over here."

Lady Barberina suddenly examined the less ornamental side of her fan, as if it had never occurred to her before to look at it. "It must be so very odd, America," she murmured at last.

"Well, I guess in that matter we are right; over here it's a leap in the dark."

"I am sure I don't know," said the girl. She had folded her fan; she stretched out her arm mechanically and plucked a sprig of azalea.

"I guess it doesn't signify, after all," Jackson Lemon remarked. "They say that love is blind at the best." His keen

young face was bent upon hers; his thumbs were in the pockets
of his trousers; he smiled a little, showing his fine teeth. She
said nothing, but only pulled her azalea to pieces. She was
usually so quiet that this small movement looked restless.

"This is the first time I have seen you in the least without
a lot of people," he went on.

"Yes, it's very tiresome," she said.

"I have been sick of it; I didn't want to come here to-
night."

She had not met his eyes, though she knew they were seeking her own. But now she looked at him a moment. She had
never objected to his appearance, and in this respect she had
no repugnance to overcome. She liked a man to be tall and
handsome, and Jackson Lemon was neither; but when she was
sixteen, and as tall herself as she was to be at twenty, she had
been in love (for three weeks) with one of her cousins, a little
fellow in the Hussars, who was shorter even than the American, shorter consequently than herself. This proved that distinction might be independent of stature—not that she ever
reasoned it out. Jackson Lemon's facial spareness, his bright
little eye, which seemed always to be measuring things, struck
her as original, and she thought them very cutting, which
would do very well for a husband of hers. As she made this
reflection, of course it never occurred to her that she herself
might be cut; she was not a sacrificial lamb. She perceived that
his features expressed a mind—a mind that would be rather
effective. She would never have taken him for a doctor;
though, indeed, when all was said, that was very negative and
didn't account for the way he imposed himself.

"Why, then, did you come?" she asked, in answer to his
last speech.

"Because it seems to me after all better to see you in this
way than not to see you at all; I want to know you better."

"I don't think I ought to stay here," said Lady Barberina,
looking round her.

"Don't go till I have told you I love you," murmured the young man.

She made no exclamation, indulged in no start; he could not see even that she changed colour. She took his request with a noble simplicity, with her head erect and her eyes lowered.

"I don't think you have a right to tell me that."

"Why not?" Jackson Lemon demanded. "I wish to claim the right; I wish you to give it to me."

"I can't—I don't know you. You have said it yourself."

"Can't you have a little faith? That will help us to know each other better. It's disgusting, the want of opportunity; even at Pasterns I could scarcely get a walk with you. But I have the greatest faith in you. I feel that I love you, and I couldn't do more than that at the end of six months. I love your beauty—I love you from head to foot. Don't move, please don't move." He lowered his tone; but it went straight to her ear, and it must be believed that it had a certain eloquence. For himself, after he had heard himself say these words, all his being was in a glow. It was a luxury to speak to her of her beauty; it brought him nearer to her than he had ever been. But the colour had come into her face, and it seemed to remind him that her beauty was not all. "Everything about you is sweet and noble," he went on; "everything is dear to me. I am sure you are good. I don't know what you think of me; I asked Lady Beauchemin to tell me, and she told me to judge for myself. Well, then, I judge you like me. Haven't I a right to assume that till the contrary is proved? May I speak to your father? That's what I want to know. I have been waiting; but now what should I wait for longer? I want to be able to tell him that you have given me some hope. I suppose I ought to speak to him first. I meant to, to-morrow, but meanwhile, to-night, I thought I would just put this in. In my country it wouldn't matter particularly. You must see all that over there for yourself. If you should tell me not to speak to your father, I wouldn't; I would wait. But I like better to ask your leave to speak to him than to ask his to speak to you."

His voice had sunk almost to a whisper; but, though it trembled, his emotion gave it peculiar intensity. He had the same attitude, his thumbs in his trousers, his attentive head, his smile, which was a matter of course; no one would have imagined what he was saying. She had listened without moving, and at the end she raised her eyes. They rested on his a moment, and he remembered, a good while later, the look which passed her lids.

"You may say anything that you please to my father, but I don't wish to hear any more. You have said too much, considering how little idea you have given me before."

"I was watching you," said Jackson Lemon.

Lady Barberina held her head higher, looking straight at him. Then, quite seriously, "I don't like to be watched," she remarked.

"You shouldn't be so beautiful, then. Won't you give me a word of hope?" he added.

"I have never supposed I should marry a foreigner," said Lady Barberina.

"Do you call me a foreigner?"

"I think your ideas are very different, and your country is different; you have told me so yourself."

"I should like to show it to you; I would make you like it."

"I am not sure what you would make me do," said Lady Barberina, very honestly.

"Nothing that you don't want."

"I am sure you would try," she declared, with a smile.

"Well," said Jackson Lemon, "after all, I am trying now."

To this she simply replied she must go to her mother, and he was obliged to lead her out of the conservatory. Lady Canterville was not immediately found, so that he had time to murmur as they went, "Now that I have spoken, I am very happy."

"Perhaps you are happy too soon," said the girl.

"Ah, don't say that, Lady Barb."

"Of course I must think of it."

"Of course you must!" said Jackson Lemon. "I will speak to your father to-morrow."

"I can't fancy what he will say."

"How can he dislike me?" the young man asked, in a tone which Lady Beauchemin, if she had heard him, would have been forced to attribute to his general affectation of the jocose. What Lady Beauchemin's sister thought of it is not recorded; but there is perhaps a clue to her opinion in the answer she made him after a moment's silence: "Really, you know, you *are* a foreigner!" With this she turned her back upon him, for she was already in her mother's hands. Jackson Lemon said a few words to Lady Canterville; they were chiefly about its being very hot. She gave him her vague, sweet attention, as if he were saying something ingenious of which she missed the point. He could see that she was thinking of the doings of her daughter Agatha, whose attitude toward the contemporary young man was wanting in the perception of differences—a madness without method; she was evidently not occupied with Lady Barberina, who was more to be trusted. This young woman never met her suitor's eyes again; she let her own rest, rather ostentatiously, upon other objects. At last he was going away without a glance from her. Lady Canterville had asked him to come to lunch on the morrow, and he had said he would do so if she would promise him he should see his lordship. "I can't pay you another visit until I have had some talk with him," he said.

"I don't see why not; but if I speak to him I dare say he will be at home," she answered.

"It will be worth his while!"

Jackson Lemon left the house reflecting that as he had never proposed to a girl before he could not be expected to know how women demean themselves in this emergency. He had heard, indeed, that Lady Barb had had no end of offers; and though he thought it probable that the number was exaggerated, as it always is, it was to be supposed that her way of appearing suddenly to have dropped him was but the usual behaviour for the occasion.

III

AT her mother's the next day she was absent from luncheon, and Lady Canterville mentioned to him (he didn't ask) that she had gone to see a dear old great-aunt, who was also her godmother, and who lived at Roehampton. Lord Canterville was not present, but our young man was informed by his hostess that he had promised her he would come in exactly at three o'clock. Jackson Lemon lunched with Lady Canterville and the children, who appeared in force at this repast, all the younger girls being present, and two little boys, the juniors of the two sons who were in their teens. Jackson, who was very fond of children, and thought these absolutely the finest in the world—magnificent specimens of a magnificent brood, such as it would be so satisfactory in future days to see about his own knee—Jackson felt that he was being treated as one of the family, but was not frightened by what he supposed the privilege to imply. Lady Canterville betrayed no consciousness whatever of his having mooted the question of becoming her son-in-law, and he believed that her eldest daughter had not told her of their talk the night before. This idea gave him pleasure; he liked to think that Lady Barb was judging him for herself. Perhaps, indeed, she was taking counsel of the old lady at Roehampton: he believed that he was the sort of lover of whom a godmother would approve.

Godmothers in his mind were mainly associated with fairy-tales (he had had no baptismal sponsors of his own); and that point of view would be favourable to a young man with a great deal of gold who had suddenly arrived from a foreign country—an apparition, surely, sufficiently elfish. He made up his mind that he should like Lady Canterville as a mother-in-law; she would be too well-bred to meddle. Her husband came in at three o'clock, just after they had left the table, and said to Jackson Lemon that it was very good in him to have waited.

"I haven't waited," Jackson replied, with his watch in his hand; "you are punctual to the minute."

I know not how Lord Canterville may have judged his young friend, but Jackson Lemon had been told more than once in his life that he was a very good fellow, but rather too literal. After he had lighted a cigarette in his lordship's "den," a large brown apartment on the ground-floor, which partook at once of the nature of an office and of that of a harness-room (it could not have been called in any degree a library), he went straight to the point in these terms: "Well now, Lord Canterville, I feel as if I ought to let you know without more delay that I am in love with Lady Barb, and that I should like to marry her." So he spoke, puffing his cigarette, with his conscious but unextenuating eye fixed on his host.

No man, as I have intimated, bore better being looked at than this noble personage; he seemed to bloom in the envious warmth of human contemplation, and never appeared so fault-less as when he was most exposed. "My dear fellow, my dear fellow," he murmured, almost in disparagement, stroking his ambrosial beard from before the empty fireplace. He lifted his eyebrows, but he looked perfectly good-natured.

"Are you surprised, sir?" Jackson Lemon asked.

"Why, I suppose any one is surprised at a man wanting one of his children. He sometimes feels the weight of that sort of thing so much, you know. He wonders what the devil

another man wants of them." And Lord Canterville laughed
pleasantly out of the copious fringe of his lips.

"I only want one of them," said Jackson Lemon, laughing
too, but with a lighter organ.

"Polygamy would be rather good for the parents. However,
Louisa told me the other night that she thought you were
looking the way you speak of."

"Yes, I told Lady Beauchemin that I love Lady Barb, and
she seemed to think it was natural."

"Oh yes, I suppose there's no want of nature in it! But,
my dear fellow, I really don't know what to say."

"Of course you'll have to think of it." Jackson Lemon, in
saying this, felt that he was making the most liberal concession to the point of view of his interlocutor; being perfectly aware that in his own country it was not left much to
the parents to think of.

"I shall have to talk it over with my wife."

"Lady Canterville has been very kind to me; I hope she
will continue."

"My dear fellow, we are excellent friends. No one could
appreciate you more than Lady Canterville. Of course we
can only consider such a question on the—a—the highest
grounds. You would never want to marry without knowing,
as it were, exactly what you are doing. I, on my side, naturally,
you know, am bound to do the best I can for my own child.
At the same time, of course, we don't want to spend our time
in—a—walking round the horse. We want to keep to the
main line." It was settled between them after a little that
the main line was that Jackson Lemon knew to a certainty the
state of his affections and was in a position to pretend to the
hand of a young lady who, Lord Canterville might say—of
course, you know, without any swagger—had a right to
expect to do well, as the women call it.

"I should think she had," Jackson Lemon said; "she's a
beautiful type."

Lord Canterville stared a moment. "She is a clever, well-grown girl, and she takes her fences like a grasshopper. Does she know all this, by the way?" he added.

"Oh yes, I told her last night."

Again Lord Canterville had the air, unusual with him, of returning his companion's scrutiny. "I am not sure that you ought to have done that, you know."

"I couldn't have spoken to you first—I couldn't," said Jackson Lemon. "I meant to, but it stuck in my crop."

"They don't in your country, I guess," his lordship returned, smiling.

"Well, not as a general thing; however, I find it very pleasant to discuss with you now." And in truth it was very pleasant. Nothing could be easier, friendlier, more informal, than Lord Canterville's manner, which implied all sorts of equality, especially that of age and fortune, and made Jackson Lemon feel at the end of three minutes almost as if he too were a beautifully preserved and somewhat straitened nobleman of sixty, with the views of a man of the world about his own marriage. The young American perceived that Lord Canterville waived the point of his having spoken first to the girl herself, and saw in this indulgence a just concession to the ardour of young affection. For Lord Canterville seemed perfectly to appreciate the sentimental side—at least so far as it was embodied in his visitor—when he said, without deprecation: "Did she give you any encouragement?"

"Well, she didn't box my ears. She told me that she would think of it, but that I must speak to you. But, naturally, I shouldn't have said what I did to her if I hadn't made up my mind during the last fortnight that I am not disagreeable to her."

"Ah, my dear young man, women are odd cattle!" Lord Canterville exclaimed, rather unexpectedly. "But of course you know all that," he added in an instant; "you take the general risk."

"I am perfectly willing to take the general risk; the particular risk is small."

"Well, upon my honour I don't really know my girls. You see a man's time, in England, is tremendously taken up; but I dare say it's the same in your country. Their mother knows them—I think I had better send for their mother. If you don't mind I'll just suggest that she join us here."

"I'm rather afraid of you both together, but if it will settle it any quicker——" said Jackson Lemon. Lord Canterville rang the bell, and, when a servant appeared, despatched him with a message to her ladyship. While they were waiting, the young man remembered that it was in his power to give a more definite account of his pecuniary basis. He had simply said before that he was abundantly able to marry; he shrank from putting himself forward as a billionaire. He had a fine taste, and he wished to appeal to Lord Canterville primarily as a gentleman. But now that he had to make a double impression, he bethought himself of his millions, for millions were always impressive. "I think it only fair to let you know that my fortune is really very considerable," he remarked.

"Yes, I dare say you are beastly rich," said Lord Canterville.

"I have about seven millions."

"Seven millions?"

"I count in dollars; upwards of a million and a half sterling."

Lord Canterville looked at him from head to foot, with an air of cheerful resignation to a form of grossness which threatened to become common. Then he said, with a touch of that inconsequence of which he had already given a glimpse: "What the deuce, then, possessed you to turn doctor?"

Jackson Lemon coloured a little, hesitated, and then replied, quickly: "Because I had the talent for it."

"Of course, I don't for a moment doubt of your ability; but don't you find it rather a bore?"

"I don't practise much. I am rather ashamed to say that."

"Ah, well, of course, in your country it's different. I dare say you've got a door-plate, eh?"

"Oh yes, and a tin sign tied to the balcony!" said Jackson Lemon, smiling.

"What did your father say to it?"

"To my going into medicine? He said he would be hanged if he'd take any of my doses. He didn't think I should succeed; he wanted me to go into the house."

"Into the House—a——" said Lord Canterville, hesitating a little. "Into your Congress—yes, exactly."

"Ah, no, not so bad as that. Into the store," Jackson Lemon replied, in the candid tone in which he expressed himself when, for reasons of his own, he wished to be perfectly national.

Lord Canterville stared, not venturing, even for the moment, to hazard an interpretation; and before a solution had presented itself Lady Canterville came into the room.

"My dear, I thought we had better see you. Do you know he wants to marry our second girl?" It was in these simple terms that her husband acquainted her with the question.

Lady Canterville expressed neither surprise nor elation; she simply stood there, smiling, with her head a little inclined to the side, with all her customary graciousness. Her charming eyes rested on those of Jackson Lemon, and though they seemed to show that she had to think a little of so serious a proposition, his own discovered in them none of the coldness of calculation. "Are you talking about Barberina?" she asked in a moment, as if her thoughts had been far away.

Of course they were talking about Barberina, and Jackson Lemon repeated to her ladyship what he had said to the girl's father. He had thought it all over, and his mind was quite made up. Moreover, he had spoken to Lady Barb.

"Did she tell you that, my dear?" asked Lord Canterville, while he lighted another cigar.

She gave no heed to this inquiry, which had been vague and

accidental on his lordship's part, but simply said to Jackson
Lemon that the thing was very serious, and that they had
better sit down for a moment. In an instant he was near her
on the sofa on which she had placed herself, still smiling and
looking up at her husband with an air of general meditation,
in which a sweet compassion for every one concerned was
apparent.

"Barberina has told me nothing," she said, after a little.

"That proves she cares for me!" Jackson Lemon exclaimed
eagerly.

Lady Canterville looked as if she thought this almost too
ingenious, almost professional; but her husband said cheerfully, jovially: "Ah, well, if she cares for you, I don't
object."

This was a little ambiguous; but before Jackson Lemon had
time to look into it, Lady Canterville asked gently: "Should
you expect her to live in America?"

"Oh, yes; that's my home, you know."

"Shouldn't you be living sometimes in England?"

"Oh, yes, we'll come over and see you." The young man
was in love, he wanted to marry, he wanted to be genial, and
to commend himself to the parents of Lady Barb; at the same
time it was in his nature not to accept conditions, save in so
far as they exactly suited him, to tie himself, or, as they said
in New York, to give himself away. In any transaction he preferred his own terms to those of any one else. Therefore, the
moment Lady Canterville gave signs of wishing to extract a
promise, he was on his guard.

"She'll find it very different; perhaps she won't like it," her
ladyship suggested.

"If she likes me, she'll like my country," said Jackson
Lemon, with decision.

"He tells me he has got a plate on his door," Lord Canterville remarked humorously.

"We must talk to her, of course; we must understand how

she feels," said his wife, looking more serious than she had done as yet.

"Please don't discourage her, Lady Canterville," the young man begged; "and give me a chance to talk to her a little more myself. You haven't given me much chance, you know."

"We don't offer our daughters to people, Mr Lemon," Lady Canterville was always gentle, but now she was a little majestic.

"She isn't like some women in London, you know," said Jackson Lemon's host, who seemed to remember that to a discussion of such importance he ought from time to time to contribute a word of wisdom. And Jackson Lemon, certainly, if the idea had been presented to him, would have said that, No, decidedly, Lady Barberina had not been thrown at him.

"Of course not," he declared, in answer to her mother's remark. "But, you know, you mustn't refuse them too much, either; you mustn't make a poor fellow wait too long. I admire her, I love her, more than I can say; I give you my word of honour for that."

"He seems to think that settles it," said Lord Canterville, smiling down at the young American, very indulgently, from his place before the cold chimney-piece.

"Of course that's what we desire, Philip," her ladyship returned, very nobly.

"Lady Barb believes it; I am sure she does!" Jackson Lemon exclaimed. "Why should I pretend to be in love with her if I am not?"

Lady Canterville received this inquiry in silence, and her husband, with just the least air in the world of repressed impatience, began to walk up and down the room. He was a man of many engagements, and he had been closeted for more than a quarter of an hour with the young American doctor. "Do you imagine you should come often to England?" Lady

Canterville demanded, with a certain abruptness, returning to that important point.

"I'm afraid I can't tell you that; of course we shall do whatever seems best." He was prepared to suppose they should cross the Atlantic every summer: that prospect was by no means displeasing to him; but he was not prepared to give any such pledge to Lady Canterville, especially as he did not believe it would really be necessary. It was in his mind, not as an overt pretension, but as a tacit implication, that he should treat with Barberina's parents on a footing of perfect equality; and there would somehow be nothing equal if he should begin to enter into engagements which didn't belong to the essence of the matter. They were to give their daughter, and he was to take her: in this arrangement there would be as much on one side as on the other. But beyond this he had nothing to ask of them; there was nothing he wished them to promise, and his own pledges, therefore, would have no equivalent. Whenever his wife should wish it, she should come over and see her people. Her home was to be in New York; but he was tacitly conscious that on the question of absences he should be very liberal. Nevertheless, there was something in the very grain of his character which forbade that he should commit himself at present in respect to times and dates.

Lady Canterville looked at her husband, but her husband was not attentive; he was taking a peep at his watch. In a moment, however, he threw out a remark to the effect that he thought it a capital thing that the two countries should become more united, and there was nothing that would bring it about better than a few of the best people on both sides pairing off together. The English, indeed, had begun it; a lot of fellows had brought over a lot of pretty girls, and it was quite fair play that the Americans should take their pick. They were all one race, after all; and why shouldn't they make one society—the best on both sides, of course? Jackson Lemon smiled as he recognised Lady Marmaduke's philosophy, and

he was pleased to think that Lady Beauchemin had some influence with her father; for he was sure the old gentleman
(as he mentally designated his host) had got all this from her,
though he expressed himself less happily than the cleverest of
his daughters. Our hero had no objection to make to it,
especially if there was anything in it that would really help his
case. But it was not in the least on these high grounds that he
had sought the hand of Lady Barb. He wanted her not in
order that her people and his (the best on both sides!) should
make one society; he wanted her simply because he wanted
her. Lady Canterville smiled; but she seemed to have another
thought.

"I quite appreciate what my husband says; but I don't see
why poor Barb should be the one to begin."

"I dare say she'll like it," said Lord Canterville, as if he
were attempting a short cut. "They say you spoil your
women awfully."

"She's not one of their women yet," her ladyship remarked,
in the sweetest tone in the world; and then she added, without
Jackson Lemon's knowing exactly what she meant, "It seems
so strange."

He was a little irritated; and perhaps these simple words
added to the feeling. There had been no positive opposition
to his suit, and Lord and Lady Canterville were most kind;
but he felt that they held back a little, and though he had not
expected them to throw themselves on his neck, he was rather
disappointed, his pride was touched. Why should they hesitate? He considered himself such a good *parti*. It was not so
much the old gentleman, it was Lady Canterville. As he saw
the old gentleman look, covertly, a second time at his watch,
he could have believed he would have been glad to settle the
matter on the spot. Lady Canterville seemed to wish her
daughter's lover to come forward more, to give certain assurances and guarantees. He felt that he was ready to say or do
anything that was a matter of proper form; but he couldn't

take the tone of trying to purchase her ladyship's consent, penetrated as he was with the conviction that such a man as he could be trusted to care for his wife rather more than an impecunious British peer and *his* wife could be supposed (with the lights he had acquired in English society) to care even for the handsomest of a dozen children. It was a mistake on Lady Canterville's part not to recognise that. He humoured her mistake to the extent of saying, just a little drily, "My wife shall certainly have everything she wants."

"He tells me he is disgustingly rich," Lord Canterville added, pausing before their companion with his hands in his pockets.

"I am glad to hear it; but it isn't so much that," she answered, sinking back a little on her sofa. If it was not that, she did not say what it was, though she had looked for a moment as if she were going to. She only raised her eyes to her husband's face, as if to ask for inspiration. I know not whether she found it, but in a moment she said to Jackson Lemon, seeming to imply that it was quite another point: "Do you expect to continue your profession?"

He had no such intention, so far as his profession meant getting up at three o'clock in the morning to assuage the ills of humanity; but here, as before, the touch of such a question instantly stiffened him. "Oh, my profession! I am rather ashamed of that matter. I have neglected my work so much, I don't know what I shall be able to do, once I am really settled at home."

Lady Canterville received these remarks in silence; fixing her eyes again upon her husband's face. But this nobleman was really not helpful; still with his hands in his pockets, save when he needed to remove his cigar from his lips, he went and looked out of the window. "Of course we know you don't practise, and when you're a married man you will have less time even than now. But I should really like to know if they call you Doctor over there."

"Oh yes, universally. We are nearly as fond of titles as your people."

"I don't call that a title."

"It's not so good as duke or marquis, I admit; but we have to take what we have got."

"Oh, bother, what does it signify?" Lord Canterville demanded, from his place at the window. "I used to have a horse named Doctor, and a devilish good one too."

"You may call me bishop, if you like," said Jackson Lemon, laughing.

Lady Canterville looked grave, as if she did not enjoy this pleasantry. "I don't care for any titles," she observed; "I don't see why a gentleman shouldn't be called Mr."

It suddenly appeared to Jackson Lemon that there was something helpless, confused, and even slightly comical, in the position of this noble and amiable lady. The impression made him feel kindly; he too, like Lord Canterville, had begun to long for a short cut. He relaxed a moment, and leaning toward his hostess, with a smile and his hands on his little knees, he said softly, "It seems to me a question of no importance; all I desire is that you should call me your son-in-law."

Lady Canterville gave him her hand, and he pressed it almost affectionately. Then she got up, remarking that before anything was decided she must see her daughter, she must learn from her own lips the state of her feelings. "I don't like at all her not having spoken to me already," she added.

"Where has she gone—to Roehampton? I dare say she has told it all to her godmother," said Lord Canterville.

"She won't have much to tell, poor girl!" Jackson Lemon exclaimed. "I must really insist upon seeing with more freedom the person I wish to marry."

"You shall have all the freedom you want, in two or three days," said Lady Canterville. She smiled with all her sweetness; she appeared to have accepted him, and yet still to be making tacit assumptions. "Are there not certain things to be talked of first?"

"Certain things, dear lady?"

Lady Canterville looked at her husband, and though he was still at his window, this time he felt it in her silence, and had to come away and speak. "Oh, she means settlements, and that kind of thing." This was an allusion which came with a much better grace from him.

Jackson Lemon looked from one of his companions to the other; he coloured a little, and gave a smile that was perhaps a trifle fixed. "Settlements? We don't make them in the United States. You may be sure I shall make a proper provision for my wife."

"My dear fellow, over here—in our class, you know, it's the custom," said Lord Canterville, with a richer brightness in his face at the thought that the discussion was over.

"I have my own ideas," Jackson answered, smiling.

"It seems to me it's a question for the solicitors to discuss," Lady Canterville suggested.

"They may discuss it as much as they please," said Jackson Lemon, with a laugh. He thought he saw his solicitors discussing it! He had indeed his own ideas. He opened the door for Lady Canterville, and the three passed out of the room together, walking into the hall in a silence in which there was just a tinge of awkwardness. A note had been struck which grated and scratched a little. A pair of brilliant footmen, at their approach, rose from a bench to a great altitude, and stood there like sentinels presenting arms. Jackson Lemon stopped, looking for a moment into the interior of his hat, which he had in his hand. Then, raising his keen eyes, he fixed them a moment on those of Lady Canterville, addressing her, instinctively, rather than her husband. "I guess you and Lord Canterville had better leave it to me!"

"We have our traditions, Mr Lemon," said her ladyship, with nobleness. "I imagine you don't know——" she murmured.

Lord Canterville laid his hand on the young man's shoulder. "My dear boy, those fellows will settle it in three minutes."

"Very likely they will!" said Jackson Lemon. Then he asked of Lady Canterville when he might see Lady Barb.

She hesitated a moment, in her gracious way. "I will write you a note."

One of the tall footmen, at the end of the impressive vista, had opened wide the portals, as if even he were aware of the dignity to which the little visitor had virtually been raised. But Jackson lingered a moment; he was visibly unsatisfied, though apparently so little unconscious that he was unsatisfying. "I don't think you understand me."

"Your ideas are certainly different," said Lady Canterville.

"If the girl understands you, that's enough!" Lord Canterville exclaimed in a jovial, detached, irrelevant way.

"May not *she* write to me?" Jackson asked of her mother. "I certainly must write to her, you know, if you won't let me see her."

"Oh yes, you may write to her, Mr Lemon."

There was a point for a moment in the look that he gave Lady Canterville, while he said to himself that if it were necessary he would transmit his notes through the old lady at Roehampton. "All right, good-bye; you know what I want, at any rate." Then, as he was going, he turned and added: "You needn't be afraid that I won't bring her over in the hot weather!"

"In the hot weather?" Lady Canterville murmured, with vague visions of the torrid zone, while the young American quitted the house with the sense that he had made great concessions.

His host and hostess passed into a small morning-room, and (Lord Canterville having taken up his hat and stick to go out again) stood there a moment, face to face.

"It's clear enough he wants her," said his lordship, in a summary manner.

"There's something so odd about him," Lady Canterville answered. "Fancy his speaking so about settlements!"

"You had better give him his head; he'll go much quieter."

"He's so obstinate—very obstinate; it's easy to see that. And he seems to think a girl in your daughter's position can be married from one day to the other—with a ring and a new frock—like a housemaid."

"Well, of course, over there, that's the kind of thing. But he seems really to have a most extraordinary fortune; and every one does say their women have *carte blanche*."

"*Carte blanche* is not what Barb wishes; she wishes a settlement. She wants a definite income; she wants to be safe."

Lord Canterville stared a moment. "Has she told you so? I thought you said——" And then he stopped. "I beg your pardon," he added.

Lady Canterville gave no explanation of her inconsistency. She went on to remark that American fortunes were notoriously insecure; one heard of nothing else; they melted away like smoke. It was their duty to their child to demand that something should be fixed.

"He has a million and a half sterling," said Lord Canterville. "I can't make out what he does with it."

"She ought to have something very handsome," his wife remarked.

"Well, my dear, you must settle it: you must consider it; you must send for Hilary. Only take care you don't put him off; it may be a very good opening, you know. There is a great deal to be done out there; I believe in all that," Lord Canterville went on, in the tone of a conscientious parent.

"There is no doubt that he *is* a doctor—in those places," said Lady Canterville, musingly.

"He may be a pedlar for all I care."

"If they should go out, I think Agatha might go with them," her ladyship continued, in the same tone, a little disconnectedly.

"You may send them all out if you like. Good-bye!" And Lord Canterville kissed his wife.

But she detained him a moment, with her hand on his arm. "Don't you think he is very much in love?"

"Oh yes, he's very bad; but he's a clever little beggar."

"She likes him very much," Lady Canterville announced, rather formally, as they separated.

IV

JACKSON LEMON had said to Sidney Feeder in the Park that he would call on Mr and Mrs Freer; but three weeks elapsed before he knocked at their door in Jermyn Street. In the meantime he had met them at dinner, and Mrs Freer had told him that she hoped very much he would find time to come and see her. She had not reproached him, nor shaken her finger at him; and her clemency, which was calculated, and very characteristic of her, touched him so much (for he was in fault; she was one of his mother's oldest and best friends), that he very soon presented himself. It was on a fine Sunday afternoon, rather late, and the region of Jermyn Street looked forsaken and inanimate; the native dulness of the landscape appeared in all its purity. Mrs Freer, however, was at home, resting on a lodging-house sofa—an angular couch, draped in faded chintz—before she went to dress for dinner. She made the young man very welcome; she told him she had been thinking of him a great deal; she had wished to have a chance to talk with him. He immediately perceived what she had in mind, and then he remembered that Sidney Feeder had told him what it was that Mr and Mrs Freer took upon themselves to say. This had provoked him at the time, but he had forgotten it afterward; partly because he became aware, that same evening, that he did wish to marry the "young marchioness," and partly because since then he had had much greater annoyances. Yes, the poor young man, so conscious of liberal intensions, of a large way of looking at the future, had had much to irritate and disgust him. He had seen the mistress of his affections but three or four times, and he had received letters from Mr Hilary, Lord Canterville's solicitor, asking him, in terms the most obsequious, it is true, to designate some gentleman of the law with whom the preliminaries of his marriage to Lady Barberina Clement might be arranged. He had given Mr Hilary the name of such a functionary, but he had written by the same post to his own solicitor (for whose services in other matters he had had much occasion, Jackson Lemon being distinctly contentious), instructing him that he was at liberty to meet Mr Hilary, but not at liberty to entertain any proposals as to this odious English idea of a settlement. If marrying Jackson Lemon were not settlement enough, then Lord and Lady Canterville had better alter their point of view. It was quite out of the question that he should alter his. It would perhaps be difficult to explain the strong aversion that he entertained to the introduction into his prospective union of this harsh diplomatic element; it was as if they mistrusted him, suspected him; as if his hands were to be tied, so that he could not handle his own fortune as he thought best. It was not the idea of parting with his money that displeased him, for he flattered himself that he had plans of expenditure for his wife beyond even the imagination of her distinguished parents. It struck him even that they were fools not to have perceived that they should make a much better thing of it by leaving him perfectly free. This intervention of the solicitor was a nasty little English tradition—totally at variance with the large spirit of American habits—to which he would not submit. It was not his way to submit when he disapproved: why should he change his way on this occasion, when the matter lay so near him? These reflections, and a hundred more, had flowed freely through his mind for several days before he called in

Jermyn Street, and they had engendered a lively indignation and a really bitter sense of wrong. As may be imagined, they had infused a certain awkwardness into his relations with the house of Canterville, and it may be said of these relations that they were for the moment virtually suspended. His first interview with Lady Barb, after his conference with the old couple, as he called her august elders, had been as tender as he could have desired. Lady Canterville, at the end of three days, had sent him an invitation—five words on a card—asking him to dine with them to-morrow, quite *en famille*. This had been the only formal intimation that his engagement to Lady Barb was recognised; for even at the family banquet, which included half a dozen outsiders, there had been no allusion on the part either of his host or his hostess to the subject of their conversation in Lord Canterville's den. The only allusion was a wandering ray, once or twice, in Lady Barberina's eyes. When, however, after dinner, she strolled away with him into the music-room, which was lighted and empty, to play for him something out of *Carmen*, of which he had spoken at table, and when the young couple were allowed to enjoy for upwards of an hour, unmolested, the comparative privacy of this rich apartment, he felt that Lady Canterville definitely counted upon him. She didn't believe in any serious difficulties. Neither did he, then; and that was why it was a nuisance there should be a vain appearance of them. The arrangements, he supposed Lady Canterville would have said, were pending, and indeed they were; for he had already given orders in Bond Street for the setting of an extraordinary number of diamonds. Lady Barb, at any rate, during that hour he spent with her, had had nothing to say about arrangements; and it had been an hour of pure satisfaction. She had seated herself at the piano and had played perpetually, in a soft incoherent manner, while he leaned over the instrument, very close to her, and said everything that came into his head. She was very bright and serene, and she looked at him as if she liked him very much.

This was all he expected of her, for it did not belong to the cast of her beauty to betray a vulgar infatuation. That beauty was more delightful to him than ever; and there was a softness about her which seemed to say to him that from this moment she was quite his own. He felt more than ever the value of such a possession; it came over him more than ever that it had taken a great social outlay to produce such a mixture. Simple and girlish as she was, and not particularly quick in the give and take of conversation, she seemed to him to have a part of the history of England in her blood; she was a *résumé* of generations of privileged people, and of centuries of rich country-life. Between these two, of course, there was no allusion to the question which had been put into the hands of Mr Hilary, and the last thing that occurred to Jackson Lemon was that Lady Barb had views as to his settling a fortune upon her before their marriage. It may appear singular, but he had not asked himself whether his money operated upon her in any degree as a bribe; and this was because, instinctively, he felt that such a speculation was idle,—the point was not to be ascertained,—and because he was willing to assume that it was agreeable to her that she should continue to live in luxury. It was eminently agreeable to him that he might enable her to do so. He was acquainted with the mingled character of human motives, and he was glad that he was rich enough to pretend to the hand of a young woman who, for the best of reasons, would be very expensive. After that happy hour in the music-room he had ridden with her twice; but he had not found her otherwise accessible. She had let him know, the second time they rode, that Lady Canterville had directed her to make, for the moment, no further appointment with him; and on his presenting himself, more than once at the house, he had been told that neither the mother nor the daughter was at home; it had been added that Lady Barberina was staying at Roehampton. On giving him that information in the Park, Lady Barb had looked at him with a mute reproach—there was always a certain superior dumbness in her eyes—as if he were exposing her to an annoyance that she ought to be spared; as if he were taking an eccentric line on a question that all well-bred people treated in the conventional way. His induction from this was not that she wished to be secure about his money, but that, like a dutiful English daughter, she received her opinions (on points that were indifferent to her) ready-made from a mamma whose fallibility had never been exposed. He knew by this that his solicitor had answered Mr Hilary's letter, and that Lady Canterville's coolness was the fruit of this correspondence. The effect of it was not in the least to make him come round, as he phrased it; he had not the smallest intention of doing that. Lady Canterville had spoken of the traditions of her family; but he had no need to go to his family for his own. They resided within himself; anything that he had definitely made up his mind to, acquired in an hour a kind of legendary force. Meanwhile, he was in the detestable position of not knowing whether or no he were engaged. He wrote to Lady Barb to inquire—it being so strange that she should not receive him; and she answered in a very pretty little letter, which had to his mind a sort of bygone quality, an old-fashioned freshness, as if it might have been written in the last century by Clarissa or Amelia: she answered that she did not in the least understand the situation; that, of course, she would never give him up; that her mother had said that there were the best reasons for their not going too fast; that, thank God, she was yet young, and could wait as long as he would; but that she begged he wouldn't write her anything about money-matters, as she could never comprehend them. Jackson felt that he was in no danger whatever of making this last mistake; he only noted how Lady Barb thought it natural that there should be a discussion; and this made it vivid to him afresh that he had got hold of a daughter of the Crusaders. His ingenious mind could appreciate this hereditary assumption perfectly, at the same time that, to

light his own footsteps, it remained entirely modern. He
believed—or he thought he believed—that in the end he
should marry Barberina Clement on his own terms; but in
the interval there was a sensible indignity in being challenged
and checked. One effect of it, indeed, was to make him desire
the girl more keenly. When she was not before his eyes in the
flesh, she hovered before him as an image; and this image
had reasons of its own for being a radiant picture. There were
moments, however, when he wearied of looking at it; it was
so impalpable and thankless, and then Jackson Lemon, for
the first time in his life, was melancholy. He felt alone in
London, and very much out of it, in spite of all the acquaintances he had made, and the bills he had paid; he felt the need
of a greater intimacy than any he had formed (save, of course,
in the case of Lady Barb). He wanted to vent his disgust, to
relieve himself, from the American point of view. He felt
that in engaging in a contest with the great house of Canterville he was, after all, rather single. That singleness was, of
course, in a great measure an inspiration; but it pinched him
a little at moments. Then he wished his mother had been in
London, for he used to talk of his affairs a great deal with this
delightful parent, who had a soothing way of advising him in
the sense he liked best. He had even gone so far as to wish he
had never laid eyes on Lady Barb and had fallen in love with
some transatlantic maiden of a similar composition. He presently came back, of course, to the knowledge that in the
United States there was—and there could be—nothing similar
to Lady Barb; for was it not precisely as a product of the
English climate and the British constitution that he valued her?
He had relieved himself, from his American point of view,
by speaking his mind to Lady Beauchemin, who confessed
that she was very much vexed with her parents. She agreed
with him that they had made a great mistake; they ought to
have left him free; and she expressed her confidence that that
freedom would be for her family, as it were, like the silence

of the sage, golden. He must excuse them; he must remember
that what was asked of him had been their custom for centuries. She did not mention her authority as to the origin of
customs, but she assured him that she would say three words
to her father and mother which would make it all right. Jackson answered that customs were all very well, but that intelligent people recognised, when they saw it, the right occasion
for departing from them; and with this he awaited the result
of Lady Beauchemin's remonstrance. It had not as yet been
perceptible, and it must be said that this charming woman was
herself much bothered. When, on her venturing to say to her
mother that she thought a wrong line had been taken with
regard to her sister's *prétendant*, Lady Canterville had replied
that Mr Lemon's unwillingness to settle anything was in itself
a proof of what they had feared, the unstable nature of his
fortune (for it was useless to talk—this gracious lady could
be very decided—there could be no serious reason but that
one): on meeting this argument, as I say, Jackson's protectress
felt considerably baffled. It was perhaps true, as her mother
said, that if they didn't insist upon proper guarantees Barberina might be left in a few years with nothing but the stars
and stripes (this odd phrase was a quotation from Mr Lemon)
to cover her. Lady Beauchemin tried to reason it out with
Lady Marmaduke; but these were complications unforeseen
by Lady Marmaduke in her project of an Anglo-American
society. She was obliged to confess that Mr Lemon's fortune
could not have the solidity of long-established things; it was
a very new fortune indeed. His father had made the greater
part of it all in a lump, a few years before his death, in the
extraordinary way in which people made money in America;
that, of course, was why the son had those singular professional attributes. He had begun to study to be a doctor very
young, before his expectations were so great. Then he had
found he was very clever, and very fond of it; and he had
kept on, because, after all, in America, where there were no

country-gentlemen, a young man had to have something to do, don't you know? And Lady Marmaduke, like an enlightened woman, intimated that in such a case she thought it in much better taste not to try to sink anything. "Because, in America, don't you see," she reasoned, "you can't sink it—nothing *will* sink. Everything is floating about—in the newspapers." And she tried to console her friend by remarking that if Mr Lemon's fortune was precarious, it was at all events so big. That was just the trouble for Lady Beauchemin; it was so big, and yet they were going to lose it. He was as obstinate as a mule; she was sure he would never come round. Lady Marmaduke declared that he would come round; she even offered to bet a dozen pair of *gants de Suède* on it; and she added that this consummation lay quite in the hands of Barberina. Lady Beauchemin promised herself to converse with her sister; for it was not for nothing that she herself had felt the international contagion.

Jackson Lemon, to dissipate his chagrin, had returned to the sessions of the medical congress, where, inevitably, he had fallen into the hands of Sidney Feeder, who enjoyed in this disinterested assembly a high popularity. It was Doctor Feeder's earnest desire that his old friend should share it, which was all the more easy as the medical congress was really, as the young physician observed, a perpetual symposium. Jackson Lemon entertained the whole body—entertained it profusely, and in a manner befitting one of the patrons of science rather than its humbler votaries; but these dissipations only made him forget for a moment that his relations with the house of Canterville were anomalous. His great difficulty punctually came back to him, and Sidney Feeder saw it stamped upon his brow. Jackson Lemon, with his acute inclination to open himself, was on the point, more than once, of taking the sympathetic Sidney into his confidence. His friend gave him easy opportunity; he asked him what it was he was thinking of all the time, and whether the young

marchioness had concluded she couldn't swallow a doctor.
These forms of speech were displeasing to Jackson Lemon,
whose fastidiousness was nothing new; but it was for even
deeper reasons that he said to himself that, for such complicated cases as his, there was no assistance in Sidney Feeder. To
understand his situation one must know the world; and the
child of Cincinnati didn't know the world—at least the world
with which his friend was now concerned.

"Is there a hitch in your marriage? Just tell me that,"
Sidney Feeder had said, taking everything for granted, in a
manner which was in itself a proof of great innocence. It is
true he had added that he supposed he had no business to ask;
but he had been anxious about it ever since hearing from Mr
and Mrs Freer that the British aristocracy was down on the
medical profession. "Do they want you to give it up? Is that
what the hitch is about? Don't desert your colours, Jackson.
The elimination of pain, the mitigation of misery, constitute
surely the noblest profession in the world."

"My dear fellow, you don't know what you are talking
about," Jackson observed, for answer to this. "I haven't told
any one I was going to be married; still less have I told any
one that any one objected to my profession. I should like to
see them do it. I have got out of the swim to-day, but I don't
regard myself as the sort of person that people object to. And
I do expect to do something, yet."

"Come home, then, and do it. And excuse me if I say that
the facilities for getting married are much greater over there."

"You don't seem to have found them very great."

"I have never had time. Wait till my next vacation, and
you will see."

"The facilities over there are too great. Nothing is good
but what is difficult," said Jackson Lemon, in a tone of artificial sententiousness that quite tormented his interlocutor.

"Well, they have got their backs up, I can see that. I'm
glad you like it. Only if they despise your profession, what

will they say to that of your friends? If they think you are
queer, what would they think of me?" asked Sidney Feeder,
the turn of whose mind was not, as a general thing, in the least
sarcastic, but who was pushed to this sharpness by a conviction that (in spite of declarations which seemed half an
admission and half a denial) his friend was suffering himself
to be bothered for the sake of a good which might be
obtained elsewhere without bother. It had come over him
that the bother was of an unworthy kind.

"My dear fellow, all that is idiotic." That had been Jackson Lemon's reply; but it expressed but a portion of his
thoughts. The rest was inexpressible, or almost; being connected with a sentiment of rage at its having struck even so
genial a mind as Sidney Feeder's that, in proposing to marry
a daughter of the highest civilisation, he was going out of his
way—departing from his natural line. Was he then so ignoble,
so pledged to inferior things, that when he saw a girl who
(putting aside the fact that she had not genius, which was
rare, and which, though he prized rarity, he didn't want)
seemed to him the most complete feminine nature he had
known, he was to think himself too different, too incongruous,
to mate with her? He would mate with whom he chose; that
was the upshot of Jackson Lemon's reflections. Several days
elapsed, during which everybody—even the pure-minded,
like Sidney Feeder—seemed to him very abject.

I relate all this to show why it was that in going to see Mrs
Freer he was prepared much less to be angry with people
who, like the Dexter Freers, a month before, had given it out
that he was engaged to a peer's daughter, than to resent the
insinuation that there were obstacles to such a prospect. He
sat with Mrs Freer alone for half an hour in the sabbatical
stillness of Jermyn Street. Her husband had gone for a walk
in the Park; he always walked in the Park on Sunday. All the
world might have been there, and Jackson and Mrs Freer in
sole possession of the district of St James's. This perhaps

had something to do with making him at last rather confidential; the influences were conciliatory, persuasive. Mrs Freer was extremely sympathetic; she treated him like a person she had known from the age of ten; asked his leave to continue recumbent; talked a great deal about his mother; and seemed almost for a while to perform the kindly functions of that lady. It had been wise of her from the first not to allude, even indirectly, to his having neglected so long to call; her silence on this point was in the best taste. Jackson Lemon had forgotten that it was a habit with her, and indeed a high accomplishment, never to reproach people with these omissions. You might have left her alone for two years, her greeting was always the same; she was never either too delighted to see you or not delighted enough. After a while, however, he perceived that her silence had been to a certain extent a reference; she appeared to take for granted that he devoted all his hours to a certain young lady. It came over him for a moment that his country people took a great deal for granted; but when Mrs Freer, rather abruptly, sitting up on her sofa, said to him, half simply, half solemnly, "And now, my dear Jackson, I want you to tell me something!"—he perceived that after all she didn't pretend to know more about the impending matter than he himself did. In the course of a quarter of an hour—so appreciatively she listened—he had told her a good deal about it. It was the first time he had said so much to any one, and the process relieved him even more than he would have supposed. It made certain things clear to him, by bringing them to a point—above all, the fact that he had been wronged. He made no allusion whatever to its being out of the usual way that, as an American doctor, he should sue for the hand of a marquis's daughter; and this reserve was not voluntary, it was quite unconscious. His mind was too full of the offensive conduct of the Cantervilles, and the sordid side of their want of confidence. He could not imagine that while he talked to Mrs Freer—and it amazed him afterward that he should have

chattered so; he could account for it only by the state of his
nerves—she should be thinking only of the strangeness of
the situation he sketched for her. She thought Americans as
good as other people, but she didn't see where, in American
life, the daughter of a marquis would, as she phrased it, work
in. To take a simple instance,—they coursed through Mrs
Freer's mind with extraordinary speed—would she not always
expect to go in to dinner first? As a novelty, over there, they
might like to see her do it, at first; there might be even a pressure for places for the spectacle. But with the increase of every
kind of sophistication that was taking place in America, the
humorous view to which she would owe her safety might
not continue to be taken; and then where would Lady Barberina be? This was but a small instance; but Mrs Freer's
vivid imagination—much as she lived in Europe, she knew
her native land so well—saw a host of others massing themselves behind it. The consequence of all of which was that
after listening to him in the most engaging silence, she raised
her clasped hands, pressed them against her breast, lowered
her voice to a tone of entreaty, and, with her perpetual little
smile, uttered three words: "My dear Jackson, don't—don't
—don't."

"Don't what?" he asked, staring.

"Don't neglect the chance you have of getting out of it;
it would never do."

He knew what she meant by his chance of getting out of it;
in his many meditations he had, of course, not overlooked
that. The ground the old couple had taken about settlements
(and the fact that Lady Beauchemin had not come back to
him to tell him, as she promised, that she had moved them,
proved how firmly they were rooted) would have offered
an all-sufficient pretext to a man who should have repented
of his advances. Jackson Lemon knew that; but he knew at the
same time that he had not repented. The old couple's want of
imagination did not in the least alter the fact that Barberina

was, as he had told her father, a beautiful type. Therefore he simply said to Mrs Freer that he didn't in the least wish to get out of it; he was as much in it as ever, and he intended to remain there. But what did she mean, he inquired in a moment, by her statement that it would never do? Why wouldn't it do? Mrs Freer replied by another inquiry—Should he really like her to tell him? It wouldn't do, because Lady Barb would not be satisfied with her place at dinner. She would not be content—in a society of commoners—with any but the best; and the best she could not expect (and it was to be supposed that he did not expect her) always to have.

"What do you mean by commoners?" Jackson Lemon demanded, looking very serious.

"I mean you, and me, and my poor husband, and Dr Feeder," said Mrs Freer.

"I don't see how there can be commoners where there are not lords. It is the lord that makes the commoner; and *vice versâ*."

"Won't a lady do as well? Lady Barberina—a single English girl—can make a million inferiors."

"She will be, before anything else, my wife; and she will not talk about inferiors any more than I do. I never do; it's very vulgar."

"I don't know what she'll talk about, my dear Jackson, but she will think; and her thoughts won't be pleasant—I mean for others. Do you expect to sink her to your own rank?"

Jackson Lemon's bright little eyes were fixed more brightly than ever upon his hostess. "I don't understand you; and I don't think you understand yourself." This was not absolutely candid, for he did understand Mrs Freer to a certain extent; it has been related that, before he asked Lady Barb's hand of her parents, there had been moments when he himself was not very sure that the flower of the British aristocracy would flourish in American soil. But an intimation from another person that it was beyond his power to pass off his wife—whether she were the daughter of a peer or of a shoe-maker—set all his blood on fire. It quenched on the instant his own perception of difficulties of detail, and made him feel only that he was dishonoured—he, the heir of all the ages—by such insinuations. It was his belief—though he had never before had occasion to put it forward—that his position, one of the best in the world, was one of those positions that make everything possible. He had had the best education the age could offer, for if he had rather wasted his time at Harvard, where he entered very young, he had, as he believed, been tremendously serious at Heidelberg and at Vienna. He had devoted himself to one of the noblest of professions—a pro-fession recognised as such everywhere but in England—and he had inherited a fortune far beyond the expectation of his earlier years, the years when he cultivated habits of work which alone—or rather in combination with talents that he neither exaggerated nor minimised—would have conduced to distinction. He was one of the most fortunate inhabitants of an immense, fresh, rich country, a country whose future was admitted to be incalculable, and he moved with perfect ease in a society in which he was not overshadowed by others. It seemed to him, therefore, beneath his dignity to wonder whether he could afford, socially speaking, to marry accord-ing to his taste. Jackson Lemon pretended to be strong; and what was the use of being strong it you were not pre-pared to undertake things that timid people might find diffi-cult? It was his plan to marry the woman he liked, and not to be afraid of her afterward. The effect of Mrs Freer's doubt of his success was to represent to him that his own character would not cover his wife's; she couldn't have made him feel otherwise if she had told him that he was marrying beneath him, and would have to ask for indulgence. "I don't believe you know how much I think that any woman who marries me will be doing very well," he added, directly.

"I am very sure of that; but it isn't so simple—one's being an American," Mrs Freer rejoined, with a little philosophic sigh.

"It's whatever one chooses to make it."

"Well, you'll make it what no one has done yet, if you take that young lady to America and make her happy there."

"Do you think it's such a very dreadful place?"

"No, indeed; but she will."

Jackson Lemon got up from his chair, and took up his hat and stick. He had actually turned a little pale, with the force of his emotion; it had made him really quiver that his marriage to Lady Barberina should be looked at as too high a flight. He stood a moment leaning against the mantelpiece, and very much tempted to say to Mrs Freer that she was a vulgar-minded old woman. But he said something that was really more to the point: "You forget that she will have her consolations."

"Don't go away, or I shall think I have offended you. You can't console a wounded marchioness."

"How will she be wounded? People will be charming to her."

"They will be charming to her—charming to her!" These words fell from the lips of Dexter Freer, who had opened the door of the room and stood with the knob in his hand, putting himself into relation to his wife's talk with their visitor. This was accomplished in an instant. "Of course I know whom you mean," he said, while he exchanged greetings with Jackson Lemon. "My wife and I—of course you know we are great busybodies—have talked of your affair, and we differ about it completely: she sees only the dangers, and I see the advantages."

"By the advantages he means the fun for us," Mrs Freer remarked, settling her sofa-cushions.

Jackson looked with a certain sharp blankness from one of these disinterested judges to the other; and even yet they did not perceive how their misdirected familiarities wrought upon him. It was hardly more agreeable to him to know that the husband wished to see Lady Barb in America, than to know that the wife had a dread of such a vision; for there was that in Dexter Freer's face which seemed to say that the thing would take place somehow for the benefit of the spectators. "I think you both see too much—a great deal too much," he answered, rather coldly.

"My dear young man, at my age I can take certain liberties," said Dexter Freer. "Do it—I beseech you to do it; it has never been done before." And then, as if Jackson's glance had challenged this last assertion, he went on: "Never, I assure you, this particular thing. Young female members of the British aristocracy have married coachmen and fishmongers, and all that sort of thing; but they have never married you and me."

"They certainly haven't married you," said Mrs Freer.

"I am much obliged to you for your advice." It may be thought that Jackson Lemon took himself rather seriously; and indeed I am afraid that if he had not done so there would have been no occasion for my writing this little history. But it made him almost sick to hear his engagement spoken of as a curious and ambiguous phenomenon. He might have his own ideas about it—one always had about one's engagement: but the ideas that appeared to have peopled the imagination of his friends ended by kindling a little hot spot in each of his cheeks. "I would rather not talk any more about my little plans," he added to Dexter Freer. "I have been saying all sorts of absurd things to Mrs Freer."

"They have been most interesting," that lady declared. "You have been very stupidly treated."

"May she tell me when you go?" her husband asked of the young man.

"I am going now; she may tell you whatever she likes."

"I am afraid we have displeased you," said Mrs Freer; "I

have said too much what I think. You must excuse me, it's all for your mother."

"It's she whom I want Lady Barberina to see!" Jackson Lemon exclaimed, with the inconsequence of filial affection.

"Deary me!" murmured Mrs Freer.

"We shall go back to America to see how you get on," her husband said; "and if you succeed, it will be a great precedent."

"Oh, I shall succeed!" And with this he took his departure. He walked away with the quick step of a man labouring under a certain excitement; walked up to Piccadilly and down past Hyde Park Corner. It relieved him to traverse these distances, for he was thinking hard, under the influence of irritation; and locomotion helped him to think. Certain suggestions that had been made him in the last half hour rankled in his mind, all the more that they seemed to have a kind of representative value, to be an echo of the common voice. If his prospects wore that face to Mrs Freer, they would probably wear it to others; and he felt a sudden need of showing such others that they took a pitiful measure of his position. Jackson Lemon walked and walked till he found himself on the highway of Hammersmith. I have represented him as a young man of much strength of purpose, and I may appear to undermine this plea when I relate that he wrote that evening to his solicitor that Mr Hilary was to be informed that he would agree to any proposals for settlements that Mr Hilary should make. Jackson's strength of purpose was shown in his deciding to marry Lady Barberina on any terms. It seemed to him, under the influence of his desire to prove that he was not afraid—so odious was the imputation—that terms of any kind were very superficial things. What was fundamental, and of the essence of the matter, would be to marry Lady Barb and carry everything out.

V

"On Sundays, now, you might be at home," Jackson Lemon said to his wife in the following month of March, more than six months after his marriage.

"Are the people any nicer on Sundays than they are on other days?" Lady Barberina replied, from the depths of her chair, without looking up from a stiff little book.

He hesitated a single instant before answering: "I don't know whether they are, but I think you might be."

"I am as nice as I know how to be. You must take me as I am. You knew when you married me that I was not an American."

Jackson Lemon stood before the fire, towards which his wife's face was turned and her feet were extended; stood there some time, with his hands behind him and his eyes dropped a little obliquely upon the bent head and richly-draped figure of Lady Barberina. It may be said without delay that he was irritated, and it may be added that he had a double cause. He felt himself to be on the verge of the first crisis that had occurred between himself and his wife—the reader will perceive that it had occurred rather promptly—and he was annoyed at his annoyance. A glimpse of his state of mind before his marriage has been given to the reader, who will remember that at that period Jackson Lemon somehow regarded himself as lifted above possibilities of irritation. When one was strong, one was not irritable; and a union with a kind of goddess would of course be an element of strength. Lady Barb was a goddess still, and Jackson Lemon admired his wife as much as the day he led her to the altar; but I am not sure that he felt so strong.

"How do you know what people are?" he said in a moment. "You have seen so few; you are perpetually denying yourself. If you should leave New York to-morrow you would know wonderfully little about it."

"It's all the same," said Lady Barb; "the people are all exactly alike."

"How can you tell? You never see them."

"Didn't I go out every night for the first two months we were here?"

"It was only to about a dozen houses—always the same; people, moreover, you had already met in London. You have got no general impressions."

"That's just what I have got; I had them before I came. Every one is just the same; they have just the same names— just the same manners."

Again, for an instant, Jackson Lemon hesitated; then he said, in that apparently artless tone of which mention has already been made, and which he sometimes used in London during his wooing: "Don't you like it over here?"

Lady Barb raised her eyes from her book. "Did you expect me to like it?"

"I hoped you would, of course. I think I told you so."

"I don't remember. You said very little about it; you seemed to make a kind of mystery. I knew, of course, you expected me to live here, but I didn't know you expected me to like it."

"You thought I asked of you the sacrifice, as it were."

"I am sure I don't know," said Lady Barb. She got up from her chair and tossed the volume she had been reading into the empty seat. "I recommend you to read that book," she added.

"Is it interesting?"

"It's an American novel."

"I never read novels."

"You had better look at that one; it will show you the kind of people you want me to know."

"I have no doubt it's very vulgar," said Jackson Lemon; "I don't see why you read it."

"What else can I do? I can't always be riding in the Park; I hate the Park," Lady Barb remarked.

"It's quite as good as your own," said her husband.

She glanced at him with a certain quickness, her eyebrows slightly lifted. "Do you mean the park at Pasterns?"

"No; I mean the park in London."

"I don't care about London. One was only in London a few weeks."

"I suppose you miss the country," said Jackson Lemon. It was his idea of life that he should not be afraid of anything, not be afraid, in any situation, of knowing the worst that was to be known about it; and the demon of a courage with which discretion was not properly commingled prompted him to take soundings which were perhaps not absolutely necessary for safety, and yet which revealed unmistakable rocks. It was useless to know about rocks if he couldn't avoid them; the only thing was to trust to the wind.

"I don't know what I miss. I think I miss everything!" This was his wife's answer to his too curious inquiry. It was not peevish, for that is not the tone of a goddess; but it expressed a good deal—a good deal more than Lady Barb, who was rarely eloquent, had expressed before. Nevertheless, though his question had been precipitate, Jackson Lemon said to himself that he might take his time to think over what his wife's little speech contained; he could not help seeing that the future would give him abundant opportunity for that. He was in no hurry to ask himself whether poor Mrs Freer, in Jermyn Street, might not, after all, have been right in saying that, in regard to marrying the product of an English caste, it was not so simple to be an American doctor—might avail little even, in such a case, to be the heir of all the ages. The transition was complicated, but in his bright mind it was rapid, from the brush of a momentary contact with such ideas to certain considerations which led him to say, after an instant, to his wife, "Should you like to go down into Connecticut?"

"Into Connecticut?"

"That's one of our States; it's about as large as Ireland. I'll take you there if you like."

"What does one do there?"

"We can try and get some hunting."

"You and I alone?"

"Perhaps we can get a party to join us."

"The people in the State?"

"Yes; we might propose it to them."

"The tradespeople in the towns?"

"Very true; they will have to mind their shops," said Jackson Lemon. "But we might hunt alone."

"Are there any foxes?"

"No; but there are a few old cows."

Lady Barb had already perceived that her husband took it into his head once in a while to laugh at her, and she was aware that the present occasion was neither worse nor better than some others. She didn't mind it particularly now, though in England it would have disgusted her; she had the consciousness of virtue—an immense comfort—and flattered herself that she had learned the lesson of an altered standard of fitness; there were, moreover, so many more disagreeable things in America than being laughed at by one's husband. But she pretended to mind it, because it made him stop, and above all it stopped discussion, which with Jackson was so often jocular, and none the less tiresome for that. "I only want to be left alone," she said, in answer—though, indeed, it had not the manner of an answer—to his speech about the cows. With this she wandered away to one of the windows which looked out on the Fifth Avenue. She was very fond of these windows, and she had taken a great fancy to the Fifth Avenue, which, in the high-pitched winter weather, when everything sparkled, was a spectacle full of novelty. It will be seen that she was not wholly unjust to her adoptive country: she found it delightful to look out of the window. This was a pleasure she had enjoyed in London only in the most furtive manner; it was not the kind of thing that girls did in England. Besides, in London, in Hill Street, there was nothing particular to see; but in the Fifth Avenue everything and every one went by, and observation was made consistent with dignity by the masses of brocade and lace in which the windows were draped, which, somehow, would not have been tidy in England, and which made an ambush without concealing the brilliant day. Hundreds of women—the curious women of New York, who were unlike any that Lady Barb had hitherto seen—passed the house every hour, and her ladyship was infinitely entertained and mystified by the sight of their clothes. She spent a good deal more time than she was aware of in this amusement; and if she had been addicted to returning upon herself, or asking herself for an account of her conduct—an inquiry which she did not, indeed, completely neglect, but treated very cursorily—it would have made her smile sadly to think what she appeared mainly to have come to America for, conscious though she was that her tastes were very simple, and that so long as she didn't hunt, it didn't much matter what she did.

Her husband turned about to the fire, giving a push with his foot to a log that had fallen out of its place. Then he said—and the connection with the words she had just uttered was apparent enough—"You really must be at home on Sundays, you know. I used to like that so much in London. All the best women here do it. You had better begin to-day. I am going to see my mother; if I meet any one I will tell them to come."

"Tell them not to talk so much," said Lady Barb, among her lace curtains.

"Ah, my dear," her husband replied, "it isn't every one that has your concision!" And he went and stood behind her in the window, putting his arm round her waist. It was as much of a satisfaction to him as it had been six months before, at the time the solicitors were settling the matter, that this flower of an ancient stem should be worn upon his own breast; he still thought its fragrance a thing quite apart, and it was as clear as day to him that his wife was the handsomest woman in New York. He had begun, after their arrival, by telling her this very often; but the assurance brought no colour to her cheek, no light to her eyes; to be the handsomest woman in New York evidently did not seem to her a position in life. Moreover, the reader may be informed that, oddly enough, Lady Barb did not particularly believe this assertion. There were some very pretty women in New York, and without in the least wishing to be like them—she had seen no woman in America whom she desired to resemble—she envied some of their elements. It is probable that her own finest points were those of which she was most unconscious. But her husband was aware of all of them; nothing could exceed the minuteness of his appreciation of his wife. It was a sign of this that after he had stood behind her a moment he kissed her very tenderly. "Have you any message for my mother?" he asked.

"Please give her my love. And you might take her that book."

"What book?"

"That nasty one I have been reading."

"Oh, bother your books," said Jackson Lemon, with a certain irritation, as he went out of the room.

There had been a good many things in her life in New York that cost Lady Barb an effort; but sending her love to her mother-in-law was not one of these. She liked Mrs Lemon better than any one she had seen in America; she was the only person who seemed to Lady Barb really simple, as she understood that quality. Many people had struck her as homely and rustic, and many others as pretentious and vulgar; but in

Jackson's mother she had found the golden mean of a simplicity which, as she would have said, was really nice. Her sister, Lady Agatha, was even fonder of Mrs Lemon; but then Lady Agatha had taken the most extraordinary fancy to every one and everything, and talked as if America were the most delightful country in the world. She was having a lovely time (she already spoke the most beautiful American), and had been, during the winter that was just drawing to a close, the most prominent girl in New York. She had gone out at first with her sister; but for some weeks past Lady Barb had let so many occasions pass, that Agatha threw herself into the arms of Mrs Lemon, who found her extraordinarily quaint and amusing and was delighted to take her into society. Mrs Lemon, as an old woman, had given up such vanities; but she only wanted a motive, and in her good nature she ordered a dozen new caps and sat smiling against the wall while her little English maid, on polished floors, to the sound of music, cultivated the American step as well as the American tone. There was no trouble, in New York, about going out, and the winter was not half over before the little English maid found herself an accomplished diner, rolling about, without any chaperon at all, to banquets where she could count upon a bouquet at her plate. She had had a great deal of correspondence with her mother on this point, and Lady Canterville at last withdrew her protest, which in the meantime had been perfectly useless. If was ultimately Lady Canterville's feeling that if she had married the handsomest of her daughters to an American doctor, she might let another become a professional *raconteuse* (Agatha had written to her that she was expected to talk so much), strange as such a destiny seemed for a girl of nineteen. Mrs Lemon was even a much simpler woman than Lady Barberina thought her; for she had not noticed that Lady Agatha danced much oftener with Herman Longstraw than with any one else. Jackson Lemon, though he went little to balls, had discovered this truth, and he looked slightly preoccupied when, after he had sat five minutes with his mother on the Sunday afternoon through which I have invited the reader to trace so much more than (I am afraid) is easily apparent of the progress of this simple story, he learned that his sister-in-law was entertaining Mr Longstraw in the library. He had called half an hour before, and she had taken him into the other room to show him the seal of the Cantervilles, which she had fastened to one of her numerous trinkets (she was adorned with a hundred bangles and chains), and the proper exhibition of which required a taper and a stick of wax. Apparently he was examining it very carefully, for they had been absent a good while. Mrs Lemon's simplicity was further shown by the fact that she had not measured their absence; it was only when Jackson questioned her that she remembered.

Herman Longstraw was a young Californian who had turned up in New York the winter before, and who travelled on his moustache, as they were understood to say in his native State. This moustache, and some of the accompanying features, were very ornamental; several ladies in New York had been known to declare that they were as beautiful as a dream. Taken in connection with his tall stature, his familiar good-nature, and his remarkable Western vocabulary, they constituted his only social capital; for of the two great divisions, the rich Californians and the poor Californians, it was well known to which he belonged. Jackson Lemon looked at him as a slightly mitigated cowboy, and was somewhat vexed at his dear mother, though he was aware that she could scarcely figure to herself what an effect such an accent as that would produce in the halls of Canterville. He had no desire whatever to play a trick on the house to which he was allied, and knew perfectly that Lady Agatha had not been sent to America to become entangled with a Californian of the wrong denomination. He had been perfectly willing to bring her; he thought, a little vindictively, that this would operate as a hint to her parents as to what he might have been inclined to do if they had not sent Mr Hilary after him. Herman Longstraw, according to the legend, had been a trapper, a squatter, a miner, a pioneer—had been everything that one could be in the romantic parts of America, and had accumulated masses of experience before the age of thirty. He had shot bears in the Rockies and buffaloes on the plains; and it was even believed that he had brought down animals of a still more dangerous kind, among the haunts of men. There had been a story that he owned a cattle-ranch in Arizona; but a later and apparently more authentic version of it, though it represented him as looking after the cattle, did not depict him as their proprietor. Manÿ of the stories told about him were false; but there is no doubt that his moustache, his good-nature and his accent were genuine. He danced very badly; but Lady Agatha had frankly told several persons that that was nothing new to her; and she liked (this, however, she did not tell) Mr Herman Longstraw. What she enjoyed in America was the revelation of freedom; and there was no such proof of freedom as conversation with a gentleman who dressed in skins when he was not in New York, and who, in his usual pursuits, carried his life (as well as that of other people) in his hand. A gentleman whom she had sat next to at a dinner in the early part of her stay in New York, remarked to her that the United States were the paradise of women and mechanics; and this had seemed to her at the time very abstract, for she was not conscious, as yet, of belonging to either class. In England she had been only a girl; and the principal idea connected with that was simply that, for one's misfortune, one was not a boy. But presently she perceived that New York was a paradise; and this helped her to know that she must be one of the people mentioned in the axiom of her neighbour—people who could do whatever they wanted, had a voice in everything, and made their taste and their ideas felt. She saw that it was great fun to be a woman in America, and that this was the best way to enjoy the New York winter—the wonderful, brilliant New York winter, the queer, long-shaped, glittering city, the heterogeneous hours, among which you couldn't tell the morning from the afternoon or the night from either of them, the perpetual liberties and walks, the rushings-out and the droppings-in, the intimacies, the endearments, the comicalities, the sleigh-bells, the cutters, the sunsets on the snow, the ice-parties in the frosty clearness, the bright, hot, velvety houses, the bouquets, the bonbons, the little cakes, the big cakes, the irrepressible inspirations of shopping, the innumerable luncheons and dinners that were offered to youth and innocence, the quantities of chatter of quantities of girls, the perpetual motion of the German, the suppers at restaurants after the play, the way in which life was pervaded by Delmonico and Delmonico by the sense that though one's hunting was lost and this so different, it was almost as good—and in all, through all, a kind of suffusion of bright, loud, friendly sound, which was very local, but very human.

Lady Agatha at present was staying, for a little change, with Mrs Lemon, and such adventures as that were part of the pleasure of her American season. The house was too close; but physically the girl could bear anything, and it was all she had to complain of; for Mrs Lemon, as we know, thought her a bonnie little damsel, and had none of those old-world scruples in regard to spoiling young people to which Lady Agatha now perceived that she herself, in the past, had been unduly sacrificed. In her own way—it was not at all her sister's way—she liked to be of importance; and this was assuredly the case when she saw that Mrs Lemon had apparently nothing in the world to do (after spending a part of the morning with her servants) but invent little distractions (many of them of the edible sort) for her guest. She appeared to have certain friends, but she had no society to speak of, and the people who came into her house came principally to see Lady Agatha. This, as we have seen, was strikingly the case with Herman Longstraw. The whole situation gave Lady Agatha a great feeling of success—success of a new and unexpected kind. Of course, in England, she had been born successful, in a manner, in coming into the world in one of the most beautiful rooms at Pasterns; but her present triumph was achieved more by her own effort (not that she had tried very hard) and by her merit. It was not so much what she said (for she could never say half as much as the girls in New York), as the spirit of enjoyment that played in her fresh young face, with its pointless curves, and shone in her gray English eyes. She enjoyed everything, even the street-cars, of which she made liberal use; and more than everything she enjoyed Mr Longstraw and his talk about buffaloes and bears. Mrs Lemon promised to be very careful, as soon as her son had begun to warn her; and this time she had a certain understanding of what she promised. She thought people ought to make the matches they liked; she had given proof of this in her late behaviour to Jackson, whose own union was, in her opinion, marked with all the arbitrariness of pure love. Nevertheless, she could see that Herman Longstraw would probably be thought rough in England; and it was not simply that he was so inferior to Jackson, for, after all, certain things were not to be expected. Jackson Lemon was not oppressed with his mother-in-law, having taken his precautions against such a danger; but he was aware that he should give Lady Canterville a permanent advantage over him if, while she was in America, her daughter Agatha should attach herself to a mere moustache.

It was not always, as I have hinted, that Mrs Lemon entered completely into the views of her son, though in form she never failed to subscribe to them devoutly. She had never yet, for instance, apprehended his reason for marrying Lady Barberina Clement. This was a great secret, and Mrs Lemon was determined that no one should ever know it. For herself, she was sure that, to the end of time, she should not discover Jackson's reason. She could never ask about it, for that of course would betray her. From the first she had told him she was delighted; there being no need of asking for explanations then, as the young lady herself, when she should come to know her, would explain. But the young lady had not yet explained; and after this, evidently, she never would. She was very tall, very handsome, she answered exactly to Mrs Lemon's prefigurement of the daughter of a lord, and she wore her clothes, which were peculiar, but, to her, remarkably becoming, very well. But she did not elucidate; we know ourselves that there was very little that was explanatory about Lady Barb. So Mrs Lemon continued to wonder, to ask herself, "Why that one, more than so many others, who would have been more natural?" The choice appeared to her, as I have said, very arbitrary. She found Lady Barb very different from other girls she had known, and this led her almost immediately to feel sorry for her daughter-in-law. She said to herself that Barb was to be pitied if she found her husband's people as peculiar as his mother found *her;* for the result of that would be to make her very lonesome. Lady Agatha was different, because she seemed to keep nothing back; you saw all there was of her, and she was evidently not home-sick. Mrs Lemon could see that Barberina was ravaged by this last passion and was too proud to show it. She even had a glimpse of the ultimate truth; namely, that Jackson's wife had not the comfort of crying, because that would have amounted to a confession that she had been idiotic enough to believe in advance that, in an American town, in the society of doctors, she should escape such pangs. Mrs Lemon treated her with the greatest gentleness—all the gentleness that was due to a young woman who was in the unfortunate position of having been married one couldn't tell why. The world, to Mrs Lemon's view, contained two great departments—that of persons, and that of things; and she believed that you must take an interest either in one or the other. The incomprehensible thing in Lady Barb was that she cared for neither side of the show. Her house apparently inspired her with no curiosity and no enthusiasm, though it had been thought magnificent enough to be described in successive columns of the American newspapers; and she never spoke of her furniture or her domestics, though she had a prodigious supply of such possessions. She was the same with regard to her acquaintance, which was immense, inasmuch as every one in the place had called on her. Mrs Lemon was the least critical woman in the world; but it had sometimes exasperated her just a little that her daughter-in-law should receive every one in New York in exactly the same way. There were differences, Mrs Lemon knew, and some of them were of the highest importance; but poor Lady Barb appeared never to suspect them. She accepted every one and everything, and asked no questions. She had no curiosity about her fellow-citizens, and as she never assumed it for a moment, she gave Mrs Lemon no opportunity to enlighten her. Lady Barb was a person with whom you could do nothing unless she gave you an opening; and nothing would have been more difficult than to enlighten her against her will. Of course she picked up a little knowledge; but she confounded and transposed American attributes in the most extraordinary way. She had a way of calling every one Doctor; and Mrs Lemon could scarcely convince her that this distinction was too precious to be so freely bestowed. She had once said to her mother-in-law that in New York there was nothing to know people by, their names were so very monotonous; and Mrs Lemon had entered into this enough to see that there was something that stood out a good deal in Barberina's own prefix. It is probable that during her short stay in New York complete justice was not done Lady Barb; she never got credit, for instance, for repressing her annoyance at the aridity of the social nomenclature, which seemed to her hideous. That little speech to her mother was the most reckless sign she gave of it; and there were few things that contributed more to the good conscience she habitually enjoyed, than her self-control on this particular point.

Jackson Lemon was making some researches, just now, which took up a great deal of his time; and, for the rest, he passed his hours abundantly with his wife. For the last three months, therefore, he had seen his mother scarcely more than once a week. In spite of researches, in spite of medical societies, where Jackson, to her knowledge, read papers, Lady Barb had more of her husband's company than she had counted upon at the time she married. She had never known a married pair to be so much together as she and Jackson; he appeared to expect her to sit with him in the library in the morning. He had none of the occupations of gentlemen and noblemen in England, for the element of politics appeared to be as absent as the hunting. There were politics in Washington, she had been told, and even at Albany, and Jackson had proposed to introduce her to these cities; but the proposal, made to her once at dinner before several people, had excited such cries of horror that it fell dead on the spot. "We don't want you to see anything of that kind," one of the ladies had said, and Jackson had appeared to be discouraged—that is if, in regard to Jackson, one could really tell.

"Pray, what is it you want me to see?" Lady Barb had asked on this occasion.

"Well, New York; and Boston, if you want to very much —but not otherwise; and Niagara; and, more than anything, Newport."

Lady Barb was tired of their eternal Newport; she had heard of it a thousand times, and felt already as if she had lived there half her life; she was sure, moreover, that she should hate it. This is perhaps as near as she came to having a lively conviction on any American subject. She asked herself whether she was then to spend her life in the Fifth Avenue, with alternations of a city of villas (she detested villas), and wondered whether that was all the great American country had to offer her. There were times when she thought that she should like the backwoods, and that the Far West might

be a resource; for she had analysed her feelings just deep
enough to discover that when she had—hesitating a good
deal—turned over the question of marrying Jackson Lemon,
it was not in the least of American barbarism that she was
afraid; her dread was of American civilisation. She believed
the little lady I have just quoted was a goose; but that did not
make New York any more interesting. It would be reckless to
say that she suffered from an overdose of Jackson's company,
because she had a view of the fact that he was much her most
important social resource. She could talk to him about England;
about her own England, and he understood more or less what
she wished to say, when she wished to say anything, which
was not frequent. There were plenty of other people who
talked about England; but with them the range of allusion
was always the hotels, of which she knew nothing, and the
shops, and the opera, and the photographs: they had a mania
for photographs. There were other people who were always
wanting her to tell them about Pasterns, and the manner of life
there, and the parties; but if there was one thing Lady Barb
disliked more than another, it was describing Pasterns. She
had always lived with people who knew, of themselves, what
such a place would be, without demanding these pictorial
efforts, proper only, as she vaguely felt, to persons belonging
to the classes whose trade was the arts of expression. Lady
Barb, of course, had never gone into it; but she knew that in
her own class the business was not to express, but to enjoy;
not to represent, but to be represented—though, indeed, this
latter liability might convey offence; for it may be noted that
even for an aristocrat Jackson Lemon's wife was aristocratic.

Lady Agatha and her visitor came back from the library
in course of time, and Jackson Lemon felt it his duty to be
rather cold to Herman Longstraw. It was not clear to him
what sort of a husband his sister-in-law would do well to look
for in America—if there were to be any question of husbands;
but as to this he was not bound to be definite, provided he

should rule out Mr Longstraw. This gentleman, however, was not given to perceive shades of manner; he had little observation, but very great confidence.

"I think you had better come home with me," Jackson said to Lady Agatha; "I guess you have stayed here long enough."

"Don't let him say that, Mrs Lemon!" the girl cried. "I like being with you so very much."

"I try to make it pleasant," said Mrs Lemon. "I should really miss you now; but perhaps it's your mother's wish." If it was a question of defending her guest from ineligible suitors, Mrs Lemon felt, of course, that her son was more competent than she; though she had a lurking kindness for Herman Longstraw, and a vague idea that he was a gallant, genial specimen of young America.

"Oh, mamma wouldn't see any difference!" Lady Agatha exclaimed, looking at Jackson with pleading blue eyes. "Mamma wants me to see every one; you know she does. That's what she sent me to America for; she knew it was not like England. She wouldn't like it if I didn't sometimes stay with people; she always wanted us to stay at other houses. And she knows all about you, Mrs Lemon, and she likes you immensely. She sent you a message the other day, and I am afraid I forgot to give it you—to thank you for being so kind to me and taking such a lot of trouble. Really she did, but I forgot it. If she wants me to see as much as possible of America, it's much better I should be here than always with Barb—it's much less like one's own country. I mean it's much nicer— for a girl," said Lady Agatha, affectionately, to Mrs Lemon, who began also to look at Jackson with a kind of tender argumentativeness.

"If you want the genuine thing, you ought to come out on the plains," Mr Longstraw interposed, with smiling sincerity. "I guess that was your mother's idea. Why don't you all come out?" He had been looking intently at Lady Agatha while the remarks I have just repeated succeeded each other

on her lips—looking at her with a kind of fascinated appro-
bation, for all the world as if he had been a slightly slow-
witted English gentleman and the girl had been a flower of the
West—a flower that knew how to talk. He made no secret of
the fact that Lady Agatha's voice was music to him, his ear
being much more susceptible than his own inflections would
have indicated. To Lady Agatha those inflections were not displeasing, partly because, like Mr Herman himself, in general,
she had not a perception of shades; and partly because it
never occurred to her to compare them with any other tones.
He seemed to her to speak a foreign language altogether—a
romantic dialect, through which the most comical meanings
gleamed here and there.

"I should like it above all things," she said, in answer to
his last observation.

"The scenery's superior to anything round here," Mr
Longstraw went on.

Mrs Lemon, as we know, was the softest of women; but,
as an old New Yorker, she had no patience with some of the
new fashions. Chief among these was the perpetual reference,
which had become common only within a few years, to the
outlying parts of the country, the States and Territories of
which children, in her time, used to learn the names, in their
order, at school, but which no one ever thought of going to
or talking about. Such places, in Mrs Lemon's opinion, belonged to the geography-books, or at most to the literature of
newspapers, but not to society nor to conversation; and the
change—which, so far as it lay in people's talk, she thought
at bottom a mere affectation—threatened to make her native
land appear vulgar and vague. For this amiable daughter of
Manhattan, the normal existence of man, and, still more, of
woman, had been "located," as she would have said, between
Trinity Church and the beautiful Reservoir at the top of the
Fifth Avenue—monuments of which she was personally
proud; and if we could look into the deeper parts of her mind,

I am afraid we should discover there an impression that both the countries of Europe and the remainder of her own continent were equally far from the centre and the light.

"Well, scenery isn't everything," she remarked, mildly, to Mr Longstraw; "and if Lady Agatha should wish to see anything of that kind, all she has got to do is to take the boat up the Hudson."

Mrs Lemon's recognition of this river, I should say, was all that it need have been; she thought that it existed for the purpose of supplying New Yorkers with poetical feelings, helping them to face comfortably occasions like the present, and, in general, meet foreigners with confidence—part of the oddity of foreigners being their conceit about their own places.

"That's a good idea, Lady Agatha; let's take the boat," said Mr Longstraw. "I've had great times on the boats."

Lady Agatha looked at her cavalier a little with those singular, charming eyes of hers—eyes of which it was impossible to say, at any moment, whether they were the shyest or the frankest in the world; and she was not aware, while this contemplation lasted, that her brother-in-law was observing her. He was thinking of certain things while he did so, of things he had heard about the English; who still, in spite of his having married into a family of that nation, appeared to him very much through the medium of hearsay. They were more passionate than the Americans, and they did things that would never have been expected; though they seemed steadier and less excitable, there was much social evidence to show that they were more impulsive.

"It's so very kind of you to propose that," Lady Agatha said in a moment to Mrs Lemon. "I think I have never been in a ship—except, of course, coming from England. I am sure mamma would wish me to see the Hudson. We used to go in immensely for boating in England."

"Did you boat in a ship?" Herman Longstraw asked, showing his teeth hilariously, and pulling his moustaches.

"Lots of my mother's people have been in the navy." Lady Agatha perceived vaguely and good-naturedly that she had said something which the odd Americans thought odd, and that she must justify herself. Her standard of oddity was getting dreadfully dislocated.

"I really think you had better come back to us," said Jackson; "your sister is very lonely without you."

"She is much more lonely with me. We are perpetually having differences. Barb is dreadfully vexed because I like America, instead of—instead of——" And Lady Agatha paused a moment; for it just occurred to her that this might be a betrayal.

"Instead of what?" Jackson Lemon inquired.

"Instead of perpetually wanting to go to England, as she does," she went on, only giving her phrase a little softer turn; for she felt the next moment that her sister could have nothing to hide, and must, of course, have the courage of her opinions. "Of course England's best, but I dare say I like to be bad," said Lady Agatha, artlessly.

"Oh, there's no doubt you are awfully bad!" Mr Longstraw exclaimed, with joyous eagerness. Of course he could not know that what she had principally in mind was an exchange of opinions that had taken place between her sister and herself just before she came to stay with Mrs Lemon. This incident, of which Longstraw was the occasion, might indeed have been called a discussion, for it had carried them quite into the realms of the abstract. Lady Barb had said she didn't see how Agatha could look at such a creature as that —an odious, familiar, vulgar being, who had not about him the rudiments of a gentleman. Lady Agatha had replied that Mr Longstraw was familiar and rough, and that he had a twang, and thought it amusing to talk of her as "the Princess;" but that he was a gentleman for all that, and that at any rate he was tremendous fun. Her sister to this had rejoined that if he was rough and familiar he couldn't be a gentleman, inasmuch

as that was just what a gentleman meant—a man who was civil,
and well-bred, and well-born. Lady Agatha had argued that
this was just where she differed; that a man might perfectly
be a gentleman, and yet be rough, and even ignorant, so long
as he was really nice. The only thing was that he should be
really nice, which was the case with Mr Longstraw, who,
moreover, was quite extraordinarily civil—as civil as a man
could be. And then Lady Agatha made the strongest point she
had ever made in her life (she had never been so inspired) in
saying that Mr Longstraw was rough, perhaps, but not rude
—a distinction altogether wasted on her sister, who declared
that she had not come to America, of all places, to learn
what a gentleman was. The discussion, in short, had been
lively. I know not whether it was the tonic effect on them,
too, of the fine winter weather, or, on the other hand, that of
Lady Barb's being bored and having nothing else to do; but
Lord Canterville's daughters went into the question with the
moral earnestness of a pair of Bostonians. It was part of Lady
Agatha's view of her admirer that he, after all, much resembled other tall people, with smiling eyes and moustaches, who
had ridden a good deal in rough countries, and whom she
had seen in other places. If he was more familiar, he was also
more alert; still, the difference was not in himself, but in the
way she saw him—the way she saw everybody in America.
If she should see the others in the same way, no doubt they
would be quite the same; and Lady Agatha sighed a little over
the possibilities of life; for this peculiar way, especially regarded in connection with gentlemen, had become very
pleasant to her.

She had betrayed her sister more than she thought, even
though Jackson Lemon did not particularly show it in the
tone in which he said: "Of course she knows that she is
going to see your mother in the summer." His tone, rather,
was that of irritation at the repetition of a familiar idea.

"Oh, it isn't only mamma," replied Lady Agatha.

"I know she likes a cool house," said Mrs Lemon, suggestively.

"When she goes, you had better bid her good-bye," the girl went on.

"Of course I shall bid her good-bye," said Mrs Lemon, to whom, apparently, this remark was addressed.

"I shall never bid you good-bye, Princess," Herman Longstraw interposed. "I can tell you that you never will see the last of me."

"Oh, it doesn't matter about me, for I shall come back; but if Barb once gets to England she will never come back."

"Oh, my dear child," murmured Mrs Lemon, addressing Lady Agatha, but looking at her son.

Jackson looked at the ceiling, at the floor; above all, he looked very conscious.

"I hope you don't mind my saying that, Jackson dear," Lady Agatha said to him, for she was very fond of her brother-in-law.

"Ah, well, then, she shan't go, then," he remarked, after a moment, with a dry little laugh.

"But you promised mamma, you know," said the girl, with the confidence of her affection.

Jackson looked at her with an eye which expressed none even of his very moderate hilarity. "Your mother, then, must bring her back."

"Get some of your navy people to supply an ironclad!" cried Mr Longstraw.

"It would be very pleasant if the Marchioness could come over," said Mrs Lemon.

"Oh, she would hate it more than poor Barb," Lady Agatha quickly replied. It did not suit her mood at all to see a marchioness inserted into the field of her vision.

"Doesn't she feel interested, from what you have told her?" Herman Longstraw asked of Lady Agatha. But Jackson

Lemon did not heed his sister-in-law's answer; he was thinking of something else. He said nothing more, however, about
the subject of his thought, and before ten minutes were over
he took his departure, having, meanwhile, neglected also to
revert to the question of Lady Agatha's bringing her visit to
his mother to a close. It was not to speak to him of this (for,
as we know, she wished to keep the girl, and somehow could
not bring herself to be afraid of Herman Longstraw) that when
Jackson took leave she went with him to the door of the
house, detaining him a little, while she stood on the steps,
as people had always done in New York in her time, though
it was another of the new fashions she did not like, not to
come out of the parlour. She placed her hand on his arm to
keep him on the "stoop," and looked up and down into the
brilliant afternoon and the beautiful city—its chocolate-
coloured houses, so extraordinarily smooth—in which it
seemed to her that even the most fastidious people ought to be
glad to live. It was useless to attempt to conceal it; her son's
marriage had made a difference, had put up a kind of barrier.
It had brought with it a problem much more difficult than his
old problem of how to make his mother feel that she was still,
as she had been in his childhood, the dispenser of his rewards.
The old problem had been easily solved; the new one was a
visible preoccupation. Mrs Lemon felt that her daughter-in-
law did not take her seriously; and that was a part of the
barrier. Even if Barberina liked her better than any one else,
this was mostly because she liked every one else so little. Mrs
Lemon had not a grain of resentment in her nature; and it was
not to feed a sense of wrong that she permitted herself to
criticise her son's wife. She could not help feeling that his
marriage was not altogether fortunate if his wife didn't take
his mother seriously. She knew she was not otherwise remarkable than as being his mother; but that position, which was
no merit of hers (the merit was all Jackson's, in being her
son), seemed to her one which, familiar as Lady Barb appeared

to have been in England with positions of various kinds, would naturally strike the girl as a very high one, to be accepted as freely as a fine morning. If she didn't think of his mother as an indivisible part of him, perhaps she didn't think of other things either; and Mrs Lemon vaguely felt that, remarkable as Jackson was, he was made up of parts, and that it would never do that these parts should depreciate one by one, for there was no knowing what that might end in. She feared that things were rather cold for him at home when he had to explain so much to his wife—explain to her, for instance, all the sources of happiness that were to be found in New York. This struck her as a new kind of problem altogether for a husband. She had never thought of matrimony without a community of feeling in regard to religion and country; one took those great conditions for granted, just as one assumed that one's food was to be cooked; and if Jackson should have to discuss them with his wife, he might, in spite of his great abilities, be carried into regions where he would get entangled and embroiled—from which, even, possibly, he would not come back at all. Mrs Lemon had a horror of losing him in some way; and this fear was in her eyes as she stood on the steps of her house, and, after she had glanced up and down the street, looked at him a moment in silence. He simply kissed her again, and said she would take cold.

"I am not afraid of that, I have a shawl!" Mrs Lemon, who was very small and very fair, with pointed features and an elaborate cap, passed her life in a shawl, and owed to this habit her reputation for being an invalid—an idea which she scorned, naturally enough, inasmuch as it was precisely her shawl that (as she believed) kept her from being one. "Is it true Barberina won't come back?" she asked of her son.

"I don't know that we shall ever find out; I don't know that I shall take her to England."

"Didn't you promise, dear?"

"I don't know that I promised; not absolutely."

"But you wouldn't keep her here against her will?" said Mrs Lemon, inconsequently.

"I guess she'll get used to it," Jackson answered, with a lightness he did not altogether feel.

Mrs Lemon looked up and down the street again, and gave a little sigh. "What a pity she isn't American!" She did not mean this as a reproach, a hint of what might have been; it was simply embarrassment resolved into speech.

"She couldn't have been American," said Jackson, with decision.

"Couldn't she, dear?" Mrs Lemon spoke with a kind of respect; she felt that there were imperceptible reasons in this.

"It was just as she is that I wanted her," Jackson added.

"Even if she won't come back?" his mother asked, with a certain wonder.

"Oh, she has got to come back!" Jackson said, going down the steps.

VI

LADY BARB, after this, did not decline to see her New York acquaintances on Sunday afternoons, though she refused for the present to enter into a project of her husband's, who thought it would be a pleasant thing that she should entertain his friends on the evening of that day. Like all good Americans, Jackson Lemon devoted much consideration to the great question how, in his native land, society should be brought into being. It seemed to him that it would help the good cause, for which so many Americans are ready to lay down their lives, if his wife should, as he jocularly called it, open a saloon. He believed, or he tried to believe, the *salon* now possible in New York, on condition of its being reserved entirely for adults; and in having taken a wife out of a country in which social traditions were rich and ancient, he had done something towards qualifying his own house—so splendidly qualified in all strictly material respects—to be the scene of such an effort. A charming woman, accustomed only to the best in each country, as Lady Beauchemin said, what might she not achieve by being at home (to the elder generation) in an easy, early, inspiring, comprehensive way, on the evening in the week on which worldly engagements were least numerous? He laid this philosophy before Lady Barb, in pursuance of a theory that if she disliked New York on a short acquaintance, she could not fail to like it on a long one. Jackson Lemon believed in the New York mind—not so much, indeed, in its literary, artistic, or political achievements, as in its general quickness and nascent adaptability. He clung to this belief, for it was a very important piece of material in the structure that he was attempting to rear. The New York mind would throw its glamour over Lady Barb if she would only give it a chance; for it was exceedingly bright, entertaining, and sympathetic. If she would only have a *salon*, where this charming organ might expand, and where she might inhale its fragrance in the most convenient and luxurious way, without, as it were, getting up from her chair; if she would only just try this graceful, good-natured experiment (which would make every one like *her* so much, too), he was sure that all the wrinkles in the gilded scroll of his fate would be smoothed out. But Lady Barb did not rise at all to his conception, and had not the least curiosity about the New York mind. She thought it would be extremely disagreeable to have a lot of people tumbling in on Sunday evening without being invited; and altogether her husband's sketch of the Anglo-American saloon seemed to her to suggest familiarity, high-pitched talk (she had already make a remark to him about "screeching women"), and exaggerated laughter. She did not tell him—for this, somehow, it was not in her power to express, and, strangely enough, he never completely guessed it—that she was singularly deficient in any natural, or indeed acquired, understanding of what a saloon might be. She had never seen one, and for the most part she never thought of things she had not seen. She had seen great dinners, and balls, and meets, and runs, and races; she had seen garden-parties, and a lot of people, mainly women (who, however, didn't screech), at dull, stuffy teas, and distinguished companies collected in splendid castles; but all this gave her no idea of a tradition of conversation, of a social agreement that the continuity of talk, its accumulations from season to season, should not be lost. Conversation, in Lady Barb's experience, had never been continuous; in such a case it would surely have been a bore. It had been occasional and fragmentary, a trifle jerky, with allusions that were never explained; it had a dread of detail; it seldom pursued anything very far, or kept hold of it very long.

There was something else that she did not say to her husband in reference to his visions of hospitality, which was, that if she should open a saloon (she had taken up the joke as well, for Lady Barb was eminently good-natured), Mrs Vanderdecken would straightway open another, and Mrs Vanderdecken's would be the more successful of the two. This lady, for reasons that Lady Barb had not yet explored, was supposed to be the great personage in New York; there were legends of her husband's family having behind them a fabulous antiquity. When this was alluded to, it was spoken of as something incalculable, and lost in the dimness of time. Mrs Vanderdecken was young, pretty, clever, absurdly pretentious (Lady Barb thought), and had a wonderfully artistic house. Ambition, also, was expressed in every rustle of her garments; and if she was the first person in America (this had an immense sound), it was plain that she intended to remain so. It was not till after she had been several months in New York that it came over Lady Barb that this brilliant, bristling native had flung down the glove; and when the idea presented itself, lighted up by an incident which I have no space to relate, she simply blushed a little (for Mrs Vanderdecken), and held her tongue. She had not come to America to bandy words about precedence with such a woman as that. She had ceased to think about it much (of course one thought about it in England); but an instinct of self-preservation led her not to expose herself to occasions on which her claim might be tested. This, at bottom, had much to do with her having, very soon after the first flush of the honours paid her on her arrival, and which seemed to her rather grossly overdone, taken the line of scarcely going out. "They can't keep *that* up!" she had said to herself; and, in short, she would stay at home. She had a feeling that whenever she should go forth she would meet Mrs Vanderdecken, who would withhold, or deny, or contest something—poor Lady Barb could never imagine what. She did not try to, and gave little thought to all this; for she was not prone to confess to herself fears, especially fears from which terror was absent. But, as I have said, it abode within her as a presentiment that if she should set up a drawing-room in the foreign style (it was curious, in New York, how they tried to be foreign), Mrs Vanderdecken would be beforehand with her. The continuity of conversation, oh! that idea she would certainly have; there was no one so continuous as Mrs Vanderdecken. Lady Barb, as I have related, did not give her husband the surprise of telling him of these thoughts, though she had given him some other surprises. He would have been very much astonished, and perhaps, after a bit, a little encouraged, at finding that she was liable to this particular form of irritation.

On the Sunday afternoon she was visible; and on one of these occasions, going into her drawing-room late, he found her entertaining two ladies and a gentleman. The gentleman was Sidney Feeder, and one of the ladies was Mrs Vanderdecken, whose ostensible relations with Lady Barb were of the most cordial nature. If she intended to crush her (as two or three persons, not conspicuous for a narrow accuracy, gave out that she privately declared), Mrs Vanderdecken wished at least to study the weak points of the invader, to penetrate herself with the character of the English girl. Lady Barb, indeed, appeared to have a mysterious fascination for the representative of the American patriciate. Mrs Vanderdecken could not take her eyes off her victim; and whatever might be her estimate of her importance, she at least could not let her alone. "Why does she come to see me?" poor Lady Barb asked herself. "I am sure I don't want to see her; she has done enough for civility long ago." Mrs Vanderdecken had her own reasons; and one of them was simply the pleasure of looking at the Doctor's wife, as she habitually called the daughter of the Cantervilles. She was not guilty of the folly of depreciating this lady's appearance, and professed an unbounded admiration for it, defending it on many occasions against superficial people who said there were fifty women in New York that were handsomer. Whatever might have been Lady Barb's weak points, they were not the curve of her cheek and chin, the setting of her head on her throat, or the quietness of her deep eyes, which were as beautiful as if they had been blank, like those of antique busts. "The head is enchanting —perfectly enchanting," Mrs Vanderdecken used to say irrelevantly, as if there were only one head in the place. She always used to ask about the Doctor; and that was another reason why she came. She brought up the Doctor at every turn; asked if he were often called up at night; found it the greatest of luxuries, in a word, to address Lady Barb as the wife of a medical man, more or less *au courant* of her husband's patients. The other lady, on this Sunday afternoon, was a certain little Mrs Chew, whose clothes looked so new that she had the air of a walking advertisement issued by a great shop, and who was always asking Lady Barb about England, which Mrs Vanderdecken never did. The latter visitor conversed with Lady Barb on a purely American basis, with that continuity (on her own side) of which mention has already been made, while Mrs Chew engaged Sidney Feeder on topics equally local. Lady Barb liked Sidney Feeder; she only hated his name, which was constantly in her ears during the half-hour the ladies sat with her, Mrs Chew having the habit, which annoyed Lady Barb, of repeating perpetually the appellation of her interlocutor.

Lady Barb's relations with Mrs Vanderdecken consisted mainly in wondering, while she talked, what she wanted of her, and in looking, with her sculptured eyes, at her visitor's clothes, in which there was always much to examine. "Oh, Doctor Feeder!" "Now, Doctor Feeder!" "Well, Doctor Feeder,"—these exclamations, on the lips of Mrs Chew, were an undertone in Lady Barb's consciousness. When I say that she liked her husband's *confrère*, as he used to call himself, I mean that she smiled at him when he came, and gave him her hand, and asked him if he would have some tea. There was nothing nasty (as they said in London) in Lady Barb, and she would have been incapable of inflicting a deliberate snub upon a man who had the air of standing up so squarely to any work that he might have in hand. But she had nothing to say to Sidney Feeder. He apparently had the art of making her shy, more shy than usual; for she was always a little so; she discouraged him, discouraged him completely. He was not a man who wanted drawing out, there was nothing of that in him, he was remarkably copious; but Lady Barb appeared unable to follow him, and half the time, evidently, did not know what he was saying. He tried to adapt his conversation to her needs; but when he spoke of the world, of what was going on in society, she was more at sea even than when he spoke of hospitals and laboratories, and the health of the city, and the progress of science. She appeared, indeed, after her first smile, when he came in, which was always charming, scarcely to see him, looking past him, and above him, and below him, and everywhere but at him, until he got up to go

again, when she gave him another smile, as expressive of pleasure and of casual acquaintance as that with which she had
greeted his entry; it seemed to imply that they had been having
delightful talk for an hour. He wondered what the deuce
Jackson Lemon could find interesting in such a woman, and
he believed that his perverse, though gifted colleague, was not
destined to feel that she illuminated his life. He pitied Jackson,
he saw that Lady Barb, in New York, would neither assimilate nor be assimilated; and yet he was afraid to betray his
incredulity, thinking it might be depressing to poor Lemon
to show him how his marriage—now so dreadfully irrevocable
—struck others. Sidney Feeder was a man of a strenuous conscience, and he did his duty overmuch by his old friend and his
wife, from the simple fear that he should not do it enough. In
order not to appear to neglect them, he called upon Lady Barb
heroically, in spite of pressing engagements, week after week,
enjoying his virtue himself as little as he made it fruitful for
his hostess, who wondered at last what she had done to deserve
these visitations. She spoke of them to her husband, who
wondered also what poor Sidney had in his head, and yet was
unable, of course, to hint to him that he need not think it
necessary to come so often. Between Doctor Feeder's wish
not to let Jackson see that his marriage had made a difference,
and Jackson's hesitation to reveal to Sidney that his standard
of friendship was too high, Lady Barb passed a good many
of those numerous hours during which she asked herself if
she had come to America for that. Very little had ever
passed between her and her husband on the subject of Sidney
Feeder; for an instinct told her that if they were ever to have
scenes, she must choose the occasion well; and this odd person
was not an occasion. Jackson had tacitly admitted that his
friend Feeder was anything she chose to think him; he was
not a man to be guilty, in a discussion, of the disloyalty of
damning him with praise that was faint. If Lady Agatha had
usually been with her sister, Doctor Feeder would have been

better entertained; for the younger of the English visitors prided herself, after several months of New York, on understanding everything that was said, and catching every allusion, it mattered not from what lips it fell. But Lady Agatha was never at home; she had learned how to describe herself perfectly by the time she wrote to her mother that she was always "on the go." None of the innumerable victims of old-world tyranny who have fled to the United States as to a land of freedom, have ever offered more lavish incense to that goddess than this emancipated London *débutante*. She had enrolled herself in an amiable band which was known by the humorous name of "the Tearers"—a dozen young ladies of agreeable appearance, high spirits and good wind, whose most general characteristic was that, when wanted, they were to be sought anywhere in the world but under the roof that was supposed to shelter them. They were never at home; and when Sidney Feeder, as sometimes happened, met Lady Agatha at other houses, she was in the hands of the irrepressible Longstraw. She had come back to her sister, but Mr Longstraw had followed her to the door. As to passing it, he had received direct discouragement from her brother-in-law; but he could at least hang about and wait for her. It may be confided to the reader, at the risk of diminishing the effect of the only incident which in the course of this very level narrative may startle him, that he never had to wait very long.

When Jackson Lemon came in, his wife's visitors were on the point of leaving her; and he did not ask even Sidney Feeder to remain, for he had something particular to say to Lady Barb.

"I haven't asked you half what I wanted—I have been talking so much to Doctor Feeder," the dressy Mrs Chew said, holding the hand of her hostess in one of her own, and toying with one of Lady Barb's ribbons with the other.

"I don't think I have anything to tell you; I think I have

told people everything," Lady Barb answered, rather wearily.

"You haven't told *me* much!" Mrs Vanderdecken said, smiling brightly.

"What could one tell you?—you know everything," Jackson Lemon interposed.

"Ah, no; there are some things that are great mysteries for me," the lady returned. "I hope you are coming to me on the 17th," she added, to Lady Barb.

"On the 17th? I think we are going somewhere."

"Do go to Mrs Vanderdecken's," said Mrs Chew; "you will see the cream of the cream."

"Oh, gracious!" Mrs Vanderdecken exclaimed.

"Well, I don't care; she will, won't she, Doctor Feeder?— the very pick of American society." Mrs Chew stuck to her point.

"Well, I have no doubt Lady Barb will have a good time," said Sidney Feeder. "I'm afraid you miss the bran," he went on, with irrelevant jocosity, to Lady Barb. He always tried the jocose when other elements had failed.

"The bran?" asked Lady Barb, staring.

"Where you used to ride, in the Park."

"My dear fellow, you speak as if it were the circus," Jackson Lemon said, smiling; "I haven't married a mountebank!"

"Well, they put some stuff on the road," Sidney Feeder explained, not holding much to his joke.

"You must miss a great many things," said Mrs Chew, tenderly.

"I don't see what," Mrs Vanderdecken remarked, "except the fogs and the Queen. New York is getting more and more like London. It's a pity; you ought to have known us thirty years ago."

"You are the queen, here," said Jackson Lemon; "but I don't know what you know about thirty years ago."

"Do you think she doesn't go back?—she goes back to the last century!" cried Mrs Chew.

"I dare say I should have liked that," said Lady Barb; "but I can't imagine." And she looked at her husband—a look she often had—as if she vaguely wished him to do something.

He was not called upon, however, to take any violent steps, for Mrs Chew presently said: "Well, Lady Barberina, good-bye;" and Mrs Vanderdecken smiled in silence at her hostess, and addressed a farewell, accompanied very audibly with his title, to her host; and Sidney Feeder made a joke about stepping on the trains of the ladies' dresses as he accompanied them to the door. Mrs Chew had always a great deal to say at the last; she talked till she was in the street, and then she did not cease. But at the end of five minutes Jackson Lemon was alone with his wife; and then he told her a piece of news. He prefaced it, however, by an inquiry as he came back from the hall.

"Where is Agatha, my dear?"

"I haven't the least idea. In the streets somewhere, I suppose."

"I think you ought to know a little more."

"How can I know about things here? I have given her up; I can do nothing with her. I don't care what she does."

"She ought to go back to England," Jackson Lemon said, after a pause.

"She ought never to have come."

"It was not my proposal, God knows!" Jackson answered, rather sharply.

"Mamma could never know what it really is," said his wife.

"No, it has not been as yet what your mother supposed! Herman Longstraw wants to marry her. He has made me a formal proposal. I met him half an hour ago in Madison Avenue, and he asked me to come with him into the Columbia Club. There, in the billiard-room, which to-day is empty, he opened himself—thinking evidently that in laying the matter before me he was behaving with extraordinary propriety. He tells me he is dying of love, and that she is perfectly willing to go and live in Arizona."

"So she is," said Lady Barb. "And what did you tell him?"

"I told him that I was sure it would never do, and that at any rate I could have nothing to say to it. I told him explicitly, in short, what I had told him virtually before. I said that we should send Agatha straight back to England, and that if they have the courage they must themselves broach the question over there."

"When shall you send her back?" asked Lady Barb.

"Immediately; by the very first steamer."

"Alone, like an American girl?"

"Don't be rough, Barb," said Jackson Lemon. "I shall easily find some people; lots of people are sailing now."

"I must take her myself," Lady Barb declared in a moment. "I brought her out, and I must restore her to my mother's hands."

Jackson Lemon had expected this, and he believed he was prepared for it. But when it came he found his preparation was not complete; for he had no answer to make—none, at least, that seemed to him to go to the point. During these last weeks it had come over him, with a quiet, irresistible, unmerciful force, that Mrs Dexter Freer had been right when she said to him, that Sunday afternoon in Jermyn Street, the summer before, that he would find it was not so simple to be an American. Such an identity was complicated, in just the measure that she had foretold, by the difficulty of domesticating one's wife. The difficulty was not dissipated by his having taken a high tone about it; it pinched him from morning till night, like a misfitting shoe. His high tone had given him courage when he took the great step; but he began to perceive that the highest tone in the world cannot change the nature of things. His ears tingled when he reflected that if the Dexter Freers, whom he had thought alike ignoble in their

hopes and their fears, had been by ill-luck spending the winter
in New York, they would have found his predicament as
entertaining as they could desire. Drop by drop the conviction
had entered his mind—the first drop had come in the form
of a word from Lady Agatha—that if his wife should return
to England she would never again cross the Atlantic to the
West. That word from Lady Agatha had been the touch from
the outside, at which, often, one's fears crystallise. What
she would do, how she would resist—this he was not yet prepared to tell himself; but he felt, every time he looked at her,
that this beautiful woman whom he had adored was filled with
a dumb, insuperable, ineradicable purpose. He knew that if
she should plant herself, no power on earth would move her;
and her blooming, antique beauty, and the general loftiness
of her breeding, came to seem to him—rapidly—but the
magnificent expression of a dense, patient, imperturbable
obstinacy. She was not light, she was not supple, and after
six months of marriage he had made up his mind that she was
not clever; but nevertheless she would elude him. She had
married him, she had come into his fortune and his consideration—for who was she, after all? Jackson Lemon was once so
angry as to ask himself, reminding himself that in England
Lady Claras and Lady Florences were as thick as blackberries
—but she would have nothing to do, if she could help it, with
his country. She had gone in to dinner first in every house in
the place, but this had not satisfied her. It *had* been simple to be
an American, in this sense that no one else in New York had
made any difficulties; the difficulties had sprung from her
peculiar feelings, which were after all what he had married
her for, thinking they would be a fine temperamental heritage for his brood. So they would, doubtless, in the coming
years, after the brood should have appeared; but meanwhile
they interfered with the best heritage of all—the nationality
of his possible children. Lady Barb would do nothing
violent; he was tolerably certain of that. She would not return

to England without his consent; only, when she should return, it would be once for all. His only possible line, then, was not to take her back—a position replete with difficulties, because, of course, he had, in a manner, given his word, while she had given no word at all, beyond the general promise she murmured at the altar. She had been general, but he had been specific; the settlements he had made were a part of that. His difficulties were such as he could not directly face. He must tack in approaching so uncertain a coast. He said to Lady Barb presently that it would be very inconvenient for him to leave New York at that moment: she must remember that their plans had been laid for a later departure. He could not think of letting her make the voyage without him, and, on the other hand, they must pack her sister off without delay. He would therefore make instant inquiry for a chaperon, and he relieved his irritation by expressing considerable disgust at Herman Longstraw.

Lady Barb did not trouble herself to denounce this gentleman; her manner was that of having for a long time expected the worst. She simply remarked dryly, after having listened to her husband for some minutes in silence: "I would as lief she should marry Doctor Feeder!"

The day after this, Jackson Lemon closeted himself for an hour with Lady Agatha, taking great pains to set forth to her the reasons why she should not unite herself with her Californian. Jackson was kind, he was affectionate; he kissed her and put his arm round her waist, he reminded her that he and she were the best of friends, and that she had always been awfully nice to him; therefore he counted upon her. She would break her mother's heart, she would deserve her father's curse, and she would get him, Jackson, into a pickle from which no human power could ever disembroil him. Lady Agatha listened and cried, and returned his kiss very affectionately, and admitted that her father and mother would never consent to such a marriage; and when he told her that he had made

arrangements for her to sail for Liverpool (with some charming people) the next day but one, she embraced him again and
assured him that she could never thank him enough for all
the trouble he had taken about her. He flattered himself that
he had convinced, and in some degree comforted her, and
reflected with complacency that even should his wife take it
into her head, Barberina would never get ready to embark
for her native land between a Monday and a Wednesday. The
next morning Lady Agatha did not appear at breakfast; but
as she usually rose very late, her absence excited no alarm. She
had not rung her bell, and she was supposed still to be sleeping. But she had never yet slept later than midday; and as this
hour approached her sister went to her room. Lady Barb
then discovered that she had left the house at seven o'clock
in the morning, and had gone to meet Herman Longstraw at a
neighbouring corner. A little note on the table explained it
very succinctly, and put beyond the power of Jackson Lemon
and his wife to doubt that by the time this news reached them
their wayward sister had been united to the man of her preference as closely as the laws of the State of New York could
bind her. Her little note set forth that as she knew she
should never be permitted to marry him, she had determined
to marry him without permission, and that directly after the
ceremony, which would be of the simplest kind, they were
to take a train for the far West. Our history is concerned only
with the remote consequences of this incident, which made,
of course, a great deal of trouble for Jackson Lemon. He went
to the far West in pursuit of the fugitives, and overtook them
in California; but he had not the audacity to propose to them
to separate, as it was easy for him to see that Herman Longstraw was at least as well married as himself. Lady Agatha
was already popular in the new States, where the history of her
elopement, emblazoned in enormous capitals, was circulated
in a thousand newspapers. This question of the newspapers
had been for Jackson Lemon one of the most definite results

of his sister-in-law's *coup de tête*. His first thought had been of the public prints, and his first exclamation a prayer that they should not get hold of the story. But they did get hold of it, and they treated the affair with their customary energy and eloquence. Lady Barb never saw them; but an affectionate friend of the family, travelling at that time in the United States, made a parcel of some of the leading journals, and sent them to Lord Canterville. This missive elicited from her ladyship a letter addressed to Jackson Lemon which shook the young man's position to the base. The phials of an unnameable vulgarity had been opened upon the house of Canterville, and his mother-in-law demanded that in compensation for the affronts and injuries that were being heaped upon her family, and bereaved and dishonoured as she was, she should at least be allowed to look on the face of her other daughter. "I suppose you will not, for very pity, be deaf to such a prayer as that," said Lady Barb; and though shrinking from recording a second act of weakness on the part of a man who had such pretensions to be strong, I must relate that poor Jackson, who blushed dreadfully over the newspapers, and felt afresh, as he read them, the force of Mrs Freer's terrible axiom—poor Jackson paid a visit to the office of the Cunarders. He said to himself afterward that it was the newspapers that had done it; he could not bear to appear to be on their side; they made it so hard to deny that the country was vulgar, at a time when one was in such need of all one's arguments. Lady Barb, before sailing, definitely refused to mention any week or month as the date of their pre-arranged return to New York. Very many weeks and months have elapsed since then, and she gives no sign of coming back. She will never fix a date. She is much missed by Mrs Vanderdecken, who still alludes to her—still says the line of the shoulders was superb; putting the statement, pensively, in the past tense. Lady Beauchemin and Lady Marmaduke are much disconcerted; the international project has not, in their view, received an impetus.

Jackson Lemon has a house in London, and he rides in the park with his wife, who is as beautiful as the day, and a year ago presented him with a little girl, with features that Jackson already scans for the look of race—whether in hope or fear, to-day, is more than my muse has revealed. He has occasional scenes with Lady Barb, during which the look of race is very visible in her own countenance; but they never terminate in a visit to the Cunarders. He is exceedingly restless, and is constantly crossing to the Continent; but he returns with a certain abruptness, for he cannot bear to meet the Dexter Freers, and they seem to pervade the more comfortable parts of Europe. He dodges them in every town. Sidney Feeder feels very badly about him; it is months since Jackson has sent him any "results." The excellent fellow goes very often, in a consolatory spirit, to see Mrs Lemon; but he has not yet been able to answer her standing question: "Why that girl more than another?" Lady Agatha Longstraw and her husband arrived a year ago in England, and Mr Longstraw's personality had immense success during the last London season. It is not exactly known what they live on, though it is perfectly known that he is looking for something to do. Meanwhile it is as good as known that Jackson Lemon supports them.

THE AUTHOR OF "BELTRAFFIO"

I

Much as I wished to see him, I had kept my letter of introduction for three weeks in my pocket-book. I was nervous and timid about meeting him—conscious of youth and ignorance, convinced that he was tormented by strangers, and especially by my country-people, and not exempt from the suspicion that he had the irritability as well as the brilliancy of genius. Moreover, the pleasure, if it should occur (for I could scarcely believe it was really at hand), would be so great that I wished to think of it in advance, to feel that it was in my pocket, not to mix it with satisfactions more superficial and usual. In the little game of new sensations that I was playing with my ingenuous mind, I wished to keep my visit to the author of *Beltraffio* as a trump-card. It was three years after the publication of that fascinating work, which I had read over five times, and which now, with my riper judgment, I admire on the whole as much as ever. This will give you about the date of my first visit (of any duration) to England; for you will not have forgotten the commotion—I may even say the scandal —produced by Mark Ambient's masterpiece. It was the most complete presentation that had yet been made of the gospel of art; it was a kind of æsthetic war-cry. People had endeavoured to sail nearer to "truth" in the cut of their sleeves and the shape of their sideboards; but there had not as yet been, among English novels, such an example of beauty of execution and value of subject. Nothing had been done in that line from the point of view of art for art. This was my own point of view, I may mention, when I was twenty-five;

whether it is altered now I won't take upon myself to say—especially as the discerning reader will be able to judge for himself. I had been in England a twelvemonth before the time to which I began by alluding, and had learned then that Mr Ambient was in distant lands—was making a considerable tour in the East. So there was nothing to do but to keep my letter till I should be in London again. It was of little use to me to hear that his wife had not left England and, with her little boy, their only child, was spending the period of her husband's absence—a good many months—at a small place they had down in Surrey. They had a house in London which was let. All this I learned, and also that Mrs Ambient was charming (my friend, the American poet, from whom I had my introduction, had never seen her, his relations with the great man being only epistolary); but she was not, after all, though she had lived so near the rose, the author of *Beltraffio*, and I did not go down into Surrey to call on her. I went to the Continent, spent the following winter in Italy, and returned to London in May. My visit to Italy opened my eyes to a good many things, but to nothing more than the beauty of certain pages in the works of Mark Ambient. I had every one of his productions in my portmanteau—they are not, as you know, very numerous, but he had preluded to *Beltraffio* by some exquisite things—and I used to read them over in the evening at the inn. I used to say to myself that the man who drew those characters and wrote that style understood what he saw and knew what he was doing. This is my only reason for mentioning my winter in Italy. He had been there much in former years, and he was saturated with what painters call the "feeling" of that classic land. He expressed the charm of the old hill-cities of Tuscany, the look of certain lonely grass-grown places which, in the past, had echoed with life; he understood the great artists, he understood the spirit of the Renaissance, he understood everything. The scene of one of his earlier novels was laid in Rome, the scene of another in

Florence, and I moved through these cities in company with the figures whom Mark Ambient had set so firmly upon their feet. This is why I was now so much happier even than before in the prospect of making his acquaintance.

At last, when I had dallied with this privilege long enough, I despatched to him the missive of the American poet. He had already gone out of town; he shrank from the rigour of the London season, and it was his habit to migrate on the first of June. Moreover, I had heard that this year he was hard at work on a new book, into which some of his impressions of the East were to be wrought, so that he desired nothing so much as quiet days. This knowledge, however, did not prevent me—*cet âge est sans pitié*—from sending with my friend's letter a note of my own, in which I asked Mr Ambient's leave to come down and see him for an hour or two, on a day to be designated by himself. My proposal was accompanied with a very frank expression of my sentiments, and the effect of the whole projectile was to elicit from the great man the kindest possible invitation. He would be delighted to see me, especially if I should turn up on the following Saturday and could remain till the Monday morning. We would take a walk over the Surrey commons, and I should tell him all about the other great man, the one in America. He indicated to me the best train, and it may be imagined whether on the Saturday afternoon I was punctual at Waterloo. He carried his benevolence to the point of coming to meet me at the little station at which I was to alight, and my heart beat very fast as I saw his handsome face, surmounted with a soft wide-awake, and which I knew by a photograph long since enshrined upon my mantelshelf, scanning the carriage-windows as the train rolled up. He recognised me as infallibly as I had recognised him; he appeared to know by instinct how a young American of an æsthetic turn would look when much divided between eagerness and modesty. He took me by the hand, and smiled at me, and said, "You must be—a—*you*, I think!" and asked if I should mind going on foot to his house, which would take but a few minutes. I remember thinking it a piece of extraordinary affability that he should give directions about the conveyance of my bag, and feeling altogether very happy and rosy, in fact quite transported, when he laid his hand on my shoulder as we came out of the station. I surveyed him, askance, as we walked together; I had already—I had indeed instantly—seen that he was a delightful creature. His face is so well known that I needn't describe it; he looked to me at once an English gentleman and a man of genius, and I thought that a happy combination. There was just a little of the Bohemian in his appearance; you would easily have guessed that he belonged to the guild of artists and men of letters. He was addicted to velvet jackets, to cigarettes, to loose shirt-collars, to looking a little dishevelled. His features, which were fine but not perfectly regular, are fairly enough represented in his portraits; but no portrait that I have seen gives any idea of his expression. There were so many things in it, and they chased each other in and out of his face. I have seen people who were grave and gay in quick alternation; but Mark Ambient was grave and gay at one and the same moment. There were other strange oppositions and contradictions in his slightly faded and fatigued countenance. He seemed both young and old, both anxious and indifferent. He had evidently had an active past, which inspired one with curiosity, and yet it was impossible not to be more curious still about his future. He was just enough above middle height to be spoken of as tall, and rather lean and long in the flank. He had the friend-liest, frankest manner possible, and yet I could see that he was shy. He was thirty-eight years old at the time *Beltraffio* was published. He asked me about his friend in America, about the length of my stay in England, about the last news in London and the people I had seen there; and I remember looking for the signs of genius in the very form of his ques-tions—and thinking I found it. I liked his voice. There was genius in his house, too, I thought, when we got there; there was imagination in the carpets and curtains, in the pictures and books, in the garden behind it, where certain old brown walls were muffled in creepers that appeared to me to have been copied from a masterpiece of one of the pre-Raphaelites. That was the way many things struck me at that time, in England; as if they were reproductions of something that existed primarily in art or literature. It was not the picture, the poem, the fictive page, that seemed to me a copy; these things were the originals, and the life of happy and distinguished people was fashioned in their image. Mark Ambient called his house a cottage, and I perceived afterwards that he was right; for if it had not been a cottage it must have been a villa, and a villa, in England at least, was not a place in which one could fancy him at home. But it was, to my vision, a cottage glorified and translated; it was a palace of art, on a slightly reduced scale—it was an old English demesne. It nestled under a cluster of magnificent beeches, it had little creaking lattices that opened out of, or into, pendent mats of ivy, and gables, and old red tiles, as well as a general aspect of being painted in water-colours and inhabited by people whose lives would go on in chapters and volumes. The lawn seemed to me of extraordinary extent, the garden-walls of incalculable height, the whole air of the place delightfully still, and private, and proper to itself. "My wife must be somewhere about," Mark Ambient said, as we went in. "We shall find her perhaps; we have got about an hour before dinner. She may be in the garden. I will show you my little place."

We passed through the house, and into the grounds, as I should have called them, which extended into the rear. They covered but three or four acres, but, like the house, they were very old and crooked, and full of traces of long habitation, with inequalities of level and little steps—mossy and cracked were these—which connected the different parts with each other. The limits of the place, cleverly dissimulated, were muffled in the deepest verdure. They made, as I remember, a kind of curtain at the farther end, in one of the folds of which, as it were, we presently perceived, from afar, a little group. "Ah, there she is!" said Mark Ambient; "and she has got the boy." He made this last remark in a tone slightly different from any in which he yet had spoken. I was not fully aware of it at the time, but it lingered in my ear and I afterwards understood it.

"Is it your son?" I inquired, feeling the question not to be brilliant.

"Yes, my only child. He is always in his mother's pocket. She coddles him too much." It came back to me afterwards, too—the manner in which he spoke these words. They were not petulant; they expressed rather a sudden coldness, a kind of mechanical submission. We went a few steps further, and then he stopped short, and called the boy, beckoning to him repeatedly.

"Dolcino, come and see your daddy!" There was something in the way he stood still and waited that made me think he did it for a purpose. Mrs Ambient had her arm round the child's waist, and he was leaning against her knee; but though he looked up at the sound of his father's voice, she gave no sign of releasing him. A lady, apparently a neighbour, was seated near her, and before them was a garden-table, on which a tea-service had been placed.

Mark Ambient called again, and Dolcino struggled in the maternal embrace, but he was too tightly held, and after two or three fruitless efforts he suddenly turned round and buried his head deep in his mother's lap. There was a certain awkwardness in the scene; I thought it rather odd that Mrs Ambient should pay so little attention to her husband. But I would not for the world have betrayed my thought, and, to conceal it, I observed that it must be such a pleasant thing to have tea in the garden. "Ah, she won't let him come!" said Mark Ambient, with a sigh; and we went our way till we reached the two ladies. He mentioned my name to his wife, and I noticed that he addressed her as "My dear," very genially, without any trace of resentment at her detention of the child. The quickness of the transition made me vaguely ask myself whether he were henpecked—a shocking conjecture, which I instantly dismissed. Mrs Ambient was quite such a wife as I should have expected him to have; slim and fair, with a long neck and pretty eyes and an air of great refinement. She was a little cold, and a little shy; but she was very sweet, and she had a certain look of race, justified by my afterwards learning that she was "connected" with two or three great families. I have seen poets married to women of whom it was difficult to conceive that they should gratify the poetic fancy —women with dull faces and glutinous minds, who were none the less, however, excellent wives. But there was no obvious incongruity in Mark Ambient's union. Mrs Ambient, delicate and quiet, in a white dress, with her beautiful child at her side, was worthy of the author of a work so distinguished as *Beltraffio*. Round her neck she wore a black velvet ribbon, of which the long ends, tied behind, hung down her back, and to which, in front, was attached a miniature portrait of her little boy. Her smooth, shining hair was confined in a net. She gave me a very pleasant greeting, and Dolcino—I thought this little name of endearment delightful—took advantage of her getting up to slip away from her and go to his father, who said nothing to him, but simply seized him and held him high in his arms for a moment, kissing him several times. I had lost no time in observing that the child, who was not more than seven years old, was extraordinarily beautiful. He had the face of an angel—the eyes, the hair, the more than mortal bloom, the smile of innocence. There was something touching, almost alarming, in his beauty, which seemed to be composed of elements too fine and pure for the breath of this world. When I spoke to him, and he came and held out his hand and smiled at me, I felt a sudden pity for him, as if he had been an orphan, or a changeling, or stamped with some social stigma. It was impossible to be, in fact, more exempt from these misfortunes, and yet, as one kissed him, it was hard to keep from murmuring "Poor little devil!" though why one should have applied this epithet to a living cherub is more than I can say. Afterwards, indeed, I knew a little better; I simply discovered that he was too charming to live, wondering at the same time that his parents should not have perceived it, and should not be in proportionate grief and despair. For myself, I had no doubt of his evanescence, having already noticed that there is a kind of charm which is like a death-warrant. The lady who had been sitting with Mrs Ambient was a jolly, ruddy personage, dressed in velveteen and rather limp feathers, whom I guessed to be the vicar's wife—our hostess did not introduce me—and who immediately began to talk to Ambient about chrysanthemums. This was a safe subject, and yet there was a certain surprise for me in seeing the author of *Beltraffio* even in such superficial communion with the Church of England. His writings implied so much detachment from that institution, expressed a view of life so profane, as it were, so independent, and so little likely, in general, to be thought edifying, that I should have expected to find him an object of horror to vicars and their ladies—of horror repaid on his own part by good-natured but brilliant mockery. This proves how little I knew as yet of the English people and their extraordinary talent for keeping up their forms, as well as of some of the mysteries of Mark Ambient's hearth and home. I found afterwards that he had, in his study, between smiles and cigar-smoke, some wonderful comparisons for his clerical neighbours; but meanwhile the chrysanthemums were a source of harmony, for he and the vicaress were equally fond of them, and I was surprised at the knowledge they exhibited of this interesting plant. The lady's visit, however, had presumably already been long, and she presently got up, saying she must go, and kissed Mrs

Ambient. Mark started to walk with her to the gate of the grounds, holding Dolcino by the hand.

"Stay with me, my darling," Mrs Ambient said to the boy, who was wandering away with his father.

Mark Ambient paid no attention to the summons, but Dolcino turned round and looked with eyes of shy entreaty at his mother. "Can't I go with papa?"

"Not when I ask you to stay with me."

"But please don't ask me, mamma," said the child, in his little clear, new voice.

"I must ask you when I want you. Come to me, my darling." And Mrs Ambient, who had seated herself again, held out her long, slender hands.

Her husband stopped, with his back turned to her, but without releasing the child. He was still talking to the vicaress, but this good lady, I think, had lost the thread of her attention. She looked at Mrs Ambient and at Dolcino, and then she looked at me, smiling very hard, in an extremely fixed, cheerful manner.

"Papa," said the child, "mamma wants me not to go with you."

"He's very tired—he has run about all day. He ought to be quiet till he goes to bed. Otherwise he won't sleep." These declarations fell successively and gravely from Mrs Ambient's lips.

Her husband, still without turning round, bent over the boy and looked at him in silence. The vicaress gave a genial, irrelevant laugh, and observed that he was a precious little pet. "Let him choose," said Mark Ambient. "My dear little boy, will you go with me or will you stay with your mother?"

"Oh, it's a shame!" cried the vicar's lady, with increased hilarity.

"Papa, I don't think I can choose," the child answered, making his voice very low and confidential. "But I have been a great deal with mamma to-day," he added in a moment.

"And very little with papa! My dear fellow, I think you have chosen!" And Mark Ambient walked off with his son, accompanied by re-echoing but inarticulate comments from my fellow-visitor.

His wife had seated herself again, and her fixed eyes, bent upon the ground, expressed for a few moments so much mute agitation that I felt as if almost any remark from my own lips would be a false note. But Mrs Ambient quickly recovered herself, and said to me civilly enough that she hoped I didn't mind having had to walk from the station. I reassured her on this point, and she went on, "We have got a thing that might have gone for you, but my husband wouldn't order it."

"That gave me the pleasure of a walk with him," I rejoined.

She was silent a minute, and then she said, "I believe the Americans walk very little."

"Yes, we always run," I answered, laughingly.

She looked at me seriously, and I began to perceive a certain coldness in her pretty eyes. "I suppose your distances are so great."

"Yes; but we break our marches! I can't tell you what a pleasure it is for me to find myself here," I added. "I have the greatest admiration for Mr Ambient."

"He will like that. He likes being admired."

"He must have a very happy life, then. He has many worshippers."

"Oh yes, I have seen some of them," said Mrs Ambient, looking away, very far from me, rather as if such a vision were before her at the moment. Something in her tone seemed to indicate that the vision was scarcely edifying, and I guessed very quickly that she was not in sympathy with the author of *Beltraffio*. I thought the fact strange, but, somehow, in the glow of my own enthusiasm, I didn't think it important; it only made me wish to be rather explicit about that enthusiasm.

"For me, you know," I remarked, "he is quite the greatest of living writers."

"Of course I can't judge. Of course he's very clever," said Mrs Ambient, smiling a little.

"He's magnificent, Mrs Ambient! There are pages in each of his books that have a perfection that classes them with the greatest things. Therefore, for me to see him in this familiar way—in his habit as he lives—and to find, apparently, the man as delightful as the artist, I can't tell you how much too good to be true it seems, and how great a privilege I think it." I knew that I was gushing, but I couldn't help it, and what I said was a good deal less than what I felt. I was by no means sure that I should dare to say even so much as this to Ambient himself, and there was a kind of rapture in speaking it out to his wife, which was not affected by the fact that, as a wife, she appeared peculiar. She listened to me with her face grave again, and with her lips a little compressed, as if there were no doubt, of course, that her husband was remarkable, but at the same time she had heard all this before and couldn't be expected to be particularly interested in it. There was even in her manner an intimation that I was rather young, and that people usually got over that sort of thing. "I assure you that for me this is a red-letter day," I added.

She made no response, until after a pause, looking round her, she said abruptly, though gently, "We are very much afraid about the fruit this year."

My eyes wandered to the mossy, mottled, garden-walls, where plum-trees and pear-trees, flattered and fastened upon the rusty bricks, looked like crucified figures with many arms. "Doesn't it promise well?" I inquired.

"No, the trees look very dull. We had such late frosts."

Then there was another pause. Mrs Ambient kept her eyes fixed on the opposite end of the grounds, as if she were watching for her husband's return with the child. "Is Mr Ambient fond of gardening?" it occurred to me to inquire, irresistibly impelled as I felt myself, moreover, to bring the conversation constantly back to him.

"He is very fond of plums," said his wife.

"Ah, well then, I hope your crop will be better than you fear. It's a lovely old place," I continued. "The whole character of it is that of certain places that he describes. Your house is like one of his pictures."

"It's a pleasant little place. There are hundreds like it."

"Oh, it has got his tone," I said laughing, and insisting on my point the more that Mrs Ambient appeared to see in my appreciation of her simple establishment a sign of limited experience.

It was evident that I insisted too much. "His tone?" she repeated, with a quick look at me and as lightly heightened colour.

"Surely he has a tone, Mrs Ambient."

"Oh yes, he has indeed! But I don't in the least consider that I am living in one of his books; I shouldn't care for that, at all," she went on, with a smile which had in some degree the effect of converting my slightly sharp protest into a joke deficient in point." I am afraid I am not very literary," said Mrs Ambient. "And I am not artistic."

"I am very sure you are not stupid nor *bornée*," I ventured to reply, with the accompaniment of feeling immediately afterwards that I had been both familiar and patronising. My only consolation was in the reflection that it was she, and not I, who had begun it. She had brought her idiosyncrasies into the discussion.

"Well, whatever I am, I am very different from my husband. If you like him, you won't like me. You needn't say anything. Your liking me isn't in the least necessary."

"Don't defy me!" I exclaimed.

She looked as if she had not heard me, which was the best thing she could do; and we sat some time without further speech. Mrs Ambient had evidently the enviable English quality of being able to be silent without being restless. But at last she spoke; she asked me if there seemed to be many people in town. I gave her what satisfaction I could on this point, and we talked a little about London and of some pictures it presented at that time of the year. At the end of this I came back, irrepressibly, to Mark Ambient.

"Doesn't he like to be there now? I suppose he doesn't find the proper quiet for his work. I should think his things had been written, for the most part, in a very still place. They suggest a great stillness, following on a kind of tumult—don't you think so? I suppose London is a tremendous place to collect impressions, but a refuge like this, in the country, must be much better for working them up. Does he get many of his impressions in London, do you think?" I proceeded from point to point, in this malign inquiry, simply because my hostess, who probably thought me a very pushing and talkative young man, gave me time; for when I paused—I have not represented my pauses—she simply continued to let her eyes wander, and, with her long fair fingers, played with the medallion on her neck. When I stopped altogether, however, she was obliged to say something, and what she said was that she had not the least idea where her husband got his impressions. This made me think her, for a moment, positively disagreeable; delicate and proper and rather aristocratically dry as she sat there. But I must either have lost the impression a moment later, or been goaded by it to further aggression, for I remember asking her whether Mr Ambient was in a good vein of work, and when we might look for the appearance of the book on which he was engaged. I have every reason now to know that she thought me an odious person.

She gave a strange, small laugh as she said, "I'm afraid you think I know a great deal more about my husband's work than I do. I haven't the least idea what he is doing," she added presently, in a slightly different, that is, a more explanatory, tone; as if she recognised in some degree the enormity of her confession. "I don't read what he writes!"

She did not succeed (and would not, even had she tried much harder) in making it seem to me anything less than monstrous. I stared at her, and I think I blushed. "Don't you admire his genius? Don't you admire *Beltraffio?*"

She hesitated a moment, and I wondered what she could possibly say. She did not speak—I could see—the first words that rose to her lips; she repeated what she had said a few minutes before. "Oh, of course he's very clever!" And with this she got up; her husband and little boy had reappeared. Mrs Ambient left me and went to meet them; she stopped and had a few words with her husband, which I did not hear, and which ended in her taking the child by the hand and returning to the house with him. Her husband joined me in a moment, looking, I thought, the least bit conscious and constrained, and said that if I would come in with him he would show me my room. In looking back upon these first moments of my visit to him, I find it important to avoid the error of appearing to have understood his situation from the first, and to have seen in him the signs of things which I learnt only afterwards. This later knowledge throws a backward light, and makes me forget that at least on the occasion of which I am speaking now (I mean that first afternoon), Mark Ambient struck me as a fortunate man. Allowing for this, I think he was rather silent and irresponsive as we walked back to the house—though I remember well the answer he made to a remark of mine in relation to his child.

"That's an extraordinary little boy of yours," I said. "I have never seen such a child."

"Why do you call him extraordinary?"

"He's so beautiful—so fascinating. He's like a little work of art."

He turned quickly, grasping my arm an instant. "Oh, don't call him that, or you'll—you'll———!" And in his hesitation he broke off, suddenly, laughing at my surprise. But immediately afterwards he added, "You will make his little future very difficult."

I declared that I wouldn't for the world take any liberties with his little future—it seemed to me to hang by threads of such delicacy. I should only be highly interested in watching it. "You Americans are very sharp," said Ambient. "You notice more things than we do."

"Ah, if you want visitors who are not struck with you, you shouldn't ask me down here!"

He showed me my room, a little bower of chintz, with open windows where the light was green, and before he left me he said irrelevantly, "As for my little boy, you know, we shall probably kill him between us, before we have done with him!" And he made this assertion as if he really believed it, without any appearance of jest, with his fine, near-sighted, expressive eyes looking straight into mine.

"Do you mean by spoiling him?"

"No—by fighting for him!"

"You had better give him to me to keep for you," I said. "Let me remove the apple of discord."

I laughed, of course, but he had the air of being perfectly serious. "It would be quite the best thing we could do. I should be quite ready to do it."

"I am greatly obliged to you for your confidence."

Mark Ambient lingered there, with his hands in his pockets. I felt, within a few moments, as if I had, morally speaking, taken several steps nearer to him. He looked weary, just as he faced me then, looked preoccupied, and as if there were something one might do for him. I was terribly conscious of the limits of my own ability, but I wondered what such a service might be—feeling at bottom, however, that the only thing I could do for him was to like him. I suppose he guessed this, and was grateful for what was in my mind; for he went on presently, "I haven't the advantage of being an American. But I also notice a little, and I have an idea that—a——" here he smiled and laid his hand on my shoulder, "that even apart from your nationality, you are not destitute of intelligence! I have only known you half an hour, but—a——" And here he hesitated again. "You are very young, after all."

"But you may treat me as if I could understand you!" I said; and before he left me to dress for dinner he had virtually given me a promise that he would.

When I went down into the drawing-room—I was very punctual—I found that neither my hostess nor my host had appeared. A lady rose from a sofa, however, and inclined her head as I rather surprisedly gazed at her. "I dare say you don't know me," she said, with a modern laugh. "I am Mark Ambient's sister." Whereupon I shook hands with her—saluting her very low. Her laugh was modern—by which I mean that it consisted of the vocal agitation which, between people who meet in drawing-rooms, serves as the solvent of social mysteries, the medium of transitions; but her appearance was—what shall I call it?—mediæval. She was pale and angular, with a long, thin face, inhabited by sad, dark eyes, and black hair intertwined with golden fillets and curious chains. She wore a faded velvet robe, which clung to her when she moved, fashioned, as to the neck and sleeves, like the garments of old Venetians and Florentines. She looked pictorial and melancholy, and was so perfect an image of a type which I—in my ignorance—supposed to be extinct, that while she rose before me I was almost as much startled as if I had seen a ghost. I afterwards perceived that Miss Ambient was not incapable of deriving pleasure from the effect she produced, and I think this sentiment had something to do with her sinking again into her seat, with her long, lean, but not ungraceful arms locked together in an archaic manner on her knees, and her mournful eyes addressing themselves to me with an intentness which was an earnest of what they were destined subsequently to inflict upon me. She was a singular, self-conscious, artificial creature, and I never, subsequently-more than half penetrated her motives and mysteries. Of one thing I am sure, however: that they were considerably less extraordinary than her appearance announced. Miss Ambient was a restless, yearning spinster, consumed with the love of Michael-Angelesque attitudes and mystical robes; but I am pretty sure she had not in her nature those depths of un-utterable thought which, when you first knew her, seemed to look out from her eyes and to prompt her complicated gestures. Those features, in especial, had a misleading elo-quence; they rested upon you with a far-off dimness, an air of obstructed sympathy, which was certainly not always a key to the spirit of their owner; and I suspect that a young lady could not really have been so dejected and disillusioned as Miss Ambient looked, without having committed a crime for which she was consumed with remorse or parted with a hope which she could not sanely have entertained. She had, I believe, the usual allowance of vulgar impulses; she wished to be looked at, she wished to be married, she wished to be thought original. It costs me something to speak in this irreverent manner of Mark Ambient's sister, but I shall have still more disagreeable things to say before I have finished my little anecdote, and moreover—I confess it—I owe the young lady a sort of grudge. Putting aside the curious cast of her face, she had no natural aptitude for an artistic development—she had little real intelligence. But her affectations rubbed off on her brother's renown, and as there were plenty of people who dis-approved of him totally, they could easily point to his sister as a person formed by his influence. It was quite possible to regard her as a warning, and she had done him but little good with the world at large. He was the original, and she was the inevitable imitation. I think he was scarcely aware of the impression she produced—beyond having a general idea that she made up very well as a Rossetti; he was used to her, and he was sorry for her—wishing she would marry and observing that she didn't. Doubtless I take her too seriously, for she did me no harm—though I am bound to add that I feel I can only half account for her. She was not so mystical as she looked, but she was a strange, indirect, uncomfortable, embarrassing woman. My story will give the reader at best so very small a knot to untie that I need not hope to excite his curiosity by delaying to remark that Mrs Ambient hated her sister-in-law. This I only found out afterwards, when I found out some other things. But I mention it at once, for I shall perhaps not seem to count too much on having enlisted the imagination of the reader if I say that he will already have guessed it. Mrs Ambient was a person of conscience, and she endeavoured to behave properly to her kinswoman, who spent a month with her twice a year; but it required no great insight to discover that the two ladies were made of a very different paste, and that the usual feminine hypocrisies must have cost them, on either side, much more than the usual effort. Mrs Ambient, smooth-haired, thin-lipped, perpetually fresh, must have regarded her crumpled and dishevelled visitor as a very stale joke; she herself was not a Rossetti, but a Gainsborough or a Lawrence, and she had in her appearance no elements more romantic than a cold, ladylike candour, and a well-starched muslin dress. It was in a garment, and with an expression, of this kind, that she made her entrance, after I had exchanged a few words with Miss Ambient. Her husband presently followed her, and there being no other company we went to dinner. The impression I received from that repast is present to me still. There were elements of oddity in my companions, but they were vague and latent, and didn't interfere with my delight. It came mainly, of course, from Ambient's talk, which was the most brilliant and interesting I had ever heard. I know not whether he laid himself out to dazzle a rather juvenile pilgrim from over the sea; but it matters little, for it was very easy for him to shine. He was almost better as a talker than as a writer; that is, if the extraordinary finish of his written prose be really, as some people have maintained, a fault. There was such a kindness in him, however, that I have no doubt it gave him ideas to see me sit open-mouthed, as I suppose I did. Not so the two ladies, who not only were very nearly dumb from beginning to the end of the meal, but who had not the air of being struck with such an exhibition of wit and knowledge. Mrs Ambient, placid and detached, met neither my eye nor her husband's; she attended to her dinner, watched the servants, arranged the puckers in her dress, exchanged at wide intervals a remark with her sister-in-law, and while she slowly rubbed her white hands, between the courses, looked out of the window at the first signs of twilight —the long June day allowing us to dine without candles. Miss Ambient appeared to give little direct heed to her brother's discourse; but, on the other hand, she was much engaged in watching its effect upon me. Her lustreless pupils continued to attach themselves to my countenance, and it was only her air of belonging to another century that kept them from being importunate. She seemed to look at me across the ages, and the interval of time diminished the realism of the performance. It was as if she knew in a general way that her brother must be talking very well, but she herself was so rich in ideas that she had no need to pick them up, and was at liberty to see what would become of a young American when subjected to a high æsthetic temperature. The temperature was æsthetic, certainly, but it was less so than I could have desired, for I was unsuccessful in certain little attempts to make Mark Ambient talk about himself. I tried to put him on the ground of his own writings, but he slipped through my fingers every time and shifted the saddle to one of his contemporaries. He talked about Balzac and Browning, and what was being done in foreign countries, and about his recent tour in the East, and the extraordinary forms of life that one saw in that part of the world. I perceived that he had reasons for not wishing to descant upon literature, and suffered him without protest to deliver himself on certain social topics, which he treated with extraordinary humour and with constant revelations of that power of ironical portraiture of which his books are full. He had a great deal to say about London, as London appears to the observer who doesn't fear the accusation of cynicism, during the high-pressure time—from April to July—of its peculiarities. He flashed his faculty of making the fanciful real and the real fanciful over the perfunctory pleasures and desperate exertions of so many of his compatriots, among whom there were evidently not a few types for which he had little love. London bored him, and he made capital sport of it; his only allusion, that I can remember, to his own work was his saying that he meant some day to write an immense grotesque epic of London society. Miss Ambient's perpetual gaze seemed to say to me, "Do you perceive how artistic we are? frankly now, is it possible to be more artistic than this? You surely won't deny that we are remarkable." I was irritated by her use of the plural pronoun, for she had no right to pair herself with her brother; and moreover, of course, I could not see my way to include Mrs Ambient. But there was no doubt that (for that matter) they were all remarkable, and, with all allowances, I had never heard anything so artistic. Mark Ambient's conversation seemed to play over the whole field of knowledge and taste; it made me feel that this at last was real talk, that this was distinction, culture, experience.

After the ladies had left us he took me into his study, to smoke, and here I led him on to gossip freely enough about himself. I was bent upon proving to him that I was worthy to listen to him, upon repaying him (for what he had said to me before dinner) by showing him how perfectly I understood. He liked to talk, he liked to defend his ideas (not that I attacked them), he liked a little perhaps—it was a pardonable weakness—to astonish the youthful mind and to feel its admiration and sympathy. I confess that my own youthful mind was considerably astonished at some of his speeches;

he startled me and he made me wince. He could not help forgetting, or rather he couldn't know, how little personal contact I had had with the school in which he was master; and
he promoted me at a jump, as it were, to the study of its inner-
most mysteries. My trepidations, however, were delightful;
they were just what I had hoped for, and their only fault was
that they passed away too quickly, for I found that, as regards
most things, I very soon seized Mark Ambient's point of view.
It was the point of view of the artist to whom every mani-
festation of human energy was a thrilling spectacle, and who
felt for ever the desire to resolve his experience of life into a
literary form. On this matter of the passion for form—the
attempt at perfection, the quest for which was to his mind the
real search for the holy grail, he said the most interesting,
the most inspiring things. He mixed with them a thousand illustrations from his own life, from other lives that he had known,
from history and fiction, and, above all, from the annals of
the time that was dear to him beyond all periods—the Italian
cinque-cento. I saw that in his books he had only said half of his
thought, and what he had kept back—from motives that I
deplored when I learnt them later—was the richer part. It was
his fortune to shock a great many people, but there was not a
grain of bravado in his pages (I have always maintained it,
though often contradicted), and at bottom the poor fellow,
an artist to his finger-tips, and regarding a failure of completeness as a crime, had an extreme dread of scandal. There are
people who regret that having gone so far he did not go
further; but I regret nothing (putting aside two or three of the
motives I just mentioned), for he arrived at perfection, and I
don't see how you can go beyond that. The hours I spent in
his study—this first one and the few that followed it; they
were not, after all, so numerous—seem to glow, as I look
back on them, with a tone which is partly that of the brown
old room, rich, under the shaded candlelight where we sat
and smoked, with the dusky, delicate bindings of valuable

books; partly that of his voice, of which I still catch the echo, charged with the images that came at his command. When we went back to the drawing-room we found Miss Ambient alone in possession of it; and she informed us that her sister-in-law had a quarter of an hour before been called by the nurse to see Dolcino, who appeared to be a little feverish.

"Feverish! how in the world does he come to be feverish?" Ambient asked. "He was perfectly well this afternoon."

"Beatrice says you walked him about too much—you almost killed him."

"Beatrice must be very happy—she has an opportunity to triumph!" Mark Ambient said, with a laugh of which the bitterness was just perceptible.

"Surely not if the child is ill," I ventured to remark, by way of pleading for Mrs Ambient.

"My dear fellow, you are not married—you don't know the nature of wives!" my host exclaimed.

"Possibly not; but I know the nature of mothers."

"Beatrice is perfect as a mother," said Miss Ambient, with a tremendous sigh and her fingers interlaced on her embroidered knees.

"I shall go up and see the child," her brother went on. "Do you suppose he's asleep?"

"Beatrice won't let you see him, Mark," said the young lady, looking at me, though she addressed our companion.

"Do you call that being perfect as a mother?" Ambient inquired.

"Yes, from her point of view."

"Damn her point of view!" cried the author of *Beltraffio*. And he left the room; after which we heard him ascend the stairs.

I sat there for some ten minutes with Miss Ambient, and we, naturally, had some conversation, which was begun, I think, by my asking her what the point of view of her sister-in-law could be.

"Oh, it's so very odd," she said. "But we are so very odd, altogether. Don't you find us so? We have lived so much abroad. Have you people like us in America?"

"You are not all alike, surely; so that I don't think I understand your question. We have no one like your brother—I may go so far as that."

"You have probably more persons like his wife," said Miss Ambient, smiling.

"I can tell you that better when you have told me about her point of view."

"Oh yes—oh yes. Well, she doesn't like his ideas. She doesn't like them for the little boy. She thinks them undesirable."

Being quite fresh from the contemplation of some of Mark Ambient's *arcana*, I was particularly in a position to appreciate this announcement. But the effect of it was to make me (after staring a moment) burst into laughter, which I instantly checked when I remembered that there was a sick child above.

"What has that infant to do with ideas?" I asked. "Surely, he can't tell one from another. Has he read his father's novels?"

"He's very precocious and very sensitive, and his mother thinks she can't begin to guard him too early." Miss Ambient's head drooped a little to one side, and her eyes fixed themselves on futurity. Then, suddenly, there was a strange alteration in her face; she gave a smile that was more joyless than her gravity—a conscious, insincere smile, and added, "When one has children, it's a great responsibility—what one writes."

"Children are terrible critics," I answered. "I am rather glad I haven't got any."

"Do you also write then? And in the same style as my brother? And do you like that style? And do people appreciate it in America? I don't write, but I think I feel." To these and various other inquiries and remarks the young lady treated me, till we heard her brother's step in the hall again and Mark

Ambient reappeared. He looked flushed and serious, and I supposed that he had seen something to alarm him in the condition of his child. His sister apparently had another idea; she gazed at him a moment as if he were a burning ship on the horizon, and simply murmured—"Poor old Mark!"

"I hope you are not anxious," I said.

"No, but I am disappointed. She won't let me in. She has locked the door, and I'm afraid to make a noise." I suppose there might have been something ridiculous in a confession of this kind, but I liked my new friend so much that for me it didn't detract from his dignity. "She tells me—from behind the door—that she will let me know if he is worse."

"It's very good of her," said Miss Ambient.

I had exchanged a glance with Mark in which it is possible that he read that my pity for him was untinged with contempt—though I know not why he should have cared; and as, presently, his sister got up and took her bedroom candlestick, he proposed that we should go back to his study. We sat there till after midnight; he put himself into his slippers, into an old velvet jacket, lighted an ancient pipe and talked considerably less than he had done before. There were longish pauses in our communion, but they only made me feel that we had advanced in intimacy. They helped me, too, to understand my friend's personal situation, and to perceive that it was by no means the happiest possible. When his face was quiet, it was vaguely troubled; it seemed to me to show that for him, too, life was a struggle, as it has been for many other men of genius. At last I prepared to leave him, and then, to my ineffable joy, he gave me some of the sheets of his forthcoming book—it was not finished, but he had indulged in the luxury, so dear to writers of deliberation, of having it "set up," from chapter to chapter, as he advanced—he gave me, I say, the early pages, the *prémices*, as the French have it, of this new fruit of his imagination, to take to my room and look over at my leisure. I was just quitting him when the door of his study was noiselessly pushed open, and Mrs Ambient stood before us. She looked at us a moment with her candle in her hand, and then she said to her husband that as she supposed he had not gone to bed she had come down to tell him that Dolcino was more quiet and would probably be better in the morning. Mark Ambient made no reply; he simply slipped past her, in the doorway, as if he were afraid she would seize him in his passage, and bounded upstairs, to judge for himself of his child's condition. Mrs Ambient looked slightly discomfited, and for a moment I thought she was going to give chase to her husband. But she resigned herself, with a sigh, while her eyes wandered over the lamp-lit room, where various books, at which I had been looking, were pulled out of their places on the shelves, and the fumes of tobacco seemed to hang in mid-air. I bade her good-night, and then, without intention, by a kind of fatality, the perversity which had already made me insist unduly on talking with her about her husband's achievements, I alluded to the precious proof-sheets with which Ambient had entrusted me, and which I was nursing there under my arm. "It is the opening chapters of his new book," I said. "Fancy my satisfaction at being allowed to carry them to my room!"

She turned away, leaving me to take my candlestick from the table in the hall; but before we separated, thinking it apparently a good occasion to let me know once for all—since I was beginning, it would seem, to be quite "thick" with my host—that there was no fitness in my appealing to her for sympathy in such a case; before we separated, I say, she remarked to me, with her quick, round, well-bred utterance, "I daresay you attribute to me ideas that I haven't got. I don't take that sort of interest in my husband's proof-sheets. I consider his writings most objectionable!"

II

I HAD some curious conversation the next morning with Miss Ambient, whom I found strolling in the garden before breakfast. The whole place looked as fresh and trim, amid the twitter of the birds, as if, an hour before, the housemaids had been turned into it with their dustpans and feather-brushes. I almost hesitated to light a cigarette, and was doubly startled when, in the act of doing so, I suddenly perceived the sister of my host, who had, in any case, something of the oddity of an apparition, standing before me. She might have been posing for her photograph. Her sad-coloured robe arranged itself in serpentine folds at her feet; her hands locked themselves listlessly together in front; and her chin rested upon a *cinquecento* ruff. The first thing I did, after bidding her good morning, was to ask her for news of her little nephew—to express the hope that she had heard he was better. She was able to gratify this hope, and spoke as if we might expect to see him during the day. We walked through the shrubberies together, and she gave me a great deal of information about her brother's *ménage*, which offered me an opportunity to mention to her that his wife had told me, the night before, that she thought his productions objectionable.

"She doesn't usually come out with that so soon!" Miss Ambient exclaimed, in answer to this piece of gossip.

"Poor lady, she saw that I am a fanatic."

"Yes, she won't like you for that. But you mustn't mind, if the rest of us like you! Beatrice thinks a work of art ought to have a 'purpose.' But she's a charming woman—don't you think her charming?—she's such a type of the lady."

"She's very beautiful," I answered; while I reflected that though it was true, apparently, that Mark Ambient was mismated, it was also perceptible that his sister was perfidious. She told me that her brother and his wife had no other difference but this one, that she thought his writings immoral and his influence pernicious. It was a fixed idea; she was afraid of these things for the child. I answered that it was not a trifle —a woman's regarding her husband's mind as a well of corruption; and she looked quite struck with the novelty of my remark. "But there hasn't been any of the sort of trouble that there so often is among married people," she said. "I suppose you can judge for yourself that Beatrice isn't at all—well, whatever they call it when a woman misbehaves herself. And Mark doesn't make love to other people, either. I assure you he doesn't! All the same, of course, from her point of view, you know, she has a dread of my brother's influence on the child—on the formation of his character, of his principles. It is as if it were a subtle poison, or a contagion, or something that would rub off on Dolcino when his father kisses him or holds him on his knee. If she could, she would prevent Mark from ever touching him. Every one knows it; visitors see it for themselves; so there is no harm in my telling you. Isn't it excessively odd? It comes from Beatrice's being so religious, and so tremendously moral, and all that. And then, of course, we mustn't forget," my companion added, unexpectedly, "that some of Mark's ideas are—well, really—rather queer!"

I reflected, as we went into the house, where we found Ambient unfolding the *Observer* at the breakfast-table, that none of them were probably quite so queer as his sister. Mrs Ambient did not appear at breakfast, being rather tired with her ministrations, during the night, to Dolcino. Her husband mentioned, however, that she was hoping to go to church. I afterwards learned that she did go, but I may as well announce without delay that he and I did not accompany her. It was while the church-bell was murmuring in the distance that the author of *Beltraffio* led me forth for the ramble he had spoken of in his note. I will not attempt to say where we went, or to describe what we saw. We kept to the fields and copses and commons, and breathed the same sweet air as the nibbling donkeys and the browsing sheep, whose woolliness seemed to me, in those early days of my acquaintance with English objects, but a part of the general texture of the small, dense landscape, which looked as if the harvest were gathered by the shears. Everything was full of expression for Mark Ambient's visitor—from the big, bandy-legged geese, whose whiteness was a "note," amid all the tones of green, as they wandered beside a neat little oval pool, the foreground of a thatched and white-washed inn, with a grassy approach and a pictorial sign—from these humble wayside animals to the crests of high woods which let a gable or a pinnacle peep here and there, and looked, even at a distance, like trees of good company, conscious of an individual profile. I admired the hedgerows, I plucked the faint-hued heather, and I was for ever stopping to say how charming I thought the thread-like footpaths across the fields, which wandered, in a diagonal of finer grain, from one smooth stile to another. Mark Ambient was abundantly good-natured, and was as much entertained with my observations as I was with the literary allusions of the landscape. We sat and smoked upon stiles, broaching paradoxes in the decent English air; we took short cuts across a park or two, where the bracken was deep, and my companion nodded to the old woman at the gate; we skirted rank covers, which rustled here and there as we passed, and we stretched ourselves at last on a heathery hillside where, if the sun was not too hot, neither was the earth too cold, and where the country lay beneath us in a rich blue mist. Of course I had already told Ambient what I thought of his new novel, having the previous night read every word of the opening chapters before I went to bed.

"I am not without hope of being able to make it my best," he said, as I went back to the subject, while we turned up our heels to the sky. "At least the people who dislike my prose—

and there are a great many of them, I believe—will dislike
this work most." This was the first time I had heard him allude
to the people who couldn't read him—a class which is supposed always to sit heavy upon the consciousness of the man
of letters. A man organised for literature, as Mark Ambient
was, must certainly have had the normal proportion of sensi-
tiveness, of irritability; the artistic *ego*, capable in some cases
of such monstrous development, must have been, in his composition, sufficiently erect and definite. I will not therefore go
so far as to say that he never thought of his detractors, or that
he had any illusions with regard to the number of his admirers (he could never so far have deceived himself as to believe he was popular); but I may at least affirm that adverse
criticism, as I had occasion to perceive later, ruffled him visibly
but little, that he had an air of thinking it quite natural he
should be offensive to many minds, and that he very seldom
talked about the newspapers—which, by the way, were
always very stupid in regard to the author of *Beltraffio*. Of
course he may have thought about them—the newspapers—
night and day; the only point I wish to make is that he didn't
show it; while, at the same time, he didn't strike one as a
man who was on his guard. I may add that, as regards his hope
of making the work on which he was then engaged the best of
his books, it was only partly carried out. That place belongs,
incontestably, to *Beltraffio*, in spite of the beauty of certain
parts of its successor. I am pretty sure, however, that he had,
at the moment of which I speak, no sense of failure; he was
in love with his idea, which was indeed magnificent, and
though for him, as (I suppose) for every artist, the act of execution had in it as much torment as joy, he saw his work
growing a little every day and filling out the largest plan he
had yet conceived. "I want to be truer than I have ever been,"
he said, settling himself on his back, with his hands clasped
behind his head; "I want to give an impression of life itself.
No, you may say what you will. I have always arranged

things too much, always smoothed them down and rounded them off and tucked them in—done everything to them that life doesn't do. I have been a slave to the old superstitions."

"You a slave, my dear Mark Ambient? You have the freest imagination of our day!"

"All the more shame to me to have done some of the things I have! The reconciliation of the two women in *Ginistrella*, for instance—which could never really have taken place. That sort of thing is ignoble; I blush when I think of it! This new affair must be a golden vessel, filled with the purest distillation of the actual; and oh, how it bothers me, the shaping of the vase —the hammering of the metal! I have to hammer it so fine, so smooth; I don't do more than an inch or two a day. And all the while I have to be so careful not to let a drop of the liquor escape! When I see the kind of things that Life does, I despair of ever catching her peculiar trick. She has an impudence, Life! If one risked a fiftieth part of the effects she risks! It takes ever so long to believe it. You don't know yet, my dear fellow. It isn't till one has been watching Life for forty years that one finds out half of what she's up to! Therefore one's earlier things must inevitably contain a mass of rot. And with what one sees, on one side, with its tongue in its cheek, defying one to be real enough, and on the other the *bonnes gens* rolling up their eyes at one's cynicism, the situation has elements of the ludicrous which the artist himself is doubtless in a position to appreciate better than any one else. Of course one mustn't bother about the *bonnes gens*," Mark Ambient went on, while my thoughts reverted to his lady-like wife, as interpreted by his remarkable sister.

"To sink your shaft deep, and polish the plate through which people look into it—that's what your work consists of," I remember remarking.

"Ah, polishing one's plate—that is the torment of execution!" he exclaimed, jerking himself up and sitting forward. "The effort to arrive at a surface—if you think a surface necessary—some people don't, happily for them! My dear fellow, if you could see the surface I dream of—as compared with the one with which I have to content myself. Life is really too short for art—one hasn't time to make one's shell ideally hard. Firm and bright—firm and bright!—the devilish thing has a way, sometimes, of being bright without being firm. When I rap it with my knuckles it doesn't give the right sound. There are horrible little flabby spots where I have taken the second-best word, because I couldn't for the life of me think of the best. If you knew how stupid I am sometimes! They look to me now like pimples and ulcers on the brow of beauty!"

"That's very bad—very bad," I said, as gravely as I could.

"Very bad? It's the highest social offence I know; it ought —it absolutely ought—I'm quite serious—to be capital. If I knew I should be hanged else, I should manage to find the best word. The people who couldn't—some of them don't know it when they see it—would shut their inkstands, and we shouldn't be deluged by this flood of rubbish!"

I will not attempt to repeat everything that passed between us or to explain just how it was that, every moment I spent in his company, Mark Ambient revealed to me more and more that he looked at all things from the standpoint of the artist, felt all life as literary material. There are people who will tell me that this is a poor way of feeling it, and I am not concerned to defend my statement—having space merely to remark that there is something to be said for any interest which makes a man feel so much. If Mark Ambient did really, as I suggested above, have imaginative contact with "all life," I, for my part, envy him his *arrière-pensée*. At any rate it was through the receipt of this impression of him that by the time we returned I had acquired the feeling of intimacy I have noted. Before we got up for the homeward stretch he alluded to his wife's having once—or perhaps more than once—asked him whether he should like Dolcino to read *Beltraffio*. I think he was unconscious at the moment of all that this conveyed to me—as well, doubtless, of my extreme curiosity to hear what he had replied. He had said that he hoped very much Dolcino would read all his works—when he was twenty; he should like him to know what his father had done. Before twenty it would be useless—he wouldn't understand them.

"And meanwhile do you propose to hide them—to lock them up in a drawer?" Mrs Ambient had inquired.

"Oh no; we must simply tell him that they are not intended for small boys. If you bring him up properly, after that he won't touch them."

To this Mrs Ambient had made answer that it would be very awkward when he was about fifteen, and I asked her husband if it was his opinion in general, then, that young people should not read novels.

"Good ones—certainly not!" said my companion. I suppose I had had other views, for I remember saying that, for myself, I was not sure it was bad for them—if the novels were "good" enough. "Bad for *them*, I don't say so much!" Ambient exclaimed. "But very bad, I am afraid, for the novel." That oblique, accidental allusion to his wife's attitude was followed by a franker style of reference as we walked home. "The difference between us is simply the opposition between two distinct ways of looking at the world, which have never succeeded in getting on together, or making any kind of common ménage, since the beginning of time. They have borne all sorts of names, and my wife would tell you it's the difference between Christian and Pagan. I may be a pagan, but I don't like the name—it sounds sectarian. She thinks me, at any rate, no better than an ancient Greek. It's the difference between making the most of life and making the least—so that you'll get another better one in some other time and place. Will it be a sin to make the most of that one too, I wonder? and shall we have to be bribed off in the future state, as well as in the present? Perhaps I care too much for

beauty—I don't know; I delight in it, I adore it, I think of it
continually, I try to produce it, to reproduce it. My wife
holds that we shouldn't think too much about it. She's always
afraid of that—always on her guard. I don't know what she
has got on her back! And she's so pretty, too, herself! Don't
you think she's lovely? She was, at any rate, when I married
her. At that time I wasn't aware of that difference I speak of
—I thought it all came to the same thing: in the end, as they
say. Well, perhaps it will in the end. I don't know what the
end will be. Moreover, I care for seeing things as they are;
that's the way I try to show them in my novels. But you
mustn't talk to Mrs Ambient about things as they are. She
has a mortal dread of things as they are."

"She's afraid of them for Dolcino," I said: surprised a
moment afterwards at being in a position—thanks to Miss
Ambient—to be so explanatory; and surprised even now that
Mark shouldn't have shown visibly that he wondered what the
deuce I knew about it. But he didn't; he simply exclaimed, with
a tenderness that touched me—

"Ah, nothing shall ever hurt *him!*" He told me more
about his wife before we arrived at the gate of his house, and
if it be thought that he was querulous, I am afraid I must
admit that he had some of the foibles as well as the gifts of the
artistic temperament; adding, however, instantly, that hitherto, to the best of my belief, he had very rarely complained.
"She thinks me immoral—that's the long and short of it,"
he said, as we paused outside a moment, and his hand rested
on one of the bars of his gate; while his conscious, expressive,
perceptive eyes—the eyes of a foreigner, I had begun to
account them, much more than of the usual Englishman—
viewing me now evidently as quite a familiar friend, took part
in the declaration. "It's very strange, when one thinks it all
over, and there's a grand comicality in it which I should like
to bring out. She is a very nice woman, extraordinarily well
behaved, upright, and clever, and with a tremendous lot of

good sense about a good many matters. Yet her conception of a novel—she has explained it to me once or twice, and she doesn't do it badly, as exposition—is a thing so false that it makes me blush. It is a thing so hollow, so dishonest, so lying, in which life is so blinked and blinded, so dodged and disfigured, that it makes my ears burn. It's two different ways of looking at the whole affair," he repeated, pushing open the gate. "And they are irreconcilable!" he added with a sigh. We went forward to the house, but on the walk, half way to the door, he stopped, and said to me, "If you are going into this kind of thing, there's a fact you should know beforehand; it may save you some disappointment. There's a hatred of art —there's a hatred of literature!" I looked up at the charming house, with its genial colour and crookedness, and I answered with a smile that those evil passions might exist, but that I should never have expected to find them there. "Oh, it doesn't matter, after all," he said, laughing; which I was glad to hear, for I was reproaching myself with having excited him.

If I had, his excitement soon passed off, for at lunch he was delightful; strangely delightful, considering that the difference between himself and his wife was, as he had said, irreconcilable. He had the art, by his manner, by his smile, by his natural kindliness, of reducing the importance of it in the common concerns of life, and Mrs Ambient, I must add, lent herself to this transaction with a very good grace. I watched her, at table, for further illustrations of that fixed idea of which Miss Ambient had spoken to me; for in the light of the united revelations of her sister-in-law and her husband, she had come to seem to me a very singular personage. I am obliged to say that the signs of a fanatical temperament were not more striking in my hostess than before; it was only after a while that her air of incorruptible conformity, her tapering, monosyllabic correctness, began to appear to be themselves a cold, thin flame. Certainly, at first, she looked like a woman with as few passions as possible; but if she had a passion at all, it

would be that of Philistinism. She might have been, for there
are guardian-spirits, I suppose, of all great principles—the
angel of propriety. Mark Ambient, apparently, ten years
before, had simply perceived that she was an angel, without
asking himself of what. He had been quite right in calling my
attention to her beauty. In looking for the reason why he
should have married her, I saw, more than before, that she
was, physically speaking, a wonderfully cultivated human
plant—that she must have given him many ideas and images.
It was impossible to be more pencilled, more garden-like,
more delicately tinted and petalled.

If I had had it in my heart to think Ambient a little of a
hypocrite for appearing to forget at table everything he had
said to me during our walk, I should instantly have cancelled
such a judgment on reflecting that the good news his wife was
able to give him about their little boy was reason enough for
his sudden air of happiness. It may have come partly, too,
from a certain remorse at having complained to me of the fair
lady who sat there—a desire to show me that he was after all
not so miserable. Dolcino continued to be much better, and
he had been promised he should come down stairs after he
had had his dinner. As soon as we had risen from our own
meal Ambient slipped away, evidently for the purpose of
going to his child; and no sooner had I observed this than I
became aware that his wife had simultaneously vanished. It
happened that Miss Ambient and I, both at the same moment,
saw the tail of her dress whisk out of a doorway—which led
the young lady to smile at me, as if I now knew all the secrets
of the place. I passed with her into the garden, and we sat
down on a dear old bench which rested against the west wall
of the house. It was a perfect spot for the middle period of a
Sunday in June, and its felicity seemed to come partly from
an antique sun-dial which, rising in front of us and forming
the centre of a small, intricate parterre, measured the moments
ever so slowly, and made them safe for leisure and talk. The

garden bloomed in the suffused afternoon, the tall beeches stood still for an example, and, behind and above us, a rose-tree of many seasons, clinging to the faded grain of the brick, expressed the whole character of the scene in a familiar, exquisite smell. It seemed to me a place for genius to have every sanction, and not to encounter challenges and checks. Miss Ambient asked me if I had enjoyed my walk with her brother, and whether we had talked of many things.

"Well, of most things," I said, smiling, though I remembered that we had not talked of Miss Ambient.

"And don't you think some of his theories are very peculiar?"

"Oh, I guess I agree with them all." I was very particular, for Miss Ambient's entertainment, to guess.

"Do you think art is everything?" she inquired in a moment.

"In art, of course I do!"

"And do you think beauty is everything?"

"I don't know about its being everything. But it's very delightful."

"Of course it is difficult for a woman to know how far to go," said my companion. "I adore everything that gives a charm to life. I am intensely sensitive to form. But sometimes I draw back—don't you see what I mean?—I don't quite see where I shall be landed. I only want to be quiet, after all," Miss Ambient continued, in a tone of stifled yearning which seemed to indicate that she had not yet arrived at her desire. "And one must be good, at any rate, must not one?" she inquired, with a cadence apparently intended for an assurance that my answer would settle this recondite question for her. It was difficult for me to make it very original, and I am afraid I repaid her confidence with an unblushing platitude. I remember, moreover, appending to it an inquiry, equally destitute of freshness, and still more wanting perhaps in tact, as to whether she did not mean to go to church, as that was an

obvious way of being good. She replied that she had performed this duty in the morning, and that for her, on Sunday
afternoon, supreme virtue consisted in answering the week's
letters. Then suddenly, without transition, she said to me,
"It's quite a mistake about Dolcino being better. I have seen
him, and he's not at all right."

"Surely his mother would know, wouldn't she?" I suggested.

She appeared for a moment to be counting the leaves on
one of the great beeches. "As regards most matters, one can
easily say what, in a given situation, my sister-in-law would
do. But as regards this one, there are strange elements at
work."

"Strange elements? Do you mean in the constitution of the
child?"

"No, I mean in my sister-in-law's feelings."

"Elements of affection, of course; elements of anxiety. Why
do you call them strange?"

She repeated my words. "Elements of affection, elements of
anxiety. She is very anxious."

Miss Ambient made me vaguely uneasy—she almost
frightened me, and I wished she would go and write her
letters. "His father will have seen him now," I said, "and if
he is not satisfied he will send for the doctor."

"The doctor ought to have been here this morning. He
lives only two miles away."

I reflected that all this was very possibly only a part of the
general tragedy of Miss Ambient's view of things; but I asked
her why she hadn't urged such a necessity upon her sister-
in-law. She answered me with a smile of extraordinary significance, and told me that I must have very little idea of what
her relations with Beatrice were; but I must do her the justice
to add that she went on to make herself a little more compre-
hensible by saying that it was quite reason enough for her
sister not to be alarmed that Mark would be sure to be. He

was always nervous about the child, and as they were pre-
destined by nature to take opposite views, the only thing for
Beatrice was to cultivate a false optimism. If Mark were not
there, she would not be at all easy. I remembered what he had
said to me about their dealings with Dolcino—that between
them they would put an end to him; but I did not repeat this
to Miss Ambient: the less so that just then her brother emerged
from the house, carrying his child in his arms. Close behind
him moved his wife, grave and pale; the boy's face was turned
over Ambient's shoulder, towards his mother. We got up to
receive the group, and as they came near us Dolcino turned
round. I caught, on his enchanting little countenance, a smile
of recognition, and for the moment would have been quite
content with it. Miss Ambient, however, received another
impression, and I make haste to say that her quick sensibility,
in which there was something maternal, argues that in spite
of her affectations there was a strain of kindness in her. "It
won't do at all—it won't do at all," she said to me under her
breath. "I shall speak to Mark about the doctor."

The child was rather white, but the main difference I saw
in him was that he was even more beautiful than the day before.
He had been dressed in his festal garments—a velvet suit and
a crimson sash—and he looked like a little invalid prince, too
young to know condescension, and smiling familiarly on his
subjects.

"Put him down, Mark, he's not comfortable," Mrs Ambient said.

"Should you like to stand on your feet, my boy?" his
father asked.

"Oh yes; I'm remarkably well," said the child.

Mark placed him on the ground; he had shining, pointed
slippers, with enormous bows. "Are you happy now, Mr
Ambient?"

"Oh yes, I am particularly happy," Dolcino replied. The
words were scarcely out of his mouth when his mother caught

him up, and in a moment, holding him on her knees, she took
her place on the bench where Miss Ambient and I had been
sitting. This young lady said something to her brother, in
consequence of which the two wandered away into the garden together. I remained with Mrs Ambient; but as a servant
had brought out a couple of chairs I was not obliged to seat
myself beside her. Our conversation was not animated, and I,
for my part, felt there would be a kind of hypocrisy in my
trying to make myself agreeable to Mrs Ambient. I didn't
dislike her—I rather admired her; but I was aware that I
differed from her inexpressibly. Then I suspected, what I
afterwards definitely knew and have already intimated, that
the poor lady had taken a dislike to me; and this of course was
not encouraging. She thought me an obtrusive and even de-
praved young man, whom a perverse Providence had dropped upon their quiet lawn to flatter her husband's worst
tendencies. She did me the honour to say to Miss Ambient,
who repeated the speech, that she didn't know when she had
seen her husband take such a fancy to a visitor; and she
measured, apparently, my evil influence by Mark's appreciation of my society. I had a consciousness, not yet acute, but
quite sufficient, of all this; but I must say that if it chilled my
flow of small-talk, it didn't prevent me from thinking that the
beautiful mother and beautiful child, interlaced there against
their background of roses, made a picture such as I perhaps
should not soon see again. I was free, I supposed, to go into
the house and write letters, to sit in the drawing-room, to
repair to my own apartment and take a nap; but the only use
I made of my freedom was to linger still in my chair and say
to myself that the light hand of Sir Joshua might have painted
Mark Ambient's wife and son. I found myself looking perpetually at Dolcino, and Dolcino looked back at me, and
that was enough to detain me. When he looked at me he
smiled, and I felt it was an absolute impossibility to abandon
a child who was smiling at one like that. His eyes never

wandered; they attached themselves to mine, as if among all the small incipient things of his nature there was a desire to say something to me. If I could have taken him upon my own knee he perhaps would have managed to say it; but it would have been far too delicate a matter to ask his mother to give him up, and it has remained a constant regret for me that on that Sunday afternoon I did not, even for a moment, hold Dolcino in my arms. He had said that he felt remarkably well, and that he was especially happy; but though he may have been happy, with his charming head pillowed on his mother's breast and his little crimson silk legs depending from her lap, I did not think he looked well. He made no attempt to walk about; he was content to swing his legs softly and strike one as languid and angelic.

Mark came back to us with his sister; and Miss Ambient, making some remark about having to attend to her correspondence, passed into the house. Mark came and stood in front of his wife, looking down at the child, who immediately took hold of his hand, keeping it while he remained. "I think Allingham ought to see him," Ambient said; "I think I will walk over and fetch him."

"That's Gwendolen's idea, I suppose," Mrs Ambient replied, very sweetly.

"It's not such an out-of-the-way idea, when one's child is ill."

"I'm not ill, papa; I'm much better now," Dolcino remarked.

"Is that the truth, or are you only saying it to be agreeable? You have a great idea of being agreeable, you know."

The boy seemed to meditate on this distinction, this imputation, for a moment; then his exaggerated eyes, which had wandered, caught my own as I watched him, "Do *you* think me agreeable?" he inquired, with the candour of his age and with a smile that made his father turn round to me, laughing, and ask, mutely, with a glance, "Isn't he adorable?"

"Then why don't you hop about, if you feel so lusty?" Ambient went on, while the boy swung his hand.

"Because mamma is holding me close!"

"Oh yes; I know how mamma holds you when I come near!" Ambient exclaimed, looking at his wife.

She turned her charming eyes up to him, without deprecation or concession, and after a moment she said, "You can go for Allingham if you like. I think myself it would be better. You ought to drive."

"She says that to get me away," Ambient remarked to me, laughing; after which he started for the doctor's.

I remained there with Mrs Ambient, though our conversation had more pauses than speeches. The boy's little fixed white face seemed, as before, to plead with me to stay, and after a while it produced still another effect, a very curious one, which I shall find it difficult to express. Of course I expose myself to the charge of attempting to give fantastic reasons for an act which may have been simply the fruit of a native want of discretion; and indeed the traceable consequences of that perversity were too lamentable to leave me any desire to trifle with the question. All I can say is that I acted in perfect good faith, and that Dolcino's friendly little gaze gradually kindled the spark of my inspiration. What helped it to glow were the other influences—the silent, suggestive garden-nook, the perfect opportunity (if it was not an opportunity for that, it was an opportunity for nothing), and the plea that I speak of, which issued from the child's eyes and seemed to make him say, "The mother that bore me and that presses me here to her bosom—sympathetic little organism that I am—has really the kind of sensibility which she has been represented to you as lacking; if you only look for it patiently and respectfully. How is it possible that she shouldn't have it? how is it possible that *I* should have so much of it (for I am quite full of it, dear strange gentleman), if it were not also in some degree in her? I am my father's child, but I am also my

mother's, and I am sorry for the difference between them!"
So it shaped itself before me, the vision of reconciling Mrs
Ambient with her husband, of putting an end to their great
disagreement. The project was absurd, of course, for had I
not had his word for it—spoken with all the bitterness of
experience—that the gulf that divided them was well-nigh
bottomless? Nevertheless, a quarter of an hour after Mark had
left us, I said to his wife that I couldn't get over what she
told me the night before about her thinking her husband's
writings "objectionable." I had been so very sorry to hear it,
had thought of it constantly, and wondered whether it were
not possible to make her change her mind. Mrs Ambient gave
me rather a cold stare—she seemed to be recommending me
to mind my own business. I wish I had taken this mute counsel,
but I did not. I went on to remark that it seemed an immense
pity so much that was beautiful should be lost upon her.

"Nothing is lost upon me," said Mrs Ambient. "I know
they are very beautiful."

"Don't you like papa's books?" Dolcino asked, addressing
his mother, but still looking at me. Then he added to me,
"Won't you read them to me, American gentleman?"

"I would rather tell you some stories of my own," I said.
"I know some that are very interesting."

"When will you tell them—to-morrow?"

"To-morrow, with pleasure, if that suits you."

Mrs Ambient was silent at this. Her husband, during our
walk, had asked me to remain another day; my promise to her
son was an implication that I had consented; and it is not
probable that the prospect was agreeable to her. This ought,
doubtless, to have made me more careful as to what I said
next; but all I can say is that it didn't. I presently observed
that just after leaving her, the evening before, and after hearing her apply to her husband's writings the epithet I had
already quoted, I had, on going up to my room, sat down to
the perusal of those sheets of his new book which he had been

so good as to lend me. I had sat entranced till nearly three in
the morning—I had read them twice over. "You say you
haven't looked at them. I think it's such a pity you shouldn't.
Do let me beg you to take them up. They are so very remarkable. I'm sure they will convert you. They place him in—
really—such a dazzling light. All that is best in him is there.
I have no doubt it's a great liberty, my saying all this; but
excuse me, and *do* read them!"

"Do read them, mamma!" Dolcino repeated. "Do read
them!"

She bent her head and closed his lips with a kiss. "Of course
I know he has worked immensely over them," she said; and
after this she made no remark, but sat there looking thoughtful, with her eyes on the ground. The tone of these last words
was such as to leave me no spirit for further aggression, and
after expressing a fear that her husband had not found the
doctor at home, I got up and took a turn about the grounds.
When I came back ten minutes later, she was still in her place,
watching her boy, who had fallen asleep in her lap. As I drew
near she put her finger to her lips, and a moment afterwards
she rose, holding the child, and murmured something about
its being better that he should go up stairs. I offered to carry
him, and held out my hands to take him; but she thanked
me and turned away, with the child seated on her arm, his
head on her shoulder. "I am very strong," she said, as she
passed into the house, and her slim, flexible figure bent back-
wards with the filial weight. So I never touched Dolcino.

I betook myself to Ambient's study, delighted to have a
quiet hour to look over his books by myself. The windows
were open into the garden, the sunny stillness, the mild light
of the English summer, filled the room, without quite chasing
away the rich, dusky air which was a part of its charm, and
which abode in the serried shelves where old morocco exhaled
the fragrance of curious learning, and in the brighter intervals
where medals and prints and miniatures were suspended upon

a surface of faded stuff. The place had both colour and quiet; I thought it a perfect room for work, and went so far as to say to myself that if it were mine, to sit and scribble in, there was no knowing but that I might learn to write as well as the author of *Beltraffio*. This distinguished man did not turn up, and I rummaged freely among his treasures. At last I took down a book that detained me a while, and seated myself in a fine old leather chair, by the window, to turn it over. I had been occupied in this way for half an hour—a good part of the afternoon had waned—when I become conscious of another presence in the room, and, looking up from my quarto, saw that Mrs Ambient, having pushed open the door in the same noiseless way that marked—or disguised—her entrance the night before, had advanced across the threshold. On seeing me she stopped; she had not, I think, expected to find me. But her hesitation was only of a moment; she came straight to her husband's writing-table, as if she were looking for something. I got up and asked her if I could help her. She glanced about an instant, and then put her hand upon a roll of papers which I recognised, as I had placed it in that spot in the morning, on coming down from my room.

"Is this the new book?" she asked, holding it up.

"The very sheets, with precious annotations."

"I mean to take your advice." And she tucked the little bundle under her arm. I congratulated her cordially, and ventured to make of my triumph, as I presumed to call it, a subject of pleasantry. But she was perfectly grave, and turned away from me, as she had presented herself, without a smile; after which I settled down to my quarto again, with the reflection that Mrs Ambient was a queer woman. My triumph, too, suddenly seemed to me rather vain. A woman who couldn't smile in the right place would never understand Mark Ambient. He came in at last in person, having brought the doctor back with him. "He was away from home," Mark said, "and I went after him—to where he was supposed to be. He had left the place, and I followed him to two or three others, which accounts for my delay." He was now with Mrs Ambient, looking at the child, and was to see Mark again before leaving the house. My host noticed, at the end of ten minutes, that the proof-sheets of his new book had been removed from the table, and when I told him, in reply to his question as to what I knew about them, that Mrs Ambient had carried them off to read, he turned almost pale for an instant with surprise. "What has suddenly made her so curious?" he exclaimed; and I was obliged to tell him that I was at the bottom of the mystery. I had had it on my conscience to assure her that she really ought to know of what her husband was capable. "Of what I am capable? *Elle ne s'en doute que trop!*" said Ambient, with a laugh; but he took my meddling very good-naturedly, and contented himself with adding that he was very much afraid she would burn up the sheets, with his emendations, of which he had no duplicate. The doctor paid a long visit in the nursery, and before he came down I retired to my own quarters, where I remained till dinner-time. On entering the drawing-room at this hour I found Miss Ambient in possession, as she had been the evening before.

"I was right about Dolcino," she said as soon as she saw me, with a strange little air of triumph. "He is really very ill."

"Very ill! Why, when I last saw him, at four o'clock, he was in fairly good form."

"There has been a change for the worse—very sudden and rapid—and when the doctor got here he found diphtheritic symptoms. He ought to have been called, as I knew, in the morning, and the child oughtn't to have been brought into the garden."

"My dear lady, he was very happy there," I answered, much appalled.

"He would be happy anywhere. I have no doubt he is happy now, with his poor little throat in a state——" She dropped her voice as her brother came in, and Mark let us know that, as a matter of course, Mrs Ambient would not appear. It was true that Dolcino had developed diphtheritic symptoms, but he was quiet for the present, and his mother was earnestly watching him. She was a perfect nurse, Mark said, and the doctor was coming back at ten o'clock. Our dinner was not very gay; Ambient was anxious and alarmed, and his sister irritated me by her constant tacit assumption, conveyed in the very way she nibbled her bread and sipped her wine, of having "told me so." I had had no disposition to deny anything she told me, and I could not see that her satisfaction in being justified by the event made poor Dolcino's throat any better. The truth is that, as the sequel proved, Miss Ambient had some of the qualities of the sibyl, and had therefore, perhaps, a right to the sibylline contortions. Her brother was so preoccupied that I felt my presence to be an indiscretion, and was sorry I had promised to remain over the morrow. I said to Mark that, evidently, I had better leave them in the morning; to which he replied that, on the contrary, if he was to pass the next days in the fidgets my company would be an extreme relief to him. The fidgets had already begun for him, poor fellow, and as we sat in his study with our cigars, after dinner, he wandered to the door whenever he heard the sound of the doctor's wheels. Miss Ambient, who shared this apartment with us, gave me at such moments significant glances; she had gone up stairs before rejoining us, to ask after the child. His mother and his nurse gave a tolerable account of him; but Miss Ambient found his fever high and his symptoms very grave. The doctor came at ten o'clock, and I went to bed after hearing from Mark that he saw no present cause for alarm. He had made every provision for the night, and was to return early in the morning.

I quitted my room at eight o'clock the next day, and as I came down stairs saw, through the open door of the house, Mrs Ambient standing at the front gate of the grounds, in colloquy with the physician. She wore a white dressing-gown, but her shining hair was carefully tucked away in its net, and in the freshness of the morning, after a night of watching, she looked as much "the type of the lady" as her sister-in-law had described her. Her appearance, I suppose, ought to have reassured me; but I was still nervous and uneasy, so that I shrank from meeting her with the necessary question about Dolcino. None the less, however, was I impatient to learn how the morning found him; and as Mrs Ambient had not seen me, I passed into the grounds by a roundabout way, and, stopping at a further gate, hailed the doctor just as he was driving away. Mrs Ambient had returned to the house before he got into his gig.

"Excuse me—but, as a friend of the family, I should like very much to hear about the little boy."

The doctor, who was a stout, sharp man, looked at me from head to foot, and then he said, "I'm sorry to say I haven't seen him."

"Haven't seen him?"

"Mrs Ambient came down to meet me as I alighted, and told me that he was sleeping so soundly, after a restless night, that she didn't wish him disturbed. I assured her I wouldn't disturb him, but she said he was quite safe now and she could look after him herself."

"Thank you very much. Are you coming back?"

"No, sir; I'll be hanged if I come back!" exclaimed Dr Allingham, who was evidently very angry. And he started his horse again with the whip.

I wandered back into the garden, and five minutes later Miss Ambient came forth from the house to greet me. She explained that breakfast would not be served for some time, and that she wished to catch the doctor before he went away. I informed her that this functionary had come and departed, and I repeated to her what he had told me about his dismissal. This made Miss Ambient very serious—very serious indeed—and she sank into a bench, with dilated eyes, hugging her elbows with crossed arms. She indulged in many ejaculations, she confessed that she was infinitely perplexed, and she finally told me what her own last news of her nephew had been. She had sat up very late—after me, after Mark—and before going to bed had knocked at the door of the child's room, which was opened to her by the nurse. This good woman had admitted her, and she had found Dolcino quiet, but flushed and "unnatural," with his mother sitting beside his bed. "She held his hand in one of hers," said Miss Ambient, "and in the other—what do you think?—the proof-sheets of Mark's new book! She was reading them there, intently: did you ever hear of anything so extraordinary? Such a very odd time to be reading an author whom she never could abide!" In her agitation Miss Ambient was guilty of this vulgarism of speech, and I was so impressed by her narrative that it was only in recalling her words later that I noticed the lapse. Mrs Ambient had looked up from her reading with her finger on her lips—I recognised the gesture she had addressed to me in the afternoon—and, though the nurse was about to go to rest, had not encouraged her sister-in-law to relieve her of any part of her vigil. But certainly, then, Dolcino's condition was far from reassuring—his poor little breathing was most painful; and what change could have taken place in him in those few hours that would justify Beatrice in denying the physician access to him? This was the moral of Miss Ambient's anecdote—the moral for herself at least. The moral for me, rather, was that it *was* a very singular time for Mrs Ambient to be going into a novelist she had never appreciated and who had simply happened to be recommended to her by a young American she disliked. I thought of her sitting there in the sick-chamber in the still hours of the night, after the nurse had left her, turning over those pages of genius and wrestling with their magical influence.

I must relate very briefly the circumstances of the rest of my visit to Mark Ambient—it lasted but a few hours longer —and devote but three words to my later acquaintance with him. That lasted five years—till his death—and was full of interest, of satisfaction, and, I may add, of sadness. The main thing to be said with regard to it is, that I had a secret from him. I believe he never suspected it, though of this I am not absolutely sure. If he did, the line he had taken, the line of absolute negation of the matter to himself, shows an immense effort of the will. I may tell my secret now, giving it for what it is worth, now that Mark Ambient has gone, that he has begun to be alluded to as one of the famous early dead, and that his wife does not survive him; now, too, that Miss Ambient, whom I also saw at intervals during the years that followed, has, with her embroideries and her attitudes, her necromantic glances and strange intuitions, retired to a Sisterhood, where, as I am told, she is deeply immured and quite lost to the world.

Mark came into breakfast after his sister and I had for some time been seated there. He shook hands with me in silence, kissed his sister, opened his letters and newspapers, and pretended to drink his coffee. But I could see that these movements were mechanical, and I was little surprised when, suddenly he pushed away everything that was before him, and with his head in his hands and his elbows on the table, sat staring strangely at the cloth.

"What is the matter *fratello mio?*" Miss Ambient inquired, peeping from behind the urn.

He answered nothing, but got up with a certain violence and strode to the window. We rose to our feet, his sister and I, by a common impulse, exchanging a glance of some alarm, while he stared for a moment into the garden. "In heaven's name, what has got possession of Beatrice?" he cried at last, turning round with an almost haggard face. And he looked from one of us to the other; the appeal was addressed to me as well as to his sister.

Miss Ambient gave a shrug. "My poor Mark, Beatrice is always—Beatrice!"

"She has locked herself up with the boy—bolted and barred the door—she refuses to let me come near him!" Ambient went on.

"She refused to let the doctor see him an hour ago!" Miss Ambient remarked, with intention, as they say on the stage.

"Refused to let the doctor see him? By heaven, I'll smash in the door!" And Mark brought his fist down upon the table, so that all the breakfast-service rang.

I begged Miss Ambient to go up and try to have speech of her sister-in-law, and I drew Mark out into the garden. "You're exceedingly nervous, and Mrs Ambient is probably right," I said to him. "Women know—women should be supreme in such a situation. Trust a mother—a devoted mother, my dear friend!" With such words as these I tried to soothe and comfort him, and, marvellous to relate, I succeeded, with the help of many cigarettes, in making him walk about the garden and talk, or listen at least to my own ingenious chatter, for nearly an hour. At the end of this time Miss Ambient returned to us, with a very rapid step, holding her hand to her heart.

"Go for the doctor, Mark; go for the doctor this moment!"

"Is he dying—has she killed him?" poor Ambient cried, flinging away his cigarette.

"I don't know what she has done! But she's frightened, and now she wants the doctor."

"He told me he would be hanged if he came back," I felt myself obliged to announce.

"Precisely—therefore Mark himself must go for him, and not a messenger. You must see him and tell him it's to save your child. The trap has been ordered—it's ready."

"To save him? I'll save him, please God!" Ambient cried, bounding with his great strides across the lawn.

As soon as he had gone I felt that I ought to have volunteered in his place, and I said as much to Miss Ambient; but she checked me by grasping my arm quickly, while we heard the wheels of the dog-cart rattle away from the gate. "He's off—he's off—and now I can think! To get him away—while I think—while I think!"

"While you think of what, Miss Ambient?"

"Of the unspeakable thing that has happened under this roof!"

Her manner was habitually that of such a prophetess of ill that my first impulse was to believe I must allow here for a great exaggeration. But in a moment I saw that her emotion was real. "Dolcino *is* dying then—he is dead?"

"It's too late to save him. His mother has let him die! I tell you that, because you are sympathetic, because you have imagination," Miss Ambient was good enough to add, interrupting my expression of horror. "That's why you had the idea of making her read Mark's new book!"

"What has that to do with it? I don't understand you—your accusation is monstrous."

"I see it all—I'm not stupid," Miss Ambient went on, heedless of the harshness of my tone. "It was the book that finished her—it was that decided her!"

"Decided her? Do you mean she has murdered her child?" I demanded, trembling at my own words.

"She sacrificed him—she determined to do nothing to make him live. Why else did she lock herself up—why else did she turn away the doctor? The book gave her a horror, she determined to rescue him—to prevent him from ever being touched. He had a crisis at two o'clock in the morning. I know this from the nurse, who had left her then, but whom, for a short time, she called back. Dolcino got much worse, but she insisted on the nurse's going back to bed, and after that she was alone with him for hours."

"Do you pretend that she has no pity—that she's insane?"

"She held him in her arms—she pressed him to her breast, not to see him; but she gave him no remedies—she did nothing the doctor ordered. Everything is there, untouched. She has had the honesty not even to throw the drugs away!"

I dropped upon the nearest bench, overcome with wonder and agitation: quite as much at Miss Ambient's terrible lucidity as at the charge she made against her sister-in-law. There was an amazing coherency in her story, and it was dreadful to me to see myself figuring in it as so proximate a cause. "You are a very strange woman, and you say strange things."

"You think it necessary to protest—but you are quite ready to believe me. You have received an impression of my sister-in-law, you have guessed of what she is capable."

I do not feel bound to say what concession on this point I made to Miss Ambient, who went on to relate to me that within the last half-hour Beatrice had had a revulsion; that she was tremendously frightened at what she had done; that her fright itself betrayed her; and that she would now give heaven and earth to save the child. "Let us hope she will!" I said, looking at my watch and trying to time poor Ambient; whereupon my companion repeated, in a singular tone, "Let us hope so!" When I asked her if she herself could do nothing, and whether she ought not to be with her sister-in-law, she replied, "You had better go and judge; she is like a wounded tigress!" I never saw Mrs Ambient till six months after this, and therefore cannot pretend to have verified the comparison. At the latter period she was again the type of the lady. "She'll be nicer to him after this," I remember Miss Ambient saying, in response to some quick outburst (on my part) of compassion for her brother. Although I had been in the house but thirty-six hours this young lady had treated me with extraordinary confidence, and there was therefore a certain demand which, as an intimate, I might make of her. I extracted from her a pledge that she would never say to her brother what she had just said to me; she would leave him to form his own theory of his wife's conduct. She agreed with me that there was misery enough in the house without her contributing a new anguish, and that Mrs Ambient's proceedings might be explained, to her husband's mind, by the extravagance of a jealous devotion.

Poor Mark came back with the doctor much sooner than we could have hoped, but we knew, five minutes afterward, that they arrived too late. Poor little Dolcino was more exquisitely beautiful in death than he had been in life. Mrs Ambient's grief was frantic; she lost her head and said strange things. As for Mark's—but I will not speak of that. *Basta*, as he used to say. Miss Ambient kept her secret—I have already had occasion to say that she had her good points—but it rankled in her conscience like a guilty participation, and, I imagine, had something to do with her retiring ultimately to a Sisterhood. And, *à propos* of consciences, the reader is now in a position to judge of my compunction for my effort to convert Mrs Ambient. I ought to mention that the death of her child in some degree converted her. When the new book came out—it was long delayed—she read it over as a whole, and her husband told me that a few months before her death—she failed rapidly after losing her son, sank into a consumption, and faded away at Mentone—during those few supreme weeks she even dipped into *Beltraffio*.

PANDORA

I

IT has long been the custom of the North German Lloyd steamers, which convey passengers from Bremen to New York, to anchor for several hours in the pleasant port of Southampton, where their human cargo receives many additions. An intelligent young German, Count Otto Vogelstein, hardly knew, a few years ago, whether to condemn this custom or approve it. He leaned over the bulwarks of the *Donau* as the American passengers crossed the plank—the travellers who embark at Southampton are mainly of that nationality—and curiously, indifferently, vaguely, through the smoke of his cigar, saw them absorbed in the huge capacity of the ship, where he had the agreeable consciousness that his own nest was comfortably made. To watch from a point of vantage the struggles of later comers—of the uninformed, the unprovided, the bewildered—is an occupation not devoid of sweetness, and there was nothing to mitigate the complacency with which our young friend gave himself up to it; nothing, that is, save a natural benevolence which had not yet been extinguished by the consciousness of official greatness. For Count Vogelstein was official, as I think you would have seen from the straightness of his back, the lustre of his light, elegant spectacles, and something discreet and diplomatic in the curve of his moustache, which looked as if it might well contribute to the principal function, as cynics say, of the lips —the concealment of thought. He had been appointed to the secretaryship of the German legation at Washington, and in these first days of the autumn he was going to take possession of his post. He was a model character for such a purpose—serious, civil, ceremonious, stiff, inquisitive, stuffed with knowledge, and convinced that at present the German empire is the country in the world most highly evolved. He was quite aware, however, of the claims of the United States, and that this portion of the globe presented an enormous field for study. The process of inquiry had already begun, in spite of his having as yet spoken to none of his fellow-passengers; for Vogelstein inquired not only with his tongue—he inquired with his eyes (that is, with his spectacles), with his ears, with his nose, with his palate, with all his senses and organs.

He was an excellent young man, and his only fault was that he had not a high sense of humour. He had enough, however, to suspect this deficiency, and he was aware that he was about to visit a highly humorous people. This suspicion gave him a certain mistrust of what might be said of him; and if circumspection is the essence of diplomacy, our young aspirant promised well. His mind contained several millions of facts, packed too closely together for the light breeze of the imagination to draw through the mass. He was impatient to report himself to his superior in Washington, and the loss of time in an English port could only incommode him, inasmuch as the study of English institutions was no part of his mission. But, on the other hand, the day was charming; the blue sea, in Southampton Water, pricked all over with light, had no movement but that of its infinite shimmer. And he was by no means sure that he should be happy in the United States, where doubtless he should find himself soon enough disembarked. He knew that this was not an important question and that happiness was an unscientific term, which he was ashamed to use even in the silence of his thoughts. But lost in the inconsiderate crowd, and feeling himself neither in his own country nor in that to which he was in a manner accredited, he was reduced to his mere personality; so that, for the moment, to fill himself out, he tried to have an opinion on the subject of this delay to which the German steamer was subjected in English waters. It appeared to him that it might be proved to be considerably greater than the occasion demanded.

Count Vogelstein was still young enough in diplomacy to think it necessary to have opinions. He had a good many, indeed, which had been formed without difficulty; they had been received ready-made from a line of ancestors who knew what they liked. This was, of course—and he would have admitted it—an unscientific way of furnishing one's mind. Our young man was a stiff conservative, a Junker of Junkers; he thought modern democracy a temporary phase, and expected to find many arguments against it in the United States. In regard to these things, it was a pleasure to him to feel that, with his complete training, he had been taught thoroughly to appreciate the nature of evidence. The ship was heavily laden with German emigrants, whose mission in the United States differed considerably from Count Otto's. They hung over the bulwarks, densely grouped; they leaned forward on their elbows for hours, with their shoulders on a level with their ears; the men in furred caps, smoking long-bowled pipes, the women with babies hidden in their shawls. Some were yellow Germans and some were black, and all of them looked greasy and matted with the sea-damp. They were destined to swell the current of western democracy, and Count Vogelstein doubtless said to himself that they would not improve its quality. Their numbers, however, were striking, and I know not what he thought of the nature of this evidence.

The passengers who came on board at Southampton were not of the greasy class; they were for the most part American families who had been spending the summer, or a longer period, in Europe. They had a great deal of luggage, innumerable bags and rugs and hampers and sea-chairs, and were composed largely of ladies of various ages, a little pale with anticipation, wrapped in striped shawls, and crowned with very high hats and feathers. They darted to and fro across the gangway, looking for each other and for their scattered parcels; they separated and reunited, they exclaimed and declared, they eyed with dismay the occupants of the steerage, who seemed numerous enough to sink the vessel, and their voices sounded faint and far as they rose to Vogelstein's ear over the tarred sides of the ship. He observed that in the new contingent there were many young girls, and he remembered what a lady in Dresden had once said to him— that America was a country of girls. He wondered whether he should like that, and reflected that it would be a question to study, like everything else. He had known in Dresden an American family, in which there were three daughters who used to skate with the officers; and some of the ladies now coming on board seemed to him of that same habit, except that in the Dresden days feathers were not worn quite so high.

At last the ship began to creak and slowly budge, and the delay at Southampton came to an end. The gangway was removed, and the vessel indulged in the awkward evolutions which were to detach her from the land. Count Vogelstein had finished his cigar, and he spent a long time in walking up and down the upper deck. The charming English coast passed before him, and he felt that this was the last of the old world. The American coast also might be pretty—he hardly knew what one would expect of an American coast; but he was sure it would be different. Differences, however, were half the charm of travel. As yet, indeed, there were very few on the steamer. Most of his fellow-passengers appeared to be of the same persuasion, and that persuasion the least to be mistaken. They were Jews and commercial, to a man. And by this time they had lighted their cigars and put on all manner of seafaring caps, some of them with big ear-lappets, which somehow had the effect of bringing out their peculiar facial type. At last the new voyagers began to emerge from below and to look about them, vaguely, with that suspicious expression of face which is to be perceived in the newly embarked, and which, as directed to the receding land, resembles that of a person who begins to perceive that he is the victim of a trick. Earth and ocean, in such glances, are made the subject of a general objection, and many travellers, in these circumstances, have an air at once duped and superior, which seems to say that they could easily go ashore if they would.

It still wanted two hours of dinner, and, by the time Vogelstein's long legs had measured three or four miles on the deck, he was ready to settle himself in his sea-chair and draw from his pocket a Tauchnitz novel by an American author whose pages, he had been assured, would help to prepare him. On the back of his chair his name was painted in rather large letters, this being a precaution taken at the recommendation of a friend, who had told him that on the American steamers the passengers—especially the ladies—thought nothing of pilfering one's little comforts. His friend had even said that in his place he would have his coronet painted. This cynical adviser had added that the Americans are greatly impressed by a coronet. I know not whether it was scepticism or modesty, but Count Vogelstein had omitted this ensign of his rank; the precious piece of furniture which, on the Atlantic voyage, is depended upon to remain steady among general concussions, was emblazoned simply with his title and name. It happened, however, that the blazonry was huge; the back of the chair was covered with enormous German characters. This time there can be no doubt; it was modesty that caused the secretary of the legation, in placing himself, to turn this portion of his seat outward, away from the eyes of his companions—to present it to the balustrade of the deck. The ship was passing the Needles—the beautiful outermost point of the Isle of Wight. Certain tall white cones of rock rose out of the purple sea; they flushed in the afternoon light, and their vague rosiness gave them a kind of human expression, in face of the cold expanse towards which the ship was turned; they seemed to say farewell, to be the last note of a peopled world.

Vogelstein saw them very comfortably from his place, and after a while he turned his eyes to the other quarter, where the sky and sea, between them, managed to make so poor an opposition. Even his American novelist was more amusing than that, and he prepared to return to this author.

In the great curve which it described, however, his glance was arrested by the figure of a young lady who had just ascended to the deck, and who paused at the mouth of the companion-way. In itself this was not an extraordinary phenomenon; but what attracted Vogelstein's attention was the fact that the young person appeared to have fixed her eyes on him. She was slim, brightly dressed, and rather pretty. Vogelstein remembered in a moment that he had noticed her among the people on the wharf at Southampton. She very soon saw that he was looking at her; whereupon she began to move along the deck with a step which seemed to indicate that she was coming straight towards him. Vogelstein had time to wonder whether she could be one of the girls he had known at Dresden; but he presently reflected that they would now be much older than this. It was true they came straight towards one, like that. This young lady, however, was no longer looking at him, and though she passed near him it was now tolerably clear that she had come upstairs simply to take a general survey. She was a quick, handsome, competent girl, and she wished to see what one could think of the ship, of the weather, of the appearance of England from such a position as that; possibly even of one's fellow-passengers. She satisfied herself promptly on these points, and then she looked about, while she walked, as if she were in search of a missing object; so that Vogelstein presently saw this was what she really had come up for. She passed near him again, and this time she almost stopped, with her eyes bent upon him attentively. He thought her conduct remarkable, even after he had perceived that it was not at his face, with its yellow moustache, she was looking, but at the chair on which he was

seated. Then those words of his friend came back to him,—
the speech about the people, especially the ladies, on the
American steamers taking to themselves one's little belongings.
Especially the ladies, he might well say; for here was one who
apparently wished to pull from under him the very chair he
was sitting on. He was afraid she would ask him for it, so he
pretended to read, without meeting her eye. He was conscious that she hovered near him, and he was curious to see
what she would do. It seemed to him strange that such a nice-
looking girl (for her appearance was really charming) should
endeavour by acts so flagrant to attract the attention of a
secretary of legation. At last it became evident to him that
she was trying to look round a corner, as it were, trying to see
what was written on the back of his chair. "She wants to find
out my name; she wants to see who I am!" This reflection
passed through his mind, and caused him to raise his eyes.
They rested on her own—which for an appreciable moment
she did not withdraw. The latter were brilliant and expressive,
and surmounted a delicate aquiline nose, which, though
pretty, was perhaps just a trifle too hawk-like. It was the oddest
coincidence in the world; the story Vogelstein had taken up
treated of a flighty, forward little American girl, who plants
herself in front of a young man in the garden of an hotel. Was
not the conduct of this young lady a testimony to the truth-
fulness of the tale, and was not Vogelstein himself in the position of the young man in the garden? That young man ended
by speaking to his invader (as she might be called), and after
a very short hesitation Vogelstein followed his example. "If
she wants to know who I am, she is welcome," he said to himself; and he got out of the chair, seized it by the back, and,
turning it round, exhibited the superscription to the girl.
She coloured slightly, but she smiled and read his name, while
Vogelstein raised his hat.

"I am much obliged to you. That's all right," she remarked,
as if the discovery had made her very happy.

It seemed to him indeed all right that he should be Count Otto Vogelstein; this appeared even a rather flippant mode of disposing of the fact. By way of rejoinder, he asked her if she desired his seat.

"I am much obliged to you; of course not. I thought you had one of our chairs, and I didn't like to ask you. It looks exactly like one of ours; not so much now as when you sit in it. Please sit down again. I don't want to trouble you. We have lost one of ours, and I have been looking for it everywhere. They look so much alike; you can't tell till you see the back. Of course I see there will be no mistake about yours," the young lady went on, with a frank smile. "But we have such a small name—you can scarcely see it," she added, with the same friendly intention. "Our name is Day. If you see that on anything, I should be so obliged if you will tell me. It isn't for myself, it's for my mother; she is so dependent on her chair, and that one I am looking for pulls out so beautifully. Now that you sit down again and hide the lower part, it does look just like ours. Well, it must be somewhere. You must excuse me; I am much obliged to you."

This was a long and even confidential speech for a young woman, presumably unmarried, to make to a perfect stranger; but Miss Day acquitted herself of it with perfect simplicity and self-possession. She held up her head and stepped away, and Vogelstein could see that the foot she pressed upon the clean, smooth deck was slender and shapely. He watched her disappear through the trap by which she had ascended, and he felt more than ever like the young man in his American tale. The girl in the present case was older and not so pretty, as he could easily judge, for the image of her smiling eyes and speaking lips still hovered before him. He went back to his book with the feeling that it would give him some information about her. This was rather illogical, but it indicated a certain amount of curiosity on the part of Count Vogelstein. The girl in the book had a mother, it appeared, and so had this young lady; the former had also a brother, and he now remembered that he had noticed a young man on the wharf—a young man in a high hat and a white overcoat—who seemed united to Miss Day by this natural tie. And there was some one else too, as he gradually recollected, an older man, also in a high hat, but in a black overcoat—in black altogether—who completed the group, and who was presumably the head of the family. These reflections would indicate that Count Vogelstein read his volume of Tauchnitz rather interruptedly. Moreover, they represented a considerable waste of time; for was he not to be afloat in an oblong box, for ten days, with such people, and could it be doubted that he should see a great deal of them?

It may as well be said without delay that he did see a great deal of them. I have depicted with some precision the circumstances under which he made the acquaintance of Miss Day, because the event had a certain importance for this candid Teuton; but I must pass briefly over the incidents that immediately followed it. He wondered what it was open to him, after such an introduction, to do with regard to her, and he determined he would push through his American tale and discover what the hero did. But in a very short time he perceived that Miss Day had nothing in common with the heroine of that work, save a certain local quality and the fact that the male sex was not terrible to her. Her local quality, indeed, he took rather on trust than apprehended for himself. She was a native of a small town in the interior of the American continent; and a lady from New York, who was on the ship, and with whom he had a good deal of conversation, assured him Miss Day was exceedingly provincial. How this lady ascertained the fact did not appear, for Vogelstein observed that she held no communication with the girl. It is true that she threw some light on her processes by remarking to him that certain Americans could tell immediately who other Americans were, leaving him to judge whether or no she herself belonged to the discriminating class. She was a Mrs

Dangerfield, a handsome, confidential, insinuating woman,
and Vogelstein's talk with her took a turn that was almost
philosophic. She convinced him, rather effectually, that even
in a great democracy there are human differences, and that
American life was full of social distinctions, of delicate shades,
which foreigners are often too stupid to perceive. Did he
suppose that every one knew every one else, in the biggest
country in the world, and that one was not as free to choose
one's company there as in the most monarchical communities?
She laughed these ideas to scorn, as Vogelstein tucked her
beautiful furred coverlet (they reclined together a great deal
in their elongated chairs) well over her feet. How free an
American lady was to choose her company she abundantly
proved by not knowing any one on the steamer but Count
Otto.

He could see for himself that Mr and Mrs Day had not her
peculiar stamp. They were fat, plain, serious people, who sat
side by side on the deck for hours, looking straight before
them. Mrs Day had a white face, large cheeks, and small eyes;
her forehead was surrounded with a multitude of little tight
black curls, and her lips and cheeks moved as if she had always
a lozenge in her mouth. She wore entwined about her head
an article which Mrs Dangerfield spoke of as a "nuby"—a
knitted pink scarf which covered her coiffure and encircled
her neck, leaving among its convolutions a hole for her perfectly expressionless face. Her hands were folded on her
stomach, and in her still, swathed figure her little bead-like
eyes, which occasionally changed their direction, alone represented life. Her husband had a stiff gray beard on his chin,
and a bare, spacious upper lip, to which constant shaving had
imparted a kind of hard glaze. His eyebrows were thick and
his nostrils wide, and when he was uncovered, in the saloon,
it was visible that his grizzled hair was dense and perpen-
dicular. He might have looked rather grim and truculent, if
it had not been for the mild, familiar, accommodating gaze

with which his large, light-coloured pupils—the leisurely eyes of a silent man—appeared to consider surrounding objects. He was evidently more friendly than fierce, but he was more diffident than friendly. He liked to look at you, but he would not have pretended to understand you much nor to classify you, and would have been sorry that it should put you under an obligation. He and his wife spoke sometimes, but they seldom talked, and there was something passive and patient about them, as if they were victims of a spell. The spell, however, was evidently pleasant; it was the fascination of prosperity, the confidence of security, which sometimes makes people arrogant, but which had had such a different effect upon this simple, satisfied pair, in which further development of every kind appeared to have been arrested.

Mrs Dangerfield told Count Vogelstein that every morning, after breakfast, the hour at which he wrote his journal, in his cabin, the old couple were guided upstairs and installed in their customary corner by Pandora. This she had learned to be the name of their elder daughter, and she was immensely amused by her discovery. "Pandora"—that was in the highest degree typical; it placed them in the social scale, if other evidence had been wanting; you could tell that a girl was from the interior—the mysterious interior about which Vogelstein's imagination was now quite excited—when she had such a name as that. This young lady managed the whole family, even a little the small beflounced sister, who, with bold, pretty, innocent eyes, a torrent of fair, silky hair, a crimson fez, such as is worn by male Turks, very much askew on top of it, and a way of galloping and straddling about the ship in any company she could pick up (she had long, thin legs, very short skirts, and stockings of every tint), was going home, in elaborate French clothes, to resume an interrupted education. Pandora overlooked and directed her relatives; Vogelstein could see that for himself, could see that she was very active and decided, that she had in a high degree the

sentiment of responsibility, and settled most of the questions
that could come up for a family from the interior. The voyage was remarkably fine, and day after day it was possible to
sit there under the salt sky and feel one's self rounding the great
curves of the globe. The long deck made a white spot in the
sharp black circle of the ocean and in the intense sea-light,
while the shadow of the smoke-steamers trembled on the
familiar floor, the shoes of fellow-passengers, distinctive now,
and in some cases irritating, passed and repassed, accompanied, in the air so tremendously "open," that rendered all
voices weak and most remarks rather flat, by fragments of
opinion on the run of the ship. Vogelstein by this time had
finished his little American story, and now definitely judged
that Pandora Day was not at all like the heroine. She was of
quite another type; much more serious and preoccupied, and
not at all keen, as he had supposed, about making the acquaintance of gentlemen. Her speaking to him that first afternoon
had been, he was bound to believe, an incident without
importance for herself, in spite of her having followed it up
the next day by the remark, thrown at him as she passed, with
a smile that was almost familiar, "It's all right, sir. I have
found that old chair!" After this she had not spoken to him
again, and had scarcely looked at him. She read a great deal,
and almost always French books, in fresh yellow paper; not
the lighter forms of that literature, but a volume of Sainte-
Beuve, of Renan, or at the most, in the way of dissipation, of
Alfred de Musset. She took frequent exercise, and almost
always walked alone, not, apparently, having made many
friends on the ship, and being without the resource of her
parents, who, as has been related, never budged out of the
cosy corner in which she planted them for the day.

Her brother was always in the smoking-room, where
Vogelstein observed him, in very tight clothes, his neck en-
encircled with a collar like a palisade. He had a sharp little
face, which was not disagreeable; he smoked enormous cigars,

and began his drinking early in the day; but his appearance
gave no sign of these excesses. As regards euchre and poker
and the other distractions of the place, he was guilty of none.
He evidently understood such games in perfection, for he
used to watch the players, and even at moments impartially
advise them; but Vogelstein never saw the cards in his hand.
He was referred to as regards disputed points, and his opinion
carried the day. He took little part in the conversation, usually
much relaxed, that prevailed in the smoking-room, but from
time to time he made, in his soft, flat, youthful voice, a remark
which everyone paused to listen to, and which was greeted
with roars of laughter. Vogelstein, well as he knew English,
could rarely catch the joke; but he could see, at least, that these
were the most transcendent flights of American humour. The
young man, in his way, was very remarkable, for, as Vogelstein heard some one say once, after the laughter had subsided,
he was only nineteen. If his sister did not resemble the dreadful little girl in the tale I have so often mentioned, there was,
for Vogelstein, at least an analogy between young Mr Day
and a certain small brother—a candy-loving Madison,
Hamilton, or Jefferson—who, in the Tauchnitz volume, was
attributed to that unfortunate maid. This was what the little
Madison would have grown up to at nineteen, and the im-
provement was greater than might have been expected.

The days were long, but the voyage was short, and it had
almost come to an end before Count Vogelstein yielded to an
attraction peculiar in its nature and finally irresistible, and, in
spite of Mrs Dangerfield's warnings, sought an opportunity
for a little continuous talk with Miss Pandora Day. To mention this sentiment without mentioning sundry other impressions of his voyage, with which it had nothing to do, is perhaps to violate proportion and give a false idea; but to pass it
by would be still more unjust. The Germans, as we know, are
a transcendental people, and there was at last a vague fascination for Vogelstein in this quick, bright, silent girl, who

could smile and turn vocal in an instant, who imparted a sort of originality to the filial character, and whose profile was delicate as she bent it over a volume which she cut as she read, or presented it, in absent-minded attitudes, at the side of the ship, to the horizon they had left behind. But he felt it to be a pity, as regards a possible acquaintance with her, that her parents should be heavy little burghers, that her brother should not correspond to Vogelstein's conception of a young man of the upper class, and that her sister should be a Daisy Miller *en herbe*. Repeatedly warned by Mrs Dangerfield, the young diplomatist was doubly careful as to the relations he might form at the beginning of his sojourn in the United States. Mrs Dangerfield reminded him, and he had made the observation himself, in other capitals, that the first year, and even the second, is the time for prudence. One is ignorant of proportions and values; one is exposed, lonely, thankful for attention; and one may give one's self away to people who afterwards prove a great encumbrance. Mrs Dangerfield struck a note which resounded in Vogelstein's imagination. She assured him that if he didn't "look out" he would be falling in love with some American girl with an impossible family. In America, when one fell in love with a girl, there was nothing to be done but marry her, and what should he say, for instance, to finding himself a near relation of Mr and Mrs P. W. Day? (These were the initials inscribed on the back of the two chairs of that couple.) Vogelstein felt the peril, for he could immediately think of a dozen men he knew who had married American girls. There appeared now to be a constant danger of marrying the American girl; it was something one had to reckon with, like the rise in prices, the telephone, the discovery of dynamite, the Chassepôt rifle, the socialistic spirit; it was one of the complications of modern life.

It would doubtless be too much to say that Vogelstein was afraid of falling in love with Pandora Day, a young woman who was not strikingly beautiful, and with whom he had

talked, in all, but ten minutes. But, as I say, he went so far as
to wish that the human belongings of a girl whose independ-
ence appeared to have no taint either of fastness, as they said
in England, or of subversive opinion, and whose nose was so
very well bred, should not be a little more distinguished.
There was something almost comical in her attitude toward
these belongings; she appeared to regard them as a care, but
not as an interest; it was as if they had been entrusted to her
honour and she had engaged to convey them safe to a certain
point; she was detached and inadvertent; then, suddenly, she
remembered, repented, and came back to tuck her parents into
their blankets, to alter the position of her mother's umbrella, to
tell them something about the run of the ship. These little
offices were usually performed deftly, rapidly, with the mini-
mum of words, and when their daughter came near them, Mr
and Mrs Day closed their eyes placidly, like a pair of household dogs that expect to be scratched. One morning she
brought up the captain to present to them. She appeared to
have a private and independent acquaintance with this officer,
and the introduction to her parents had the air of a sudden
inspiration. It was not so much an introduction as an exhibition, as if she were saying to him, "This is what they look
like; see how comfortable I make them. Aren't they rather
queer little people? But they leave me perfectly free. Oh, I can
assure you of that. Besides, you must see it for yourself."
Mr and Mrs Day looked up at the captain with very little
change of countenance; then looked at each other in the same
way. He saluted and bent towards them a moment; but Pandora shook her head, she seemed to be answering for them;
she made little gestures as if she were explaining to the captain
some of their peculiarities, as, for instance, that they wouldn't
speak. They closed their eyes at last; she appeared to have a
kind of mesmeric influence on them, and Miss Day walked
away with the commander of the ship, who treated her with
evident consideration, bowing very low, in spite of his

supreme position, when, presently after, they separated. Vogelstein could see that she was capable of making an impression; and the moral of our episode is that in spite of Mrs Dangerfield, in spite of the resolutions of his prudence, in spite of the meagreness of the conversation that had passed between them, in spite of Mr and Mrs Day and the young man in the smoking-room, she had fixed his attention.

It was the evening after the scene with the captain that he joined her, awkwardly, abruptly, irresistibly, on the deck, where she was pacing to and fro alone, the evening being mild and brilliant and the stars remarkably fine. There were scattered talkers and smokers, and couples, unrecognisable, that moved quickly through the gloom. The vessel dipped, with long, regular pulsations; vague and spectral, under the stars, with its swaying pinnacles spotted here and there with lights, it seemed to rush through the darkness faster than by day. Vogelstein had come up to walk, and as the girl brushed past him he distinguished Pandora's face (with Mrs Dangerfield he always spoke of her as Pandora) under the veil that seemed intended to protect it from the sea-damp. He stopped, turned, hurried after her, threw away his cigar, and asked her if she would do him the honour to accept his arm. She declined his arm, but accepted his company, and he walked with her for an hour. They had a great deal of talk, and he remembered afterwards some of the things she said. There was now a certainty of the ship getting into dock the next morning but one, and this prospect afforded an obvious topic. Some of Miss Day's expressions struck him as singular; but, of course, as he knew, his knowledge of English was not nice enough to give him a perfect measure.

"I am not in a hurry to arrive; I am very happy here," she said. "I'm afraid I shall have such a time putting my people through."

"Putting them through?"

"Through the custom-house. We have made so many

purchases. Well, I have written to a friend to come down, and
perhaps he can help us. He's very well acquainted with the
head. Once I'm chalked, I don't care. I feel like a kind of
black-board by this time, any way. We found them awful in
Germany."

Vogelstein wondered whether the friend she had written
to was her lover, and if she were betrothed to him, especially
when she alluded to him again as "that gentleman that is
coming down." He asked her about her travels, her impressions, whether she had been long in Europe, and what she
liked best; and she told him that they had gone abroad, she
and her family, for a little fresh experience. Though he found
her very intelligent he suspected she gave this as a reason
because he was a German and she had heard that Germans
were fond of culture. He wondered what form of culture
Mr and Mrs Day had brought back from Italy, Greece, and
Palestine (they had travelled for two years and been everywhere), especially when their daughter said, "I wanted
father and mother to see the best things. I kept them three
hours on the Acropolis. I guess they won't forget that!" Perhaps it was of Pheidias and Pericles they were thinking, Vogelstein reflected, as they sat ruminating in their rugs. Pandora
remarked also that she wanted to show her little sister everything while she was young; remarkable sights made so much
more impression when the mind was fresh; she had read
something of that sort in Goethe, somewhere. She had wanted
to come herself when she was her sister's age; but her father
was in business then, and they couldn't leave Utica. Vogelstein thought of the little sister frisking over the Parthenon
and the Mount of Olives, and sharing for two years, the years
of the schoolroom, this extraordinary odyssey of her parents,
and wondered whether Goethe's dictum had been justified
in this case. He asked Pandora if Utica were the seat of her
family; if it were a pleasant place; if it would be an interesting
city for him, as a stranger, to see. His companion replied

frankly that it was horrid, but added that all the same she would ask him to "come and visit us at our home," if it were not that they should probably soon leave it.

"Ah! You are going to live elsewhere?"

"Well, I am working for New York. I flatter myself I have loosened them while we have been away. They won't find Utica the same; that was my idea. I want a big place, and, of course, Utica——" And the girl broke off, with a little sigh.

"I suppose Utica is small?" Vogelstein suggested.

"Well, no, it's middle-sized. I hate anything middling," said Pandora Day. She gave a light, dry laugh, tossing back her head a little as she made this declaration. And looking at her askance, in the dusk, as she trod the deck that vaguely swayed, he thought there was something in her air and port that carried out such a spirit.

"What is her social position?" he inquired of Mrs Dangerfield the next day. "I can't make it out at all, it is so contradictory. She strikes me as having so much cultivation and so much spirit. Her appearance, too, is very neat. Yet her parents are little burghers. That is easily seen."

"Oh, social position!" Mrs Dangerfield exclaimed, nodding two or three times, rather portentously. "What big expressions you use! Do you think everybody in the world has a social position? That is reserved for an infinitely small minority of mankind. You can't have a social position at Utica, any more than you can have an opera-box. Pandora hasn't got any; where should she have found it? Poor girl, it isn't fair of you to ask such questions as that."

"Well," said Vogelstein, "if she is of the lower class, that seems to be very—very——" And he paused a moment, as he often paused in speaking English, looking for his word.

"Very what, Count Vogelstein?"

"Very significant, very representative."

"Oh, dear, she isn't of the lower class," Mrs Dangerfield murmured, helplessly.

"What is she, then?"

"Well, I'm bound to admit that since I was at home last she is a novelty. A girl like that, with such people—it's a new type."

"I like novelties," said Count Vogelstein, smiling, with an air of considerable resolution. He could not, however, be satisfied with an explanation that only begged the question; and when they disembarked in New York, he felt, even amid the confusion of wharf and the heaps of disembowelled baggage, a certain acuteness of regret at the idea that Pandora and her family were about to vanish into the unknown. He had a consolation, however: it was apparent that for some reason or other—illness or absence from town—the gentleman to whom she had written had not, as she said, come down. Vogelstein was glad—he couldn't have told you why—that this sympathetic person had failed her; even though without him Pandora had to engage single-handed with the United States custom-house. Vogelstein's first impression of the western world was received on the landing-place of the German steamers, at Jersey City—a huge wooden shed, covering a wooden wharf which resounded under the feet, palisaded with rough-hewn, slanting piles, and bestrewn with masses of heterogeneous luggage. At one end, towards the town, was a row of tall, painted palings, behind which he could distinguish a press of hackney-coachmen, brandishing their whips and awaiting their victims, while their voices rose, incessant, with a sharp, strange sound, at once fierce and familiar. The whole place, behind the fence, appeared to bristle and resound. Out there was America, Vogelstein said to himself, and he looked towards it with a sense that he ought to muster resolution. On the wharf people were rushing about amid their trunks, pulling their things together, trying to unite their scattered parcels. They were heated and angry, or

else quite bewildered and discouraged. The few that had succeeded in collecting their battered boxes had an air of flushed
indifference to the efforts of their neighbours, not even looking at people with whom they had been intimate on the
steamer. A detachment of the officers of the customs was in
attendance, and energetic passengers were engaged in attempts
to draw them towards their luggage or to drag heavy pieces
towards them. These functionaries were good-natured and
taciturn, except when occasionally they remarked to a pas-
senger whose open trunk stared up at them, imploring, that
they were afraid the voyage had had a good deal of sameness.
They had a friendly, leisurely, speculative way of performing
their office, and if they perceived a victim's name written on
the portmanteau, they addressed him by it, in a tone of old
acquaintance. Vogelstein found, however, that if they were
familiar, they were not indiscreet. He had heard that in
America all public functionaries were the same, that there was
not a different *tenue*, as they said in France, for different positions; and he wondered whether at Washington the President
and ministers, whom he expected to see, would be like that.

He was diverted from these speculations by the sight of
Mr and Mrs Day, who were seated side by side upon a trunk,
encompassed, apparently, by the accumulations of their tour.
Their faces expressed more consciousness of surrounding
objects than he had hitherto perceived, and there was an air
of placid expansion in the mysterious couple which suggested
that this consciousness was agreeable. Mr and Mrs Day, as they
would have said, were glad to get back. At a little distance,
on the edge of the dock, Vogelstein remarked their son, who
had found a place where, between the sides of two big ships,
he could see the ferryboats pass; the large, pyramidal, low-
laden ferryboats of American waters. He stood there, patient
and considering, with his small neat foot on a coil of rope, his
back to everything that had been disembarked, his neck elongated in its polished cylinder, while the fragrance of his big

cigar mingled with the odour of the rotting piles, and his little sister, beside him, hugged a huge post and tried to see how far she could crane over the water without falling in. Vogelstein's servant, an Englishman (he had taken him for practice in the language), had gone in pursuit of an examiner; he had got his things together and was waiting to be released, fully expecting that for a person of his importance the ceremony would be brief. Before it began he said a word to young Mr Day, taking off his hat at the same time to the little girl, whom he had not yet greeted, and who dodged his salute by swinging herself boldly outwards, to the dangerous side of the pier. She was not much "formed" yet, but she was evidently as light as a feather.

"I see you are kept waiting, like me. It is very tiresome," Count Vogelstein said.

The young man answered without looking behind him. "As soon as we begin we shall go straight. My sister has written to a gentleman to come down."

"I have looked for Miss Day to bid her good-bye," Vogelstein went on; "but I don't see her."

"I guess she has gone to meet that gentleman; he's a great friend of hers."

"I presume he's her lover!" the little girl broke out. "She was always writing to him, in Europe."

Her brother puffed his cigar in silence for a moment. "That was only for this. I'll tell on you," he presently added.

But the younger Miss Day gave no heed to his announcement; she addressed herself to Vogelstein. "This is New York; I like it better than Utica."

Vogelstein had no time to reply, for his servant had arrived with one of the emissaries of the customs; but as he turned away he wondered, in the light of the child's preference, about the towns of the interior. He was very well treated. The officer who took him in hand, and who had a large straw hat and a diamond breastpin, was quite a man of the world, and

in reply to the formal declarations of the Count only said,
"Well, I guess it's all right; I guess I'll just pass you;" and
he distributed, freely, a dozen chalk-marks. The servant had
unlocked and unbuckled various pieces, and while he was
closing them the officer stood there wiping his forehead and
conversing with Vogelstein. "First visit to our country,
Count?—quite alone—no ladies? Of course the ladies are
what we are after." It was in this manner he expressed himself, while the young diplomatist wondered what he was waiting for, and whether he ought to slip something into his palm.
But Vogelstein's visitor left him only a moment in suspense;
he presently turned away, with the remark, very quietly
uttered, that he hoped the Count would make quite a stay; upon
which the young man saw how wrong he should have been
to offer him a tip. It was simply the American manner, and it
was very amicable, after all. Vogelstein's servant had secured
a porter, with a truck, and he was about to leave the place
when he saw Pandora Day dart out of the crowd and address
herself, with much eagerness, to the functionary who had
just liberated him. She had an open letter in her hand, which
she gave him to read, and he cast his eyes over it, deliberately,
stroking his beard. Then she led him away to where her
parents sat upon their luggage. Vogelstein sent off his servant
with the porter, and followed Pandora, to whom he really
wished to say a word in farewell. The last thing they had said
to each other on the ship was that they should meet again on
shore. It seemed improbable, however, that the meeting would
occur anywhere but just here on the dock; inasmuch as Pandora was decidedly not in society, where Vogelstein would be,
of course, and as, if Utica was not—he had her sharp little
sister's word for it—as agreeable as what was about him there,
he would be hanged if he would go to Utica. He overtook
Pandora quickly; she was in the act of introducing the customs-
officer to her parents, quite in the same manner in which she
had introduced the captain of the steamer. Mr and Mrs Day

got up and shook hands with him, and they evidently all prepared to have a little talk. "I should like to introduce you to my brother and sister," he heard the girl say; and he saw her look about her for these appendages. He caught her eye as she did so, and advanced, with his hand outstretched, reflecting the while that evidently the Americans, whom he had always heard described as silent and practical, were not unversed in certain social arts. They dawdled and chattered like so many Neapolitans.

"Good-bye, Count Vogelstein," said Pandora, who was a little flushed with her various exertions, but did not look the worse for it. "I hope you'll have a splendid time, and appreciate our country."

"I hope you'll get through all right," Vogelstein answered, smiling and feeling himself already more idiomatic.

"That gentleman is sick that I wrote to," she rejoined; "isn't it too bad? But he sent me down a letter to a friend of his, one of the examiners, and I guess we won't have any trouble. Mr Lansing, let me make you acquainted with Count Vogelstein," she went on, presenting to her fellow-passenger the wearer of the straw hat and the breast-pin, who shook hands with the young German as if he had never seen him before. Vogelstein's heart rose for an instant to his throat. He thanked his stars that he had not offered a tip to the friend of a gentleman who had often been mentioned to him, and who had been described by a member of Pandora's family as her lover.

"It's a case of ladies this time," Mr Lansing remarked to Vogelstein, with a smile which seemed to confess, surreptitiously, and as if neither party could be eager, to recognition.

"Well, Mr Bellamy says you'll do anything for *him*," Pandora said, smiling very sweetly at Mr Lansing. "We haven't got much; we have been gone only two years."

Mr Lansing scratched his head a little, behind, with a movement which sent his straw hat forward in the direction of his nose. "I don't know as I would do anything for him that I wouldn't do for you," he responded, returning the smile of the girl. "I guess you had better open that one." And he gave a little affectionate kick to one of the trunks.

"Oh, mother, isn't he lovely! It's only your sea-things," Pandora cried, stooping over the coffer instantly, with the key in her hand.

"I don't know as I like showing them," Mrs Day murmured, modestly.

Vogelstein made his German salutation to the company in general, and to Pandora he offered an audible good-bye, which she returned in a bright, friendly voice, but without looking round, as she fumbled at the lock of her trunk.

"We'll try another, if you like," said Mr Lansing, laughing.

"Oh no, it has got to be this one! Good-bye, Count Vogelstein. I hope you'll judge us correctly!"

The young man went his way and passed the barrier of the dock. Here he was met by his servant, with a face of consternation which led him to ask whether a cab were not forthcoming.

"They call 'em 'acks 'ere, sir," said the man, "and they're beyond everything. He wants thirty shillings to take you to the inn."

Vogelstein hesitated a moment. "Couldn't you find a German?"

"By the way he talks he *is* a German!" said the man; and in a moment Count Vogelstein began his career in America by discussing the tariff of hackney-coaches in the language of the fatherland.

II

VOGELSTEIN went wherever he was asked, on principle, partly to study American society, and partly because, in Washington, pastimes seemed to him not so numerous that one could afford to neglect occasions. Of course, at the end of two winters he had a good many of various kinds, and his study of American society had yielded considerable fruit. When, however, in April, during the second year of his residence, he presented himself at a large party given by Mrs Bonnycastle, and of which it was believed that it would be the last serious affair of the season, his being there (and still more his looking very fresh and talkative) was not the consequence of a rule of conduct. He went to Mrs Bonnycastle's simply because he liked the lady, whose receptions were the pleasantest in Washington, and because if he didn't go there he didn't know what he should do. That absence of alternatives had become rather familiar to him in Washington—there were a great many things he did because if he didn't do them he didn't know what he should do. It must be added that in this case, even if there had been an alternative, he would still have decided to go to Mrs Bonnycastle's. If her house was not the pleasantest there, it was at least difficult to say which was pleasanter; and the complaint sometimes made of it that it was too limited, that it left out, on the whole, more people than it took in, applied with much less force when it was thrown open for a general party. Towards the end of the social year, in those soft, scented days of the Washington spring, when the air began to show a southern glow, and the little squares and circles (to which the wide, empty avenues converged according to a plan so ingenious, yet so bewildering) to flush with pink blossom and to make one wish to sit on benches—at this period of expansion and condonation Mrs Bonnycastle, who during the winter had been a good deal on the defensive, relaxed her vigilance a little, became humorously inconsistent, vernally reckless, as it were, and ceased to calculate the consequences of an hospitality which a reference to the back-files—or even to the morning's issue—of newspapers might easily show to be a mistake. But Washington life, to Vogelstein's apprehension, was paved with

mistakes; he felt himself to be in a society which was founded
on necessary lapses. Little addicted as he was to the sportive
view of existence, he had said to himself, at an early stage of
his sojourn, that the only way to enjoy the United States
would be to burn one's standards and warm one's self at the
blaze. Such were the reflections of a theoretic Teuton, who
now walked for the most part amid the ashes of his prejudices. Mrs Bonnycastle had endeavoured more than once
to explain to him the principles on which she received certain
people and ignored certain others; but it was with difficulty
that he entered into her discriminations. She perceived differences where he only saw resemblances, and both the merits
and defects of a good many members of Washington society,
as that society was interpreted to him by Mrs Bonnycastle,
he was often at a loss to understand. Fortunately she had a
fund of good humour which, as I have intimated, was apt to
come uppermost with the April blossoms, and which made
the people she did not invite to her house almost as amusing
to her as those she did. Her husband was not in politics,
though politics were much in him; but the couple had taken
upon themselves the responsibilities of an active patriotism;
they thought it right to live in America, differing therein from
a great many of their acquaintance, who only thought it
expensive. They had that burdensome heritage of foreign
reminiscence with which so many Americans are saddled;
but they carried it more easily than most of their country-
people, and you knew they had lived in Europe only by their
present exultation, never in the least by their regrets. Their
regrets, that is, were only for their ever having lived there, as
Mrs Bonnycastle once told the wife of a foreign minister. They
solved all their problems successfully, including those of
knowing none of the people they did not wish to, and of
finding plenty of occupation in a society supposed to be
meagerly provided with resources for persons of leisure.
When, as the warm weather approached, they opened both the

wings of their door, it was because they thought it would entertain them, and not because they were conscious of a pressure. Alfred Bonnycastle, all winter indeed, chafed a little at the definiteness of some of his wife's reserves; he thought that, for Washington, their society was really a little too good. Vogelstein still remembered the puzzled feeling (it had cleared up somewhat now) with which, more than a year before, he had heard Mr Bonnycastle exclaim one evening, after a dinner in his own house, when every guest but the German secretary, who often sat late with the pair, had departed, "Hang it, there is only a month left; let us have some fun—let us invite the President!"

This was Mrs Bonnycastle's carnival, and on the occasion to which I began my little chapter by referring, the President had not only been invited but had signified his intention of being present. I hasten to add that this was not the same functionary to whom Alfred Bonnycastle's irreverent allusion had been made. The White House had received a new tenant (the old one, then, was just leaving it), and Otto Vogelstein had had the advantage, during the first eighteen months of his stay in America, of seeing an electoral campaign, a presidential inauguration, and a distribution of spoils. He had been bewildered, during those first weeks, by finding that in the national capital, in the houses that he supposed to be the best, the head of the State was not a coveted guest; for this could be the only explanation of Mr Bonnycastle's whimsical proposal to invite him, as it were, in carnival. His successor went out a good deal, for a President.

The legislative session was over, but this made little difference in the aspect of Mrs Bonnycastle's rooms, which, even at the height of the congressional season, could not be said to overflow with the representatives of the people. They were garnished with an occasional senator, whose movements and utterances often appeared to be regarded with a mixture of alarm and indulgence, as if they would be disappointing if they were not rather odd, and yet might be dangerous if they were not carefully watched. Vogelstein had grown to have a kindness for these conscript fathers of invisible families, who had something of the toga in the voluminous folds of their conversation, but were otherwise rather bare and bald, with stony wrinkles in their faces, like busts and statues of ancient law-givers. There seemed to him something chill and exposed in their being at once so exalted and so naked; there were lonesome glances in their eyes, sometimes, as if in the social world their legislative consciousness longed for the warmth of a few comfortable laws ready-made. Members of the House were very rare, and when Washington was new to Vogelstein he used sometimes to mistake them, in the hall and on the staircases where he met them, for the functionaries engaged for the evening to usher in guests and wait at supper. It was only a little later that he perceived these functionaries were almost always impressive, and had a complexion which served as a livery. At present, however, such misleading figures were much less to be encountered than during the months of winter, and, indeed, they never were to be encountered at Mrs Bonny-castle's. At present the social vistas of Washington, like the vast fresh flatness of the lettered and numbered streets, which at this season seemed to Vogelstein more spacious and vague than ever, suggested but a paucity of political phenomena. Count Otto, that evening, knew every one, or almost every one. There were very often inquiring strangers, expecting great things, from New York and Boston, and to them, in the friendly Washington way, the young German was promptly introduced. It was a society in which familiarity reigned, and in which people were liable to meet three times a day, so that their ultimate essence became a matter of importance.

"I have got three new girls," Mrs Bonnycastle said. "You must talk to them all."

"All at once?" Vogelstein asked, reversing in imagination a position which was not unknown to him. He had often, in

Washington, been discoursed to at the same moment by several virginal voices.

"Oh no; you must have something different for each; you can't get off that way. Haven't you discovered that the American girl expects something especially adapted to herself? It's very well in Europe to have a few phrases that will do for any girl. The American girl isn't any girl; she's a remarkable individual in a remarkable genus. But you must keep the best this evening for Miss Day."

"For Miss Day!" Vogelstein exclaimed, staring. "Do you mean Pandora?"

Mrs Bonnycastle stared a moment, in return; then laughed very hard. "One would think you had been looking for her over the globe! So you know her already, and you call her by her pet name?"

"Oh no, I don't know her; that is, I haven't seen her, nor thought of her, from that day to this. We came to America in the same ship."

"Isn't she an American, then?"

"Oh yes; she lives at Utica, in the interior."

"In the interior of Utica? You can't mean my young woman then, who lives in New York, where she is a great beauty and a great success, and has been immensely admired this winter."

"After all," said Vogelstein, reflecting and a little disappointed, "the name is not so uncommon; it is perhaps another. But has she rather strange eyes, a little yellow, but very pretty, and a nose a little arched?"

"I can't tell you all that; I haven't seen her. She is staying with Mrs Steuben. She only came a day or two ago, and Mrs Steuben is to bring her. When she wrote to me to ask leave she told me what I tell you. They haven't come yet."

Vogelstein felt a quick hope that the subject of this correspondence might indeed be the young lady he had parted from on the dock at New York, but the indications seemed to point the other way, and he had no wish to cherish an illusion. It did not seem to him probable that the energetic girl who had introduced him to Mr Lansing would have the entrée of the best house in Washington; besides, Mrs Bonnycastle's guest was described as a beauty and as belonging to the brilliant city.

"What is the social position of Mrs Steuben?" it occurred to him to ask in a moment, as he meditated. He had an earnest, artless, literal way of uttering such a question as that; you could see from it that he was very thorough.

Mrs Bonnycastle broke into mocking laughter. "I am sure I don't know! What is your own?" And she left him, to turn to her other guests, to several of whom she repeated his question. Could they tell her what was the social position of Mrs Steuben? There was Count Vogelstein, who wanted to know. He instantly became aware, of course, that he ought not to have made such an inquiry. Was not the lady's place in the scale sufficiently indicated by Mrs Bonnycastle's acquaintance with her? Still, there were fine degrees, and he felt a little unduly snubbed. It was perfectly true, as he told his hostess, that, with the quick wave of new impressions that had rolled over him after his arrival in America, the image of Pandora was almost completely effaced; he had seen a great many things which were quite as remarkable in their way as the daughter of the Days. But at the touch of the idea that he might see her again at any moment she became as vivid in his mind as if they had parted but the day before; he remembered the exact shade of the eyes he had described to Mrs Bonnycastle as yellow; the tone of her voice when, at the last, she expressed the hope that he would judge America correctly. Had he judged it correctly? If he were to meet her again she doubtless would try to ascertain. It would be going much too far to say that the idea of such an ordeal was terrible to Otto Vogelstein; but it may at least be said that the thought of meeting Pandora Day made him nervous. The fact is certainly singular, but I shall not take upon myself to explain it; there

are some things that even the most philosophic historian is
not bound to account for.

He wandered into another room, and there, at the end of
five minutes, he was introduced by Mrs Bonnycastle to one
of the young ladies of whom she had spoken. This was a very
intelligent girl, who came from Boston, showing much
acquaintance with Spielhagen's novels. "Do you like them?"
Vogelstein asked, rather vaguely, not taking much interest
in the matter, as he read works of fiction only in case of a sea-
voyage. The young lady from Boston looked pensive and
concentrated; then she answered that she liked some of them,
but that there were others she did not like, and she enumer-
ated the works that came under each of these heads. Spielhagen is a voluminous writer, and such a catalogue took some
time; at the end of it, moreover, Vogelstein's question was not
answered, for he could not have told you whether she liked
Spielhagen or not. On the next topic, however, there was no
doubt about her feelings. They talked about Washington as
people talk only in the place itself, revolving about the subject in widening and narrowing circles, perching successively
on its many branches, considering it from every point of
view. Vogelstein had been long enough in America to discover that, after half a century of social neglect, Washington
had become the fashion, possessed the great advantage of
being a new resource in conversation. This was especially the
case in the months of spring, when the inhabitants of the
commercial cities came so far southward to escape that
boisterous interlude. They were all agreed that Washington
was fascinating, and none of them were better prepared to
talk it over than the Bostonians. Vogelstein originally had
been rather out of step with them; he had not seized their point
of view, had not known with what they compared this object
of their infatuation. But now he knew everything; he had
settled down to the pace; there was not a possible phase of the
discussion which could find him at a loss. There was a kind of

Hegelian element in it; in the light of these considerations the American capital took on the semblance of a monstrous, mystical *Werden*. But they fatigued Vogelstein a little, and it was his preference, as a general thing, not to engage the same evening with more than one new-comer, one visitor in the freshness of initiation. This was why Mrs Bonnycastle's expression of a wish to introduce him to three young ladies had startled him a little; he saw a certain process, in which he flattered himself that he had become proficient, but which was after all tolerably exhausting, repeated for each of the damsels. After separating from his bright Bostonian he rather evaded Mrs Bonnycastle, and contented himself with the conversation of old friends, pitched, for the most part, in a lower and more sceptical key.

At last he heard it mentioned that the President had arrived, had been some half-an-hour in the house, and he went in search of the illustrious guest, whose whereabouts at Washington parties was not indicated by a cluster of courtiers. He made it a point, whenever he found himself in company with the President, to pay him his respects; and he had not been discouraged by the fact that there was no association of ideas in the eye of the great man as he put out his hand, presidentially, and said, "Happy to see you, sir." Vogelstein felt himself taken for a mere constituent, possibly for an office-seeker; and he used to reflect at such moments that the monarchical form had its merits: it provided a line of heredity for the faculty of quick recognition. He had now some difficulty in finding the chief magistrate, and ended by learning that he was in the tea-room, a small apartment devoted to light refection, near the entrance of the house. Here Vogelstein presently perceived him, seated on a sofa, in conversation with a lady. There were a number of people about the table, eating, drinking, talking; and the couple on the sofa, which was not near it, but against the wall, in a kind of recess, looked a little withdrawn, as if they had sought seclusion and were disposed to profit by the diverted attention of the others. The President leaned back; his gloved hands, resting on either knee, made large white spots. He looked eminent, but he looked relaxed, and the lady beside him was making him laugh. Vogelstein caught her voice as he approached—he heard her say, "Well, now, remember; I consider it a promise." She was very prettily dressed, in rose-colour; her hands were clasped in her lap, and her eyes were attached to the presidential profile.

"Well, madam, in that case it's about the fiftieth promise I have given to-day."

It was just as he heard these words, uttered by her companion in reply, that Vogelstein checked himself, turned away, and pretended to be looking for a cup of tea. It was not customary to disturb the President, even simply to shake hands, when he was sitting on a sofa with a lady, and Vogelstein felt it in this case to be less possible than ever to break the rule, for the lady on the sofa was none other than Pandora Day. He had recognised her without her appearing to see him, and even in his momentary look he had perceived that she was now a person to be reckoned with. She had an air of elation, of success; she looked brilliant in her rose-coloured dress; she was extracting promises from the ruler of fifty millions of people. What an odd place to meet her, Vogelstein thought, and how little one could tell, after all, in America, who people were! He didn't wish to speak to her yet; he wished to wait a little, and learn more; but, meanwhile, there was something attractive in the thought that she was just behind him, a few yards off, that if he should turn he might see her again. It was she whom Mrs Bonnycastle had meant; it was she who was so much admired in New York. Her face was the same, yet Vogelstein had seen in a moment that she was vaguely prettier; he had recognised the arch of her nose, which suggested ambition. He took two ices, which he did not want, in order not to go away. He remembered her *entourage* on the steamer: her father and mother, the silent burghers, so little "of the world," her infant sister, so much of it, her humorous brother, with his tall hat and his influence in the smoking-room. He remembered Mrs Dangerfield's warnings—yet her perplexities too, and the letter from Mr Bellamy, and the introduction to Mr Lansing, and the way Pandora had stooped down on the dirty dock, laughing and talking, mistress of the situation, to open her trunk for the customs. He was pretty sure that she had paid no duties that day; that had been the purpose, of course, of Mr Bellamy's letter. Was she still in correspondence with this gentleman, and had he recovered from his sickness? All this passed through Vogelstein's mind, and he saw that it was quite in Pandora's line to be mistress of the situation, for there was nothing, evidently, on the present occasion that could call itself her master. He drank his tea, and as he put down his cup he heard the President, behind him, say, "Well, I guess my wife will wonder why I don't come home."

"Why didn't you bring her with you?" Pandora asked.

"Well, she doesn't go out much. Then she has got her sister staying with her—Mrs Runkle, from Natchez. She's a good deal of an invalid, and my wife doesn't like to leave her."

"She must be a very kind woman," Pandora remarked, sympathetically.

"Well, I guess she isn't spoiled yet."

"I should like very much to come and see her," said Pandora.

"Do come round. Couldn't you come some night?" the President responded.

"Well, I will come some time. And I shall remind you of your promise."

"All right. There's nothing like keeping it up. Well," said the President, "I must bid good-bye to these kind folks."

Vogelstein heard him rise from the sofa, with his companion, and he gave the pair time to pass out of the room before him, which they did with a certain impressive deliberation, people making way for the ruler of fifty millions and looking with a certain curiosity at the striking pink person at his side. When, after a few moments, Vogelstein followed them across the hall, into one of the other rooms, he saw the hostess accompany the President to the door, and two foreign ministers and a judge of the Supreme Court address themselves to Pandora Day. He resisted the impulse to join this circle; if he spoke to her at all he wished to speak to her alone. She continued, nevertheless, to occupy him, and when Mrs Bonnycastle came back from the hall he immediately approached her with an appeal. "I wish you would tell me something more about that girl—that one, opposite, in pink?"

"The lovely Day—that is what they call her, I believe? I wanted you to talk with her."

"I find she is the one I have met. But she seems to be so different here. I can't make it out."

There was something in his expression which provoked Mrs Bonnycastle to mirth. "How we do puzzle you Europeans; you look quite bewildered!"

"I am sorry I look so; I try to hide it. But, of course, we are very simple. Let me ask, then, a simple question. Are her parents also in society?"

"Parents in society! D'où tombez-vous? Did you ever hear of a girl—in rose-colour—whose parents were in society?"

"Is she, then, all alone?" Count Vogelstein inquired, with a strain of melancholy in his voice.

Mrs Bonnycastle stared at him a moment, with her laughter in her face. "You are too pathetic. Don't you know what she is? I supposed, of course, you knew."

"It's exactly what I am asking you."

"Why, she's the new type. It has only come up lately. They have had articles about it in the papers. That's the reason I told Mrs Steuben to bring her."

"The new type? What new type, Mrs Bonnycastle?" said

Vogelstein, pleadingly, and conscious that all types in America were new.

Her laughter checked her reply for a moment, and by the time she had recovered herself the young lady from Boston, with whom Vogelstein had been talking, stood there to take leave. This, for an American type, was an old one, he was sure; and the process of parting between the guest and her hostess had an ancient elaboration. Vogelstein waited a little; then he turned away and walked up to Pandora Day, whose group of interlocutors had now been reinforced by a gentleman that had held an important place in the cabinet of the late occupant of the presidential chair. Vogelstein had asked Mrs Bonnycastle if she were "all alone;" but there was nothing in Pandora's present situation that suggested isolation. She was not sufficiently alone for Vogelstein's taste; but he was impatient, and he hoped she would give him a few words to himself. She recognised him without a moment's hesitation, and with the sweetest smile, a smile that matched the tone in which she said, "I was watching you; I wondered whether you were not going to speak to me."

"Miss Day was watching him," one of the foreign ministers exclaimed, "and we flattered ourselves that her attention was all with us!"

"I mean before," said the girl, "while I was talking with the President."

At this the gentlemen began to laugh, and one of them remarked that that was the way the absent were sacrificed, even the great; while another said that he hoped Vogelstein was duly flattered.

"Oh, I was watching the President too," said Pandora. "I have got to watch *him*. He has promised me something."

"It must be the mission to England," the judge of the Supreme Court suggested. "A good position for a lady; they have got a lady at the head, over there."

"I wish they would send you to my country," one of the

foreign ministers suggested. "I would immediately get recalled."

"Why, perhaps in your country I wouldn't speak to you! It's only because you are here," the girl returned, with a gay familiarity which with her was evidently but one of the arts of defence. "You'll see what mission it is when it comes out. But I will speak to Count Vogelstein anywhere," she went on. "He is an older friend than any one here. I have known him in difficult days."

"Oh yes, on the ocean," said the young man, smiling. "On the wastery waste, in the tempest!"

"Oh, I don't mean that so much; we had a beautiful voyage, and there wasn't any tempest. I mean when I was living in Utica. That's a watery waste, if you like, and a tempest there would have been a pleasant variety."

"Your parents seemed to me so peaceful!" Vogelstein exclaimed, with a vague wish to say something sympathetic.

"Oh, you haven't seen them on shore. At Utica they were very lively. But that is no longer our home. Don't you remember I told you I was working for New York? Well, I worked—I had to work hard. But we have moved."

"And I hope they are happy," said Vogelstein.

"My father and mother? Oh, they will be, in time. I must give them time. They are very young yet; they have years before them. And you have been always in Washington?" Pandora continued. "I suppose you have found out everything about everything."

"Oh no; there are some things I can't find out."

"Come and see me, and perhaps I can help you. I am very different from what I was on the ship. I have advanced a great deal since then."

"Oh, how was Miss Day on the ship?" asked the cabinet minister of the last administration.

"She was delightful, of course," said Vogelstein.

"He is very flattering; I didn't open my mouth!" Pandora

cried. "Here comes Mrs Steuben to take me to some other place. I believe it's a literary party, near the Capitol. Everything seems so separate in Washington. Mrs Steuben is going to read a poem. I wish she would read it here; wouldn't it do as well?"

This lady, arriving, signified to Pandora the necessity of their moving on. But Miss Day's companions had various things to say to her before giving her up. She had an answer for each of them, and it was brought home to Vogelstein, as he listened, that, as she said, she had advanced a great deal. Daughter of small burghers as she was, she was really brilliant. Vogelstein turned away a little, and, while Mrs Steuben waited, asked her a question. He had made her, half an hour before, the subject of that inquiry to which Mrs Bonnycastle returned so ambiguous an answer; but this was not because he had not some direct acquaintance with Mrs Steuben, as well as a general idea of the esteem in which she was held. He had met her in various places, and he had been at her house. She was the widow of a commodore—a handsome, mild, soft, swaying woman, whom every one liked, with glossy bands of black hair and a little ringlet depending behind each ear. Some one had said that she looked like the Queen in *Hamlet*. She had written verses which were admired in the South, wore a full-length portrait of the commodore on her bosom, and spoke with the accent of Savannah. She had about her a positive odour of Washington. It had certainly been very crude in Vogelstein to question Mrs Bonnycastle about her social position.

"Do kindly tell me," he said, lowering his voice, "what is the type to which that young lady belongs. Mrs Bonnycastle tells me it's a new one."

Mrs Steuben for a moment fixed her liquid eyes upon the secretary of legation. She always seemed to be translating the prose of your speech into the finer rhythms with which her own mind was familiar. "Do you think anything is really

new?" she asked. "I am very fond of the old; you know that
is a weakness of we Southerners." The poor lady, it will be
observed, had another weakness as well. "What we often take
to be the new is simply the old under some novel form. Were
there not remarkable natures in the past? If you doubt it you
should visit the South, where the past still lingers."

Vogelstein had been struck before this with Mrs Steuben's
pronunciation of the word by which her native latitudes were
designated: transcribing it from her lips, you would have
written it (as the nearest approach) the Sooth. But, at present,
he scarcely observed this peculiarity; he was wondering,
rather, how a woman could be at once so copious and so un-
satisfactory. What did he care about the past, or even about
the Sooth? He was afraid of starting her again. He looked at
her, discouraged and helpless, as bewildered almost as Mrs
Bonnycastle had found him half an hour before; looked also
at the commodore, who, on her bosom, seemed to breathe
again with his widow's respirations. "Call it an old type, then,
if you like," he said in a moment. "All I want to know is
what type it is! It seems impossible to find out."

"You can find out by the newspapers. They have had
articles about it. They write about everything now. But it
isn't true about Miss Day. It is one of the first families. Her
great-grandfather was in the Revolution." Pandora by this
time had given her attention again to Mrs Steuben. She seemed
to signify that she was ready to move on. "Wasn't your great-
grandfather in the Revolution?" Mrs Steuben asked. "I am
telling Count Vogelstein about him."

"Why are you asking about my ancestors?" the girl demanded, smiling, of the young German. "Is that the thing
that you said just now that you can't find out? Well, if Mrs
Steuben will only be quiet you never will."

Mrs Steuben shook her head, rather dreamily. "Well, it's
no trouble for a Southerner to be quiet. There's a kind of
languor in our blood. Besides, we have to be, to-day. But I

have got to show some energy to-night. I have got to get you to the end of Pennsylvania Avenue."

Pandora gave her hand to Count Vogelstein, and asked him if he thought they should meet again. He answered that in Washington people were always meeting, and that at any rate he should not fail to come and see her. Hereupon, just as the two ladies were detaching themselves, Mrs Steuben remarked that if Count Vogelstein and Miss Day wished to meet again the picnic would be a good chance—the picnic that she was getting up for the following Thursday. It was to consist of about twenty bright people, and they would go down the Potomac to Mount Vernon. Vogelstein answered that, if Mrs Steuben thought him bright enough, he should be delighted to join the party; and he was told the hour for which the tryst was taken.

He remained at Mrs Bonnycastle's after every one had gone, and then he informed this lady of his reason for waiting. Would she have mercy on him and let him know, in a single word, before he went to rest—for without it rest would be impossible—what was this famous type to which Pandora Day belonged?

"Gracious, you don't mean to say you have not found out that type yet!" Mrs Bonnycastle exclaimed, with a return of her hilarity. "What have you been doing all the evening? You Germans may be thorough, but you certainly are not quick!"

It was Alfred Bonnycastle who at last took pity on him. "My dear Vogelstein, she is the latest, freshest fruit of our great American evolution. She is the self-made girl!"

Vogelstein gazed a moment. "The fruit of the great American Revolution? Yes, Mrs Steuben told me her great-grandfather——" But the rest of his sentence was lost in the explosion of Mrs Bonnycastle's mirth. He bravely continued his interrogation, however, and, desiring his host's definition to be defined, inquired what the self-made girl might be.

"Sit down, and we'll tell you all about it," Mrs Bonny-castle said. "I like talking this way after a party's over. You can smoke, if you like, and Alfred will open another window. Well, to begin with, the self-made girl is a new feature. That, however, you know. In the second place, she isn't self-made at all. We all help to make her, we take such an interest in her."

"That's only after she is made!" Alfred Bonnycastle broke in. "But it's Vogelstein that takes an interest. What on earth has started you up so on the subject of Miss Day?"

Vogelstein explained, as well as he could, that it was merely the accident of his having crossed the ocean in the steamer with her; but he felt the inadequacy of this account of the matter, felt it more than his hosts, who could know neither how little actual contact he had had with her on the ship, how much he had been affected by Mrs Dangerfield's warnings, nor how much observation at the same time he had lavished on her. He sat there half an hour, and the warm, dead stillness of the Washington night—nowhere are the nights so silent—came in at the open windows, mingled with a soft, sweet, earthy smell—the smell of growing things. Before he went away he had heard all about the self-made girl, and there was something in the picture that almost inspired him. She was possible, doubtless, only in America; American life had smoothed the way for her. She was not fast nor emancipated nor crude nor loud, and there was not in her, of necessity at least, a grain of the stuff of which the adventuress is made. She was simply very successful, and her success was entirely personal. She had not been born with the silver spoon of social opportunity; she had grasped it by honest exertion. You knew her by many different signs, but chiefly, infallibly, by the appearance of her parents. It was her parents that told the story; you always saw that her parents could never have made her. Her attitude with regard to them might vary, in innumerable ways; the great fact on her own side being that she had lifted herself from a lower social plane, done it all herself, and done it by the simple lever of her personality. In this view, of course, it was to be expected that she should leave the authors of her being in the shade. Sometimes she had them in her wake, lost in the bubbles and the foam that showed where she had passed; sometimes, as Alfred Bonnycastle said, she let them slide; sometimes she kept them in close confinement; sometimes she exhibited them to the public in discreet glimpses, in prearranged attitudes. But the general characteristic of the self-made girl was that, though it was frequently understood that she was privately devoted to her kindred, she never attempted to impose them on society, and it was striking that she was much better than they. They were almost always solemn and portentous, and they were for the most part of a deathly respectability. She was not necessarily snobbish, unless it was snobbish to want the best. She didn't cringe, she didn't make herself smaller than she was; on the contrary, she took a stand of her own, and attracted things to herself. Naturally, she was possible only in America, only in a country where certain competitions were absent. The natural history of this interesting creature was at last completely exhibited to Vogelstein, who, as he sat there in the animated stillness, with the fragrant wreath of the western world in his nostrils, was convinced of what he had already suspected, that conversation in the United States is much more psychological than elsewhere. Another thing, as he learned, that you knew the self-made girl by was her culture, which was perhaps a little too obvious. She had usually got into society more or less by reading, and her conversation was apt to be garnished with literary allusions, even with sudden quotations. Vogelstein had not had time to observe this element in a developed form in Pandora Day; but Alfred Bonnycastle said that he wouldn't trust her to keep it under in a *tête-à-tête*. It was needless to say that these young persons had always been to Europe; that was usually the first thing they did. By this means they

sometimes got into society in foreign lands before they did
so at home; it was to be added, on the other hand, that this
resource was less and less valuable; for Europe, in the United
States, had less and less prestige, and people in the latter
country now kept a watch on that roundabout road. All this
applied perfectly to Pandora Day—the journey to Europe,
the culture (as exemplified in the books she read on the ship),
the effacement of the family. The only thing that was excep-
tional was the rapidity with which she had advanced; for the
jump she had taken since he left her in the hands of Mr
Lansing struck Vogelstein, even after he had made all allowance for the abnormal homogeneity of American society, as
really considerable. It took all her cleverness to account for
it. When she moved her family from Utica, the battle appeared
virtually to have been gained.

Vogelstein called on her the next day, and Mrs Steuben's
blackamoor informed him, in the communicative manner of
his race, that the ladies had gone out to pay some visits and
look at the Capitol. Pandora apparently had not hitherto
examined this monument, and the young man wished he had
known the evening before of her omission, so that he might
have offered to be her initiator. There is too obvious a connection for me to attempt to conceal it between his regret
and the fact that in leaving Mrs Steuben's door he reminded
himself that he wanted a good walk, and took his way along
Pennsylvania Avenue. His walk had become fairly good by the
time he reached the great white edifice which unfolds its repeated colonnades and uplifts its isolated dome at the end of
a long vista of saloons and tobacco-shops. He slowly climbed
the great steps, hesitating a little, and wondering why he had
come there. The superficial reason was obvious enough, but
there was a real one behind it which seemed to Vogelstein
rather wanting in the solidity that should characterise the
motives of an emissary of Prince Bismarck. The superficial
reason was a belief that Mrs Steuben would pay her visit first—

it was probably only a question of leaving cards—and bring her young friend to the Capitol at the hour when the yellow afternoon light gives a tone to the blankness of its marble walls. The Capitol was a splendid building, but it was rather wanting in tone. Vogelstein's curiosity about Pandora Day had been much more quickened than checked by the revelations made to him in Mrs Bonnycastle's drawing-room. It was a relief to see the young lady classified; but he had a desire, of which he had not been conscious before, to judge really to the end how well a girl could make herself. His calculations had been just, and he had wandered about the rotunda for only ten minutes, looking again at the paintings, commemorative of national history, which occupy its panels, and at the simulated sculptures, so touchingly characteristic of early American taste, which adorn its upper reaches, when the charming women he had hoped for presented themselves in charge of a licensed guide. He went to meet them, and did not conceal from them that he had marked them for his own. The encounter was happy on both sides, and he accompanied them through the queer and endless interior, through labyrinths of white, bare passages, into legislative and judicial halls. He thought it a hideous place; he had seen it all before, and he asked himself what he was doing *dans cette galère*. In the lower House there were certain bedaubed walls, in the basest style of imitation, which made him feel faintly sick; there was a lobby adorned with artless prints and photographs of eminent congressmen, which was too serious for a joke and too comical for anything else.

But Pandora was greatly interested; she thought the Capitol very fine; it was easy to criticise the details, but as a whole it was the most impressive building she had ever seen. She was very good company; she had constantly something to say, but she never insisted too much; it was impossible to be less heavy, to drag less, in the business of walking behind a cicerone. Vogelstein could see, too, that she wished to improve her mind; she looked at the historical pictures, at the uncanny statues of local worthies, presented by the different States—they were of different sizes, as if they had been "numbered," in a shop—she asked questions of the conductor, and in the chamber of the Senate requested him to show her the chairs of the gentlemen from New York. She sat down in one of them, though Mrs Steuben told her *that* senator (she mistook the chair, dropping into another State) was a horrid old thing. Throughout the hour that he spent with her Vogelstein seemed to see how it was that she had made herself. They walked about afterwards on the magnificent terrace that surrounds the Capitol, the great marble table on which it stands, and made vague remarks (Pandora's were the most definite) about the yellow sheen of the Potomac, the hazy hills of Virginia, the far-gleaming pediment of Arlington, the raw, confused-looking country. Washington was beneath them, bristling and geometrical; the long lines of its avenues seemed to stretch into national futures. Pandora asked Vogelstein if he had ever been to Athens, and, on his replying in the affirmative, inquired whether the eminence on which they stood did not give him an idea of the Acropolis in its prime. Vogelstein deferred the answer to this question to their next meeting; he was glad (in spite of the question) to make pretexts for seeing her again.

He did so on the morrow; Mrs Steuben's picnic was still three days distant. He called on Pandora a second time, and he met her every evening in the Washington world. It took very little of this to remind him that he was forgetting both Mrs Dangerfield's warnings and the admonitions—long familiar to him—of his own conscience. Was he in peril of love? Was he to be sacrificed on the altar of the American girl—an altar at which those other poor fellows had poured out some of the bluest blood in Germany, and at which he had declared himself that he would never seriously worship? He decided that he was not in real danger; that he had taken his

precautions too well. It was true that a young person who
had succeeded so well for herself might be a great help to her
husband; but Vogelstein, on the whole, preferred that his
success should be his own; it would not be agreeable to him
to have the air of being pushed by his wife. Such a wife as that
would wish to push him; and he could hardly admit to himself that this was what fate had in reserve for him—to be pro-
pelled in his career by a young lady who would perhaps
attempt to talk to the Kaiser as he had heard her the other
night talk to the President. Would she consent to relinquish
relations with her family, or would she wish still to borrow
plastic relief from that domestic background? That her family
was so impossible was to a certain extent an advantage; for if
they had been a little better the question of a rupture would
have been less easy. Vogelstein turned over these ideas in spite
of his security, or perhaps, indeed, because of it. The security
made them speculative and disinterested. They haunted him
during the excursion to Mount Vernon, which took place
according to traditions long established.

Mrs Steuben's picnickers assembled on the steamer, and were
set afloat on the big brown stream which had already seemed
to Vogelstein to have too much bosom and too little bank.
Here and there, however, he became aware of a shore where
there was something to look at, even though he was conscious
at the same time that he had of old lost great opportunities of
idyllic talk in not sitting beside Pandora Day on the deck of
the North German Lloyd. The two turned round together
to contemplate Alexandria, which for Pandora, as she declared,
was a revelation of old Virginia. She told Vogelstein that she
was always hearing about it during the civil war, years before.
Little girl as she had been at the time, she remembered all the
names that were on people's lips during those years of reitera-
tion. This historic spot had a certain picturesqueness of decay,
a reference to older things, to a dramatic past. The past of
Alexandria appeared in the vista of three or four short streets,

sloping up a hill and bordered with old brick warehouses, erected for merchandise that had ceased to come or go. It looked hot and blank and sleepy, down to the shabby water-side where tattered darkies dangled their bare feet from the edge of the rotting wharves. Pandora was even more interested in Mount Vernon (when at last its wooded bluff began to command the river) than she had been in the Capitol; and after they had disembarked and ascended to the celebrated mansion she insisted on going into every room it contained. She declared that it had the finest situation in the world, and that it was a shame they didn't give it to the President for his villeggiatura. Most of her companions had seen the house often, and were now coupling themselves, in the grounds, according to their sympathies, so that it was easy for Vogelstein to offer the benefit of his own experience to the most inquisitive member of the party. They were not to lunch for another hour, and in the interval Vogelstein wandered about with Pandora. The breath of the Potomac, on the boat, had been a little harsh, but on the softly-curving lawn, beneath the clustered trees, with the river relegated to a mere shining presence far below and in the distance, the day gave out nothing but its mildness, and the whole scene became noble and genial.

Vogelstein could joke a little on great occasions, and the present one was worthy of his humour. He maintained to his companion that the shallow, painted mansion looked like a false house, a "fly," a structure of daubed canvas, on the stage; but she answered him so well with certain economical palaces she had seen in Germany, where, as she said, there was nothing but china stoves and stuffed birds, that he was obliged to admit the home of Washington was after all really *gemüth-lich*. What he found so, in fact, was the soft texture of the day, his personal situation, the sweetness of his suspense. For suspense had decidedly become his portion; he was under a charm which made him feel that he was watching his own life and that his susceptibilities were beyond his control. It hung over him that things might take a turn, from one hour to the other, which would make them very different from what they had been yet; and his heart certainly beat a little faster as he wondered what that turn might be. Why did he come to picnics on fragrant April days with American girls who might lead him too far? Would not such girls be glad to marry a Pomeranian count? And would they, after all, talk that way to the Kaiser? If he were to marry one of them he should have to give her some lessons. In their little tour of the house Vogelstein and his companion had had a great many fellow-visitors, who had also arrived by the steamer and who had hitherto not left them an ideal privacy. But the others gradually dispersed; they circled about a kind of showman, who was the authorised guide, a big, slow, genial, familiar man, with a large beard, and a humorous, edifying, patronising tone, which had immense success when he stopped here and there to make his points, to pass his eyes over his listening flock, then fix them quite above it with a meditative look, and bring out some ancient pleasantry as if it were a sudden inspiration. He made a cheerful thing even of a visit to the tomb of the *pater patriæ*. It is enshrined in a kind of grotto in the grounds, and Vogelstein remarked to Pandora that he was a good man for the place, but that he was too familiar.

"Oh, he would have been familiar with Washington," said the girl, with the bright dryness with which she often uttered amusing things.

Vogelstein looked at her a moment, and it came over him, as he smiled, that she herself probably would not have been abashed even by the hero with whom history has taken fewest liberties. "You look as if you could hardly believe that," Pandora went on. "You Germans are always in such awe of great people." And it occurred to Vogelstein that perhaps, after all, Washington would have liked her manner, which was wonderfully fresh and natural. The man with the beard was an ideal cicerone for American shrines; he played upon

the curiosity of his little band with the touch of a master, and
drew them away to see the classic ice-house where the old
lady had been found weeping in the belief that it was Washington's grave. While this monument was under inspection
Vogelstein and Pandora had the house to themselves, and they
spent some time on a pretty terrace, upon which certain windows of the second floor opened—a little roofless verandah,
which overhung in a manner, obliquely, all the magnificence
of the view—the immense sweep of the river, the artistic
plantations, the last-century garden, with its big box-hedges
and remains of old espaliers. They lingered here for nearly
half an hour, and it was in this spot that Vogelstein enjoyed
the only approach to intimate conversation that fate had in
store for him with a young woman in whom he had been
unable to persuade himself that he was not interested. It is
not necessary, and it is not possible, that I should reproduce
this colloquy; but I may mention that it began—as they
leaned against the parapet of the terrace and heard the frater-
nising voice of the showman wafted up to them from a
distance—with his saying to her, rather abruptly, that he
couldn't make out why they hadn't had more talk together
when they crossed the ocean.

"Well, I can, if you can't," said Pandora. "I would have
talked if you had spoken to me. I spoke to you first."

"Yes, I remember that," Vogelstein replied, rather awkwardly.

"You listened too much to Mrs Dangerfield."

"To Mrs Dangerfield?"

"That woman you were always sitting with; she told you
not to speak to me. I have seen her in New York; she speaks
to me now herself. She recommended you to have nothing
to do with me."

"Oh, how can you say such dreadful things?" the young
man murmured, blushing very red.

"You know you can't deny it. You were not attracted by

my family. They are charming people when you know them. I don't have a better time anywhere than I have at home," the girl went on, loyally. "But what does it matter? My family are very happy. They are getting quite used to New York. Mrs Dangerfield is a vulgar wretch; next winter she will call on me."

"You are unlike any girl I have ever seen; I don't understand you," said poor Vogelstein, with the colour still in his face.

"Well, you never will understand me, probably; but what difference does it make?"

Vogelstein attempted to tell her what difference it made, but I have not space to follow him here. It is known that when the German mind attempts to explain things it does not always reduce them to simplicity, and Pandora was first mystified, then amused, by some of her companion's revelations. At last I think she was a little frightened, for she remarked irrelevantly, with some decision, that lunch would be ready and they ought to join Mrs Steuben. He walked slowly, on purpose, as they left the house together, for he had a vague feeling that he was losing her.

"And shall you be in Washington many days yet?" he asked her as they went.

"It will all depend. I am expecting some news. What I shall do will be influenced by that."

The way she talked about expecting news made him feel, somehow, that she had a career, that she was active and independent, so that he could scarcely hope to stop her as she passed. It was certainly true that he had never seen any girl like her. It would have occurred to him that the news she was expecting might have reference to the favour she had asked of the President, if he had not already made up his mind, in the calm of meditation, after that talk with the Bonnycastles, that this favour must be a pleasantry. What she had said to him had a discouraging, a somewhat chilling, effect; nevertheless it was

not without a certain ardour that he asked of her whether,
so long as she stayed in Washington, he might not come and
see her.

"You may come as often as you like," she answered, "but
you won't care for it long."

"You try to torment me," said Vogelstein.

She hesitated a moment. "I mean that I may have some of
my family."

"I shall be delighted to see them once more."

She hesitated again. "There are some you have never
seen."

In the afternoon, returning to Washington on the steamer,
Count Vogelstein received a warning. It came from Mrs
Bonnycastle, and constituted, oddly enough, the second
occasion on which an officious female friend had, on the deck
of a vessel, advised him on the subject of Pandora Day.

"There is one thing we forgot to tell you, the other night,
about the self-made girl," Mrs Bonnycastle said. "It is never
safe to fix your affections upon her, because she has almost
always got an impediment somewhere in the background."

Vogelstein looked at her askance, but he smiled and said,
"I should understand your information—for which I am so
much obliged—a little better if I knew what you mean by
an impediment."

"Oh, I mean she is always engaged to some young man
who belongs to her earlier phase."

"Her earlier phase?"

"The time before she had made herself—when she lived at
home. A young man from Utica, say. They usually have to
wait; he is probably in a store. It's a long engagement."

"Do you mean a betrothal—to be married?"

"I don't mean anything German and transcendental. I mean
that peculiarly American institution, a precocious engagement;
to be married, of course."

Vogelstein very properly reflected that it was no use his

having entered the diplomatic career if he were not able to bear himself as if this interesting generalisation had no particular message for him. He did Mrs Bonnycastle, moreover, the justice to believe that she would not have taken up the subject so casually if she had suspected that she should make him wince. The whole thing was one of her jokes, and the notification, moreover, was really friendly. "I see, I see," he said in a moment. "The self-made girl has, of course, always had a past. Yes, and the young man in the store—from Utica —is part of her past."

"You express it perfectly," said Mrs Bonnycastle. "I couldn't say it better myself."

"But, with her present, with her future, I suppose it's all over. How do you say it in America? She lets him slide."

"We don't say it at all!" Mrs Bonnycastle cried. "She does nothing of the sort; for what do you take her? She sticks to him; that, at least, is what we expect her to do," Mrs Bonnycastle added, more thoughtfully. "As I tell you, the type is new. We haven't yet had time for complete observations."

"Oh, of course, I hope she sticks to him," Vogelstein declared simply, and with his German accent more apparent, as it always was when he was slightly agitated.

For the rest of the trip he was rather restless. He wandered about the boat, talking little with the returning revellers. Towards the last, as they drew near Washington, and the white dome of the Capitol hung aloft before them, looking as simple as a suspended snowball, he found himself, on the deck, in proximity to Mrs Steuben. He reproached himself with having rather neglected her during an entertainment for which he was indebted to her bounty, and he sought to repair his omission by a little friendly talk. But the only thing he could think of to say to her was to ask her by chance whether Miss Day were, to her knowledge, engaged.

Mrs Steuben turned her Southern eyes upon him with a look of almost romantic compassion. "To my knowledge?

Why, of course I would know! I should think you would
know too. Didn't you know she was engaged? Why, she has
been engaged since she was sixteen."

Vogelstein stared at the dome of the Capitol. "To a gentleman from Utica?"

"Yes, a native of her place. She is expecting him soon."

"Oh, I am so glad to hear it," said Vogelstein, who decidedly, for his career, had promise. "And is she going to
marry him?"

"Why, what do people get engaged for? I presume they
will marry before long."

"But why have they never done so, in so many years?"

"Well, at first she was too young, and then she thought
her family ought to see Europe—of course they could see it
better with her—and they spent some time there. And then
Mr Bellamy had some business difficulties which made him
feel as if he didn't want to marry just then. But he has given
up business, and I presume he feels more free. Of course it's
rather long, but all the while they have been engaged. It's a
true, true love," said Mrs Steuben, who had a little flute-like
way of sounding the adjective.

"Is his name Mr Bellamy?" Vogelstein asked, with his
haunting reminiscence. "D. F. Bellamy, eh? And has he been
in a store?"

"I don't know what kind of business it was; it was some
kind of business in Utica. I think he had a branch in New
York. He is one of the leading gentlemen of Utica, and very
highly educated. He is a good deal older than Miss Day. He
is a very fine man. He stands very high in Utica. I don't know
why you look as if you doubted it."

Vogelstein assured Mrs Steuben that he doubted nothing,
and indeed what she told him struck him as all the more cred-
ible, as it seemed to him eminently strange. Bellamy had been
the name of the gentleman who, a year and a half before, was
to have met Pandora on the arrival of the German steamer;

it was in Bellamy's name that she had addressed herself with such effusion to Bellamy's friend, the man in the straw hat, who was to fumble in her mother's old clothes. This was a fact which seemed to Vogelstein to finish the picture of her contradictions; it wanted at present no touch to be complete. Yet even as it hung there before him it continued to fascinate him, and he stared at it, detached from surrounding things and feeling a little as if he had been pitched out of an overturned vehicle, till the boat bumped against one of the outstanding piles of the wharf at which Mrs Steuben's party was to disembark. There was some delay in getting the steamer adjusted to the dock, during which the passengers stood watching the process, over the side and extracting what entertainment they might from the appearance of the various persons collected to receive it. There were darkies and loafers and hackmen, and also individuals with tufts on their chins, toothpicks in their mouths, their hands in their pockets, rumination in their jaws, and diamond-pins in their shirtfronts, who looked as if they had sauntered over from Pennsylvania Avenue to while away half an hour, forsaking for that interval their various postures of inclination in the porticos of the hotels and the doorways of the saloons.

"Oh, I am so glad! How sweet of you to come down!" It was a voice close to Vogelstein's shoulder that spoke these words, and the young secretary of legation had no need to turn to see from whom it proceeded. It had been in his ears the greater part of the day, though, as he now perceived, without the fullest richness of expression of which it was capable. Still less was he obliged to turn to discover to whom it was addressed, for the few simple words I have quoted had been flung across the narrowing interval of water, and a gentleman who had stepped to the edge of the dock without Vogelstein's observing him tossed back an immediate reply.

"I got here by the three o'clock train. They told me in K

Street where you were, and I thought I would come down and meet you."

"Charming attention!" said Pandora Day, with her friendly laugh; and for some moments she and her interlocutor appeared to continue the conversation only with their eyes. Meanwhile Vogelstein's, also, were not idle. He looked at Pandora's visitor from head to foot, and he was aware that she was quite unconscious of his own nearness. The gentleman before him was tall, good-looking, well-dressed; evidently he would stand well not only at Utica, but, judging from the way he had planted himself on the dock, in any position which circumstances might compel him to take up. He was about forty years old; he had a black moustache and a business-like eye. He waved a gloved hand at Pandora, as if, when she exclaimed, "Gracious, ain't they long!" to urge her to be patient. She was patient for a minute, and then she asked him if he had any news. He looked at her an instant in silence, smiling, after which he drew from his pocket a large letter with an official seal, and shook it jocosely above his head. This was discreetly, covertly done. No one appeared to observe the little interview but Vogelstein. The boat was now touching the wharf, and the space between the pair was inconsiderable.

"Department of State?" Pandora asked, dropping her voice.

"That's what they call it."

"Well, what country?"

"What's your opinion of the Dutch?" the gentleman asked, for an answer.

"Oh, gracious!" cried Pandora.

"Well, are you going to wait for the return trip?" said the gentleman.

Vogelstein turned away, and presently Mrs Steuben and her companions disembarked together. When this lady entered a carriage with Pandora, the gentleman who had spoken to the girl followed them; the others scattered, and Vogelstein, declining with thanks a "lift" from Mrs Bonnycastle, walked home alone, in some intensity of meditation. Two days later he saw in a newspaper an announcement that the President had offered the post of Minister to Holland to D. F. Bellamy, of Utica; and in the course of a month he heard from Mrs Steuben that Pandora's long engagement had terminated at the nuptial altar. He communicated this news to Mrs Bonnycastle, who had not heard it, with the remark that there was now ground for a new induction as to the self-made girl.

A NOTE ON THE TEXT

In preparing these tales for publication, the editor had to choose between James's original magazine texts, those published in book form soon afterwards and those revised and rewritten for the New York Edition. The obvious choice, it seemed to him, was the original book form of the story where there was one. In that form it had the benefit of revision from magazine to volume; and in that form it was best known to James's generation. It seemed to the editor that in a chronological edition of James's shorter fictions, the New York Edition texts had no relevance. They belong exclusively to the edition for which they were designed; particularly since the revisions were often made several decades after the original publication.

The original magazine and newspaper publications of the tales in this volume were as follows:

"The Siege of London," *Cornhill Magazine*, January–February 1883.

"The Impressions of a Cousin," *Century Magazine*, November–December 1883.

"Lady Barberina," *Century Magazine*, May–July 1884.

"The Author of 'Beltraffio'," *English Illustrated Magazine*, June–July 1884.

"Pandora," *New York Sun*, 1 and 8 June 1884.

"The Siege of London" was first reprinted in the volume of that name published in Boston in 1883, and the text of this first book publication has been used here. "The Impressions of a Cousin" and "Lady Barberina" were reprinted first in Boston and then in London in *Tales of Three Cities* in 1884.

"The Author of 'Beltraffio'" and "Pandora" were reprinted first in Boston in *The Author of Beltraffio* and then in London in *Stories Revived* in 1885. For these last four tales the London text has been preferred to that which appeared in Boston three or four months earlier and with less supervision by the author.

For the complete bibliography of the tales the reader is referred to *A Bibliography of the Writings of Henry James* by Leon Edel and Dan H. Laurence (second edition, revised, London, 1961) in the Soho Bibliographies published by Rupert Hart-Davis.

DATE DUE

GAYLORD			PRINTED IN U.S.A.